WHO'S OUT THERE

A NOVEL

WESTLEY SMITH

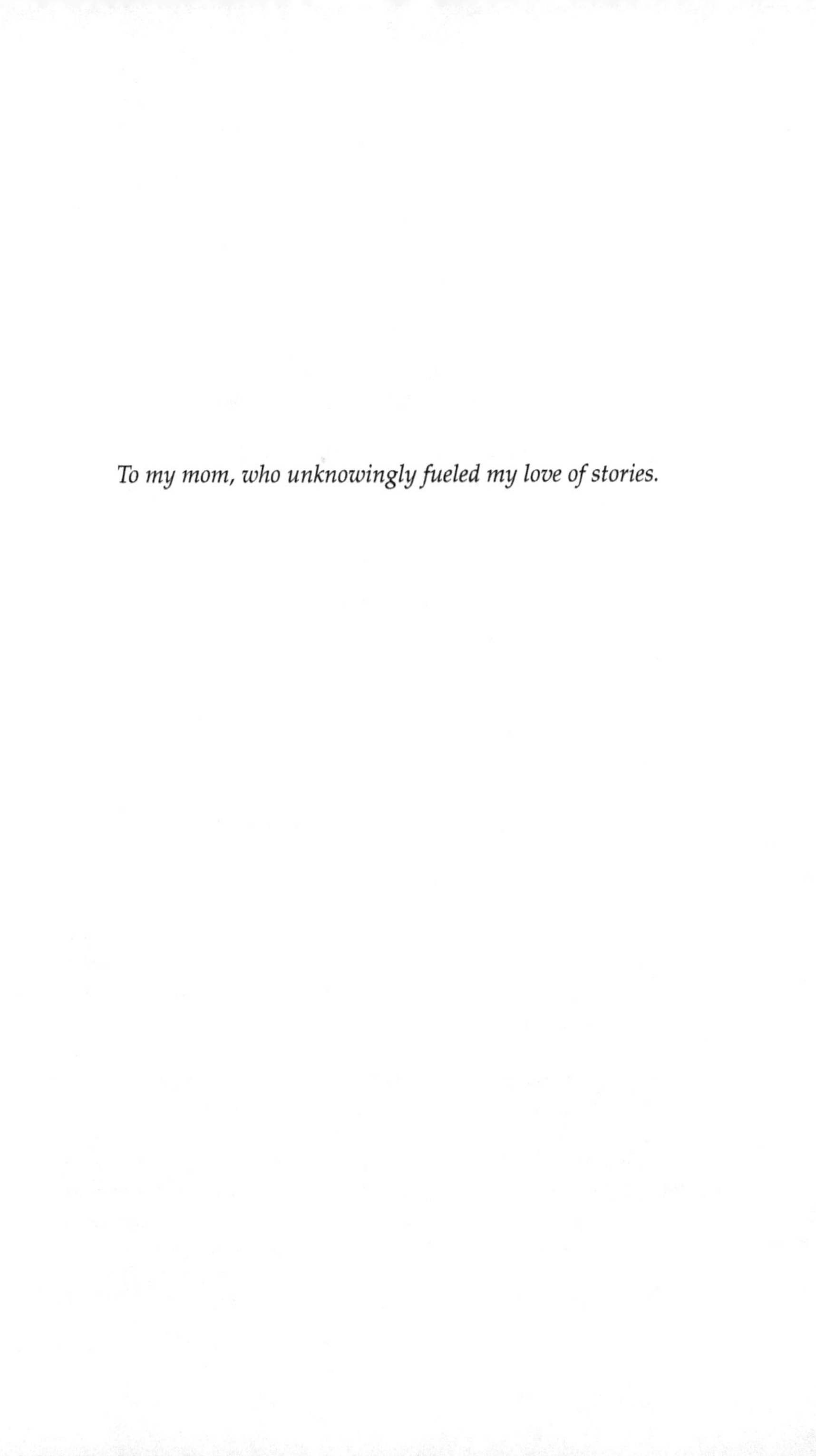

To my mom, who unknowingly fueled my love of stories.

Copyright © 2026 Westley Smith

Who's Out There
ISBN: 978-1-958370-31-5 (paperback)
ISBN: 978-1-958370-32-2 (eBook)

Published by Manta Press, Ltd.
Pickerington, OH 43147

Cover Design by Krystal Penney
Author photo by Laurie Smith

First Edition

All rights reserved. No part of this book may be reproduced in any form or by any means, electronic or mechanical, including photocopying, recording, or by any information storage system, without the written permission of the publisher.

No part of this book may be used or reproduced in any manner for the purpose of training artificial intelligence technologies or systems.

This book is a work of fiction. Names, characters, places and events portrayed are either the product of the author's imagination or are used fictitiously. Any resemblance to actual persons, living or dead, events or locales is entirely coincidental.

Printed in the United States of America

CHAPTER 1

God, it's cold. Rumor Shoff checks his digital watch. 10:45 p.m. The Marburg State Park ranger won't start his nightly rounds for another fifteen minutes. It will take him at least half an hour to forty-five minutes, to reach this end of the park. Rumor has plenty of time to accomplish his task.

Perfect.

At the bed of his Ford F-150, he lifts a duffel bag with R. Shoff sewn into the canvas and throws the strap over his shoulder. He pulls the trucker's cap tighter to his balding head, the air rushes through its vented rear and prickles his dome. Chills walk up his skin. He zips his coat to his chin. *Christ, it must be near zero with the windchill.* The crisp, dry air burns his throat, and the scent of the oncoming snowstorm tickles his nose.

He's alone in the Serpentine Trail parking lot. Only the forest trees are watching. Silent observers who won't tell a soul what he is up to—even after killing plenty of their kin.

Good. But Rumor needs to move. If caught by the park ranger at a quarter to eleven, he'll arrest Rumor and charge him with trespassing on state land after dark. That's the least of Rumor's concerns. What's in his duffel bag, however, is.

Heaving the strap to a more comfortable position on his shoulder, Rumor starts toward a large ranch-style gate serving as the entryway onto Serpentine Trail. The white moonlight casts the gate's arch onto the gravel trail winding its way through the forest like a snake, past the Shoff Family Cemetery, and down to the shoreline of Lake Clarke, directly across from the abandoned summer camp.

Rumor starts past the gate and into the forest, the moonlight has trouble penetrating the leafless trees; the branches so thick and interwoven they block all but a few streaks of white light cutting through the bare canopy. But Rumor doesn't need a flashlight to guide him; he's taken this trail many times to get to the cemetery—day and night—before the land was stolen from his father.

Rumor's face grows warm even in the bitter cold at the thought of the Pennsylvania Department of Conservation and Natural Resources (DCNR) stealing his father's land. The DCNR came to his father a year and a half ago with an offer to buy thirty-two acres of woodlands that made up the southwestern shore of Lake Clarke, excluding the small plot of land on which the Shoff Family Cemetery rests. *No sir! Uncle Sam won't pick up the tab to take care of that.* They planned to add to Marburg State Park's already sizable acreage. With his father's refusal to sell, the DCNR made an eminent domain claim—the right of the government or its agencies to expropriate private property for public use. His father sued. But it was a losing battle from the start, and the courts ruled in favor of the DCNR, forcing his father to surrender the land with zero compensation.

The DCNR can claim eminent domain or whatever fancy legal jargon the lawyers invented to sugarcoat the truth, but to Rumor, it was theft—plain and simple.

The trail curves sharply to the right, and the Shoff Family Cemetery appears on the left. Behind an old wrought iron fence, fifteen tombstones jut from the forest floor like crooked white teeth. The wind blows with a haunting whistle. The bare branches sway back and forth, casting long shadows across the front of the tombstones that look like skeleton fingers caressing the grave markers. Rumor pauses by the gate. Even in the shadowy darkness, he spots his mother's tombstone. Feels his heart ache.

Fuck cancer.

Rumor starts again. The gravel trail fades away and turns to dirt, worn-down over time by hikers making their way to the lakebed on the backside of the hill. He hasn't been past the cemetery since August 1997 and doesn't want to go down there now. Still, the DCNR needed to pay for what they had done. And by God, Rumor was going to collect in spades, even if that meant scaring up the memory of that dead girl he and his father discovered the morning of the camp massacre.

Along the shoreline, where the cold water of Lake Clarke laps at the rocks and bankside like a soft kiss, Rumor pauses to catch his breath. The smell of mud and fishy water mixes with the crisp night air that smells both clean and repugnant to him. The full white moon is visible above, and its reflection ripples across the water. In the open, the cold wind cuts across the lake bowl. It stings Rumor's face and makes his nose leak. He slides the sleeve of his jacket under his nose and sniffs back a glob of snot. The last time he stood there was the morning of the massacre at Camp Southwoods, when he was six.

Across the inlet of water, the steel cable *tinks* against the flagpole in the courtyard at Camp Southwoods. It's a lonely, eerie sound that causes Rumor to shiver, as if a ghostly voice speaks from the past. The moonlight casts an eerie white glow across the rundown mess hall, tucked between two identical shotgun-style buildings—the boys' and girls' bunkhouses. The dilapidated structures stand out against the clear northeastern sky—though it's about to be overtaken by the dark snow clouds rolling in from the South.

The ghost-town vibe of Camp Southwoods still resonates with

residual energy from the grisly murders in the early morning hours of August 5, 1997. Rumor's stomach churns as the vivid memory unpacks itself and his eyes drift to where they found the girl, washed up on the shore. She was lying on her side, facing away from them, her brown hair tangled with lake weeds, wet leaves, and interwoven sticks. On the back of her yellow T-shirt was a word in large red letters: COUNSELOR. Rumor thought she was sleeping. But when his father rolled her over to check on her, Rumor saw her pretty face was split from her hairline to her mouth, leaving a fleshy fissure where the axe had struck her. On either side of that gory canyon, two lifeless, milky-white eyes were locked on him in a death stare. An arrow was through the swell of her left breast. Deep lacerations scarred her forearms, and the first two fingers on her right hand were gone. She was from Camp Southwoods, just across the inlet—the torn and bloody yellow T-shirt with the camp's name and logo affirmed this.

Rumor remembers screaming in horror at the sight of the dead camp counselor. Then, his father was next to him, hurrying them back up the trail to call the police.

Her name was Alice King, and how she ended up there raises the hackles on Rumor's neck. He tugs his coat closer. But she wasn't the only camp counselor found slain. Kurt MacReady, Virginia Steel, and Ted Charno also met their demise at the hands of fifteen-year-old Douglas Lee Carver, who, for reasons unknown, decided to hunt them down with a bow and arrow (taken from the camp's archery range) before stealing their faces with a violent strike with an axe. Three of the victims, Rumor has learned in his research of the murders, were disposed of quickly. But Alice King had valiantly fought back. Sadly, she fell to Carver's wrath by the lake before washing up a few feet from where Rumor now stood.

Since the murders, a local legend arose of a curse on Lake Clarke and a curse on Marburg State Park itself. Locals claim to see shadow people on the trails or around the camp, hear whispering and laughing, and see lights emanating from the rundown cabins. The lore has grown exponentially over the years. So much so that locals have reimagined an old nursery rhyme, "Bye, Baby Bunting," to scare the bejesus out of one another for nearly three decades. Rumor knew it well:

> *Little counselor running,*
> *Douggie Carver's gone a-hunting*
> *Gonna catch that counselor,*
> *Gonna cleave that counselor,*
> *Little counselor done running.*

But those campfire tales are just that…tales. *You have work to do.* Rumor checks his watch. 10:55 p.m. *Get your ass moving.*

He continues to follow the trail south along the lake to an area known as Ice Fisherman's Cove. It's a favorite spot for ice fishermen to set up because the water freezes fast and hard in the winter. By a large oak tree leaning dangerously over the trail, Rumor drops the duffel bag and squats beside it. He unzips the bag and pulls out a gardening shovel. A battery-operated DeWalt drill with a three-inch wooden drill bit in its jaws. A 350ml syringe. And a bottle of Tardon—an herbicide that kills woody plants. He drops to his knees at the oak's base and begins clearing away a small patch of earth with the shovel. The January ground is frozen and tough to dig up. Perspiration dampens his back even in the cold. But he's persistent, despite the challenging work, and continues removing the earth until the oak's root system is bare.

He rechecks his watch. 11:10 p.m.

Need to hurry this up.

With the drill, Rumor bores into the oak's most prominent root. Once done, he opens the Tardon bottle, takes out the syringe, dips the wide plastic needle into the herbicide, and extracts a barrel full of blue liquid.

What was that? Footsteps?

Rumor searches the trail ahead but sees no one in the moonlight. *It could be an animal. A deer?*

The legend of Camp Southwoods, and its murderous boogieman, has lit his imagination. *Stop it. There ain't any ghosts in these woods. I'm alone.*

Rumor shakes the silly thought away, plunges the 350ml of Tardon into the root, and empties the barrel. *Drink it up.* The Tardon kills the trees slowly over several weeks. He's poisoned many trees around the park. Some are on trails like this one. Some in parking lots where a tree collapse could damage structures, costing the DCNR a lot of money in time and repairs. That's just what Rumor wants. He refills the hole with dirt, replaces his equipment in the duffel bag, and stands.

Gazing upon the oak leaning precariously over the trail, Rumor knows it's just a matter of time before it topples. He smiles jovially. Poisoning the trees is only one of the many subterfuges Rumor has committed around the park: clogging the toilets in the guests' facilities, wrecking the well pumps so the park didn't have water for drinking and cleaning, dumping trashcans, spray painting obscenities on the public pavilions. He even lit a few fires that burnt some acres on the park's western side in late September. *Maybe I'll drill holes in the canoes this summer. Or put wasps' nests in the garbage cans. Or poison the drinking water.* He has little concern about someone getting hurt from his shenanigans: *people are collateral damage.* Pride flows through his veins, pure like holy water, warming him. He's giving it to the man for stealing his father's land.

But the warmth is quickly blown away as another gust of wind howls across the lake. Rumor shivers and looks at his watch again. 11:22 p.m. *Time to get going.*

He returns to where the trail winds back into the woods, past the Shoff Cemetery, and eventually to the parking lot. The desolate *tink, tink, tink* of the cable snapping against the flagpole at the abandoned campground cuts across the inlet.

Footsteps! On the trail again.

Someone is *there!* Cold fear shoots through him and tightens his chest like a clenched fist. *I can't get caught. Not now. Not when there's so much more to do.*

He ducks behind a large white sycamore and checks his watch. 11:29 p.m. The park ranger may be down there, checking for trespassers or even looking for him after finding his pickup in the Serpentine Trail parking lot. Or it might be a few local kids hiking to the abandoned campground to get high, drink, or make out. They might even tell each other ghost stories about Carver's victims haunting the area.

Rumor peers around the tree and scans the trail from which he just came. No one lingers about. The tightness in his chest eases. Still, he tries to tune out the wind and focus on the sounds of approaching footsteps. But if they were there and not a figment of his imagination, they're gone now. He lets out a slow, grateful breath and feels the tension in his muscles relax.

Rumor steps out from behind the tree. He's about to turn away when he sees a human silhouette step off the trail and duck into the forest about twenty-five yards away.

I'm seeing things, he thinks, as his balls shrivel into his pelvis and goose pimples rise from his feet to his scalp. He's heard stories about hikers seeing shadow people on the trail, ducking in and around trees. Is that what he's seeing now? A shadow person? *No! There's no one out there. It's the wind causing the tree branches to swing and the shadows to move, nothing more.* He swallows. His throat is dry like dust. *But you heard footsteps—twice now —and saw the shadow. Someone or something is out here with you. Maybe one of Carver's victims?* An unseen frozen hand clasps upon his lungs in a powerful, vicelike grip.

Fuck this!

Rumor turns on his heels to bolt up the trail when a loose rock gives way, and his right foot slips out from underneath him. He loses his grip on the duffel bag, which slides from his shoulder into the dark somewhere, and falls hard on his right elbow. The impact with the unforgiving ground peels the flesh back, and the sting of cold air bites at the raw, bleeding wound. He stifles a scream. He can't risk someone hearing. Through the discomfort, he pulls himself to his feet and darts up the trail toward the dark, concealing woods where he'll be safe from…well, whatever it was that he saw duck off the trail.

He doesn't stop or look back until he's far enough from the shoreline, hidden deep within the woods where no one—man or ghost—can see him. He bends at the waist to catch his breath, to allow his heart rate to slow. It beats in his ears like a sinister drum. He now understands what it must be like for people who say they've seen Bigfoot or the Loch Ness Monster…

"A ghost," Rumor whispers in the dark.

Of course, Rumor will never admit ghosts are real. Just like Bigfoot and the Loch Ness Monster are nothing more than stories made up by fringe outliers looking for attention. What he saw tonight were moving shadows, brought on by the wind and an overactive imagination. Rumor feels that the only ghosts down there are memories.

Then why were you running?

He doesn't entertain this thought and looks at his watch. 11:40 p.m. *Christ! I need to—*

My duffel bag! It isn't slung over his shoulder. *You must've dropped it when you fell.* His bloody elbow begins to thump with discomfort at his carelessness. *How could you be so stupid!* He can't leave it behind. If found, the Rangers will easily link the tree poisoning and the vandalisms back to him because his damn name is stitched on the side.

No. Leaving the duffel bag isn't an option.

Rumor gazes down the trail into the dark hollow and listens for footsteps again. But only the breeze blows through the trees, rustling what leaves remain on the branches. He's positive that everything he's experiencing—the footsteps, the shadowy figure —is a manifestation brought on by the camp's violent history and his memories of that fateful day. His head was full of enough lore about Carver and Camp Southwoods to trick anyone's brain into thinking someone was out there, maybe even following him.

Steeling himself against his fears—real or imaginary—Rumor takes a step. Then another. Soon he's heading back toward the lake to find the duffel bag. In his mind, he keeps repeating:

They're only stories.

CHAPTER 2

Two and a half miles outside Marburg State Park, Ranger Colt Mitcham finishes his breakfast at the Route 206 Diner. A gust of wind rushes past the diner, flicking the lights and silencing all discussion. The storm front is here. It's just a matter of time before it unleashes its fury. There's a sigh of relief when the lights stay on, and everyone returns to their breakfast and conversation. But for Colt, the storm's not only bringing lousy weather but bad memories, memories that are as raw as an open wound. He swallows the last of his coffee to wash the anticipation—anxiety?—away.

It's not like last July.

He stands and adjusts his gun belt. The heft of the .357 Smith & Wesson Model 627 on his right hip is like lugging a brick. Most Pennsylvania State Rangers carry a Glock .9mm nowadays. But Colt prefers a revolver because it won't jam in a pinch like a semi-auto could. He pulls a twenty from a fold of bills in his green cargo pants and lays it on the counter with the check. He takes pleasure in tipping his servers well.

As Colt slips on his jacket, he sees Bill Hardy, the diner's owner, step out of the kitchen. He's a tall, portly man with a thick gray beard and hair that reminds Colt of Jerry Garcia, the lead singer of the Grateful Dead. His white T-shirt is stained with food spatter, oil, and butter splotches. His face is red, and beads of sweat roll down his brow and soak into a 1980s-style blue sweatband that one might see in a Jane Fonda workout video. He spots Colt and starts toward him.

"I was hoping I'd catch you before you left. Got stuck in the kitchen. Wasn't expecting the rush this morning."

"You have quite the crowd."

"Has to be the weather. Brings out the crazy in everyone."

"What can I do for you?" Colt zips up the ranger jacket.

"You said I should tell you if I saw Rumor Shoff around. Well, he was in here last night. Alone."

As head of the Marburg State Park's Ranger Rescue Unit, a position he's only six months into, Colt's responsibility is to ensure the safety of the park, its guests, and the wildlife that call it home. But over the past year, the park has had its share of vandalisms, each increasingly worse than the last. Colt knew only two people who would resort to such tactics. One was Darryl Shoff, a sixty-five-year-old man. The other was his thirty-three-year-old son, Rumor, who Colt felt was in better physical shape to commit the crimes, though not without his daddy's blessing. The DCNR was on his ass about apprehending those responsible. The amount spent on repairs and overtime pay strained the park's budget, and the bean counters weren't happy about it. *Shit rolls downhill.* So, Colt asked locals like Bill to watch for Rumor and Darryl and tell him if they saw or said something he should know about.

"What time?" Colt asks.

"Came in around eight thirty, left a little after nine."

"Say anything?"

Bill shakes his head. "Nah. Had some liver and onions. Glass of Coke. Paid his check and left."

"Which way'd he go?"

"West, up 206."

"Toward the park?"

Bill nods.

Colt considers this. With the Shoffs' contention with the DCNR, he feels they're most likely the culprits responsible for the mischief. The problem is that Colt has no solid evidence to make an arrest. Just a hunch. And a hunch isn't worth squat in a court of law. But what's even more worrisome is that whoever's committing the crimes has been able to skirt the park's nightly patrol.

How's that possible?

Colt's cell phone rings.

Ranger Station 2 - Marburg State Park

Calling...

Colt answers.

"Hey, Colt," Ranger Flint Wheeler says in a voice that concerns him. "Another tree came down."

Colt's shoulders slump. *That's the fifth one this week.*

"Where?"

"That big red oak next—" The connection crackles and Colt suspects the wind is interfering with the phone lines. The back of his head begins to ache with worry. "...orama Building."

Though the connection is distorted, Colt knows the tree Flint references is the seventy-five-foot, nearly two-hundred-year-old red oak. It sat next to the Panorama Building that overlooked Lake Clarke on Dedication Hill, and it could have hit the building on its way to the ground.

"All right. Call maintenance. Let 'em know what's going on."

"Will do," Flint says. "I'm heading over...to...eck...ow."

The line crackles again.

"No. Stay at RS2. I'm on my way." He pauses momentarily, waiting for Flint's response, biting his lip. "Flint, you still there? Flint?"

The line is dead.

Goddamnit!

Colt's neck burns hot, and his lips press tight with irritation. He doesn't need Flint Wheeler to abandon his post at RS2. And they don't need the phone lines to go down like they had last July when Hurricane Phillis, a Cat 2 coastal storm, hit. As a result, the park could not contact outside emergency crews after a distress call came in from someone claiming to be stuck at the top of the Rocks—a cliff north of Snyder Point.

Maynard Barrett's horrified scream fills the space between Colt's ears, instantly transporting him back to the night he lost his boss, mentor, and friend. *We should've never gone up there.* The Rocks were treacherous, even during the day. Still, in the middle of a hurricane, and at night, it became another world. A miserable, unforgiving hellscape that took Maynard's life with one misplaced step. Had Colt's backpack not gotten snagged on a downed tree, causing him to lag behind Maynard on the trail to the top of the Rocks, he would've been there too...

"Everything okay?" Bill asks cautiously. He's noticed the change in Colt's demeanor.

Colt blinks from his reverie, Maynard's scream still echoes through his mind. He slips the phone back into his pocket, looks at Bill, and forces himself to smile.

"Everything's fine."

Inside Marburg State Park, Colt pulls the Ford Interceptor SUV to a stop at the mouth of Dedication Road. Lance Sawyer is there, removing a wooden barricade from the bed of a maintenance pickup, the bar of swirling yellow caution lights atop catching the first fine flakes of snow. Lance places the barricade in the center of the road to block public access to the Panorama Building and Dedication Hill beyond. Across the front of the barricade, it says: ROAD CLOSED. Colt rolls down his window. The whine of chainsaws cuts above the wind, and he worries again that the tree has hit the Panorama Building. Lance turns and waves at him, then reaches into his pocket, pulls out his cell, and checks it. He frowns at the screen and then hurries to the driver's side door.

"Morning," Lance says. He's a wiry guy, about five-eleven with a scruffy dark brown beard and long, untamable hair that sticks out from under his well-worn Yankees baseball cap.

"Morning. Flint called. Said the red oak came down."

"Yeah," Lance says. He hitches a thumb over his shoulder. "Tripp and Amos are up there now, cutting it apart. Flint's up there, too. I'll assist as soon as I get these barricades set up." He pauses and studies Colt with an apprehensive gaze. "That's the fifth tree this week that went over."

Colt nods, aware that two trees were found across Long Head Trail. One across Band Shell Road. And another had come down in the boat launch area, off Black Rock Road at the south end of the lake, just before the road dead ends at the Serpentine Trail parking lot. The result, Colt knew after seeing the black bark and rotted cores, was poison. Now the two-hundred-year-old red oak next to the Panorama Building. *Had it been poisoned like the others?*

He thinks about Rumor Shoff at the Route 206 Diner the previous night. Could Rumor be poisoning the trees? It's possible. But like with the other vandalisms they've dealt with for the last year, he has no hard proof that Rumor is responsible.

"We were lucky," Lance says.

But maybe not the next time.

"You mind moving the barricade? I'm going to go up and look," Colt says.

"Sure." Lance glances back at his cell phone. Again, he frowns.

"Something wrong?"

"No signal. Joey asked me to keep her in the loop."

"Why not use the CB in the pickup?"

"Eh." Lance sighs and shakes his head. "Someone flattened the tires on all the maintenance pickups and disabled the CBs last night. Luckily, we had enough spare tires in the shed to get one pickup up and running this morning." Lance taps the pickup's hood. "But this CB's done." He holds up the cell. "Why I was trying to use this to keep Joey informed."

Colt bites his lower lip. The anger and irritation boil in his belly. He was tired of cleaning up after a vandalism spree and having the DCNR down his throat about getting the clowns responsible. But targeting the maintenance pickups…that was a new one.

"Don't worry about keeping Joey informed. I'll tell her what's happening when I get to RS1." Colt points to the road in front of him. "The barricade."

"Oh, right."

After Lance moves the barricade, Colt steps on the gas and proceeds. In the rearview mirror, he watches Lance replace it and then move back to the pickup to get the second one.

Steering the SUV around a bend in the road, Colt sees the eight-foot-by-four-foot slab of rough-cut granite between the bare trees at the top of Dedication Hill, the highest point on that side of the park. The monument is for the victims of Douglas Lee Carver, whose names are engraved into the granite's smooth surface.

Colt was seventeen when the murders at Camp Southwoods happened, a senior in high school. The murders were all over the local news at the time, and the fuss around the trial afterward. Though the investigators found the murder weapons (a bow and arrow and a hatchet) under Carver's bunk with his bloody fingerprints on both, it should have been an open-and-shut case. But there was a crux going into the trial. Because of Carver's age, fifteen, and his inability to comprehend what he had done, the judge ordered him to undergo psychiatric evaluations. After countless tests and assessments by doctors and psychologists, Carver was deemed unfit to stand trial, lacking the mental cognitive abilities to understand his actions. He was sentenced to Haven Hurst Mental Hospital for the Criminally Insane, where he spent the last twenty-six years of his life. The victim's parents felt justice wasn't served and that Carver got off easy after the brutality of his murders. They wanted a harsher punishment. A retrial was fought for. The state didn't pursue it.

Under the shadow of Dedication Hill, Colt comes to a four-way intersection. To the right is Fishhook Drive, which leads to the Marina by the lake. To the left are the parking lots and the public restrooms, shuttered for the winter. Ahead is the Panorama Building. Colt continues through the intersection and stops behind a Mack Granite plow truck, its hopper full of a sand-and-salt mixture. Beside the plow is a white Ford Interceptor SUV, with the words MARBURG PARK RANGER in green across the sides, identical to the one Colt's driving. He can go no further. The red oak that proudly stood next to the Panorama Building for nearly two hundred years lies across the road. Debris from the tree litters the area around it like a bomb has exploded. Though it's painful to see the beautiful, old tree down, Colt's thankful it's fallen in the opposite direction and not into the Panorama Building.

What a nightmare that would be.

Colt gets out. He notices the head of the maintenance department, Marion "Tripp" Thatcher, has a crowbar wedged under a large branch of the fallen red oak to keep it off the ground while Amos Kent cuts through it with a chainsaw so it doesn't ground out and dull the teeth. It's a tough, time-consuming job. He's done enough tree felling and stacking at his cabin to understand and sympathize with Tripp and Amos's backbreaking work under these miserable conditions.

The SUV's door opens and closes. Out of the corner of his eye, Colt notices Flint Wheeler limp around the front. Flint is fifty-three years old and has been with the park for twenty-two years, longer than anyone else. He has broad shoulders and a barrel chest, making him look like a professional powerlifter. His salt-and-pepper beard matches his hair, hidden under the green bush hat he always wears this time of year. His limp has progressively worsened over time. And, this morning, it looks incredibly uncomfortable. Colt understands it was from an old hiking injury. Flint grimaces with each step he takes.

"I told you to stay at RS2," Colt says.

"You did? The message didn't come through."

"Who's manning the radio at RS2?"

All ranger stations were always to have at least one ranger monitoring the phones and long-range radios in case of an emergency.

"Dusty."

"He was supposed to be clearing Trail Loop One this morning. And you were supposed to clear Trail Loop Two after that." Colt aims to have the park buttoned up before the snowfall picks up. That means all buildings need safeguarding, the trails and playgrounds shut down to the public, and all park guests off the premises.

"He can start as soon as I get back." Flint glances at the fallen tree. "Thought I'd secure the scene until you got here."

"Thanks. But I got it now. Get back to RS2 so Dusty can start clearing Trail Loop One. I want both trails closed before this storm fully opens up."

Flint bites his lower lip to keep himself from saying something regrettable. With only six months into his leadership role, Colt realizes there are still kinks between everyone, an adjustment from Maynard's management style to his own. Flint isn't unlikable, but he can be a challenge to work with, especially when Colt gives him direct orders. He wonders if Flint's inability to follow orders is because of a personal issue. If that's the case, Colt must address it before it becomes problematic. Colt knows he must prove himself to his team as a capable leader, as much as they need to prove themselves reliable to him when given their orders. Flint is testing boundaries.

"Yes, sir."

Flint turns and limps back to the SUV. He starts it up, and Colt watches him drive off. He puts his issues with Flint out of his mind, for the time being, and starts toward the fallen tree. The wind gusts and smells of gasoline and chain oil. It reminds Colt of being at home, cutting, chopping, and stacking wood for his wood stove. Amos kills his chainsaw and motions to Tripp once he realizes Colt's there.

Tripp waves, removes his safety glasses, and starts toward him. Tripp's tall and lean, with naturally wavy gray hair that falls to his shoulders. It's currently hidden under the hood of his red-and-black flannel jacket. His narrow face is weathered, skin tan from the year-round outdoor work. The crow's feet around his blue-green eyes give them a keen look like he's always one step ahead of everyone else. The wind lifts his gray handlebar mustache like a kite about to catch flight. As he approaches, Tripp reaches into the breast pocket of his jacket and pulls out his cigar case, an anniversary gift from his late wife, Aleja. The gold initials MTT gleam on the front, even though there's no sunlight breaking through the clouds. Lifting off the lid, Tripp removes a La Aroma de Cuba cigar—*it's a good smoke*, Tripp always says when talking about cigars he enjoys. He's quite the cigar connoisseur, talking Colt's ear off over his love of a good smoke on more than one occasion.

"This is the fifth tree this week, Colt." Tripp angles his eyes at him.

"Yeah." *Everyone keeps saying that as if I'm unaware.* The wind nips at Colt's face and stings his skin.

"So, what are you going to do about it?"

"What would you like me to do?"

"Arrest Rumor! He's behind all this. It's only a matter of time before someone gets hurt or killed. And this isn't all that the prick did last night. Lance tell you about the flat tires and CBs?"

Colt sighs and nods. "Look, as much as I believe Rumor's responsible for the vandalisms, I don't have any proof. Can't arrest the man without some hard evidence linking him to the crimes."

"That might've just changed."

"What's that supposed to mean?"

A shit-eating grin works across Tripp's face and his eyes twinkle. The intrigue he's privy to delights him.

"What's up, Tripp? You only smile like that when you know something I don't."

"Go talk to Joey," Tripp says, slipping the cigar into his mouth. "She'll fill you in."

"Fill me in about what?" Colt stuffs his hands into his pants and cups his thighs for warmth.

Tripp puts a butane lighter on the cigar's end and puffs. The strong, pungent aroma causes Colt's nose to wrinkle. He's aware there are people, like Tripp, who love the smell of fine tobacco. He's not one of them. The smoke tickles his nose and makes his eyes water. *Maybe I'm allergic.*

"Jus go twlk to her," Tripp says. The stogie in his mouth causes the words to come out mushy.

Colt rolls his eyes. He's about to tell Tripp to quit being coy and let him in on what he knows, but Amos Kent shouts out.

"Hey, you guys need to come and look at this!"

Colt and Tripp meet each other's troubled gaze. The tone of Amos's voice is like he's just uncovered some grave secret. *What now?* They hurry over to where Amos stands by the base of the fallen red oak.

Amos Kent is a large Black man built like a brick shithouse, as Colt's Aunt Sunny would have said. He's an imposing figure at six-five and nearly three hundred pounds of hard muscle. Yet, he's quiet and modest, with kind almond-shaped eyes. He's a single father of an eleven-year-old daughter whose mother ran off with a guy she met online while Amos was at work, leaving him to raise her alone. But, as the saying goes, make lemonade when life gives you lemons. Amos did just that. He could be angry at the world because of the cards he was dealt, but Amos made the best of his situation. He's one of the hardest-working people Colt has ever met, and he respects Amos for not letting life get him down. Colt believes that he does what's asked of him—both in his personal life and at his job in the maintenance department—and never makes a fuss—something many people nowadays could use a lesson on.

"What's up?" Colt steps beside Amos with Tripp in tow.

"Look here." Amos points to the red oak's split stump.

Colt deduces that the wind is most likely the culprit that brought the tree down—a sharp, blade-like stump from where it snapped, the only reminder that it ever stood there. However, the center is black with decay. Someone had fed the tree poison, just like the others they found this week. The poison had yet to reach the outer rings of the red oak—trees die from the bottom up and from the inside out—so there was no way to know the red oak was weakened from the toxin it was fed.

Colt takes a deep breath and gazes across the lake, past the two islands—Long and Round—to the northern hills above Snyder Point. The now obsolete wooden fire tower is visible above the pines, carpeting the ridgeline around it. In a few hours, the whiteout will be so thick they won't be able to see Snyder Point, let alone ten feet in front of their faces.

"Time for you to go have that talk with Joey," Tripp says.

Time for you to go have that talk with Joey.

Tripp's haunting words rattle around in Colt's head as he climbs back in the SUV. What did Joey know about Rumor? She had said nothing to him last night at the motel, so how could she know anything?

Heading west on 206, Colt passes Camp Southwoods Road on his way to Ranger Station One. A yellow gate blocks the road to the public. A white sign with bold red letters attached to it reads NO TRESPASSING! VIOLATORS WILL BE ARRESTED! The overgrown and twisting road beyond led to the abandoned campgrounds, and at one time, also connected Route 206 and Route 9 before it was inaccessible.

After the Carver murders, the DCNR shut down the camp, along with the entire southeastern side of the park, to visitors. The gate and sign are there to deter people from exploring the abandoned summer camp. *Fat lotta good it does.* Cold had run dozens of trespassers out of there wanting to see where Douglas Lee Carver lay waste to four young souls. He knows the stories about Camp Southwoods being haunted; the claims of seeing ghostly apparitions—shadow people—hearing screams, moaning, and whispering voices from beyond the grave. The crime, the legend born from it, and the area are ripe for people who believe in such nonsense. *They're just stories.* Still, the legend invites all sorts of people—from ghost hunters to true crime podcasters to weirdos with a hard-on for the macabre—to the park to investigate. But the camp is strictly off-limits. No exceptions are made. However, if the state is serious about keeping people away, they must tear the camp down and leave the area alone. It's the only way.

Yet, the DCNR wanted to reopen the camp.

They had phoned Colt a month ago to get his opinion. He disagreed, feeling it would exhume a past that is better left buried. It was a sacred place where people died; it should be left alone. Alas, the decision was above his pay grade. He had no say in the matter.

Coming off the hill, the SUV begins to cross the bridge over Lake Clarke. A strong gust of wind slams into the side, forcing it across the double yellow line. *Whoa!* Colt quickly course-corrects and continues, making a mental note to keep his hands at ten and two on the wheel so he doesn't lose control again. He shivers, thinking about the storm worsening as the day goes on.

Lake Clarke is a massive body of water covering 1,275 acres with twenty-six miles of shoreline. It is a migrating area for waterfowl and shorebirds. The lake is a popular spot for sail boaters—who dock their boats at the Marina during the summer months—as well as motorboaters and water skiers. Fishermen love the lake for ice and warm water fishing, and it's not uncommon to see them along the shore or in boats from sunup to sundown when the park officially closes to the public. In the summer, Colt believes there isn't a prettier sight than the lake with the sun sparkling off the warm water. But at that very moment, as he's crossing over it, he thinks the lake looks like a moody bitch—dark and angry, much like it had last summer just before Hurricane Phillis hit.

He exits the bridge, turns right into Ranger Station One (RS1), and parks the SUV in the back lot. The maintenance building is directly across from RS1. The maintenance crew calls the building *The Shed*, even though it is nearly a hundred feet long, thirty feet wide, and twenty-five feet high. Beside the building are three maintenance pickups sitting on their rims, the tires flat.

Irritation blossoms. Colt exits the SUV and hurries across the lot to the first maintenance pickup. He examines the driver's side front tire. There's a small puncture hole in the front wall. Whoever did this—be it Rumor or not—looks to have used a screwdriver or maybe an ice pick to penetrate the tires.

This shit's getting out of hand. It has to end.

Colt opens the pickup's door and looks at the CB radio. The microphone is on the seat, and the cord is neatly cut from the radio as if by knife or scissors.

He slams the door, his anger sears into outrage, and he heads for RS1.

Inside, Colt finds Josephine "Joey" Walsh working at the front desk. His heart skips in her presence, like when he first met her. He knows the Shawnee side of her heritage attracts him physically to her. The long and straight raven-color hair (which is in a no-nonsense ponytail), high cheekbones, and reddish-brown skin. Her green ranger uniform matches Colt's. She is stunning in her uniform. The green heightens her skin tone and perfectly fits her tight, athletic physique.

They met five years ago. Introduced by Maynard, she was a greener-than-goose's-shit rookie with zero ranger experience but eager to learn the ropes. Intelligent, forthright, and honest were qualities Colt loves about her personality. Couple her inner beauty and exotic looks, and it was hard not to be attracted to her. But there was a toughness to Joey that Colt didn't see in all female rangers; she had an intolerance for bullshit and was quick to stand up for herself, especially in the man-driven field of park rangers. They had remained professional for years, even if their interactions were playful flirtiness.

For Colt, this was fine. He was, by nature, a loner—a simple man with simple needs. But Josephine Walsh complicated that life in ways he had not foreseen after Maynard's death. His addiction to her is like his addiction to air. And, to some extent, that addiction pesters him, like the smoker who loves cigarettes but knows he should quit. The air, he needs. The worry of them getting caught seeing each other, he doesn't.

The DCNR has strict rules against park rangers dating. They especially do not like commanding officers sleeping with their subordinates, which Colt has been doing with Joey for the last six months. If the DCNR found out, they would both lose their jobs.

So, they kept their relationship a secret and met at a motel off I-95 two or three times a week.

Still, Colt knows it's his fault for the predicament he finds himself in. He should not have let Joey into his home after Maynard's funeral. He should have asked her to leave. But he was grateful for the company. For God's sake, he was hurting, miserable, and very vulnerable. Had he been there when Maynard slipped on those wet rocks, he might've been able to reach out and grab him before he fell. But he wasn't. *Stuck on a goddamn tree branch.* The diversion her presence brought him that evening was welcome. It kept him from thinking about Maynard's terrible decision to mount a rescue mission for the hiker during the hurricane, something Colt was vehemently against.

What the hell were you thinking, Maynard?

Their hookup that first night had been nothing more than a way to suppress their collective grief. That's at least what he and Joey told each other as they lay nude on the floor of Colt's cabin. But was Maynard's death the excuse they needed to give in to their carnal needs—needs they always had for one another since their first introduction.

"Morning, everyone," Colt nears the front desk, where Joey fills out an incident report for the vandalism of the maintenance trucks. Behind her, across the room at the communications desk with a cup of coffee and a stack of Oreos for dipping, is Porter Barrett, Maynard's only son. He turns and nods at Colt. For a moment, Colt thinks Maynard has come back from the dead. The older Porter gets, the more he resembles his father with a mop of dark black hair, a square jaw with a dimple in the center, and a pair of cunning steel-blue eyes. Colt turns his attention back to Joey. "Tripp said I needed to speak with you?"

She looks up from the paperwork. Something flickers in her gold-brown eyes that burrows under his skin like a tick.

Joey clears her throat.

"Norm found Rumor Shoff's pickup in the Serpentine Trail parking lot last night."

Norm Roberts works the graveyard shift, patrolling the park from eleven at night to seven in the morning. Since Route 206 cuts directly through Marburg State Park, connecting the towns of Jackson and Hopewell, part of Norm's job is to assist local authorities with wildlife or auto incidents within park limits at night.

"Was Rumor pulled in for trespassing?" Colt glances past Joey to the small seven-by-seven holding cell in the back of the ranger station, but he doesn't see Rumor. A worrisome look pinches her face when he turns back to her. "What?"

"Rumor wasn't in the truck, Colt. There's no sign of him anywhere, according to Norm."

Colt remembers his conversation with Bill Hardy. Hardy had seen Rumor leave the Route 206 Diner a little after nine last evening, heading toward the park. Now, Rumor's truck was found in the Serpentine Trail lot. The fallen tree by the Panorama Building. The flat tires. The cut CBs. None of these incidents are a coincidence. *Rumor has to be responsible.* But where is Rumor now? And why didn't he hightail it out of the park before Norm found his pickup?

What are you up to, Rumor?

"So…he's been in the park all night?" Colt feels a slight tremor skip across his chest.

"All I can tell you is that his truck was there all night. Doesn't mean Rumor was in the park all night."

"Doesn't mean he wasn't, either." Colt's face warms at the thought of having to search for him with a storm about to burst. "Norm still around?"

"In the locker room."

"Send him into Maynard's—my—office when he comes out."

Colt starts toward the office, but Porter speaks before he can step away from the front desk.

"Rumor isn't our only concern. Word just came in over the radio from Ohiopyle State Park. Their phones and power are down, and they are operating on only a generator. They're also reporting sustained winds between forty and fifty miles an hour, with gusts reaching upward of seventy. It's only going to get worse." He pauses, and his face tightens with a troubled thought. "I'm concerned we'll lose our power and the phones, too."

"I hear you, Porter. And I know you're worried about a repeat of July." Colt sure is. He tries to quell the broken distress call from entering his mind, but it's in the front of his brain before he can stop it. *Help! Can any…ear me?* He blinks away the auditory memory of that tragic day and studies Porter. It's been hard for Colt to process Maynard's death, playing the events repeatedly in his mind as if he could magically change their outcome, but he can't imagine how sick with grief Porter must be. "We're going to have the park clear of guests and everything secured and locked up tight by the time the storm opens up. If the electricity and phones go down, we have the generators to power the long-distance radios if anything arises."

"As long as nothing happens to the antenna again," Porter says in a melancholy tone.

When the hurricane hit the park, the sustained winds were upward of sixty-five miles an hour. They took the nearly thirty-year-old long-range antenna down as if it were made of straw, effectively cutting off their communications outside the three-mile radius of their short-range CBs. Had the radios been functioning, they might have gotten help up to the Rocks to save Maynard's life. But even if they had, saving Maynard after his fall was impossible.

"It'll be alright." Colt places his hand on Porter's shoulder and squeezes. "Just keep us posted on any news updates you get."

"Will do."

Colt walks past him. He hopes his words ease Porter's worries a bit. It's been a tough six months for the younger Barrett, and with another severe storm on the horizon, those raw wounds were reopening. Colt feels his strain, too, but he stitches them before the memories get the best of him.

Colt closes the office door behind him. He needs a moment of solitude to wrap his head around the eventful morning. He sinks into the desk chair. The day's weight has already tensed his muscles. Though it's Colt's office, it still feels like Maynard's to him. Sure, all of Maynard's personal stuff—family pictures, knick-knacks, hunting trophies—are gone, but Colt left everything as it was when Maynard was in charge. He couldn't bring himself to change anything. It felt wrong. Like he was abandoning Maynard's memory if he moved the desk or shifted the filing and gun cabinets to another wall. Or removed Maynard's beloved whiteboard where he wrote the ranger schedules—something Colt does at the beginning of each month. So, he left the office as Maynard had. It was comfortable. Familiar. Not only to him, but to everyone working in the park. They all needed stability until the wounds of that day healed.

A knock at the door brings Colt from his thoughts. Norm Roberts—stout, thick black hair, face like a pug—is standing there.

"You wanted to see me?" Norm steps into the office.

"Heard you found Rumor Shoff's pickup last night in the Serpentine Trail parking lot, but no sign of Rumor."

"True. Got down there just after eleven thirty. No sign of him."

"You check the cemetery?"

"Sure did."

"What about the lake? You hike down there and look around?"

"Yeah. Went the whole way over to Ice Fisherman's Cove. There was no sign of him anywhere. Maybe he met up with someone and left his truck there overnight."

Colt nods. Ridesharing has increased in popularity with the rise in gas prices. It was a plausible theory that Rumor had hitched a ride with someone. But there was one thing about this scenario that bothered him.

"It's not a park-and-ride location," Colt says. "There are signs all around saying no overnight parking."

"Have it towed then," Norm replies with a shrug. "Anything else?"

Colt slowly shakes his head. *Maybe I'm overreacting. Maybe Rumor did hitch a ride with a friend, or perhaps he had car trouble and was forced to leave it there overnight.*

"No. Get out of here."

Norm nods, turns, and exits the office. On his way out of RS1, he says goodbye to Porter and Joey.

"Joey." Colt pushes himself up from the chair and meets her by the front desk. "Call Adam's Towing. Have them come and pick up Rumor's—

The front door to RS1 bursts open. A blast of arctic air snatches the room in its wintery paw. Darryl Shoff shuffles in like a drunk walking into a saloon looking to settle a score.

"Where's my son!" he screams.

CHAPTER 3

"Where is he?" Darryl asks through his false teeth. He looks at the holding cell in the back of RS1. "Rumor! You back there, boy? Speak up if you are."

"Rumor's not here, Darryl. Though his pickup was found in the Serpentine Trail parking lot last night. Know anything about that?" Joey asks. Like everyone else, she suspects Rumor and his father are responsible for terrorizing the park over the last year.

"'Course not!"

"Then how'd you know to come here?"

Darryl squares his shoulders and settles his beady, dark eyes on her, flaring with irritation. Anger pulsates off him in hot waves that chap Joey's skin like windburn.

"You sayin' I'm a liar?"

"When the shoe fits," Joey claps back. *You know damn well Rumor was in the park last night and what he was doing here.*

Darryl's upper lip raises like a wolf about to bite. Having dealt with hostile men, both in the park and out of it, Joey feels Darryl would like to slap her across the face for how she spoke to him. *A woman should know her place,* Darryl might say afterward. *Misogynistic prick.*

"All right. Spill it, Darryl. What was Rumor up to last night?" Colt intervenes.

"How should I know? He's a thirty-three-year-old man. I'm not his keeper anymore."

"When was the last time you saw him?"

Darryl hikes his narrow shoulders. He's of medium height—five-eight—and lean like a chicken except for his pot gut. His face is rubbery with fleshy jaws, and the soft skin under his eyes droops like a sad clown. The false teeth don't fit on his gums and give his lips a curvature like the end of a duck's beak. What hair that's left on his head is white and horseshoed around the bottom of his skull. A fur-trimmed plaid hat with flaps to keep his small ears warm covers the balding.

"Maybe he was out visitin' his momma. She's buried in the Shoff Cemetery, ya know."

"He's not allowed at the cemetery after dark," Colt says.

"The cemetery *is* our land! He's allowed on it any damn time he wants." Darryl spits on the floor between Colt's boots.

Gross. Joey wrinkles her nose.

"I'm not getting into a land dispute with you today," Colt says, ignoring the spitting, the low class of Darryl Shoff. "I've got enough to worry about before this storm hits."

"Well, I ain't leavin' until we find my son. Got it, Buster?" Darryl crosses his arms defiantly.

If Rumor is missing, as Darryl claims, he must feel helpless. Even a miserable old cuss like him still has some semblance of a heart. Still, it's hard for Joey to empathize with Darryl Shoff, and Rumor, for that matter, after everything they had put the park through. She was not a vindictive woman by nature—there had been a drive inside her to help those in need since she was a little girl—but Rumor had made his bed and now it was time to let him sleep in it.

"Isn't anyone lookin' for him after findin' his pickup?" Darryl's eyes, large like saucers with concern, dart around the room for confirmation that at least an attempt to search for his son is underway.

"Norm said he checked around down there. But no Rumor," Colt replies.

"You've got to be kiddin' me! You left him out there? In this cold?"

"If he's out there," Colt counters. "Maybe he met a friend and left his truck down there overnight—which I might add is illegal."

"He wasn't meetin' anyone last night."

"Then what was he doing down there?" Joey asks.

"Like I said, maybe he was visiting his momma."

Joey doesn't believe that. Not for a second. Rumor was up to something last night, and it didn't include visiting his mother's grave. Colt takes a long breath and lets it out slowly. What's coming next is inevitable: a search for Rumor—who most likely put himself in whatever situation he finds himself in.

"Porter?" Colt finally says after a long moment of contemplation. Porter Barrett jumps to his feet and meets Colt by the front desk. "Grab your gear. You're with me."

Colt turns to Joey. She knows he's about to tell her to stay there and monitor the phones and radio, but she speaks before he has a chance.

"No offense to Porter, but I should be the one to go. If Rumor's hurt, I'm the best medic on the team."

All rangers working in the park have a standard first aid certification. However, Joey was the only certified EMT. Before becoming a Marburg State Park ranger, she worked as a Harrisburg paramedic for five years. Burnt out from the horror show she found herself in night after night—treating gunshot wounds and stabbing victims, DUI-related accidents, and drug overdoses—she needed out. She saw enough death and sadness in those five years as a night-shift critter to last her a lifetime. She decided to follow in her father's footsteps and become a park ranger. Like Charles Walsh, who Joey resembles, she found serenity in nature—a contrast from working the streets of Harrisburg, where she washed blood out of the ambulance after each shift.

Colt nods knowingly. He glances at Porter.

"She's right," Porter agrees. "If Rumor *is* out there, and he *is* injured, Joey's the best person to have with you."

Colt looks back at her.

"Okay. Grab your gear." He turns to Porter. "Contact Flint and Dusty at RS2. And Wyatt at RS3. Let 'em know what's going on and tell 'em to watch for Rumor on their ends of the park."

"Will do, Boss."

Joey is in the back seat of the SUV while Colt drives. Darryl is beside Colt and complains about how the DCNR stole his land and that the *United States is turning to Socialism.* She tries to tune him out. His shrill voice irritates her ears—*he sounds like a Grey go-away-bird, whyyy-whaah*—and he's speaking louder than he has to, which makes her head hurt. She wants to tell him to shut his trap. At least the government didn't take everything from them like they had from the Shawnee—their land, language, culture…their lives. But instead, she looks out the window at the passing forest and tries to drown out his incessant moaning with other thoughts. Black Rock Road cuts along the park's southwestern edge before it dead ends at the Serpentine Trail parking lot.

"And the state wanted to offer me fifty-five grand for over thirty acres. And do you know what Rumor said?" When Colt doesn't acknowledge Darryl, he continues. "He says, *Daddy, they tryin' to stick it to us. That price, for that amount of land, is a slap in the face.* You know what, the boy was right."

Whyyy-whaaah!

Joey notices Colt glance at her in the rearview mirror. The look in his eyes tells her he's concerned about Rumor and getting all of them back before the storm unleashes. An icy chill tickles the back of her neck. She'd seen that same nervous gaze just before he and

Maynard set off to find the stranded hiker, after the distress call. That was July 15. Six months ago. *We don't need a repeat of July.*

She tunes back into the conversation Darryl's having with himself.

"Then the state counteroffers, after I sue them for trying to steal my land through Eminent Domain, with sixty-five thousand dollars. So, they weren't willing to pay me sixty-five grand off the bat—which is ten thousand more than the fifty-five (*no shit,* Joey thinks)—but then they're all about upping the offer after the courts get invol—"

Joey has heard enough and returns to her thoughts.

She was in RS1 when Dusty Albert answered the broken distress call that came in after five o'clock that July afternoon. By then, the storm had already taken the phones and powerlines down, and RS1 was running off the generator. Maynard wanted to mount a rescue immediately. Colt strongly objected, saying it was too dangerous with the wind and rain to hike up to the Rocks. Trails were washing out, and trees were coming down left and right. But Maynard wouldn't listen, which was so unlike him.

She had immediately taken a liking to Maynard Barrett when she first started at the park. He taught her how to conduct herself as a ranger while teaching her survival skills and the lay of the land needed to be successful in her new career. She came to think of him as the father figure she no longer had. Her father died when she was fourteen. She was raised by her mother, Casandra, a stout, blond-haired, blue-eyed Pennsylvania-Dutch woman whom Joey was glad she didn't resemble. Maynard was usually reasonable and understanding. He listened to others' points of view. A sign, at least to her, of a man who knew how to handle a situation, himself, and those who served under him. But on the day of the hurricane, something was…off with him.

Distracted is the word that floats into Joey's mind.

A bump in the road jolts Joey from her thoughts. The Serpentine Trail parking lot is ahead. Alone in the lot, about fifteen feet from the wooden archway gate is Rumor's red Ford F-150 pickup.

Colt steers the SUV to the driver's side of the F-150. As they're slowing to a stop, Darryl, all sixty-five years of him, jumps out and scuttles toward the driver's side door. He walks like a man with rickets, bowlegged and stiff in his movements. Peering through the window, Darryl doesn't find his boy inside—*if he had, he'd be frozen to death by this point*—and turns around and yells into the woods.

"*Rumor! Rumor! Ruuuuumooooor!*"

Colt slams the SUV into park and jumps out.

"Quit screaming, you loon. If Rumor's out here, we'll find him. Relax."

Darryl falls silent. But he continues to pace around the parking lot like a wild animal in a cage. His eyes search between every tree and around every rock for his boy.

Joey steps out and is hit by a strong gust of wind. The bite of the cold instantly touches her bare skin, and a deep chill hits her core, which will be with her for the rest of the day. She pops the hatch to retrieve their survival and rescue gear backpacks. Colt joins her, irritation pulses off him like radiation. He tells her to turn around and assists her into the pack's shoulder straps.

"What do you think?" she asks quietly so Darryl doesn't overhear.

"I think Rumor was up to something. Got himself in a mess he can't get himself out of."

Turning, she stares into Colt's dark blue eyes. He still holds the same look she'd seen on his face in the rearview mirror moments ago. She doesn't have to hear Colt verbalize his thoughts to know he's concerned about searching for Rumor with a blizzard knocking on their doorstep. She glances up at the dark gray clouds, and a moment of trepidation works across her body. *We need to get moving.* Colt picks up his pack and slings it effortlessly over his broad shoulders. He looks back at her. *Later*, his eyes say. *We'll talk later.*

Her attraction to Colt was undeniable from the moment they met. Her first impression was how ruggedly handsome he was, with sandy-blond hair and dark blue eyes that held the wisdom of a wise man. At six-one and well-built—a body sculpted from years of hiking and hard work in the wilderness - Colt was like a cowboy lost in the modern-day world. *An old soul*, Maynard had called him once. He was different from other men she had met, dated. He had a quiet calmness that she found fascinating and a bit mysterious. He's a hard guy to read and an even harder guy to get to open up. He isn't void of emotions but keeps them close to his heart.

But with Maynard's death, Colt grew even more inward, brooding over a situation out of his control from the start and an outcome he could not change. He stayed home on the nights he and Joey weren't together at the motel off of I-95 so no one would find out about their relationship. It hurt Joey to know he was alone. Negative thoughts can creep up on a person when alone. She wants him to let the floodgates open and spill his soul to her about what happened that night on the Rocks, something she's been after him to do since Maynard's death. But he keeps everything bottled up and corked. The only time she'd seen him weep was at Maynard's funeral and then, later, after the funeral when Joey felt the need to go to his home and comfort him. *He has no one.* It's what she told herself, convinced herself, on the way there. She knew better than to go, to allow him to cry on her shoulder, into her neck; his hot tears running down her chest, circling her breasts. Her mistake was making that first move and kissing him.

Her "mistake"? That was only in the eyes of their employer. It's why she insisted they continue to see one another, even at the risk of their jobs, even after Colt said they should no longer see one another outside of work. A part of her finds it exciting, like they're a couple of teenagers sneaking around behind their parents' backs. Still, Joey would like to go home with the man she's head-over-heels in love with every night and not have to play the hide-and-go-fuck game to avoid losing their jobs.

Colt slams the SUV's hatch. He turns to Darryl, who resembles a lost and cold senile old man trying to figure out where he is. A moment of pity for Darryl passes through Joey, like she would for any old person in a bind. But like before, the feeling quickly passes. *This is your fault.*

"What was Rumor doing out here last night?" Joey asks. She hopes to catch Darryl in a lie with the same question - a tactic all law enforcement uses to get the truth.

"I have no idea," Darryl says, indignation rising in his voice.

"You sure you don't know?" Colt stares at Darryl with such intent that it forces the old man to look toward the trail; his eyes squint vexingly.

"Yes." Darryl shifts his hardened gaze back to Colt. "Now, are we going to stand here and freeze to death, or are we going to go and find my son?"

They pass under Serpentine Trail's wooden archway and start up the trail into the woods with Colt in the lead. Then Darryl. Joey brings up the rear. The woods close in around them, further darkening the already gloomy day and dampening Joey's mood and tolerance for the cold. She'd like to find Rumor, get back to RS1, where it was warm, and deal with him there. But she suspects that's not how this afternoon will play out.

"Could Rumor have come with a friend or met someone down here?" Colt asks.

"No. He was alone last night," Darryl grumbles.

"Did you see him?"

"No."

"Then how do you know he was alone?"

"Because I just came from his house. His girlfriend said he went out for dinner but didn't come home."

"How do you know he didn't meet someone after leaving his house?" Darryl's story is full of holes so big Joey feels she could drive a truck through them. And she's pretty sure Colt suspects the same thing.

Darryl mumbles under his breath.

"Where'd he go for dinner?" Colt asks.

"The Tavern, over in Hopewell."

Colt stops and turns to Darryl with a stern gaze that could turn the old man into stone.

"You sure about that, Darryl?"

"That's what I was told." Darryl's eyes narrow into thin slits that study Colt just as hard—*a dick-measuring contest.* "What are you getting at?"

Colt doesn't reply and turns away. He continues on the trail. Does Colt know something about where Rumor was last night? She wants to ask but decides it will be best to talk to him later. Though, she does have another question for Darryl.

"Why'd Rumor have dinner alone?"

"Because he was hungry," Darryl says, glancing over his shoulder at her.

"Yeah. But it just seems strange that he went to dinner without his girlfriend. Wasn't she home? Did they fight?"

"I don't know. Are you writing a book, Missy? You should leave that chapter out if you are."

"I'm just trying to understand what's going on."

"No. You're trying to pin something on Rumor."

Not too hard to make assumptions after you sue the park, and when you don't win, the problems start.

"Look," Darryl says, calmer now. "Maybe he and his old lady did fight, or maybe she wasn't home. She didn't say one way or the other. Jus that Rumor didn't come home last night. Boy's always been hot-headed. He gets it from me. So maybe Rumor went to cool off and had dinner by himself. Then maybe he came here to see his momma and talk to her. She always knew what to say to settle him down."

Lame excuse. And it's not very convincing. But Joey lets him talk. He might incriminate himself while he runs his mouth.

But Darryl grows quiet, and they continue silently on the trail.

Five minutes later, they come to the Shoff Cemetery. The wrought iron gate hangs ajar, rocks back and forth in the breeze, an eerie *squeak, squeak* crawls across the bare forest. Colt stops by the entrance. Darryl shuffles past him and pushes through the gate, which makes a long *squeeeeeeeeak* as the cold iron groans. He looks behind each tombstone as he moves further into the cemetery, as if he expects to find Rumor. There's a scared desperation in Darryl's eyes as he searches. Again, Joey is saddened for him. This time the feeling doesn't dissipate.

"There's blood on the gate," Colt says in a voice deep with worriment.

"Some here, too," Darryl says, standing beside the largest tombstone in the cemetery. Across the top is the name SHOFF. A dark blood trail between the O and the F has frozen to the marker on its way to the ground. A tremor passes through Joey, fearing the worst for Rumor.

She and Colt meet Darryl by the tombstone. Colt bends and examines the blood on the grave marker. His dark blue eyes travel down the stone to the ground, where more blood is frozen to the earth. When Colt shifts his gaze back to her, a grim look stitches his face, reminding her of when he returned from the Rocks without Maynard or the stranded climber.

"Is it *his* blood?" Darryl swallows, and his throat clicks.

"I don't know. It's someone's blood, that's for sure," Colt replies. But the look on his face tells Joey he believes it *could* be Rumor's.

"Rumor!" Darryl screams, his voice echoing across the forest. *"Rumor! Can you hear me, son! Rumor!"*

"Shut it!" Colt snaps. "If Rumor's hurt, and he's trying to call out, we're not going to be able to hear him over your screaming."

Darryl falls mum. He seems to grow small, inward, like a child scorned for talking out of turn.

"What do you think?" Joey asks.

Colt looks back at the blood frozen to the dead, yellow blades of grass, and starts toward the gate. He keeps his line of sight on the ground, slightly in front of him. What does he see that she doesn't? Colt's skill as a tracker is incomparable to that of other rangers in their unit, including hers. A skill Maynard taught him; one Colt's honed from years of tracking animals and humans lost in the park. After examining the ground around the gate, Colt walks parallel with the wrought iron fence and the trail, his head swinging back and forth like a pendulum. He stops at the end of the cemetery fence, looks off into the woods behind it, and then returns to them.

"There are two different blood trails," Colt says. "But I think the same person made them. The spatter marks indicate someone came up the trail from the lake, went into the cemetery, stopped at the tombstone, and doubled back. You see this." Colt bends and points between the two lines of blood droplets frozen on the dead grass. "See how the tails in one set of droplets point away from the tombstones, while the others point toward the gate?"

Joey sees the pattern now that Colt points it out. She still has so much to learn about tracking. But she also sees something that isn't trackable.

"Are you saying that whoever's blood this is, was hurt when they got here?" Colt nods bleakly. "Why would someone stop here if they were hurt?" None of this makes a lick of sense to her.

"The blood trail exiting the cemetery is interesting," Colt says. "It leads along the fencing and then off into the woods. Must've taken the old cattle trail."

"Cattle trail?" Joey asks.

"There's a path that leads back up to the parking lot." Darryl jabs his finger at the dense forest behind the cemetery. "It's how our cows used to get down to the lake for water. Rumor knows it. But why would he use it instead of the main trail to return to his truck if he was injured?"

Why indeed?

"The trail's not on any park map I've ever seen." This is the first time she's ever heard about it. For that matter, how does Colt know about it?

"It wouldn't be," Colt replies. "Since it was here before the park took over the land, Maynard and I mapped it out one afternoon in case the main trail was blocked, and we needed to get back here for an emergency. If Rumor knew it was there—"

"He does," Darryl says.

"Then he might've taken it."

"Saying it *was* Rumor, and he *was* hurt, why in God's name would he go through the woods when there's a perfectly good trail leading directly to the parking lot and his truck?" Joey turns and studies the trail. She had seen nothing obstructing it that would impede Rumor's trek to the parking lot. "And why didn't Norm say anything about blood on the trail?"

"Rumor! Rumor! Ruuuuumooooor!"

Colt doesn't tell Darryl to shut it this time. He looks at Joey instead, trouble brewing across his brow. If he has a theory on why Norm didn't say anything to them about the blood, he keeps it to himself.

"I want you to follow the main trail to the lakebed. See if you can find any signs that Rumor was down there."

Joey shifts her gaze to the trail snaking its way down the hillside to the lake below. The thought of hiking in this wind makes her wish she had kept her mouth shut when Colt asked Porter to assist. But if that wasn't enough, she'd be coming out directly across from Camp Southwoods. Five years with the park and the abandoned camp still gave her the creeps.

"What about you?" she asks, looking back at Colt.

"Darryl and I will follow the cattle trail and see what we can find."

Colt steps closer. She can smell the Old Spice cologne on his skin.

"If you find anything by the lake, call me on the CB. I'll do the same. We'll meet back here in twenty minutes, regardless. Understand?"

Joey does. Her stomach knots in a way she can't explain.

This entire situation feels…wrong.

CHAPTER 4

Colt's been quiet, focused on tracking the trail of broken branches and disruption of dead logs and rocks. The few footprints he spotted here and there in the loose dirt tell him he's correct, that someone—Rumor?—came this way. But he's worried. Snow is starting to cover the landscape, and with it, any traces of that individual, along with the ruts, divots, roots, and branches peppering the trail. They need to tread carefully. One improper step can turn or break an ankle.

"I…need…a…moment," Darryl huffs behind Colt.

Colt turns to find the old man leaning against a tree. His face is sweaty, skin ashen. He heaves air. Though Darryl appears in decent physical shape, looks can be deceiving for a man of his age. The cattle trail is rugged terrain. Couple that with worrying about his son's safety, the cold, and the hike, and it's starting to zap Darryl's energy fast. *Unless there's something internally wrong.* Colt doesn't know enough about the human body besides how to patch it up on the outside to assess Darryl's condition clinically. He thinks about telling Darryl to turn back. The storm is dropping its payload. *Time isn't on our side.* But Darryl will protest—as Colt would if he were in the man's shoes and his son was missing in these woods.

Colt recalls the hike to the Rocks with Maynard. They were lucky enough to get a quarter of the way there in an ATV until the trail became impassable with debris. From there, it was on foot, climbing over downed trees, dodging landslides, or having to sidestep the trail altogether in hopes of finding another way around a blockage or a washout. All for what? *Nothing. It was all for nothing.* Now, he finds himself in a similar situation. Only this time, it's during a blizzard instead of a hurricane. The semblance between the two incidents twists in his mind with unease.

Colt slips off his backpack, unzips it, and pulls out two water bottles. He hands one to Darryl.

"Thanks." Darryl takes the bottle from him.

Colt nods and cracks the cap on his bottle. He takes a sip, just enough to wet his whistle. Darryl, on the other hand, downs most of his water in three chugs. Colt can't help but think how greedy the man looks, not only with the water but also in life.

"You really think Rumor came this way?" Darryl asks, running his forearm across his wet lips.

"Someone did. Whoever it was followed the cattle trail, mostly."

"Whatcha mean, 'mostly'?"

"He avoided a few things here and there, large rocks and some of the bigger fallen trees that took him off the trail, but he made his way back onto it."

"Any idea why he came this way?"

"I don't know." An eerie tingling at the base of Colt's neck raises the goose bumps. He's not sure what he's sensing or why.

"Doesn't make any goddamn sense. If Rumor was hurt, why not stay on the main trail back to his truck? It's the most direct route. Why all…this?"

Colt wishes he had a solid answer. But something made him—Rumor?—take this route. *What?* And though Colt doesn't express his feelings because he doesn't want Darryl to lose hope that he'll see his boy again, a constant worry that they *are* already too late has been pecking away at him. The first twenty-four hours were critical to getting a lost hiker out of the woods in good weather conditions. They were already past the twelve-hour mark since Rumor was last seen at the Route 206 diner. With the wind, cold, and snow, and a possible injury, his chances of survival diminished with each passing minute. *If he's even still alive.*

"We need to keep moving," Colt says.

Darryl nods and pushes himself off the tree. He drops the plastic bottle on the ground as he does.

"I know you're going to pick that up," Colt says matter-of-factly.

"Easy, big fella," Darryl says, holding up his hands. "I just dropped it." He bends and picks the bottle up and stuffs it into his Carhartt's big pouch pocket. "Whatever you think about my son or me, we're not any of those the-world-is-our-garbage-can people."

"I don't think about you or Rumor at all, to be honest. Unless you're out here when you shouldn't be."

Colt turns and starts up the trail.

"You just can't drop it, can you? You think because Rumor and I were in a fight with the state to get our land back, that he must've been out here doing somethin'."

Colt snaps around.

"Then why was he out here last night, Darryl? The park is closed after sundown. You both know that."

"Like I said, maybe he was visiting his momma."

"Bullshit." Colt steps closer, staring the old man down. "I know that Rumor wasn't in Hopewell last night for dinner, like you said. He was at the Route 206 Diner—had liver and onions and washed it all down with a Coke." If Darryl knows the truth, he masks it well. "You and I know Rumor was out here for a reason last night. I'm going to find out what."

Darryl narrows his eyes, and his lips press into a thin white line. Colt knows he's trying to think of a witty retort or deflect the accusation away from his son, and possibly himself. When nothing comes to mind, he steps past Colt and begins up the trail.

"C'mon, we're losin' time."

Colt drops it there. For the moment, at least.

They continue on without speaking. Colt's thankful for this. He wants to avoid arguing with Darryl, especially about the land dispute with the DCNR while together. *Don't need any "he said, he said" bullshit finding its way into court with a frivolous lawsuit Darryl might file once we find Rumor.* Regardless, Colt saw Darryl's point of view on the matter and even sympathized with him, to a point. Darryl had every right to be upset at the DCNR for taking his land. It was wrong. Colt felt strongly about that. They should have appropriately compensated Darryl for the land, not offered him a bullshit deal they knew he'd turn down. But that was why they did it: they could use the eminent domain laws and courts to get the land for free, because Darryl wouldn't be able to afford to fight them on an appeal. Be that as it may, that didn't give the Shoffs the right to destroy public property and to put people's lives at risk with their vengeance tour through the park for the last year. It needed to stop.

With the snowflakes *clicking* on the branches and dead leaves carpeting the forest floor, they continue until the trail dips into a gully. Colt warns Darryl to watch his footing. It's slippery, and they're careful to navigate the hillside as they descend.

At the bottom of the gully, they pause a moment to catch their breath. Colt studies the hill before them. It climbs sharply before leveling off between two large boulders at the top. Though the ground is frozen solid, loose rocks and snow cover the incline. It will be a bitch to get up. The snow-dusted stones will be like walking over chunks of ice. They must tread carefully. As he starts up the hill, he ensures his feet are planted firmly and the rocks under him won't give way before pushing off to take the next step.

Colt is almost at the top of the insufferable rocky slant when he spots something.

"Up here," he says over his shoulder.

"You…find…him?" Darryl asks, panting with desperation.

Colt doesn't bother to answer and moves the rest of the way up the hill toward the right boulder, where a bloody handprint stands out on the rock's surface in stark contrast with the white world closing in around it. He kneels beside the rock and examines the print just as Darryl crests the hill behind him, wheezing like an asthmatic.

"He…definitely…came…this way." Darryl's brow is sweaty, and the gray pallor of his skin has worsened.

"Someone did," Colt replies, looking around.

"What's that…supposed…to mean? You said that…before."

"We don't know for certain if this is Rumor's blood. But if it *is*, then he's hurt. Bad. He paused here, probably to catch his breath after climbing that hill. See how the fingers are pointing downward?" Darryl nods and sweat drips off his chin. "I believe someone was sitting on the boulder and pushed off when they stood." Colt stands and surveys the snowy forest in front of them. *Frozen hell.* "We need to find whoever left that print before this storm worsens."

"Then what are we waiting for. Let's get—"

Darryl steps forward when the toe of his boot catches on something buried underneath the snow. He falls sideways into the left boulder and tries to grab onto its smooth surface to prevent himself from going over and down the embankment. His hands find only air. The top half of his body disappears behind the boulder, pulling his legs along with the rest of him. His boots shoot into the air, flinging snow from the treads in a fan pattern as he goes over the rock.

Colt runs toward the other boulder, as Darryl rolls down the hill. Twigs snap. Branches slap against Darryl's Carhartt jacket. Painful grunts explode from the old man as the air is driven from his body with each turn that impacts the hard, unforgivable earth underneath. The sounds fill Colt's ears with a brazen memory of Maynard's fall. His body sounded like wet meat when it impacted the rocks; his limbs snapped like dried wood on his way to the forest floor. Colt hadn't been able to stop Maynard's fall, and he hadn't been able to stop Darryl's, either.

On top of the boulder, Colt searches the hollow below. He spots Darryl lying on his back, snow and dirt covering his body. Darryl's face has minor nicks and cuts; one across the bridge of his nose is bleeding copiously. A familiar panic grips Colt's heart, like when he reached the top of the rocks and searched the darkness below for Maynard.

"Darryl!" he hollers.

There's no reply.

"Darryl?" The panic expands into Colt's back. There was no way a sixty-five-year-old man could survive the fall, just like Maynard hadn't. "Darryl!"

"Ye-ah," a gravelly weak voice calls back.

Colt sighs, and the tension in his chest and back eases.

"You okay?"

Darryl moves slowly, like a man awakening from a long winter's nap. Using a small tree nearby, he props his back against it, legs extended in front, hands resting on his lap. From the blank look and watery absentness in his eyes, Colt worries that he might have hit his head. He asks again if he's okay.

"I-I think so. Just…just got the wind…knocked out of…me."

"Does anything feel broken?"

Darryl looks down at himself as if this will provide the answer Colt seeks. As a result, Colt's fear intensifies. Darryl may have a concussion.

"No," Darryl slurs.

Colt scans the landscape. The hillside is a wall of snow and rocks. And Darryl has fallen below where the trail dips into the gully. Getting Darryl back to the lowest point on the trail is about a five-foot climb. Darryl's injuries might be too severe for such a feat. *I need to call for help.*

Plucking the CB from his belt, Colt says, "Colt calling RS1. Come in RS1."

Static.

He tries again.

"Porter, you there?"

More static.

A wind gust rolls over the hill—flecks of snow and ice tap Colt's jacket like bee-bees fired from a machine gun. *The storm's interfering with the short-to-long-range radio connections.* They had a similar problem while Colt and Maynard were hiking to the Rocks. But what Colt didn't know, at that time, was that the hurricane had taken down the long-range antenna, effectively cutting off communications with RS1 nearly five miles away. That helpless sadness envelopes him. It's a feeling he knows he'll never be rid of. *We should've never gone up there.*

Angry that he can't reach RS1, Colt clips the CB back onto his belt. He will have to rappel down and make sure Darryl's okay. Will he be able to walk out of there on his own? If not, Colt will need to hike back to the parking lot, get in the SUV, and return to RS1 to bring back help.

"Stay where you are. Don't move until I get down there," Colt says.

Darryl lifts his hand heavily, like it's made of iron, before letting it fall back to his lap.

Colt takes the backpack off and unzips it. He pulls out a rope, bound in a figure-eight knot. He undoes the rope from its binding, takes it to a maple tree near the hillside, and ties it off in an arborist knot. He then gathers the rest of it and tosses it over the side. It lands near Darryl's feet. When he gets Darryl up, bearing none of his appendages are broken—or worse, his skull—Colt hopes he'll be able to use the rope to pull himself up to the lowest part of the trail.

Colt slings his backpack over his shoulders and grabs the rope. He moves to the edge of the hillside, using the rope as a guideline to keep him steady so he doesn't go ass over teacup down the hill like Darryl. Snow and a few loose rocks cascade down the embankment as he kicks off and rappels to the bottom.

Once down, Colt hurries to Darryl. He appears more lucid

than a few moments ago. That's a good sign. However, the gash across Darryl's nose is a concern. Blood runs down his face, into his mouth, dots his jacket, and the snow around him.

"How are you feeling?" Colt kneels beside him and unslings the backpack. He removes his gloves, unzips the bag, and roots inside for the first aid kit.

"Like I just went rollin' down a hill like a drunk in a barrel." Darryl spits a wad of blood into the snow. "Only without the barrel."

"Can you move?" Colt opens the first aid kit, pulls out a gauze bandage, and places it across the laceration. Darryl cries, winces at the touch. Blood quickly soaks through the gauze, and Colt feels it warm his bare fingertips.

"I-I think so. Nothin' feels broken, except maybe my nose."

Colt pulls the gauze away. The pressure has stemmed the bleeding. He examines the cut and the shape of Darryl's nose. There's going to be a hell of a bruise, and a hell of a lot of pain, especially around the laceration, but it doesn't appear broken, though Colt has no real way of knowing. He tosses the blood-soaked gauze aside, reaches for another one, and places it back on Darryl's face.

"Hold." Darryl reaches up and holds the gauze gingerly to his face. Colt sits back with his legs folded under him. "I think you'll be okay. Your nose doesn't look broken. But we need to get out of here. Think you can use the rope to pull yourself back up to the lowest part of the trail?"

Darryl nods. He lifts his hand away and looks at the gauze. A trickle of blood seeps from the gash. Colt directs Darryl to keep pressure on the wound.

He gathers everything up, stuffs it into a red medical baggie from inside the first aid kit and returns it to the backpack. Once he has the pack slung over his shoulders, he reaches out for Darryl. Taking him by the forearm, Colt pulls the old man to his feet. He sways back and forth once upright. Colt steadies him until he regains his bearings, unsure of Darryl's cognitive abilities to pull himself back to the trail.

"You good?" Colt asks.

"Yep," Darryl says with a nod.

But he doesn't look well. In fact, Colt thinks he looks like a man knocking on death's door. Darryl's well-being worries him. They need to wrap this up and return to RS1, where it is warm, and Joey can examine him.

Colt guides Darryl over to the wall and hands him the rope.

"You sure you can do this?"

"I'm…fine," Darryl wheezes, about to pull himself up the wall when the CB radio on Colt's belt *bleats*.

"Colt? This is Joey. Come in, over."

Snatching the CB off his utility belt, Colt says, "Go for Colt."

"Where are you?"

"We're still on the cattle trail north of the cemetery. Where are you?"

"I'm across from the abandoned camp."

"Any sign of Rumor?"

"No." The way Joey speaks concerns him. "But I found his duffel bag."

Colt looks at Darryl and sees the worry of a father fearing the worst for his son. It was a similar look that Porter gave Colt when he came back without his father and with news that there never was a climber stuck on the Rocks. The distress call had been a hoax to get them out there. In the end, Maynard died for nothing. Was that Rumor and Darryl's handiwork, too? Colt doesn't know.

"We ran into a little trouble on our end. We'll be there as soon as we can."

CHAPTER 5

rouble? What kind of trouble? The muscles in Joey's throat constrict. She wants to ask Colt if he's okay. No, she *needs* to know if he's okay. But she suppresses the urge, fearing someone might overhear their conversation and question her excessive concern for Colt's well-being. *Remain professional.*

"Ten-four."

Joey hooks the CB back onto her belt and looks at the duffel bag at her feet. The yellow letters of R. Shoff stand out on the canvas. She had found the bag alongside the trail, tucked into a thicket of dead brush. She would never have seen the backpack if she had not spotted the yellow R against the white snow. *What the hell were you doing down here, Rumor?*

Tink, tink, tink.

The metal cable snaps off the hollow flagpole, as if warning trespassers to stay away. Across the inlet are the remains of Camp Southwoods. Even in its desertedness, Joey feels like someone is watching her from one of the abandoned cabins. Her skin crawls with unease. She keeps her eyes away from the boarded-up windows, fearing she'll see eyes staring back at her through the slats. Camp Southwoods has always unnerved her. *The willies,* Maynard called it when he showed her around the camp for the first time. Whether it's the lore, the camp's bloody and very violent history, or its malevolent boogieman, Joey keeps her distance unless she needs to run a trespasser off the land. Though she feels that most talk about seeing ghosts and hearing disembodied voices is nothing more than urban legends, the area resonates with the dreaded heaviness of what happened there. And that damn rhyme has worked to the front of her brain, on repeat like a skipping record.

Little counselor running,
Douggie Carver's gone a-hunting
Gonna catch that counselor,
Gonna cleave that counselor,
Little counselor done running.

The wind growls across the inlet, and snow pellets sting Joey's cheeks like mosquito bites. Her nose and lips are raw and wind burnt, and her eyes are teary. She wishes she had brought a pair of snow goggles or, at the very least, a facemask to keep the cold at bay.

Stupid.

She unzips the duffel bag and pushes the sides out so she can see inside. She finds a battery-operated DeWalt drill. The three-inch bit in the drill's jaws has wood lodged in the grooves. A 350ml syringe with blue liquid frozen inside the drum. There's also a gardening shovel; its blade dirty. Under the shovel is a bottle. The label faces away from her, so she can't see what its contents are. She pulls the bottle out and turns the label to face her.

Tardon.

Tardon, Joey knows, is an herbicide that kills plants like…

Trees!

Rumor's been the one poisoning the trees around the park. A swell of emotions—fury, hate, and anger—spikes her blood pressure. She thinks of the two trees they found across Long Head Trail this week. Someone could have been seriously injured or even killed while out hiking if a tree had fallen on them.

You motherfucker…

She can't do anything until Colt arrives and is about to replace the contents when something else grabs her attention inside the duffel bag.

A white piece of paper with a rubber band around a stack of what looks like eight-by-ten cards. Joey picks the cards up and sees a series of numbers written in chicken scratch down the front of the paper.

11
1215
130
245
300
415
530
645

What the hell do these numbers mean?

She removes the rubber band from the stack and lifts away the paper to find…

Photographs?

Joey's face blushes at the images.

The first eight-by-ten photograph appears to have been taken through a window, and two people are in a bed having sex. A woman is on top of a man, her head lowered, her long black hair blocking her features. The man's face is also obstructed between her bare breasts. Joey's cheeks grow hotter, and her nipples stiffen so hard they hurt. She feels like a Peeping Tom (or, in her case, a Peeping Jane), unable to look away, attracted for some sick, perverse reason to the most private, intimate moments in these people's lives. She thinks finding these photos in Rumor's duffel bag is odd but considers that maybe taking voyeuristic pictures might be Rumor's fet—

Is that…

Her stomach drops, and her warm skin turns deathly cold, like an injection of ice water was just shot into her veins.

No way. It can't…

She no longer feels the eroticism of being the voyeur, but the icky feeling of violation, while deviant eyes leer at *her* body. She pulls her jacket tighter.

Focusing on the woman's bare right hip, Joey sees a small nondescript birthmark.

Just like the birthmark on *her* right hip.

It's not just a picture of some random couple, Joey realizes, as her heart rate spikes to an uncomfortable rhythm. *It's a picture of Colt and me!*

She flips through the stack of photos like a madwoman. There are ten photographs, each a snapshot of them in various sexual positions. Her stomach churns uncomfortably from their intrusiveness, their smuttiness. Why were the photos in Rumor's bag? Did he take them? If so, how did he know about their relationship? They had kept it, and where they met, a secret. Sour bile bites at the back of her throat with her next thought:

Or so you believe.

"What did you find?"

Joey nearly jumps out of her skin at Colt's sudden appearance. She shoots to her feet, cups the pictures to keep them out of sight. Colt and Darryl stand about ten feet from her. Joey's first instinct is to charge Darryl, who has a massive cut across the bridge of his nose. She doesn't care how it got there or what happened to him, and she envisions herself grabbing hold of that bulbous and bloody piece of meat and twisting until he tells her the truth. *Why were these pictures in Rumor's bag? Did he take them? Or was it you, you sick old fuck?* But her embarrassment is too substantial to confront him. She feels nasty and desperately wants a shower to wash away the perversion that inks her skin like a tattoo.

"You, okay?" Colt asks, sensing her distress.

She fakes a smile.

"Just cold. And a little perturbed." This isn't a lie. She's upset by what she found in the bag—by the Tardon and now the pictures.

Colt studies her for a long moment, analyzes her words and body language, and searches for the truth between the lines.

She turns away so he can't get a bead on her. She doesn't need him probing her; she'll tell him about the photos if he pushes hard enough. She slips the pictures into her pocket without anyone seeing them. She *will* show them to Colt later when Darryl isn't around.

"I found it right there." Joey points to the bag at her feet just off the trail in a thick brush.

Colt and Darryl crunch through the snow toward her. But her mind is still on the photographs and who could have taken them. Yet the bigger question, Joey wonders, is *why*. Why would someone want pictures of them having sex? There has to be a reason...

Colt drops to a knee and begins going through the duffle bag. Darryl lurches up beside her. Out of the corner of her eye, she sees his pale complexion, and concern and worry are set in his tired eyes. The gash across his nose is bright red and beginning to swell. By nightfall, it will be thumping so bad he'll wish he had something more substantial than a few painkillers.

Colt stands, turns, and chucks something at Darryl, catching him in the breadbasket.

"You don't know why Rumor was out here, huh?"

Darryl turns the bottle around so the label faces him. His face remains emotionless, blank. *Practiced.*

"I don't know what this is," Darryl says.

"The hell you don't," Colt replies. "You and Rumor have been poisoning the trees."

"I have no idea what you're talking about." Darryl drops the bottle in the snow.

"Really? Well, know this, Darryl. When we find Rumor, I will arrest him for trespassing, destroying park property, and endangerment of human lives. He's going away for a long time."

"That's not all, Colt. I also found this." Joey holds up the piece of paper with the numbers written on it.

Colt's eyes flick to Darryl—fire burns in them, and his brow furrows with anger—before taking the paper from Joey and studying it.

"Know what it means?"

Colt shakes his head. He turns to Darryl and shows him the paper.

"Any idea why this was in Rumor's bag? Or what these numbers mean?"

"Nope." Darryl doesn't bother to look at the paper.

Liar. You know exactly what it is. That's why you denied it without even looking at it.

"We're done here," Colt says.

"What about Rumor? He's still out here."

Colt gathers everything in the duffel bag and slings it over his shoulder. He starts back up the trail.

"We can't just leave Rumor out here," Darryl says.

Joey agrees with Colt. *Fuck Rumor.* But what stops her from walking away and letting Rumor fend for himself is that she wants to know why the photographs were in his bag. *And I plan on asking him when I find his ass.*

"I'll stay out with Darryl and continue the search," Joey offers.

Colt turns back, mulls over her proposition. His expression says he isn't totally on board with the idea. The temperature is plunging. The snow is getting heavier. Soon it will be a whiteout, and they can't search in a whiteout. Colt knows this. So does Joey. But she'll take the risk if it means answers when they find the pervert.

"I'm with her. I told you before, I'm not leaving here until I find my son."

The radio on Colt's belt *bleeps*, and Porter's voice comes over the speaker.

"Colt, you there, over?"

Colt pulls the CB off his belt, but his hard stare remains on Darryl while he speaks.

"Where the hell have you been? I tried to radio you. We had a situation down here."

"Sorry, Colt. The message never came through. The snow and wind both picked up in the last hour or so. It's starting to interfere with the short- to long-range connections. Something's not working right with the antenna." There's a brief pause before Porter asks, "Colt, are you alone?"

Joey hears the anxiety in Porter's voice. *Something's wrong.*

"I can be."

"It might be best that you are," Porter replies.

"Give me a minute."

Colt turns and walks far enough away that Joey and Darryl can't hear his conversation with Porter. *What's going on?* The tone of Porter's voice chills her. Has someone found Rumor dead, frozen to the ground like an animal?

Colt returns a few moments later. His face holds a troubled gaze that creeps under Joey's skin and scrapes the bone. Like the night he returned with news that the distress call was nothing more than a deadly prank that cost Maynard his life.

Who would've done such a thing?

"We're heading back," Colt says, not offering details about his conversation with Porter. "All of us."

"What? You're just going to leave my boy out here?" Darryl lunges at Colt, eyes filled with fire and icy fear.

"For the moment." Colt looks at Joey. "Let's go."

What the hell is going on? She has worked with Colt for five years, has been with him on numerous search-and-rescue operations, and he's never left before the objective was complete. *Something is wrong.* Joey's teeth chatter, and it's not because of the cold.

"Then I'll look for him myself," Darryl says.

"You do that, and I'll arrest you for trespassing." Colt levels his intense, dark blue eyes on Darryl—a warning look. *You only get one.*

"You can't do that!" Darryl's face wrinkles like a prune. "This is a public park, and I can go wherever I want."

"Not today. Today, the park's closed. That means anyone caught in or around the park is subject to detention and arrest."

"That's bullshit. My son—"

"Your son got himself into this mess. Had he not been out here last night, we wouldn't have to be out here now. I've made my decision, and the search is suspended."

"You fuck," Darryl says in a low voice that's boiling with anger and utter despair. "You just sealed my boy's fate."

CHAPTER 6

Colt is quiet on the way back to RS1 to drop off Joey and Darryl. Too quiet, he knew, even for his ordinarily introverted self. He feels Joey's eyes hot on the side of his face as he drives, burning with questions about the call from Porter. He wants to tell her what they talked about; it gnaws at him like a dog to a bone. But he can't. Not yet.

In the parking lot of RS1, Colt throws the Interceptor into park and tells Darryl to go inside and wait until he returns.

"What about Rum—"

"Darryl, I'm not going to tell you again."

Darryl mumbles about his tax dollars *paying for this bullshit* and exits the SUV. He slams the door hard enough to shake the truck. Both Colt and Joey remain silent until Darryl is inside the ranger station.

"You want to tell me what's going on?"

Colt faces her.

"Tripp radioed Porter. Said he found a body on Dedication Hill."

"Oh, jeez. Rumor?"

Colt's face twists into a grim scowl.

"I don't know. Tripp wouldn't say."

A quizzical look clambers across Joey's face.

"What?" Colt asks.

"Dedication Hill is a good five miles from Serpentine Trail. How did Rumor get way up there and on foot in this weather? He would've frozen to death from the hike alone."

"We don't know if it is Rumor."

"Well, who else could it be," Joey says as if the answer should be obvious.

And it should. But something's eating away at him. Something doesn't feel right, just like it didn't feel right when they found the blood in the cemetery that led to the cattle trail. *Why would someone use it and not the main trail back to the parking lot?* It made no sense. What made him—Rumor?—take that route.

Or someone…

And why didn't Norm see the blood when he searched down there?

"When I know more, you'll know more," Colt says, blinking his thoughts away.

Joey nods. He sees the hurt flash in her eyes. But he doesn't know more than what he's already told her.

"How'd you know Rumor wasn't in Hopewell for dinner last night?"

"Because Bill Hardy saw him at the Route 206 Diner. He left around nine, heading toward the park."

"Is Darryl lying?"

"That, or Rumor's lying to him."

Joey nods and shifts her gaze to her lap. Since he found her near Ice Fisherman's Cove, with Rumor's bag, he's sensed her unease.

"You okay?"

"We need to discuss what else I found in Rumor's bag."

She pulls a stack of photographs from her pocket and passes them to him. Colt takes them and studies the picture on top before quickly flipping through the rest like a deck of cards.

"They're a bunch of dirty pictures. So what." Colt goes to hand them back.

"Take a closer look."

He studies the first photo again at Joey's insistence but doesn't understand her concern. Yes, they're crude and smutty, but he's oblivious to whatever she wants him to see. Joey leans across the center console and points at the woman's hip. A birthmark that Colt hadn't seen at first glance.

"Does that look familiar to you?"

A jolt shoots through Colt's body like he's been struck by a speeding locomotive as his eyes focus on the birthmark. He knows it intimately. He's run his lips and tongue over it numerous times.

That's…us!

His eyes flick to hers with repulsion.

"Someone knows we're seeing each other, Colt. And they know we get together at that motel off I-95. They followed us there to take those pictures."

Disgust winds its way up Colt's back at the thought of someone watching, taking pictures of them as they make love. He has questions. *So goddamn many questions.* But his mind and mouth can only articulate one: "Why?"

"To blackmail us." Joey sits back in the seat and crosses her arms over her chest. She stares out the windshield at RS1—the snow is coming down at a 20-degree slant—fuming angrily. "They were in Rumor's bag. Maybe he took them? Or maybe it was Darryl?"

Colt turns the photos upside down. He can't bear to look at them anymore.

They're silent for a long moment, the air thick with despair that their secret might see the light of day. *And if that happens…*

"We need to get rid of these," Joey finally says. She snatches the stack from his hand and stuffs them in the jacket's pocket. "I should go in there and break that old fucker's hip."

"As fun as that would be, especially after this, I think playing this close to the vest would be better. Right now, the only people who know about these photos are you and me, Rumor, and maybe Darryl. You go in there half-cocked, Darryl will deny any involvement like he always does, and you'll expose that we know. Plus, we have to consider the possibility of more photos being stored on a computer somewhere."

"Shit! I didn't even think about that."

Joey looks utterly hopeless, like she's about to fall into hysteria.

"You need to hold it together," Colt says with a no-nonsense tone. She nods, but it's a half-hearted attempt. "I mean it, Joey."

She looks back at him, eyes wet. Her pain is his pain. If these pictures find their way to the park service higher-ups, their careers and their lives will be over. And for what? So, the Shoffs can feel some vindication for the DCNR taking their land.

That's precisely the plan. But what did Rumor and Darryl think blackmailing them will accomplish? Sure, Joey and Colt will lose their jobs, but it's not like the DCNR will give them their land back because they exposed their relationship. But maybe, Colt thinks, it's not about him and Joey personally but to burn the entire system to the ground.

"What are we going to do?" she asks.

"I don't know. I'll think of something." He nervously taps his fingers on the steering wheel, but a plan eludes him. Finally, he turns to her and says, "You better get inside."

Joey nods, opens the door, and steps into the white hell.

"Keep an eye on Darryl. Make sure he doesn't leave."

"I will," she says. "And you be careful, too. This storm is just getting started."

Porter Barrett's head snaps up from the communications desk, and he flashes a wan smile as Joey enters. Irritation floods her senses when she sees him sitting there, dry and warm, with a cup of steaming coffee and a half stack of Oreos beside him. Pulling off her cap, Joey shakes the flakes off. Then she remembers her offer to go and look for Rumor, which she's glad she did in hindsight. If Porter had gone with Colt, he might've found the photos in Rumor's bag. Thank God for big favors.

Porter stands and crosses the room toward her. She removes her gloves and flexes her cold fingers. As he approaches, Joey detects his concern from his pinched face.

"What the hell happened out there?" Porter asks. "Looks like someone kicked the shit out of that old man."

She slides her pack off her shoulders and sits it on the floor. She gazes past Porter to find Darryl has slid one of the desk chairs next to the heater along the far wall. The gash across his nose is a bloody scab, and the swelling has worsened. His hands are bright red, and his fingers are splayed over the warm air vents. What concerns her is that there's a slight blueness to Darryl's lips, and he's extremely pale. He might be suffering from a mild case of hypothermia. If Colt hadn't stopped the search for Rumor when he did, Darryl wouldn't have made it another hour outside. *The cold would have got him.* Colt made the right decision, whether Darryl believes it or not. Not that he had much choice, given the circumstances that maybe Rumor was found.

"He tripped. Went down over a hillside."

"Jesus." Porter turns and looks at Darryl. When he returns his gaze to Joey, he whispers, "Did Colt tell you what Tripp found?"

Joey nods, and her eyes flip to Darryl, but he doesn't appear to be able to hear their conversation. Still, she keeps her voice low, just above a whisper.

"Yeah. We found Rumor's bag"—*filled with pictures of Colt and me*—"and a lot of blood down there."

"Rumor's blood?"

Joey shrugs.

Porter glances over his shoulder at Darryl again; the old man's not listening to their conversation. He turns back to Joey.

"If Rumor was injured, it could've been..." He lowers his voice. "His body Tripp found?"

"How in the hell did he get to Dedication Hill, if it is Rumor?" Joey replies. "It's a five-mile hike from Serpentine Trail. If he *was* injured, there's no way he could've made that walk. And in this cold?"

Porter considers this. Finally, he nods, at Joey's point. But he has no insight to what was going on, just like herself.

"What was in the bag?" Porter asks.

"Oh, the usual stuff. Shovel. Drill. Syringe. Bottle of Tardon."

"Tardon? That's an herbicide used to kill—" He meets Joey's gaze, his eyes bright as he figures out why Rumor had Tardon in his bag. "He's the one who's been poisoning the trees, hasn't he? Using the Tardon."

"Looks that way."

"That son of a..." Porter stops himself. His lips press together into a thin, white line.

Darryl had shown up insistent on finding Rumor. Joey remembers him eyeing the cells in the back of RS1. He expected to find Rumor locked up. *Because he knew what Rumor was doing out there last night and thought he'd been caught.*

"We have another problem," Porter says.

"What?"

"The storm has taken down the phone lines and the internet. It's also interfering with the new antenna, not allowing it to relay messages between the long- and short-range radios. If we lose contact with each other again..." Porter trails off.

The fear in Porter's eyes is palpable. After Maynard's funeral, he took classes on repairing the antenna and bypassing any problems to ensure the communications between the rangers were always functioning. This unique skill (offered and paid for by the park service) brought him back to Marburg State Park after his father's death, when he seriously considered hanging up his badge. He was determined not to let someone else die because the radios couldn't transmit.

But here we are. Same shit, different day.

"I'm going to the antenna shed to look," Porter says in a woeful tone. The hurt of losing his father is present on his face and makes Joey's heart ache for Maynard—*a good man taken too soon.* She swallows her pain, suppresses the bite of tears at the corners of her eyes.

"Make sure you dress warm for the hike. It's freezing. If you start to get cold, get your butt back inside."

"I'll be fine."

She's sure he will be. Porter is intelligent, quick-thinking, and an excellent person to have around if one finds oneself in a bind, just like his father was. But experience only went so far. Maynard had years under his belt, and it didn't turn out well for him.

Colt notices Tripp has an unlit stogie tucked into the corner of his mouth as he climbs down from the plow. He pulls his hood over his head and tightens the drawstrings. Colt meets him halfway up the path leading to the top of Dedication Hill.

"What the hell took you so long?" Tripp asks, ripping the cigar out of his mouth. He reaches inside his jacket and pulls out his cigar case, opens it, and slips the nub inside. "It's twelve thirty."

"I got held up," Colt replies. The pictures Joey found in Rumor's bag materialize in his mind. *How did Rumor get them?*

"I need to show you something. This way," Tripp says.

Tripp starts up the pathway, nearly running. Colt follows, trying to keep up, but the path has become slick, and, unlike Tripp, he doesn't have snow boots for traction.

At the top of the hill, Colt looks out across the white landscape. The Panorama Building and what's left of the fallen red oak are to his right. Lance and Amos are gone, presumably taking the debris down to the pit by RS3 for disposal. In the valley below, the lake is churning like a bubbling cauldron. The western shoreline, past the islands, is still visible in the haze—Snyder Point, the fire tower—but it won't be for long. It's just a matter of time before it disappears in the white.

The black granite monument at the top of the hill is in the middle of a circular flagstone enclosure. A knee-high stone wall encapsulates the area. Tripp stops in front of the monument.

"This is what I wanted to show you," Tripp says, pointing at the monument.

Colt steps beside him. Four names are precision etched into the eight-by-four-foot granite slab in memoriam to the lives Douglas Lee Carver took on August 5, 1997.

Kurt MacReady

Alice King

Ted Charno

Virginia Steel

Underneath Virginia Steel, a fifth name has been crudely carved into the black granite.

Colt shudders at the sight of the name.

Norm Roberts

There's more. The hair rises on Colt's neck as he reads over the nursery rhyme, which is also carved into the stone.

> *Little Ranger Roberts running,*
> *Douggie Carver's gone a-hunting*
> *Gonna catch that ranger,*
> *Gonna cleave that ranger,*
> *Little Ranger Roberts done running.*

"This is spooky, Colt." Tripp's voice floats through the air with an eerie tone.

"Is…" Colt's words catch in his throat. After finding the blood on the trail, he had readied himself to find Rumor's body, not… *What the hell is going on?* A gust of wind blows in his face. His eyes water. The names on the black granite smear together into a blurry mass. *Oh, God. Norm…*

"I found him on the bench. At the bottom of the hill," Tripp says sadly, his eyes heavy, cast downward.

"Are you…sure it's Norm? Over the radio, Porter didn't…"

"I told Porter no names. Didn't want it going out over an open frequency for everyone to hear."

Colt looks at the slab. Why was Norm's name there? Why was

the rhyme there? Certainly, this wasn't the work of Douglas Lee Carver. *That's impossible. Carver's locked up in Haven Hurst.*

"I should warn you," Tripp says, bringing Colt's attention back to him. "He's in pretty bad shape."

"Pretty bad shape how?"

"You'll see."

Tripp hops over the stone wall and starts down the embankment. Colt follows. His emotions ping through his body and mind like a pinball as he tries to wrap his head around what's going on.

Twenty feet from the monument, a single bench overlooks the Panorama Building and the lake beyond that. Norm's body sits upright as if he's watching the snowfall; his shoulders and the black tassel cap have a dusting of snow on them. Tripp rounds the side of the bench and stands in front of the body. His face squeezes into a tight wrinkle of horror.

Jesus, how bad is it?

Approaching the body, Colt doesn't want to believe it's Norm. But the Pennsylvania Ranger patch sewn onto the shoulder of the green jacket sticks out like a beacon, solidifying his fear. Two arrows, with blue-and-white fletchings, protrude from the body— one in the right calf and one just below the right shoulder blade. *Why would anyone want to hurt Norm?* His mind demands a reason even though one isn't presenting itself. Colt had readied himself for the grisliness of what he was about to see. But even then, he's not sure he can keep down the steak and eggs he had for breakfast.

Rounding the bench, Colt gasps.

"Oh, my God!"

"God had nothing to do with what happened to him," Tripp says gravely.

A gust of wind cuts over the hill. It pulls the tassel cap off Norm's head and sends it tumbling across the lawn before it catches in the low branches of a nearby pine tree. His face has been split in two. He's nearly unrecognizable. To Colt, though he's no pathology expert, it looks like someone struck him with an axe.

Like Carver's victims. Still, there's no mistaking it's Norm by the badge and name tag on the left side of the jacket that reads Ranger Roberts.

Colt's eyes drift past the body to the bench. He can only make out about half of what the plaque says, but he doesn't need to see all of it; he already knows whose memory it's dedicated to. The park has many in memoriam benches, honoring the deceased, bought and paid for by their families. But this one is special, and Colt believes it isn't a coincidence that Norm's body was left there to be discovered.

IN MEMORY OF
RANGER MAYNARD BARRETT

Colt turns to Tripp. He looks gaunt and fragile, every bit his sixty-five years of age.

"When did you find him?"

"About eleven thirty this morning, or thereabouts."

Colt looks at his watch. It was going on a quarter to one.

"Where were you?"

"I left to plow and lay salt once the snow started coming down."

"Why'd you come back?"

The question seems to strike a nerve with Tripp.

"To see how Lance and Amos were making out with the tree," he says, like Colt should already know why he was in the area.

"Were they still here when you arrived?"

Tripp shakes his head. "No. I assume they finished and took the logs down to the pit. So, I turned the plow around and was about to head back out when I saw..." Tripp's eyes drift back to the body and linger there. "I thought he was a park guest, enjoying the view, the snowfall. I was going to ask 'em to leave when..." He trails off and swallows; his Adam's apple bobs so deep in his throat that Colt thinks he swallowed it.

Colt studies the area around the bench. There are a few drops of frozen blood on the seat and a few more in the grass between Norm's feet.

"He wasn't killed here," Colt finally says.

"How do you know that?"

"There's not enough blood. A face wound that deep would have bled profusely. No, Norm was murdered somewhere else in the park." He rounds the bench and looks at the arrows in his body. "I would say while he was trying to escape whoever was shooting at him. He was then moved here before the snow started to fall."

"How do you know he was trying to run away?"

"The arrows. The one in the rear of his calf probably slowed him down but didn't stop him. The second shot, in the shoulder blade, took him down." Colt studies the gash that stole Norm's face. "Then the killer got up close and personal."

"Just like Douglas Lee Carver."

Colt's eyes flick to Tripp. He looks sick to his stomach, like he sometimes does when he smokes a new cigar that's too strong. Norm's murder *is* eerily similar to Douglas Lee Carver's MO.

"That's Maynard's bench," Tripp says in a haunting tone that works its way into him, seeding itself in his mind. "Of all the benches in this park, why was Norm left here for us to find?"

"I don't know," Colt says, "But this is a crime scene now. We need to secure it until someone can get to the sheriff's station in Jackson. No word of this can go out over the radio, either."

"Why? We should let the others know about Norm—"

"No," Colt cuts him off. "We don't know who might be listening to our communications."

"How could someone be listening to us?"

"Because Norm's CB...it's missing."

CHAPTER 7

solation creeps into Dusty Albert's bones as he works along Trail Loop Two while the white forest closes in around the heated ATV. Before he left RS2 he spoke to his wife Melinda on the phone and the concern in her voice about the storm twists through his psyche like a screw being driven into his brain.

"The National Weather Service is now reporting nearly forty inches with wind gusts up to seventy miles an hour. Governor Stine is supposed to declare a State of Emergency later this afternoon. By the time you head home, the worst of it will be on top of us."

Dusty reassured her that he'll be fine and that he will get home safe. Melinda always got nervous and fidgety when a bad storm came—her motherly nature was to protect her family and ensure her loved ones were home safe and sound with her. She often reminded Dusty that she doesn't want to be raising their daughter on her own because some dumbass was out driving when they shouldn't be.

"I'm not worried about your driving. I'm worried about the other idiot who thinks it's a good idea to go out in this mess."

She's right to worry. With the amount of snow that's already on the forest floor—five inches in an hour and a half—there's no doubt in Dusty's mind it will be too deep to drive through, even with a 4x4, by the time his shift ends. *At least I don't have to worry about someone else out driving in this mess.* Still, he wonders if he'll have to spend the night at RS1, snowed in with the rest of the team. That wouldn't be so bad. The bunks are comfortable. Flint is a decent cook and makes a tasty egg scramble. There are plenty of board games and a deck of cards to pass the time until the roads become passable, although he wasn't playing poker with Colt and losing all his money again. Though Dusty doesn't mind spending the night in the park, he isn't fond of being away from Melinda and Sarah overnight, not with an intense storm hitting the area. Anything could go wrong at home, and he wouldn't be there if they needed him.

"Everything okay there?" he recalls asking her, when his three-month-old baby girl, Sarah, whined in the background.

"Yes. Sarah's a little fussy this morning. Did you get the photo that I..."

A crackle in the connection.

"What did you say?"

"I *asked* if you got the photo I sent to your cell phone?"

"Sorry. The line's breaking up. You're cutting in and out."

"Oh. That's...ot good."

Dusty didn't think so, either. Most phone lines in and around the park ran through heavily wooded areas. They were easy marks for tree branch disruptions when the wind was strong. Remnants of that clusterfuck of a rescue last July bubble in his subconscious.

"Doesn't look like it. And I'm not getting a signal. Probably the storm, too."

"It was the cutest thing. She had Cheerios stuck to her chubby little cheeks."

Yet, the bad phone connection and the loss of a cell signal are not the only things causing the isolation to creep up on him. He spoke with Porter over the radio earlier, alerting him that Rumor Shoff might have an injury, or he could be stalking around the park to cause more mischief and mayhem on a day when their time and energy would be better spent elsewhere. Colt and Joey were out in this mess to find him.

He swallows dryly, the seclusion metastasizing into primal worry. He can't help but see the parallels between what's happening today and last year—a missing person, a team on a search-and-rescue mission, and a bad storm. Dusty was at RS1, operating the radio, when the distress call came in that afternoon; he remembers it as vividly as the birth of his daughter.

"Help! Can any…ear me?"

"This is Ranger Dusty Albert at Ranger Station One. I read you, but you're breaking up. Are you in need of assistance?"

"…anded…line…"

"Say again? Over."

"I'm stranded. Need…elp."

"Okay. What's your name and where are you stranded?"

"…ocks."

"Say again?"

"T…ocks…"

"I'm sorry I'm having trouble hearing you. Can you repeat your location, over?"

"The Rocks!"

Irritation itches his body like a rash. Had he heard the caller's voice clearly, Dusty might've known who was on the other end of the line. It could've been Rumor. Or Darryl. *It could have been anyone.* That was the point of the call. To distract. To manipulate. The caller knew the hurricane would interfere with the radios, masking their voice in the static like a ghost speaking through the white-noise hiss of a tape recorder. And they knew the distress call would get Maynard to mount a search-and-rescue expedition. It was brilliant in its deceptiveness.

The trail comes peerlessly close to the bank's edge before sloping fifty feet to the waterline. Because it's the end of January and there's sparse vegetation, Dusty can see Snyder Point and the old fire tower across the lake, blurry in the snowfall. Trail signs warn hikers: DANGER! DO NOT GO PAST THIS POINT. A strong gust of wind shakes the ATV, but Dusty's not worried about it blowing him down the bankside and into the icy waters below. The tight grouping of the trees would prevent that from happening. Still, he keeps his eyes on the trail and his steering on point. The last thing he needs is to be stuck out there and have to radio for help.

You'd look like a damn fool.

He drives on for another ten minutes. There's no sign of life on the trail. No deer. No squirrels or rabbits hopping about. It wasn't uncommon while it was snowing for him to see cardinals flying around—a speck of bright red in all the white—and hear them chirping in the trees as they jumped from one snowy branch to another. But even the cardinals—along with every other bird—seem to understand the magnitude of the storm and have decided to take refuge.

But most importantly, Dusty doesn't see any people. *That's a good thing. It means they're listening to the weather reports and staying home.*

The trail turns away from the bank and dips into the ravine, leveling between two large rock formations. Here, neither the radio nor the CBs will work. The rocks in the ravine prevent a signal from getting in or out. Dusty knew he was now the furthest away from help if something went wrong or he stumbled onto someone who was…

He slams his foot on the brake.

The ATV's tires lock, and it skids to a stop.

For a moment, Dusty sits there squinting through the snow, trying to understand what he's seeing. He wants to tell himself that what's hanging in front of him isn't there—*an illusion*—that this ghastly image is a manifestation in his mind. But he knows it isn't an illusion. Hot fear bubbles on his skin like painful blisters.

A deer carcass hangs above the trail. Its body is strung between two trees in an X pattern. *Why in God's name?*

Who could have done this to that poor animal? *A special kind of sick and twisted individual. Rumor?* He wouldn't put the depravity past the son of a bitch to make his point.

Dusty steps out of the ATV. A draught of wind slices through the ravine with a howl. He hardly feels the cold as distaste for the dead animal's brutal display wells up in the back of his throat. *The poor creature didn't deserve this kind of treatment.* Dusty wasn't a hunter like some of the other rangers. He found the act inhumane. He could understand the need to hunt if it meant survival—clothes, food—but not for sport and certainly not for…well, whatever the hell this was.

Dusty slumbers through the deepening snow to the carcass and stands there, stupidly staring at it strung above him. An arrow with blue-and-white fletchings protrudes from the left side of the animal's chest. It had punctured the heart. *It was probably dead before it hit the ground.* He follows the blood leaking down the deer's belly to its right rear leg, dripping off a dirty, black hoof and into a small puddle of red slush on the forest floor.

What he sees before him is something out of a horror movie. No, not a movie. *This is real life. Someone shot this animal and strung it here for one of us to find.*

Why?

The sense of someone watching him skulks up his back, and the hair on his shoulders stands straight. Gazing around the desolate, snow-covered forest, Dusty sees no one lingering amongst the trees and rocks surrounding him. *Of course, they could be hiding, and you still wouldn't see them.*

With this troubled thought and the aura of eyes leering on his every move, Dusty reaches down, undoes the safety strap of the Glock .9mm in its holster, and pulls the firearm free. He works his way back to the idling ATV and throws open the door, eager to get out of the ravine and reach someone on the radio.

Something whistles by his left ear and embeds itself into the ATV's metal roof with a *Thwack!*

Dusty jumps back. Fear sinks its fangs into him. An arrow with blue-and-white fletchings still vibrates from the impact, the bolt missing his head by less than an inch. Dusty knows with utmost certainty that it was meant to take him down.

Then, he realizes why this part of the trail had been chosen to hang the deer.

An ambush!

With the Glock in his right hand, he spins and examines the ridgeline to see where the arrow was shot from.

"Who's out there!" Dusty brings the Glock up and searches for a movement, a face amongst the trees, a flash of light from a scope along the ridgeline, anything that would tip him off to where the shot came from.

He hears another *thwack* echo off the rock walls a millisecond before a second arrow punches through his right shoulder. The force of the shot knocks Dusty back into the ATV's door. The Glock is kicked from his hand, which falls into the snow and disappears. He grabs the door for stability, his body sways back and forth as he tries to regain his footing and breath. Pain cascades down his arm and into his hand like a charley horse.

Another *thwack* breaks off the rocks. Dusty tries to duck behind the ATV's door before another arrow can strike him.

But he's too late.

The third arrow strikes him in the right side of his chest, just above his lung, clipping his clavicle and sending a firework of immense pain to every nerve. The impact throws him back into the ATV cab. Another *thwack* breaks the quiet. A fourth arrow embeds itself into Dusty's left leg, just below his groin. His scream echoes off the ravine walls and over the whine of the cold breeze.

Although he's hurt with three arrows protruding from his body, his mind is clear, hyper-focused—survival mode.

Got to get out of here. Got to…

Dusty pulls himself up by the steering wheel. The world around him is fuzzy and uneven, like he's on a tilt-a-whirl ride. His stomach lurches, and he tastes something foul on the back of his tongue—a moldy, rotten flavor that he doesn't recognize. He tells himself it's trauma his body has sustained.

It's fear…

He tries to turn himself around in the driver's seat to throw his legs in. But the arrow through his right shoulder snags on the seat as he twists his body, preventing him from getting in correctly.

But that's not all.

Dusty can no longer move his left leg. A nerve, tendon, or muscle must have been severed when the arrow hit him. It's as dead as a paperweight.

But you have to, he tells himself through the discomfort. *You have to try.* He thinks of Melinda back home. Of Sarah in her high chair with Cheerios stuck to her chubby little cheeks—if only he had been able to see the photo Melinda texted to him. *You have to make it home to them…for them!*

He takes hold of his green pant leg and tries to pull his left leg up and place it in the cab. But another jolt of fire—emanating from the arrow in his upper chest—zigzags through his body, causing his left hand to go lax, and he drops his leg. It falls back to the ground with a *thud* that kicks up snow and pain. Tears run down his cheeks, not just from the pain but the horror that he won't see his family again, and strangely, he realizes this is the first time he's cried in a long while, maybe since Maynard's funeral.

There's another *thwack*. Another arrow is coming. This one hits the ATV's metal roll bars with a *tink* directly above his head and ricochets into the woods somewhere. The kill shot. *Oh, God!* As luck would have it, he has another chance at getting into the ATV and make it out of there.

Clenching his jaw, Dusty grabs his pants again. With all his strength and a guttural scream through gritted teeth, he yanks his left leg off the ground and dumps it into the cab like a dead fish.

He's not out of the woods yet. His body is half in and half out of the ATV. He can't turn around in the seat with the arrow through his right shoulder. *Make it work. Hit the gas and go.*

Dusty lifts his right foot to stomp on the accelerator when the final arrow passes through his neck. His entire body instantly goes limp. His right foot, raised to stomp on the gas pedal, falls lifelessly on the accelerator. The ATV jumps forward. The jolt rocks Dusty's unresponsive body out of the seat and onto the snowy ground while the ATV rolls on before it stops about five feet away from where he lays.

On the ground, with the snow falling around him, Dusty realizes he can't move. Can't feel anything below his chin. Hell, he hadn't even felt the arrow pass through his neck; it must have severed his spinal column but missed anything vital that would have turned off the lights. Fear of what his life will be like without the use of his limbs consumes him in a matter of seconds—he'll no longer be able to hold his baby girl, embrace Melinda, or make love to...

Oh, Jesus, no...

But all that pales in comparison when he sees a hooded figure step out from behind a tree on the hill, a crossbow in hand. The figure reaches up and pulls down the hood. It stares at him with two empty black sockets and a mirthless, forever grin that seems to grow gleefully at what it's done. Dusty tries to scream at the sight of the figure, but from the blood in the back of his throat, only a wet gurgle escapes.

It's not real!

Dusty lies helplessly in a forming pool of blood as it steps beside him. It pulls a large, curved object with a sharp pick on one end and a long blade on the other from its side.

An ice axe.

It is real. And whatever it is, it's come to collect your soul.

CHAPTER 8

Tripp returns from the plow with a large blue tarpaulin. A strand of yellow nylon rope dangles from his right hand and slides across the top of the snow behind him like a wagging tail as he approaches Colt.

Together, they unfold the tarpaulin. They struggle to place it over Norm's body as the wind catches it like a sail and nearly rips it out of their hands. Colt holds it down while Tripp secures it to the benches' legs and backrest with the nylon rope. By the time they're finished, both men feel the fatigue in their bodies; the cold's slurping up their energy.

"Did Rumor do this?" Tripp asks, through gasps for air.

Colt shakes his head and looks at the body on the bench dedicated to Maynard's memory. Why leave the corpse on Maynard's bench, and not by the monument, especially if the murderer wants them to believe Norm was another one of Douglas Lee Carver's victims?

"Has to be him," Tripp speculates, his eyes narrow thoughtfully on the human shape under the tarp; the corners snap in the wind like a plastic bag caught on a signpost. "Unless it was his old man?"

"Colt…there? …ver." Wyatt Burke's broken voice comes through on Colt's CB.

Colt yanks the CB off his belt.

"Go for Colt."

"Need …dow…ow? Oh…?"

Colt looks at Tripp, puzzled.

"Come again, over?" Colt says back into the CB.

Static comes from the speaker in a long whine that mixes eerily with the violent wind. Dread and remoteness works through Colt's cold body like he's stuck in an icy wasteland and losing his last contact with civilization.

"C-lt…oblem…it…ver."

"Say again, Wyatt! You're breaking up."

"It's the storm interfering with the long-range to short-range connection," Tripp hollers. "We should go to the Panorama Building and use the long-range radio instead of your CB to reach Wyatt. And we should get out of this cold, too."

Colt nods. The temperature is rapidly dropping, and he feels the cold's bite work past his flesh and into his joints. He looks back at Norm on the bench under the tarpaulin. He doesn't want to leave him out here. It feels wrong, like he's leaving a man behind on the battlefield, like he had to leave Maynard behind after the fall. But Colt knows he can't move the body. He has to preserve the crime scene for the investigators and any evidence they might uncover.

Together, he and Tripp make their way through the snow and wind to the SUV. Colt drives them to the Panorama Building. They hurry under the round porch that gives nearly a 180-degree view of the lake; snow has blown across the floor, making the wood slick. Tripp rushes toward the door. He pulls his jacket aside to retrieve his keys to unlock it, but skids to a stop.

"Shit!"

"What?" Colt asks. He slips on the wooden porch floor and grabs on to the railing to keep himself from falling straight down onto his butt.

"The door's open."

Colt's eyes shoot to the door of the Panorama Building. It hangs open about two inches. Air whistles through the crack.

"That door was locked this morning. I checked this building for damages myself."

"You sure?"

"Positive."

"Stand back," Colt says, reaching for his gun.

He opens the door and cautiously steps into the Panorama Building's ballroom—where weddings, birthdays, and other events are held for those renting the place. The ballroom is cavernous and empty; the large glass windows reveal the snowy hillside and lake beyond. Colt heads to a short hallway along the back wall that leads to a kitchen, a bathroom, and finally to an office marked PRIVATE. The door is ajar, and a splash of light from inside the office cuts sharply across the floor like a knife's blade. Inside the office, he hears movements—heavy footsteps. Whoever broke into the Panorama Building is still here.

His grip on the .357 tightens, and his heart rate spikes with anticipation; each beat pounding in his temples. Are they finally going to catch Rumor in the act? *Only one way to find out.*

Colt throws the door open and charges into the office with a two-handed grip on the revolver. The light from the single desk lamp is dim, and the air is dry and musty from nonuse; the entire Panorama Building has been shuttered since Labor Day. Someone stands by the desk with their back to him, bent over the long-range radio.

"Don't move." Colt pulls the hammer and the cylinder rotates heavily in the quiet office.

"Easy, Colt," a familiar voice says. Slowly, the hands raise, and the figure turns to face him.

Colt's shock is an understatement.

"Flint!" Colt says, lowering the gun. "What the hell are you doing here?"

"I saw someone sneaking around up here from RS2. Looks like

I was right. Found this." Flint steps aside, revealing the long-range radio laying in pieces. "Someone broke in and destroyed the radio."

"Fuckin' Rumor!" Tripp steps into the room. "First, the CBs and tires in the maintenance trucks. Now, this."

"You saw someone? When was this?" Colt asks.

Flint hikes his shoulders. "An hour ago, maybe."

Tripp hurries to the desk to assess the damage to the radio.

"Can you fix it?" Colt asks, hopeful. He needs to contact Wyatt and find out what's happening at RS3. Though broken up, the sound of Wyatt's voice was cause for concern. Something is wrong. Colt's nerves twitch. *But what? Had Wyatt seen Rumor? Do they have him in custody?*

"No. It's smashed to hell and back." Tripp says.

Fuck!

"Did you get a look at whoever was up here?" Colt asks Flint.

Flint shakes his head. "No. I was in RS2 when I saw them through the binoculars briefly before they ducked around the side of the building."

"Where's your SUV?" Colt asks. "I didn't see it."

"I parked behind the public restrooms in case anyone was still there. That way, they wouldn't see or hear me coming."

Colt turns his attention to the radio and feels something work its way loose from deep inside his chest. *Who did this? Rumor?*

"Do you think this has something to do with how I found Norm?" Tripp's voice is heavy, thick with sorrow.

"Probably," Colt answers honestly. *But how does it connect?*

"What happened to Norm?" Flint asks.

A long silence grows heavier as the seconds tick by. The wind blows through the open front door with a shrill, the sound amplifying in the spacious ballroom as if an evil presence is announcing its arrival. The names on the monument, including the recent addition of Norm Roberts, and the rhyme form in Colt's mind, darken his thoughts. *Is this land cursed by Douglas Lee Carver?*

"What happened to Norm?" Flint repeats, his voice louder, demanding.

"Someone murdered him," Colt says matter-of-factly.

"What!" Flint screams. Shock works across his face as he tries to come to terms with the news of Norm's murder. His gray eyes dart back and forth in thought. Finally, he asks, "What time did you find Norm's body, Tripp?"

"Around eleven thirty this morning. Why?"

"I saw someone sneaking around up here around eleven fifteen or so this morning," Flint replies, glancing at Colt's. He shifts his gaze with a blink back to Tripp. "What about you? Did you see anyone?"

"No." Tripp shakes his head.

"And you weren't anywhere near the Panorama Building?" Flint asks.

"Only to drive by. Once I saw Lance and Amos weren't here, I turned around to leave. That's when I saw Norm's body on the hill."

"Then who did I see?" Flint asks. "Rumor?"

"Maybe," Colt says. "We haven't found him yet."

"Vandalizing the park is one thing, but...murder?" Tripp's gaze shifts from Flint to Colt. Trepidation deepens the lines of his face. "Do either of you think Rumor's capable?"

"He poisoned trees in public areas where if one of them fell, they could've killed someone," Flint says. "I say that makes him capable of murder, sure."

"But why Norm?" Colt asks.

"Maybe he saw something Rumor didn't want him to see," Tripp says.

Could Norm have seen something that Rumor didn't want him to? But if he did, and Rumor murdered him for it, then why the ruse? Why carve Norm's name on the monument below Carver's four other victims, along with the rhyme? And why leave Norm's body on Maynard's bench for them to find?

"Or maybe they were working together," Flint says.

"No way," Tripp says, shaking his head. "Norm was a decent guy. He wouldn't—"

"We don't know that," Flint interjects. "Put your personal feelings for Norm aside and think—how else would Rumor be able to get into the park at night and not get caught. He had an inside man, that's how."

Colt hadn't thought it possible for one of their own to be an accomplice to Rumor and Darryl's bullshit. He knew all of them and would vouch for their characters. He would have said Flint was off base if he had made such an outlandish suggestion yesterday. But that was yesterday. Now, he's not so sure.

"Norm? Straight-as-an-arrow, do-it-by-the-book Norm?" Tripp laughs mockingly.

"Flint has a point," Colt says. "We have to look at every possibility right now. Norm could have looked the other way so Rumor could vandalize the park at night. And then their relationship could have soured for any number of reasons."

"Looks like motive to me," Flint says. "I say we find this cocksucker and end this shit once and for all."

Colt ignores Flint's tough-guy bravado act and says, "I'll radio Dusty since he's only about a quarter of a mile away at RS2. He can contact Porter, who can then call the sheriff in Jackson and get someone out here to handle this better than we can."

"Can't exactly do that, Colt," Flint says.

"What do you mean?"

"Dusty's not at RS2."

"Then where is he, Flint?"

"Clearing Trail Loop Two."

"I thought *you* were clearing Trail Loop Two," Colt says, remembering a conversation he overheard Flint and Dusty have in the locker room yesterday about who would take which trail that morning.

Flint stares him down with such intent that Colt begins to feel an uncomfortable sweat at the base of his neck. *Is that look meant to say something?* Colt isn't sure.

"Dusty took it for me because of my knee," Flint finally says.

"That's fine, but you abandoned your post...again!"

"For a goddamn good reason!"

"Okay. Okay," Colt relents. Flint's right. His obligation as a park ranger is to check out any suspicious activity. Flint *was* doing his job when he left RS2 to investigate the Panorama Building.

The small office turns quiet. The only sound is the winds growl outside until Tripp says, "You should send someone to drive into Jackson and get the sheriff out here before this worsens, Colt."

"Might not be a bad idea, just in case the radios and phones go down," Colt replies.

"I can do it," Flint says.

"No. The storm's getting worse, and the SUVs will only be good for a few more hours before the snow's too deep to drive through. Tripp can easily make it to Jackson in the plow and bring the sheriff back, clearing the roads as he does." Colt looks at Tripp and studies his keen eyes and tan, leathery face. "You okay with that?"

"You bet your ass I am."

CHAPTER 9

Where the hell is Porter? It's a quarter to one, and he isn't back from the antenna shed yet. *Maybe he ran into a problem?* Joey wonders if she should have gone with him just to be safe. *Like you should have gone with Colt and Maynard up to the Rocks.* But, even if she was there, there was no medical treatment she could have provided Maynard to fix seven compound fractures, internal bleeding, and a shattered skull. Maynard ordered her to stay at RS1 and organize the police and EMTs once Tripp and his crew opened the eastern entrance. She was then to escort them to the Rocks to assist in getting the hiker down safely. *Only there was no hiker.* The distress call was a hoax. Someone's idea of a joke—a sick one—cost Maynard his life.

Rumor? Darryl? Were they responsible? The assumption wiggles around in her brain like a maggot. But like Maynard used to say: *Assumptions are the mother of all fuckups.* They had no proof that Rumor or Darryl had any connection to that call. To outright blame them is wrong, she knows. Still, she can't stop thinking about the coincidental connection binding everything together.

A snore brings Joey's attention to Darryl in the cell, asleep on the small cot. His mouth hangs open—a toothless pink hole of gums and tongue. His false teeth rest on his chest, rising slowly up and down with each breath. They smile sardonically at her from their perch.

Disgusting.

After Porter left, Joey examined Darryl for signs of a concussion. He was lucky his injuries weren't worse than the laceration across his nose after his tumble down the hill. Joey mended it with ointment and a bandage before telling him to lie in the holding cell and rest until Colt returned. Soon Darryl was snoring; the day's physical and mental trauma had caught up to him.

Watching Darryl now, she believes he doesn't look well; his breath is erratic and raspy. In fact, Joey thinks he looks downright ill like he's coming down with the flu. *Or pneumonia...*

She returns to her desk and falls into the chair, worn out from the cold, traipsing through the woods to try to find a man who would rather spit in her face than seek her help. Now alone in RS1, besides Darryl snoozing away in the cell, Joey pulls the photos from her pocket. The paper with the numbers is on top. She studies the numbers again before putting it aside—*what do they mean?*—and begins to look over the photos. *When were they taken?* She has no memory of the particular love-making session captured. It's not like she logs her sexual exploits with Colt down in a journal with a grade. Monday, June 14: A-, Tuesday, July 3: C+ (at best), and so on. But she wishes she could remember this one.

Was Rumor going to use them to blackmail her and Colt? What was his endgame if that's the case?

She flips through the stack and studies each photo closely to see if anything might jog her memory of that night.

But it's useless.

Nothing grabs her attention.

She slaps the photographs down on the desk, where they fan out like a deck of cards. Frustration sinks deep into her neck muscles, like a hawk's talons. She sits back in the chair and rubs the tender area. She's tired. She's hungry. She needs some caffeine to keep the engine running. Coffee will help.

She goes to the coffee pot sitting atop the filing cabinet, takes a paper cup from the stack beside it, and pours herself a cup. On her way back to the desk, she glances at the clock on the wall. 1:15 p.m. *Porter, where the hell are you?*

Next to the desk, sipping her coffee, Joey spreads the photographs out so she can study each one independently. At first, she sees only the vulgarity of the photos; the ickiness of them taken unknowingly slithers over her skin like a film of slime.

Then something jumps out at her. Something so small that she hadn't seen it earlier. An article of clothing was thrown over a chair in the motel room. She had only worn it once, for Colt, recently, not even two months ago.

There's a loud click in her brain that sounds like a shotgun racking as memories start to form in her cloudy mind.

Joey had bought a sexy nighty to wear for Colt when they met up at the motel off I-95. She wore it for only a few moments, just that one time. She remembers Colt stripping her out of it and tossing it over the chair before they fell onto the sheets naked in each other's arms. But she remembers seeing something strange that night, too.

After they were done making love, and while Colt was in the shower, Joey made her way to the vending machines to get them each a Coke when someone darted from behind the motel. From the size, she was confident it was a man. Hobbling across the parking lot, he jumped into a car. She isn't sure what color the car was, but the model might have been a late seventies or early eighties muscle car. Maybe a Camaro? She has no clue. She tries to recall the license plate number as the car speeds away in her mind, but it's a smear in her memory.

What isn't a smudge of images is that whoever she saw wore black—jacket, pants, and dark shoes. *Strange?* At the time, yes. But did it arouse suspicion that he might have been following them? Taking intimate pictures of them. No. The thought never crossed her mind.

But he was carrying something, wasn't he? Maybe it was a camera?

She can't recall, which pisses her off. The rest of her memory of the incident is foggy at best, but she's confident it was the night the photos were taken. Gathering all the photographs together, she tosses them into the desk drawer and slams it shut so hard it's like a firecracker going off.

"What's goin' on?" Darryl asks, jolted awake. His sleepy eyes shoot around the room with bewilderment until they find Joey.

"Sorry," she says, even though she's not.

Darryl runs his thick pink tongue over his lips, and a dry cough works its way up from his throat that sounds like a dog choking on a bone. Lifting his teeth from his chest, he slips them back into his mouth. Joey cringes as he works them around with his tongue until they are in place. She looks away. The thought of Darryl Shoff taking pictures of her, him running his thick tongue over those false teeth excitedly as she and Colt made love, raises the bile in the back of her throat. *Probably can't even get his pecker up anymore.*

"What time is it?" Darryl asks, swinging his feet off the bunk.

"Past one."

"Any word on my boy?"

"No." As a matter of fact, the radio's been silent since she's been back to RS1. Again, the worry that Porter caught a snag at the antenna shed runs across her mind. *You need to go and check on him.*

"When's Colt gettin' back? And when are we gonna resume the search for Rumor?" Darryl levels his eyes - small, black, and beady - on her.

The eyes of a pervert.

"I don't know."

"You don't know when Colt's gettin' back? Or you don't know when the search to find my son will resume?"

Instead of answering the question, Joey says, "How 'bout some coffee?"

Darryl considers and nods.

She pours the coffee and walks it over to Darryl on the bunk inside the cell.

"Can I ask you something?"

"It's a free country…for now." Darryl takes a sip of coffee.

"Do you or Rumor own an older Camaro?"

Darryl cautiously levels his gaze on her as if deciding whether she's working an angle, hoping he'll slip up and say something he shouldn't.

"No. Neither of us owns a Camaro," he finally says. "What's this about, anyway?"

Joey tries to conceal her disappointment. She thought she was onto something with her recent memory. He could be lying. But what if he isn't? And if he isn't, then who took the photos? And why?

"Well?" Darryl presses.

"It's nothing," Joey turns away.

She's said too much and remembers Colt telling her not to confront Darryl about the photos and tip their hand. *You need to change the directory of this conversation. Fast!*

An idea hits her.

She moves through the cell's threshold, grabs the door's steel bars, and slams it shut. It *clangs,* and the cage shakes. *The* lock falls into place with a metallic *click.*

"What are you doin'?" Darryl asks. He looks like a puppy that's been led into its pen with a treat, only to find out it was a trick to lock him in.

"Porter isn't back yet. I need to check on him at the antenna shed. And since I can't watch you while I'm gone, you stay locked in until I return."

A narrow, windy path through the woods led Joey toward the antenna shed. The snow falls hard and fast, stings her face. The wind pushes against her like a punch to the chest. The ground is covered, at least eight inches by her estimation, making the trek that much harder.

The path opens into a clearing, where a ten-by-ten-foot metal building sits on the knoll above RS1. Joey gasps for air, and her leg muscles burn from the slog through the snow. A 150-foot antenna is mounted on top of the building. The red light at the tower's tip is dark, indicative that it isn't operational.

Not good.

"Porter!" Joey calls out.

There's no response other than a banshee cry of wind. Chills dagger her soul. *Where the hell is he?*

Opening the door, the wind rips it out of her hands. It slams against the wall with a *bang* that cracks through the forest like a gunshot. She steps through the threshold into the antenna shed, grabs hold of the door, and struggles against the gale to pull the door shut behind her. It's nearly ripped out of her hands again before she can secure it.

It takes her eyes a moment to adjust to the dimly lit space. When they do, she finds it in disarray. And Porter isn't there. Her hackles rise at the sight of the place and Porter's absence. *What the hell happened here?*

The small desk has a computer monitor and a landline phone. The phone's receiver is off the hook, laying on the floor—the *urt, urt, urt,* of a disconnected line, isn't present. The monitor is broken, and the screen flips and shudders. On the back wall are several large computer servers that operate the antenna. The servers are in pieces. Shards of plastic and bits of metal litter the floor, and crunch under the tread of her boots as she nears.

On the floor, beside the servers, dark droplets like oil splotches glisten in the soft light.

But it isn't oil, Joey realizes.

It's blood!

Porter's blood?

Her heart rate ticks up, and alarm ripples through her body which causes the gooseflesh to rise. *Someone attacked Porter and disabled the long-range antenna to prevent them from communicating.*

Then, something else catches her attention.

Joey nearly screams at what's written on the wall in what she can only assume is Porter's blood.

Little Ranger Barrett running,
Douggie Carver's gone a-hunting
Gonna catch that ranger,
Gonna cleave that ranger,
Little Ranger Barrett done running.

The door snaps open. A whoosh of freezing air fills the void, sending a deathly chill into her bones that causes her entire body to quake. She spins on her heels, yanks her sidearm from its holster, and comes around with the weapon raised.

Someone is standing in the doorway. Their face a black cloak against the piercing white beyond.

"Who's there?" Joey screams over the shrieking wind, her grip already tightening on the trigger of the Glock. "Identify yourself!"

Whoever's standing in the doorway, silhouetted by the white snow wall outside, is massive: large chest, thick arms, legs, and hands. By their size alone, Joey knows this person can easily be responsible for how she found the antenna shed and the attack and disappearance of Porter. If given the opportunity, he could kill her, too. Joey's finger hardens on the trigger.

"Take it easy. Relax, Joey. Christ!"

Flint Wheeler steps into the building, the dim light scaring the shadows from his face. His cheeks and nose are rosy from the harsh wind. Flecks of snow and ice gleam like diamonds in his salt-and-pepper beard. His green bush hat has enough snow caught in the folds to melt into a pitcher of water.

"What are you doing up here?" Joey keeps the gun on him.

Flint closes the door. The air thrashing past the shed outside sounds like a turbine engine. It's a slight but welcome reprieve from the noise and the chill. When he turns to face her, a grim look tightens the skin around his eyes and mouth.

"I just came from the Panorama Building, where I saw Colt.

He told me to return to RS1 and wait with you until he got back. But you weren't there. I got worried and decided to check on you."

Joey studies Flint closely. His appearance is suspicious, especially after finding the shed a mess, the antenna nonfunctional, and Porter missing. Possibly worse, she frets. Flint showing up there out of the blue—or in this case, out of the white—was strange. *And a little coincidental.*

"How'd you know I was up here?"

"Darryl told me. He's pretty pissed that you locked him in the cage." His eyes shift to the gun. "You mind putting that thing down."

Joey lowers the Glock, relieved to know Darryl told Flint where to find her.

"Porter's missing," she says, holstering the sidearm.

"What do you mean *missing*?"

Joey steps aside, letting Flint see the carnage.

"Oh!" Flint gasps. His eyes sweep across the small space with a morbid curiosity, like how people look at a car accident on the freeway.

"Someone sabotaged the computers that run the antenna," Joey says.

Flint's eyes cut sharply to her. The flecks of worry in them perturb her. Not about what she just told him, but about something he hasn't shared with her yet.

"I found the long-range radio in the Panorama Building smashed to hell and back, too."

Joey swallows and realizes her throat is cold like she'd been sucking on dry ice. The destruction of the antenna and radios wasn't a random act of vandalism; it was done on purpose.

"I want to show you something else," Joey says, leading Flint to the blood on the floor below the rhyme.

"Is that...blood?" His eyes raise to the rhyme. "And why the hell is *that* there?"

"To scare us."

"Doing a pretty damn good job." Flint shivers. "There's something else you should know. I would let Colt break the news to you, but under the circumstances..." He licks his lips, nervous. "Norm's dead."

The news of Norm's death hits Joey like she stepped on a landmine, like when she learned of Maynard's death. She stares at Flint in a wide-eyed stupor for a long moment, unsure what to say, feel, or think. The room begins to tilt and sway as if she's in some bizarre, alternate world, where everything appears normal until the layers are peeled away, revealing the unsteadiness under her feet.

Flint notices her shell-shocked silence and continues.

"Tripp found him this morning on Dedication Hill."

Dedication Hill? Colt mentioned that Tripp had found a body when they returned to RS1. At the time, she thought Tripp had found Rumor. *You were wrong.* And, if she was wrong, then Rumor is still out there...somewhere.

But Norm?

"What hap-pened?" Joey asks, her voice breaking. Maynard's face flashes behind her eyes; she sees him smile and wink at her for the last time as he exits RS1. Though she didn't know Norm Roberts well, she feels the first sting of tears burn the backs of her eyes at the loss of another colleague.

"He was murdered."

"Murdered!" The word explodes from Joey's mouth. She had thought Rumor to be many things, but a murderer isn't one of them. Until now. Did he kill Norm and Porter? Is that why he's disabling their communications, so they cannot call for help?

Flint steps closer to her. *Too close* for Joey's comfort, given the circumstances she finds herself in with him, and says, "About eleven thirty, I saw someone sneaking around the Panorama Building. That's when I investigated and found the long-range radio destroyed." His eyes flip away. Joey follows his gaze to the servers. "Someone in this park shouldn't be here—and that someone is Rumor Shoff. That little prick is out there doing this—

did that." He points to the wall. "When we find him, I'm going to put my size thirteen boot up his ass."

Joey tries to calm herself and use her rational mind, not her emotional one, to see the situation clearly. If Rumor is responsible for what's happening today, why did he leave his duffel bag by Ice Fisherman's Cove? What about the blood on the trail? If it isn't Rumor's blood, then whose is it? *Norm's?* And why leave the rhyme on the wall? Something isn't adding up. No. There is something darker, more sinister at work here.

"What are we going to do about the radios?" There's desperation in Flint's voice, much like when he reported the downed trees blocking both park entrances, successfully cutting off anyone from getting in or out the night of the hurricane.

"The only person who could have fixed them is Porter. What can we do?" Joey replies. She suddenly feels as if the walls are closing in around her. Desperation to escape the small building's confines claws at her like a prisoner trying to dig their way out of their cell.

"We need to get the sheriff," Joey says.

"Colt sent Tripp into Jackson to bring him back, but I don't want to wait until then—not with Porter missing and…this. When we return to RS1, we *must* call the sheriff ourselves." Flint studies the rhyme like a scholar, his lips move as he reads the words silently to himself.

"We can't," Joey says, bringing Flint's attention back to her. "The landlines are down, too. We're officially cut off from reaching anyone."

CHAPTER 10

As Colt stomps up the snowy steps onto the porch of RS3, the door opens and Wyatt Burke steps out. He's a good-looking young man with reddish-brown hair and attractive emerald eyes that cause some female park guests to swoon. Today the charm in Wyatt's eyes is gone. They are dull and haunted of a man privy to a secret. Nausea swoops over Colt, and he suspects he's walking into a bigger problem than Wyatt having Rumor in custody.

"I've been trying to reach you," Wyatt says.

Was that a tremor in his voice?

"I know. I only got bits and pieces of your message. The storm's interfering. I was up on Dedication—"

"Colt, we found a body in the pit," Wyatt cuts him off.

The matter-of-fact way Wyatt relays the information knocks Colt off balance. He had expected any number of things, but this wasn't it. He takes hold of the railing to keep himself from toppling, as an indescribable feeling passes through his chest that he assumes is the physical manifestation of shock.

Another...body?

"You okay?" Wyatt asks, touching his shoulder. "All the color just drained from your face."

Colt nods. But he's unsure if he's *okay* or not. In his fifteen years with the park, he's never dealt with anything this…crazy. He was a peace officer for the park service, there to protect the public, the wildlife, and the land. Now, two dead bodies have turned up in his park. *I'm not equipped to deal with this.*

"How…how did someone get into the pit?" Colt asks, rattled. "The fence door is always locked."

"I don't think someone got into the pit as much as they were placed in there."

Colt's gaze locks onto Wyatt's. Utter dread dances through the thirty-one-year-old ranger's eyes.

"What are you telling me, Wyatt?"

But he understands. Yet, he needs to hear Wyatt say it, confirm what he already suspects, fears.

"You should talk to Lance and Amos."

Inside, Colt finds Amos in the middle of the room with a cup of coffee in his hand. He's pale and looks sick, like he ate something that didn't agree with him. The fright in his eyes is unmistakable. He never thought it possible for a man Amos's size to be that afraid. Lance sits by the window. He rubs his knuckles like a prize fighter after twelve hellish rounds that left his hands sore and swollen. His right leg bounces up and down with a nervous tick.

"What happened?" Colt asks.

Lance looks up, removes the Yankees cap, and runs a shaky hand through his hair.

"I threw a log into the pit," he says. "It knocked some debris away. That's when I saw it."

"The body?" Colt asks.

"No." Lance shakes his head. "A hand. Sticking out of the brush."

Colt glances back at Wyatt. Their eyes lock in a knowing gaze. The body was intentionally hidden in there.

"I thought it best to leave it alone until you got here, Colt," Lance says.

"And you're sure they're dead?" Colt asks.

Lance nods with a certainty that frightens him.

"Had we not come along when we did, we might not have found it until spring, when we cleaned the pit. If we even found it then," Amos says, his voice a baritone of subtle truth.

The excavator Tripp uses to clean the pit in the spring has a massive bucket. It could easily scoop the body up with the rest of the park's natural refuse, especially if it was tightly interwoven with the sticks and branches. The chances of them noticing, even when the load is put in the dump truck to be taken to the mulching plant, was slim. Whoever did this, Colt believes, knew the cleaning of the pit took place in the spring, too. And with today's snow, the body would have been hidden for days, if not weeks, by which point more refuse would be brought down, further burying the body, the cold slowing decomposition.

Colt tries to clear the jitters from his body before he speaks. He doesn't want his voice to break in front of the men looking to him for leadership. *Get it together, Mitcham.*

"What about the padlock?" Colt asks.

"It was unlocked, clipped on the latch to prevent the door from opening."

"And you didn't find this odd?" Colt knows his tone sounds accusatory, but he has to get the facts.

"Yeah. I found it odd," Lance snaps back in annoyance. "But I didn't think much of it. Thought maybe Tripp or Amos came down to get rid of some branches and forgot to lock it on their way out."

"I haven't been down here since last week after we cleared that fallen tree from Sidewinder Trail," Amos says. "When I left, the padlock was secure. Maybe Tripp?"

Colt seriously doubts Tripp would have forgotten to lock the gate. The man is meticulous to a fault that everything is done correctly around the park.

It has to be someone else! Rumor?

Colt shifts his attention to Wyatt.

"You see anything or anyone suspicious when you got here this morning?"

Wyatt shakes his head.

"No. Nothing. And the access road gate was locked."

"Are you sure?"

"Positive," Wyatt says with a nod. "I came out myself and unlocked it so they could get the pickup back to the pit."

"That doesn't mean anything," Lance says. "Anyone could get around the gate and make it to the pit. It's not like the entire area is fenced off, just the road. And at night, this place is deserted. What's important is the padlock. Whoever dumped the body either picked it or had a key."

"But only three people have keys to the pit," Wyatt says. "Two of which are in this room."

And one I sent to bring back the sheriff, Colt thinks.

While Amos and Lance head back to RS1 per Colt's orders, he and Wyatt drive to the pit to examine the body. The pit's gate is open when they arrive, and the wind drives with such force that it vibrates the chain-link fence. A lonely *ching, ching, ching* creeps across the forest. An abandoned vibe hangs in the air, reminiscent of how it feels near Camp Southwoods with the *tink* of the cable against the flagpole.

The thought of Douglas Lee Carver tiptoes across his mind again. It's an absurd thought, he knows, one better left for bad B-movies than real life. Carver was locked up. Yet Norm's name on the monument and the brutality with which he met his grisly end indicate Carver's MO. Was this some kind of misdirection Rumor was using to throw everyone off? To make it seem like Douglas Lee Carver returned to his old hunting grounds to seek new prey?

As they walk from the Interceptor to the pit, Colt's focus shifts to the open padlock. Had someone picked it or used a key? Three people working in the park have a key to access the pit anytime, including in the middle of the night.

Between Lance, Amos, and Tripp, who Colt had always found to be upstanding people, would any of them be a likely suspect? Or could one of them have passed their key along to Rumor? Could it have been stolen and returned before they noticed?

Colt forces the thought away. He doesn't want to accuse his team members of nefarious deeds. To entertain such an idea that one of them could be a murderer—a wolf in sheep's clothing - is beyond terrifying.

But you might have to, Colt tells himself begrudgingly, *and it's more rational than believing Douglas Lee Carver has returned.* The Carver rhyme singsongs through his head. *Little counselor running, Douggie Carver's gone a-hunting…*

The pit is heavy, as if the curse of Camp Southwoods has spread through the park like an infection. The sorrow that comes with death permeates the land. Colt feels it in his bones, like a cancer eating the marrow. Near the middle of the pit, Colt spots a single, pale left hand sticking up from the interwoven brush and sticks. The fingers bent like a frozen claw. Black dirt is caked under the nails, almost like whoever was down there had tried to dig themselves out. A knot tightens in his stomach.

"Who do you think it is?" Wyatt asks.

"Only one way to find out."

Colt pulls a long, slender branch from inside the pit. He smacks it on the concrete side to knock the snow away and then extends it to where the body lies under the brush. He shouldn't be doing this, but he has to know who's down there and begins to push away the brush carefully, revealing—

Oh, Christ!

Rumor Shoff lays on his back. Two arrows with blue-and-white fletchings protrude from the body—one in the right shoulder (the entire sleeve of his jacket is coated with frozen blood) and another through the center of the chest. The soft tissue of Rumor's face—lips, cheeks, and nose—is black from exposure. His eyes are milky white, and he stares lifelessly at them. Based on the body's condition, Colt believes Rumor has been there for at least twelve hours. He tries to swallow, but the tendons are constricted into immovable bands. Rumor couldn't have murdered Norm. He was long dead before Norm met his end.

"It's Rumor Shoff," Colt says gruffly.

"You sure?"

"I'm sure. His truck was found at Serpentine Trail last night, only he wasn't in it. Joey, Darryl Shoff, and I went looking for him this morning. Found blood on the trail, the cemetery, and the old cattle trail that circumvents the main one." Colt studies the arrows in Rumor's body. They have the same fletchings as the ones that took Norm down. Both were murdered with the same weapon, the same killer. "We couldn't figure out why he didn't take the main trail back to his truck if he was injured. Now I know why."

A tremor works its way across Wyatt. Colt can't decide if it's from the cold, the sight of the dead body with its milky-white eyes locked on them in a death stare, or something else.

"He was being hunted," Wyatt says in a whisper, barely audible over the wind. "Someone tried to cover him up to hide what they did."

"It wasn't just him," Colt says. "Tripp found Norm a little while ago on Dedication Hill." An audible gasp slips from Wyatt's mouth. "He had two arrows in him. Same blue-and-white fletchings, just like the ones in Rumor here."

"Are you..." Wyatt pauses and licks his lips nervously. "Are you saying that someone is out there, in the park, stalking, hunting, and killing people..." He trails off, then. "Like..."

Colt knows Wyatt wants to say Douglas Lee Carver but can't bring himself to believe it possible. The absurdity of it all is too much to fathom. Looking back to Rumor's body, Colt knows it's likely the same person is responsible for the murders, though several differences stand out to him. One: there are no signs of blunt force trauma on Rumor's body—the bloody slash that split Norm's face flashes across his mind, but he quickly buries the image away in his gray matter. Two: there is no sign of Rumor's name anywhere around the pit, like with Norm's on the monument, supposedly adding to Carver's kill count. Three: no rhyme. And finally: Rumor's body was purposely hidden in the pit, under the brush, so as not to be found. Why display Norm on Dedication Hill for them to find, but try to hide Rumor here in the pit?

Nothing makes sense.

Colt snaps to attention when a car horn belches across the forest. The sound is faint, a few miles away. But it's there, just over the howl of the wind.

"Is that a horn?" Wyatt asks.

Colt believes it's coming from the northwestern side of the park, though he can't be certain with the wind. He fears there might've been an accident somewhere on Route 206, and his heart sinks at the thought. *What next?* He returns his gaze to Rumor's body in the pit, already hidden under a fresh sheen of snow.

The horn whines over the wind. He needs to check it out and confirm no one is hurt. First, he must preserve the crime scene until Tripp gets back with the sheriff. But using a tarp like they had with Norm, isn't possible. They would need something else. And he has an idea on how to do that.

"Are those field cameras we used to track that black bear last fall still in RS3?"

A black bear was seen roaming this end of the park. But when the search for the elusive bear was unsuccessful, Maynard ordered night vision field cameras mounted around the area. The cameras operate off battery power and connect to a monitor using Bluetooth. Within two days the bear was caught, sedated, and taken to a bear sanctuary in the northwestern part of the state.

"Sure. In the storage room."

"I want you to set them up around the pit and monitor them until the police arrive. Don't let anything—human or animal—mess with this crime scene. Got it?"

"Yes, sir. But where are you going?"

"To find out where that horn is coming from."

CHAPTER 11

Tripp is a half mile from the park's eastern exit on Route 206. It's two-thirty in the afternoon, but to Tripp, it feels much later since the sun is a blotch behind the clouds. *The dark will come early tonight, crawling over the land like Black Death.* The temperature, on the Mac's dashboard, has fallen two degrees in the last hour. By nightfall, it will be somewhere in the low teens. And, by midnight, it'll be near zero or below. The thought of the extreme cold makes his old bones ache.

And the worst of the storm is yet to come.

The thought sours in Tripp's mind in more ways than one, and an unpleasant feeling begins to frost his skin as the woods close around him in a narrow white tunnel.

He glances at the black leather cigar case lying on the dashboard for some semblance of comfort. His initials MTT stand out like three gold medallions on the front. It was Aleja's last gift to him for their twenty-fifth wedding anniversary. That familiar sadness of her passing slips over his skin like a well-worn suit. *I should have known something was wrong that morning when you looked so pale, so…unlike yourself.* But Tripp had thought she was coming down with a cold or the flu, perhaps. How could he know she had an undiagnosed heart issue? Hell, Aleja herself didn't even know until the chest pains began. Two minutes later…she was gone. *Died right in my arms.* Tripp remembers the hot tears streaming down his face, the uncontrollable shaking, and the internal fear that he would be alone for the first time in twenty-six years. Truly alone. He reminds himself to quit living in the past, an issue he's been dealing with since her passing.

He returns the hurtful memories to their nearby place in his mind and shifts his focus back onto the road, the sheriff's office in Jackson. Tripp knows it will take over an hour to get there. The roads and visibility are worsening by the minute; the snow as thick as volcanic ash and the winds are as strong as the hurricane gusts last summer when Phillis hit.

Two taillights materialize out of the frozen hellscape ahead.

Tripp slams his foot on the pedal, the plow wheels lock, and the brakes squeal like pigs being slaughtered as the rear wheels fight desperately for traction until the Mac shutters to a stop.

A black Dodge Ram sits idling in the middle of the road with its driver's side door open. The snow under the tailpipe is melted from the exhaust, and the slush is stained black.

That's Norm's truck! But why is it…

Tripp sees it. The past seems to reach across time and space and seize his heart in its cold embrace. Two large maple trees have fallen across the park exit in the same place where they fell during the hurricane last July. He, Amos, and Lance tried desperately to clear the area to get emergency crews into the park to assist with the rescue at the Rocks.

"What are the odds of this happening twice?"

He jumps down from the plow into the bitter cold; the wind stings his chapped lips. The snow is shin-deep. He slogs through the snow so he can examine the blockage. Alongside the pickup, the repeated *ding* from the open door rings creepily across the snowy forest like some morbid bell calling zombies for a dinner of *braaaains.* Tripp figures that Norm must've stopped when he saw the trees blocking the exit.

The trees are piled on top of one another, and the thought of trying to pull them away with the plow crosses Tripp's mind. He has a heavy tow chain in the cab that he could wrap around them. But it would be useless. Even with the plow and a chain, there's no way he could remove the trees; they're too big, too long, and too heavy. The trees will need to be cut apart piece by piece to reopen the road, just like last time, which took them several hours to complete, even with outside help working the other side of the blockage.

Time we don't have.

With this side blocked, Tripp will have to go back through the park and use the western exit to get out. Then he'll drive ten miles around the park and another eight miles into Jackson. That will take him hours.

Fuck!

He's about to return to the plow when he spots something odd about the stump on the left side of the road. It's not splintered as if the wind had snapped the tree naturally. He feels a buckling in his chest like the bulkheads of a ship's hull failing, only instead of water rushing in, it's a flood of panic, much like he felt when word came down the line that Maynard had fallen and died. *And for what? A fucking hoax!*

He trudges through the snow to the stump and dusts the top off, exposing the evenly cut wood. Burn marks blacken the grain. Only a chainsaw can decolorize the woodgrain like that when the blade begins to dull as it rips through a tree.

Someone cut these trees down on purpose.

But why?

And the answer reveals itself like a blast of gunpowder exploding behind his eyes.

Because someone doesn't want us to leave this park.

He slowly turns to the Dodge, the *ding* of the open door a warning bell of what transpired there. Whoever did this used the blockage to get Norm out of his truck, and when he did...

He was attacked.

Exposed and vulnerable out in the open, Tripp turns, hurries back to the Mac, and climbs in before someone lurking in the forest can pick him off, too.

Tripp rips the CB off the hook and tries to call RS1.

Static.

He calls out again. Still, static is the only response.

This fucking storm!

But it's not just the storm anymore. Someone *is* in the park with them, and they have been prevented from leaving or calling for help.

He lifts the cigar case off the dash, opens it, and pulls out half a cigar. He lights it with the butane torch and takes a long drag, letting the smoke out slowly; it encapsulates the cab around him, comforts him.

Whoever's doing this could have gotten to both entrances to the park. Tripp feels his blood pressure rise. And if they did get to both entrances...

Then we're fubar.

Still, there's only one way to know for sure.

Tripp jams the cigar back into his mouth, turns the Mac around, and heads west toward the other side of the park.

CHAPTER 12

Route 206 is a white sheet. Amos tries to relax in the passenger seat while Lance drives, but he's got a firm grip on the "oh, shit" bar above his right shoulder, nonetheless. It's a treacherous drive. Even in the 4x4, an accident could happen in the blink of an eye with snow this deep and the icy condition of the road. The wind gusts are so strong that Amos feels the cab rock. Neither of them speak. Lance needs to keep his full attention on the road.

They pass Dedication Road on their right and come upon Camp Southwoods Road on the left. The bridge across Lake Clarke is directly in front of them at the bottom of the hill, snow whipping across the lanes. Drifts have built up along the small concrete guardrails. As they pass Camp Southwoods Road, Amos looks beyond the yellow gate with its ominous warning signs to the winding, overgrown road that once led to the summer camp. He's never been back to Camp Southwoods, but he knows about the Carver murders, the dead counselors, and the legend of their ghosts haunting the area. Is that what's been happening today? Is the arrival of the storm awakening a malevolent spirit that's now casting its shadow over the park and all in it?

Of course not, Amos reminds himself, thinking of the body in the pit. *Someone of flesh and blood is responsible.*

The truck nears the mouth of the bridge.

He doesn't want any part of what's going on. He wants to go home, see his daughter, and barricade them inside until the storm passes. But a dreadfulness picks away at him, like a wolf stripping flesh from bone, that getting home won't be easy.

Four simultaneous explosions punch Amos's eardrums. He sees the steering wheel rip out of Lance's hands—*oh, fuck!*—and the pickup shoots hard to the left, toward the bridge's concrete guardrail. Amos watches, helpless, as Lance tries to regain control of the pickup before they hit the guardrail. But they're going too fast on the slippery road for him to do anything.

"Hang on!" Lance screams.

The pickup sideswipes the guardrail. The driver's side mirror tears away upon impact and goes flipping through the air before landing in the angry water below. Sparks fly and mix with the snow like glitter. The sound of grinding metal pierces the air. The cab shakes Amos as if he's in a rickety roller coaster before the steering wheel rips from Lance's hand and the pickup cuts back to the right, across the lanes toward the other side of the bridge.

Amos sees the concrete barrier coming up fast, though everything in his mind seems to have grown slow as if giving his body time to react. He knows if they hit the guardrail just right, the pickup could smash through the concrete barrier and go down into Lake Clarke's murky depths, taking him and Lance with it.

Before Amos can form another thought, the pickup slams headfirst into the concrete barrier. Amos is driven forward. The hood pops up like an A-frame tent. The windshield cracks in a spider-web pattern. Steam from the punctured radiator blows out from under the hood and shoots into the air with a loud *hiss,* and the horn cries out as if the pickup knows it is hurt.

Everything goes dark and silent.

• • •

Amos fights to come out of the darkness as if he's taken a heavy-duty opioid that's held him captive in a deep sleep. A low *wailing* sound comes to his foggy mind. It reminds him of a steam whistle on some far-off train on lonely, dark tracks. Soon, the blackness begins to lift, and the wailing grows louder as if the train is nearing the station. Finally, like waking from a nightmare, his eyes snap open. For a moment, he isn't aware of where he is; everything is blurry and out of focus, like he's peering through a jar of Vaseline.

And then the accident starts to trickle back to him. *We crashed!* He blinks rapidly like a camera's shutter snapping picture after picture until his vision clears. He's still in the maintenance pickup. The seat belt has held him in place. He's staring at the floor where a scattering of objects lay by his feet—tools, paper, plastic bottles.

Lifting his head feels like he's trying to pull a ton of bricks with his neck. His left trapezius tightens into a hard knot of blistering pain that shoots into the base of his skull like a dagger.

Lance? Is he okay?

Turning to check on Lance causes another flare of discomfort at the base of Amos's skull. He grimaces and grabs at the tender area as if his hand will help soothe the pain. It won't, he knows, but he does it anyway. Like how putting a Band-Aid on a cut can sometimes make it instantly feel better.

He finds Lance bent over the steering wheel, eyes closed, and a large gash across his forehead bleeds profusely. Amos thinks he's dead—*he sure looks dead*—until he sees the slow rise and fall of Lance's chest.

Unconscious. Badly hurt. But alive.

Amos's teeth begin to chatter from the cold as much as from the shock of the accident.

I need to call for help.

He reaches for the CB. Another jolt of agony shoots through him. He cries out. Tears leak from his eyes and run down his cheeks, drip off his chin. *You can do this; just breathe.* He leans forward, grinds his teeth through his pain, and plucks the CB from its hasp below the dashboard. Only then does he remember the cord is cut, like someone knew they would crash and be unable to call for help.

Fuck!

A *whoosh* from the engine grabs Amos's attention. *Oh, no!* And the strong smell of burnt plastic and wiring floods his senses—a hot, unpleasant odor that irritates his nose. The white steam from under the wrinkled hood instantly turns black as night, and hot orange flames begin lapping from the engine compartment.

You need to get out! And you need to get Lance out and get as far away as possible before….

Amos reaches for the seat belt release. This slight movement of his neck causes sharp pain in the base of his skull again. Like an injured animal, he whimpers but persists through the discomfort and presses the seat belt release button.

Nothing happens.

He presses it again.

The belt stays in place.

He clicks it again.

And again.

And again.

Driving his thumb into the release, he stacks his hands and pushes with everything he has until his thumb feels like it's moments away from snapping backward.

Still, the seat belt won't unlatch.

Wind belts over the bridge, shakes the pickup, and fuels the flames. They grow, angry, snap like a whip. Amos feels the heat on his face, legs, and feet. The fire is spreading under the truck. If there's a rupture in the fuel line or even the tank—

Panic sets in across his body and settles on his heart. He thinks of Aisha, his daughter, who is at home and off from school because of the snow. Before work that day, Aisha made him promise that they would go sledding when he got home. It is a promise he plans to keep if he can get out. *But I can't fucking get out! I can't!*

The smell of burnt wires and oil is stronger than ever. A popping sound from deep inside the engine house causes the horn to die like a deflating balloon. Thick, black smoke starts to inch out from the vents. It burns his eyes, causes them to water uncontrollably, and chokes him as it works up his nose, down his throat, and into his lungs.

He coughs.

Through watery vision, he scans the tools between his feet. He believes he sees a screwdriver, a hammer, and maybe a pipe wrench, but his stinging eyes might be deceiving him.

Amos reaches for what he believes is the screwdriver. He might be able to drive it into the seat belt clasp and somehow dislodge the buckle. But the seat belt is locked in place from the accident, preventing him from moving more than a few inches at best.

The only way you're getting out is to cut yourself free.

Amos looks around to find something to cut the seat belt, but there's nothing.

He coughs again; the black smoke has thickened inside the cab, eating away his oxygen.

Then, through the smoke and flames, he catches sight of a hooded figure standing at the mouth of the bridge, the face hidden in the dark of the hood, watching as Amos struggles to get free. When the figure lowers the hood, Amos feels his breath catch in his throat at what is staring at him with a mirthless grin and black eyeless sockets. It can't be real. But it is, Amos knows in his heart. It's as real as death itself. Amos believes he sees the grin grow with excitement between the flames, the smoke, and the heat distortion. It's enjoying the chaos it created.

Amos pulls frantically at the seat belt again, as a guttural, manic scream that he's never heard comes from somewhere deep inside him. But the belt doesn't break free.

Why would it? It's made to keep people in. Made to keep people safe.

CHAPTER 13

Colt is driving faster than he should on less-than-safe roads. His uneasiness is reminiscent of how he felt as he and Maynard worked their way to the Rocks. He opposed the rescue, not solely because of the weather but because of this horrible feeling that something would go wrong if they made the trek. It's very similar to what Colt feels now after hearing the horn. *What the hell happened?*

"Can any…ne…ear me, over?" Flint's broken voice comes through on the SUV's short-range CB.

Colt snatches the microphone from the Interceptor's dashboard.

"Flint? Can you hear me, over?" Colt figures Flint must be within a three-mile radius for Colt to be receiving messages on the short range, but that doesn't mean that Flint is receiving his in return. The CBs were fickle that way, especially in a storm this severe.

"I got you! Colt, we got a problem." Flint comes through clearer this time, panic in his voice.

"What's going on?" Colt's grip on the microphone tightens, and spittle flies from his mouth and dots the dash.

"There was an accident on the bridge."

You've got to be fucking kidding me!

"Colt, I can see fl—" Flint's voice drowns in the static.

"Flint? Flint?"

"….it looks like a pickup! But my view is impeded by the bridge's guardrails." Flint's voice comes in again.

Colt's stomach constricts, forcing something acidic onto the back of his tongue. *Oh, sweet Jesus!*

He slams his foot down on the accelerator and hits the siren. The SUV's end loosens and starts to come around. He cuts the wheel in the opposite direction, lets off the gas, and the SUV corrects itself. He punches the gas.

"Colt, it's Joey. I'm here with Flint. We're heading to the bridge now. Where are you?"

Why's she with Flint? I told him to go back to RS2 and update Dusty.

"I'm passing Dedication Road—"

The bridge begins to take shape at the bottom of the hill. A hue of orange pulsates in the blur of white, and thick black smoke rises against the gray sky. Smoke that thick and black is never a good sign. As he nears the bridge, Colt sees that a pickup has hit the guardrail and is on fire.

But it's not just any pickup.

It's the one Lance and Amos were driving. Overwhelming alarm and urgency flood every fiber of Colt's being. Flames from under the hood snap in the wind, and black smoke blows over the truck's cab, filling it with carbon monoxide. He swallows whatever came from his stomach a moment ago and feels it slide back down into him and sink not into his stomach but deep into a pit of despair.

Is anyone hurt? Or worse, dead? He wonders if Lance was driving too fast coming off the hill and lost control. The thought reminds Colt to tap his brakes and slow the SUV, or he'd end up just like…

Something on the ground grabs Colt's attention as he nears the mouth of the bridge. At first, he's unsure what he sees poking through the snow that gleam like little metal shark fins under the Interceptor's headlights.

Then it hits Colt's brain like a shot of dopamine.

Speed spikes.

Someone had set them across the road, hoping to blow the tires of any automobile coming off the hill.

He slams on the brakes. The tires lock. Colt cuts the wheel hard to the right and the SUV careens sideways, stopping just before the tires pass over the spikes. If the headlights hadn't caught the gleam of the metal spikes, Colt would never have seen them. He would have driven over them. The tires would have blown, and he would have lost control and crashed, just like Lance and Amos had. The realization that someone had set this trap descends into his brain with sickening clarity—a trap.

It's diabolical!

Jumping out, Colt sees the spikes look similar to the ones in all Park Ranger Ford Interceptors. *Had someone stolen a set? Or was it someone with a badge who set the trap in the first place?* The thought darkens in Colt's mind. But he doesn't have the time to investigate further, not with Amos and Lance still inside the burning pickup. He sprints toward the wreckage, his feet slipping and sliding in the snow.

At the mouth of the bridge, Colt notices something written in black on the side of the concrete guardrail. He slides to a stop, his feet almost going out from under him. The words are like a vile incantation foretelling of misfortune and death.

> *Little maintenance men riding,*
> *Douggie Carver's set a trap in hiding.*
> *Gonna catch those maintenance men,*
> *Gonna dispatch those maintenance men,*
> *Little maintenance men done riding.*

Another rhyme. This one perfectly tailored to fit the crime.

Amos's scream snaps Colt from his paralysis and he tears off for the pickup.

He's about ten feet away from the inferno when he feels the heat on his face. Inside the cab, Lance is bent forward over the steering wheel. He's not moving, which causes Colt to worry that Lance didn't survive the accident. Beside him, Amos pulls frantically at his seat belt while the thick black smoke fills the cab around him. He's coughing, asphyxiating on the poison. *The belt must be jammed.*

Colt rushes to the driver's side door. "LANCE! LANCE, WAKE UP!"

Still, he's unresponsive.

"He's unconscious! And my seat belt is stuck. I need a knife to cut myself free," Amos shouts.

"Hold on!" Colt says. He reaches into his pocket, pulls out his gloves, and slips them on. He needs to get both men out, but Lance needs to be removed first since he's unconscious. The door handle is warm through his gloves; he can hear the snowflakes sizzle on contact with the hot metal. He yanks the handle.

The door doesn't budge.

Fuck! It's jammed.

Hurrying around the truck's bed toward the passenger side, Colt slips in the snow and comes down hard on his side. Pain shoots through his ribs and kicks air from his lungs. But he pays the fall little mind and pulls himself up by the bumper, snow falling off him in large patches. He buries his hand in the front pocket of his green cargo pants and retrieves his pocketknife. He hits the button on the side, and the spring-loaded five-inch blade shoots from the handle with a *click*.

At the passenger side door, Colt wrenches on the lever. The door unlatches, and he throws it open. Black smoke billows out from the cab and directly into Colt's face. He sucks in a breath and the poison settles on his lungs with a hot burning. He coughs it away.

"The driver's door is jammed," Colt screams at Amos over the roaring flames and wind. The intense heat from the fire singes his whiskers; the smell of rancid burning hair follicles wafts up his nose. "I need to get you out so I can get to Lance."

Amos nods as another coughing fit erupts.

Colt takes the strap across Amos and saws through the fabric. The belt goes lax, and Amos rips it away and slips out of the truck.

"Help me with Lance," Colt cries as he climbs into the cab.

"No time!"

Before Colt knows what's happening and can reach Lance, Amos's strong hands drag him from the cab.

"Let go! I have to get Lance out!"

"No time!" Amos shouts again.

"Yes, there is!"

He tries to pull away, but Amos's vice-like grip is impossible to break free of. The wind blows, and with it comes the smell of gasoline, and Colt understands why Amos is dragging him away from the cab.

The pickup's fuel tank is leaking.

Just as that realization settles uncomfortably in Colt's brain, the pickup explodes.

The shockwave knocks him and Amos to the ground as if an unseen giant hand has taken them off their feet. The pickup's bed lifts from the ground and it lands upside down on the concrete guardrail between the cab and the bed, breaking its back in an upside-down V. The weight of the bed pulls the cab over the side and into the icy waters below.

Lance!

Colt jumps to his feet and sprints to where the truck went over, kicking fiery wreckage out of his way as he goes, hoping, praying that somehow Lance made it out alive. Yet, the utter hopelessness of Lance's situation is a reality slap that he doesn't want to accept.

When he looks over the side, what's left of the pickup is already sinking into the icy depths.

And just like with Maynard, there wasn't anything he could do to save Lance's life.

CHAPTER 14

Joey and Flint are speeding toward the bridge when an explosion rocks the wilderness with such force that she feels the concussion pass through her chest like a malevolent spirit. A giant mushroom fireball forms above the tree line, which morphs into a black cloud blown away by the wind.

"Holy shit!" Flint shouts from the passenger seat.

They were almost back to RS1 from the antenna shed when they heard the horrible sound of screeching tires and the crunch of metal nearby. When the horn blew through the forest like an alarm for an oncoming nuclear attack, Joey knew someone had crashed.

On the bridge, Joey sees fiery pieces of wreckage from the accident dot the snow like craters on the moon's surface. The concrete barrier where the pickup struck has cracks through its smooth surface like a roadmap and is blackened from the fire. *But where's the pickup?* Flint echoes her thoughts aloud. His eyes sweep back and forth for any signs that it was ever there.

Joey's stomach clenches. She doesn't want to accept the truth. The pain is like a scalpel slicing her heart in two. The explosion. The fireball. Who was inside when the pickup exploded and went over the side into the cold, black abyss?

As they near the spot of the accident, Joey observes Colt materialize like a phantom through the snow. He pulls Amos to his feet. Both men look shell-shocked, survivors gathering themselves from the ashes of battle. A shower of relief cascades over her. *He's okay.* Colt assists Amos to the side of the bridge and leans him against the guardrail. As the Interceptor rolls to a stop, Colt lumbers toward them like a boxer who just went ten rounds with the Abominable Snowman—punch-drunk and wobbly. Joey jumps out and runs to him. She wants to wrap her arms around him, hold him, and kiss him. *For God's sake, tell him you love him!* But she does none of this. Not with Flint behind her and Amos just across the bridge.

"What happened?" she screams to Colt over the shrieking wind.

"Someone set up a fucking speed trap at the mouth of the bridge!" That was not what Joey expected to hear. The shock of this revelation twists through her body like a corkscrew. She thought whoever was driving the pickup had lost control in the snow coming off the hill and wrecked. A mistake. A tragedy. But…a speed trap? In the middle of a blizzard? *Who would have…*

"Are you sure?" Flint sounds dubious.

"Yes. Lance didn't see it since it was buried in the snow. Hell, I barely saw it. Had my headlights not caught the gleam of teeth…" Colt's face draws tight with gloom of his fate had his reaction been a moment slower.

Lance? What about Lance? Joey's eyes shoot to Amos, leaning against the guardrail. His expression is bewildered, eyes buggy with uncertainty, shock, and dread. *But Lance? Where's Lance?* She doesn't see him anywhere.

Joey looks to Colt for an answer. But the misery on his face and the sad heaviness of his dark blue eyes tells her the horrifying realism. Her throat pulls so tight she can't breathe. Lance didn't make it out of the pickup before it exploded.

She grips Colt's forearm tightly; feels the tremble of his body. She knows she shouldn't do this, not with Flint watching, but she does it anyway. She needs to touch him. To make sure he's really there. That she's not interacting with his ghost. Besides, would Flint even question her actions at that moment? She's just consoling a friend. *Nothing more than that to see here, folks.* Still, it's hard for her to hold her tears back, not just for Lance but also for Colt. He could've hit the speed trap just as easily and be lying dead at the bottom of the lake.

"Are you alright?" Joey manages to croon.

Colt gives a reassuring nod but nothing more to indicate his feelings. He turns to Amos, bent at the waist, his right hand clasped to his neck.

"Amos is hurt. Lance…well…" Colt looks back at Joey grimly. "The pickup was on fire. I had enough time to get Amos out before…before…"

Joey feels the tears well in the cups of her eyes, but she wills them not to release. *Hold fast. There will be time for that later.*

"Amos is going to pass out!" Flint darts past them.

Joey looks up in time to see Amos face-plant into the snow.

CHAPTER 15

"Hey, let me outta here!" Darryl demands as Colt and Flint burst through the door of RS1, carrying Amos, unconscious and limp in their hands. "It's against my rights to hold me in this cell!"

"Not now, Darryl," Colt says. He strains to keep a grip under Amos's arms. The six-foot-five, three-hundred-pound Amos Kent is like moving a dead bear.

Joey follows them and closes the door. The shriek of the wind dies to a quiet hum that, in other circumstances, would be therapeutic. Today, it's a death rattle.

"Hey, you. Let me out, huh?"

Joey ignores Darryl and moves through the doorway to the right.

Colt and Flint carry Amos down the hallway, like two men trying to move a refrigerator, passed the locker room and the kitchen and into the bunkroom at the far end of the hall. They ease Amos down on one of the bunks; the springs squeak from his weight.

Joey hurries to Amos's bedside and unzips his jacket. Colt assists her, freeing the unconscious man of the bulky outer layer of clothing. In the meantime, Flint has the first aid kit open and ready. He removes the automatic blood pressure cuff, slips it around Amos's thick, muscular arm, and hits the start button. The room fills with a soft drone as the bladder fills with air. Grabbing a stethoscope from the back, Joey puts it on Amos's chest and listens to his lungs and heart. Her steady gaze tells Colt that she doesn't hear anything abnormal. Relief spills over him. He had already lost two men; he wasn't sure he could handle losing a third. Though he fears this day is long from over and it's just the beginning of things to come.

"What's his BP?" Joey asks, removing the stethoscope from her ears.

"105/64," Flint replies.

"How's he doing?" Colt asks, worried. He knows Amos's blood pressure is low for a man of his size.

"He's okay. But not out of the woods yet." She pulls a small penlight from the kit, opens Amos's left eyelid, and moves the light past it for pupillary reflexes—a concussion. She repeats the process with the other eye. "I don't see anything too severe externally, few bumps and bruises. Pupillary reflexes are normal. I think he passed out from a symptom called vasovagal syncope. His blood pressure and heart rate are low. It's a common trigger for the symptom."

"And that is?" Colt asks.

"A form of fainting."

"What causes it?"

"Several things. Heat—"

"Think we can rule that one out."

"Exposure, emotional stress, pain." Joey looks at Colt with a bleakness that cuts through him. "Fear."

Fear. There was a lot of that out there on the bridge. Colt's mind flashes to Amos stuck in the truck. He can't imagine what must have been going through his mind with the fire engulfing the space around him, nibbling at his skin, ready to take a bite; all that black smoke choking off his air. It must have been agonizing believing he was moments away from asphyxiation or burning to death. *Maybe both.*

Joey looks back at Flint.

"Can you watch Amos for a moment?"

"Sure."

She stands and turns to Colt, her grim gaze morphing into something else. Anger? Irritation? He isn't sure. But something's eating away at her, something she wants to share with only him.

"We need to talk."

She takes him by the arm and leads him back into the main room of RS1. Darryl watches them as they head toward Colt's office, like a drunk in a cell in an old Western movie, arms through the bars, hands dangling, looking unkempt and mean.

"What's going on?" he demands. "And let me outta here, will ya?" They ignore his pleas and move into the office. "You can't keep me in here like an ani—"

Joey closes the door behind them. She pulls the blinds and turns back to face Colt. She's about to speak, but Colt beats her to it.

"You need to know something, Joey." Colt gets straight to it. *No sense in tiptoeing around it.* "Tripp found Norm on Dedication Hill—someone murdered him."

"I know. Flint told me." A single tear forces itself out and runs down her cheek. She pushes the tear away with the back of her hand and quickly regains her composure. "Porter's also missing."

With everything happening, Colt didn't realize Porter wasn't in the building until now. He was so preoccupied with Amos to notice Porter wasn't there. His perplexed look must tell Joey to elaborate further.

"There was something wrong with the antenna. Porter went to check it out. He was gone over an hour, and I began to worry, so I went to the shed to check on him." She pauses and swallows deep, like she's trying to dislodge a piece of food stuck in her throat. "Colt, the antenna servers were destroyed."

"What!" Despondency hits him like a boulder. His knees weaken, and he almost crumbles to the floor with the weight of defeat. But what Joey says next solidifies his worst fear: a repeat of the past.

"We're effectively cut off from reaching anyone outside the park."

"We have the landlines. We can use—"

Joey shakes her head. And with it, Colt's hopelessness builds.

"The phones are down, too, along with the internet."

"Good, God. What's next?" His shoulders slump as the bad news keeps piling up like an accident on the interstate.

"Porter's missing." Colt's heart clenches. *First Maynard. Now his son.* "I found his equipment bag in the antenna shed and… blood. I believe someone jumped him to get to the communications system." The worry lines around Joey's mouth and forehead deepen. "Colt…there was a message left." Her golden eyes are a dark yellow, almost brown, like a piece of rotten fruit, a look that tells Colt that he's already seen what she found—twice now.

"It wasn't really a message, was it?"

Joey shakes her head and recites the nursery rhyme on the antenna shed wall.

"Little Ranger Barrett running, Douggie Carver's gone a-hunting, Gonna catch that ranger, Gonna cleave that ranger, Little Ranger Barrett done running." She draws a shaky breath that rattles in her throat.

A chill fans across Colt's body. A feeling Aunt Sunny would have described as someone walking over her grave.

"Joey, I found the rhyme and Norm's name carved into the monument on Dedication Hill and another one on the bridge, after the accident."

Joey's eyebrows twitch as she tries to comprehend the motivation behind staging the crime scenes. When she looks up at him, her face is ghoulishly sallow.

"Someone wants us to believe that Norm is Carver's fifth victim."

"That's what I believe, too, making Lance victim number six. And if I hadn't gotten Amos out in time, he'd be seven."

"And Porter might be eight." Her face tightens as if a foul odor had filled the air around them. "But who would do this? Rumor?"

"Rumor isn't behind this," Colt says, shaking his head.

"You don't know that. He and Darryl could—"

"He's dead, Joey," he says bluntly. "It wasn't him."

"What!" Joey grabs his arm. "Where did you find him?"

"I didn't. Lance and Amos found him in the pit, covered with brush so he wouldn't be seen." He pries his arm from her clutches.

"Someone…murdered him, too?" Joey's eyes shift back and forth in disbelief.

"From the looks of him—and mind you, I'm no expert—he's been down there for at least twelve hours or more. Had two arrows, same blue-and-white fletchings as those I found in Norm."

"But what about the gate? The lock on the pit?"

"Someone either had the key or picked it."

"So, if it isn't Rumor doing this…then who is it?" she asks, looking up at him, eyes probing for answers he doesn't have. "And who did Flint see at the Panorama Building, if not Rumor? You don't think that Douglas—"

"No. I don't." Colt thinks of Flint. Something was bugging him about the man. "Why was Flint with you on the bridge? I told him to return to RS2."

"He showed up at the antenna shed shortly after I arrived there. That's how I found out about Norm."

"Flint was at the antenna shed?"

Joey nods.

"He said you told him to go back to RS1. When he didn't find Porter and me, Darryl told him we went to the antenna shed."

"That's bullshit. I specifically told Flint to go back to RS2. Why would he tell you that?"

"I don't know. Maybe he misheard you?" She crosses her arms over her chest as if trying to hold herself together.

Colt considers this a possibility. They were outside the Panorama Building while Colt gave Flint orders to return to RS2 and update Dusty on recent developments, who should have been back from clearing Trail Loop Two by then. Flint could have misheard him.

"Do *you* believe Flint misunderstood the order?" he asks.

Joey shifts her weight from foot to foot, uneasily. She's uncomfortable accusing a fellow ranger, particularly of murder, without proof.

"It's just…I don't know…strange that he was suddenly there, especially after I found the shed like I had. Flint believed Rumor was behind everything. But with what I know now…" She meets Colt's troubled gaze. "What are you thinking?"

Colt's quiet for a long moment before he answers.

"Flint *was* at the Panorama Building when Tripp and I arrived, standing over the smashed radio. Then he shows up at the antenna shed after you discover the servers, the blood, and the rhyme. Coincidence?"

"It could—" Joey stops midsentence. Something over Colt's shoulder has caught her attention.

"What?" Colt asks as her face turn deathly pale. "Joey, what is it?" He follows her gaze to the whiteboard on the office wall behind him. Written on it are two columns of patrol schedules that Colt wrote there at the start of the month. The column on the left was for the day shift, and the column on the right was for the night shift—Norm. It was the same system Maynard used when he was in charge, simple and easy to understand—*if it isn't broke, don't fix it*, Maynard would've said—so Colt left the system in place.

She floats past him as if the whiteboard were summoning her. From the pocket of her green slacks, she pulls a piece of paper, unfolds it, and looks between it and the whiteboard's second column—Norm's night patrol schedule.

11:00 p.m.
12:15 a.m.
1:30 a.m.
2:45 a.m.
3:00 a.m.
4:15 a.m.
5:30 a.m.
6:45 a.m.

"The numbers we found in Rumor's bag. They match the patrol times," Joey says.

He takes the paper from her and compares the numbers to those on the whiteboard. Now, Colt feels the color run from his face.

11
1215
130
245
300
415
530
645

And it hits him like a snowball to the face. This was how Rumor had evaded capture for nearly a year.

"Someone who has access to RS1 gave Rumor the nightly patrol schedules," Colt says. "That's why we could never catch him in the act!"

"We all have access. Any of us could have passed the schedules onto Rumor."

"But who among us would do that?" Colt asks, fanning the piece of paper to accentuate his point.

"Maybe the same someone who knows about our relationship. Someone who owns—or owned—a dark-colored Camaro."

"How—"

"The photos. I believe I know the night they were taken. You remember that see-through black nightie I bought?" Colt nods and can't help but give a small smile. Yes, he remembers that night—and the nightie—quite well now that Joey brings it up. "I only wore it once. It was hanging on a chair in all the photos." She pauses to collect her thoughts. "That night, while you were in the shower, I went to get us sodas from the vending machine. I saw someone dressed in dark clothing, maybe holding a camera—I couldn't tell because it was dark—jump into what I believe was a late seventies or early eighties model Camaro before hightailing it out of there. Didn't think much of it at the time, but now—"

"Now you're not so sure."

Joey's lips smooth with doubt and anger at her lapse in memory.

"I asked Darryl if either he or Rumor had a Camaro. He said no. But we can't believe anything that comes out of his mouth."

The room falls into an uncomfortable silence. Outside, the wind squeals and pushes against RS1 that it feels like the entire structure will lift off the foundation and fly through the park like Dorothy's house in *The Wizard of Oz.*

"We need help," Joey says, breaking the silence. "We're not equipped to handle this situation on our own."

Colt's thoughts exactly.

"I already sent Tripp to Jackson to bring the sheriff back."

Joey nods, though her eyes show uncertainty about Tripp's ability to make it back to the park with the sheriff before the roads become impassable.

"What about Darryl? We'll need to tell him about his son."

"We will. But first, we need to know who gave Rumor the patrol schedules. Knowing that could help us narrow down who might be behind the murders."

She agrees.

Colt shoots past her, throws open the office door, and barges up to Darryl in the cell.

"How did Rumor get ahold of the park's nightly patrol schedules?"

"I don't know what—"

"No more lies," Colt snaps. "Rumor had them in his bag, written on this piece of paper. Someone's been helping him, someone who works in this park. I want a name."

"I have no idea what you're talking about," Darryl says. The dumbfounded look on his face is like a cat that doesn't understand why you're scolding it for clawing the furniture.

"You know Rumor was here. Because he told you he was coming, didn't he?"

"Of course not."

And like the cat, Darryl falls back on his instincts. He digs deeper into the lie. He'd go to his grave before he gave himself or his boy up. *Can't get blood from a stone*, another one of Aunt Sunny's euphemisms that Colt adored.

Fuck that! Colt reaches through the bars and grabs Darryl's shirt collar. He rips him forward. Darryl's swollen nose slams into the bars and he wallows in agony.

"You're going to tell me how Rumor got the patrol schedules!" Colt shouts into Darryl's face, the piece of paper with the time schedules clenched in his fist.

"My nose! Ahhh! My fuckin'—ahhh—nose. You—uh—cocksucker, you!"

"No more games, Darryl. Talk!"

"Colt," Joey says from behind. "That's enough."

He pays her no mind.

"Talk, Darryl!" He pushes the paper with the schedule under Darryl's left eye. "How did Rumor get these?"

Darryl meets Colt's intense gaze with his own.

"You can wipe your ass with that, ranger man. I got nuttin' to say to you."

Colt releases him. Darryl stumbles back into the cell, a small stream of blood runs down his face from the reopened gash across his nose. He turns back to Joey, angered that he couldn't get Darryl to talk. She pushes a strand of dark hair off her forehead and tucks it behind her ear agitatedly, and her eyes shimmer with anger at his outburst. She's never seen that side of him before, the son of a bitch he can quickly become when the situation warrants such a response. It scares her. He knows he should apologize. First, to Darryl for losing his temper. And then to Joey for acting so irrationally, for scaring her. But they weren't in a rational situation. They were fighting for survival against an unknown enemy, and he'll do whatever he has to to keep his team members safe.

Flint hurries into the room.

"Amos is awake, Colt. And he *needs* to talk to you."

CHAPTER 16

Amos is alert and sits upright in the bed when Joey, Colt, and Flint enter the bunkroom.

"How are you feeling?" Joey asks, sitting down beside him. She reaches for the water bottle on the stand, cracks the top, and eases it to his lips. "Take only a few sips. You can have more later."

"I feel okay. My neck hurts, though." Amos says after a sip of water. He rubs the tender spot just below the right side of his skull. "Feels all knotted up."

"Probably whiplash." Joey refits the cap to the bottle and sits it back on the stand. "You'll have pain for a while."

"How long's a while?"

"Depends on the severity—days, weeks, months—"

"Years?"

Joey nods solemnly.

"Possibly a lifetime."

Amos's face darkens at the thought. Thanks to a madman trying to kill them, he'll have pain to go with the memories that will last a lifetime.

"Flint said you have something to tell us," Colt says.

Amos clears his throat and pushes himself up in the bed, wincing as he does.

"There was someone on the bridge with us. I saw 'em just after the pickup caught fire, watching, waiting for Lance and me to burn."

"You get a look at 'em?" Flint asks. "Was it Rumor?"

"Whoever it was…was…well, I don't know how to explain it." Amos looks away, lost in memory of the horrible event.

"Do the best you can," Joey places her hand on Amos's forearm.

"I just remember those black, eyeless sockets and that fucking menacing grin that grew bigger the harder I struggled to get out."

"What are you telling us, Amos?" Colt asks.

Joey feels the tiny hairs on the nape of her neck begin to rise. There's a sincerity in Amos's eyes that works under her skin; the fear of someone who knows death lurks around every acre of this park.

"It was a skeleton, Colt," Amos breathes.

"A skeleton? You didn't say anything about a skeleton," Flint says skeptically. "You might want to reevaluate Amos's condition, Joey." He chuckles at the absurdity of the idea that a skeleton was the cause of all the mayhem.

"You don't believe me?" He looks from Flint to Colt and then finally to Joey. There's an earnestness in his eyes that disconcerts her. Did he really believe he saw a skeleton out there? She wants to believe him. He's confident that what he saw wasn't a figment of his imagination. But what Amos believes he saw and what was there are two vastly different things. He was fighting for his life while trapped in the burning pickup. There was no telling what images his mind conjured up under such extreme duress.

"I'm sure whatever you think you saw was because of shock," Joey says.

Amos snatches his arm away, as if her touch repulses him.

"I'm telling you, *it* was there! On the bridge. Thriving in the chaos *it* created." Amos shifts his bulk in the bunk. Again, his face tightens into a tight pucker; tears press through his eyelashes from the discomfort.

"Easy. Just relax," Joey says, her voice low and calm. She doesn't need his agitation exacerbating his condition.

"It was there, Joey! I swear it was."

"I'm sure you just imag—"

"I didn't!" Amos fires back. His large hands form into fists. "Whatever *it* is, *it* wants us dead. We need to get out of here."

He tries to stand, but Joey forces him back down. She needs to keep him in the bunk and still.

"Get your damn hands off me, woman," Amos says in a low grumble.

Joey flings her hands up as if in surrender.

"I'm so sorry. I didn't mean…" She clears her throat. "I think it's best to lie still for a little while. You're still recovering from your…*episode*. If you try to move around too fast, you might black out again. Only this time, Amos, you might actually hurt yourself in the fall."

Amos's brown eyes reflect the state of his physical condition. He eases down on the bunk.

"You guys aren't buying this, are you?" Flint asks crassly. He glances at Joey and then to Colt.

"I know what I saw, Flint," Amos says. "So take your skepticism and shove it."

"Look, Amos. I believe that you believe you saw a skeleton. I do. But here's the thing: the last time I checked, a skeleton can't get up and move around on its own."

"Enough. Who, or whatever, is out there, is responsible for murdering Norm and Rumor and leaving the rhyme," Colt says.

"Hold on. Rumor's dead?" Flint asks. "When was anyone going to tell me?"

"I just did."

"Yeah, but—"

"But nothing. Amos and Lance found his body in the pit a few hours ago. I confirmed that it was him."

Flint tries to process the news of Rumor's murder. But that's easier said than done, Colt knows. Nothing about today was easy to understand.

"Then if it isn't Rumor…" Flint trails off.

"What rhyme?" Amos asks, confusion stilts his voice. His eyes travel around the room, looking for an answer.

"The Carver rhyme, only it was changed to fit what happened to you and Lance."

"Just like at the antenna shed," Flint says.

"And like Tripp and I found carved into the monument, along with Norm's name, on Dedication Hill."

"You and Tripp neglected to tell me that when we were at the Panorama Building," Flint says testily.

"We were dealing with other things, Flint," Colt says. He turns to Amos. "Did you see anything else that might help us narrow down who's behind this?"

"No. *It* was there only a second before it disappeared in the storm. If Lance were here, maybe he could confirm…" Amos falls back onto the bed. His mouth pulls tight, and his jaw muscles spasm as the anguish ripples through him. "I was right next to him. Why didn't I get him out after Colt cut me free? I had time."

Joey reaches out and places her hand on his forearm.

"I'm sorry, Amos."

Joey sadly knows from experience what Amos is feeling is survivor's guilt, and there isn't any first-aid treatment to fix that. Again, the shame of her not going with Colt and Maynard up to the Rocks works through her mind, even though there wasn't anything she could have done to change the outcome. But that's the thing about guilt. It's always there, in the back of your mind, pecking away at you until there's nothing left but the overwhelming hurt that you could have done more.

"He needs to rest," she says to the others.

They move to the doorway. Flint steps out into the hall with Colt while Joey hangs back and reaches for the light switch.

"On or off?" she asks.

"On," Amos says. "I don't think I can bear to be in the dark, alone, right now."

In the hall, Flint grabs ahold of Colt's elbow.

"You're not buying this shit about the skeleton, are you?"

Colt mulls the question before answering.

"I believe Amos saw *someone* on the bridge." Flint studies him with the cynicism of a man who was just told little green men were coming from outer space to invade the planet. "Okay. Maybe it wasn't a skeleton, maybe that part Amos imagined. But he saw someone out there—the same someone who's been leaving the rhymes."

Flint's still not buying a word of Amos's story.

"Is it true what you said? About finding Rumor in the pit?" Flint whispers so there isn't a chance Darryl can overhear their conversation.

"Afraid so," Colt whispers back.

"But the pit's locked."

"Someone either picked it or has a key."

"I was positive Rumor was behind this."

"So was I. Until I found him."

"Does Darryl know?"

Colt shakes his head. "No."

Joey comes up beside them. She looks ten years older. Worry pulls the frown lines across her brow and the crow's feet around her eyes into deep fissures.

"We need to be careful how we break the news to Darryl," she says. "There's no telling how he's going to react."

Colt agrees. Darryl's a loose cannon. They don't need his anger and pain being taken out on them right now.

"I say we keep it to ourselves for the time being," Flint says.

"We can't do that!" Joey replies, shaking her head. "Darryl has a right to know."

"I second that," Colt says. "We need to—"

A heavy engine rumbles outside RS1.

"What the hell is that?" Flint asks.

"Sounds like Tripp's plow," Joey says.

Colt checks his watch. A quarter past three. There's no way Tripp made it to the sheriff's station in Jackson and back in under two hours, not with the road conditions the way they are. Claustrophobia presses down on his shoulders like two strong hands holding him in a space no bigger than a coffin. He has a bad feeling that something forced Tripp's return.

Colt leads them back to the office area of RS1, just as the door opens and Tripp Thatcher walks in looking like a haggard, ghostly version of Sam Elliot.

"Tripp?" Colt says. "What happened?"

Without a word, Tripp moves past Colt, around the front desk, and makes a beeline for the coffee pot atop the filing cabinet. Joey looks at him for an explanation. But Colt doesn't have one. Tripp fumbles with the colander. His hand shakes as he pours, spilling coffee around the mug. He suspects the shaking isn't from the cold alone, but something else—something Tripp's seen in the storm.

"I need to tell you all," Tripp's eyes drift around the room, meeting their intense stares individually. "There's no easy way to say it, so I'll just lay it out. Both exits on Route 206 are blocked."

"What!" Flint erupts.

Colt feels any hope of the cavalry coming fall into the dark well of despair.

"Someone cut trees down at both exits."

"How do you know the trees were cut? That they didn't come down because of the storm? It's windy as hell out there," Flint says. Out the window, the snow is falling as thick as cake batter.

"Because I saw the stumps, Flint." Tripp takes a slurp of coffee. "Whoever did it used chainsaws to take them down, keeping us in the park. It's how they got Norm. I found his pickup at the eastern exit of the park, still running, door hanging open. He was ambushed."

"Ambushed?" Flint questions as if he didn't hear Tripp correctly.

"Take out the long-range radios and sabotage the antenna, limiting our communications to just the short-range CBs. Then block both exits, preventing any of us from leaving. Or anyone from getting in," Joey says.

"No shit," Flint scoffs. "But who's doing it?"

"I think the more important question is why?" Colt says. He pauses to align his thoughts. "Let's go over what we know so far. Norm's body was found on a park bench—Maynard's bench, to be precise—and his name was sliced into the monument under Carver's victims along with the rhyme. And Joey found blood— possibly Porter's—in the antenna shed and again the rhyme. It was also written on the bridge, after the accident."

"Are you suggesting," Flint says. A smirk grows as if something struck him funny. "Norm, Lance, and Porter were murdered by Douglas Lee Carver?"

"Why is that so hard to believe?" Darryl says from his cell. His voice is low, full of menace that causes a chill to walk up Colt's back.

The room falls silent. Outside, the wind moans, and the snow taps against the windows like the incessant clicking of the Grim Reaper's boney finger on the glass, reminding everyone of his ominous presence over the park.

"No way!" Flint answers for the group.

"Look what he did to those counselors in '97—I should know; I found one of 'em washed up on my land." Darryl frowns at the memory. "Who's to say he hasn't returned to pick up where he left off?"

"According to what I know, Carver was autistic," Colt says. "His parents brought him to the camp that summer because they believed it would help socialize him."

"And one night that same autistic kid decided to up and murder four people," Flint butts in. "Yeah, Colt, we all know the story."

"That's not the entire story."

All eyes focus on Darryl.

"What are you talking about?" Flint asks, already sounding bored with Darryl's unsubstantiated account of events.

"There were whispers about Camp Southwoods for years around the area. About what they did there. About how it was run. How they treated the kids."

Colt was with the park rangers for fifteen years, and in that time, he's never heard stories of abuse against the kids who spent their summers at Camp Southwoods. Not from Maynard. Or those in high positions in the DCNR.

"Who's *they*?" Flint asks.

"You're all in the dark about what happened down there, huh?" Darryl looks surprised, yet not. His distrust of any government agency leads him to believe they're all corrupt.

"Enlighten us," Colt says.

"The scuttlebutt is that some pretty awful shit was happening down there."

"Such as?" Joey asks.

"Physical abuse. Mental harassment. Dished out to the campers by the counselors. Of course, nothing was ever done because it was a state-owned camp."

"But the park operated from the early seventies until the late nineties. How would they get away with abusing children for so many years without anyone raising concerns?" Joey asks.

"You just answered your own question," Darryl says.

But they need no further explanation. Accusations of child abuse during those thirty years the camp was in operation weren't taken as seriously as they are nowadays. Any allegations toward the camp, or its staff, would be brushed off as nothing more than tales from unhappy campers who didn't want to be there.

"Wait," Flint says. "I've been here longer than any of you and never heard of this. And as far as I know, neither have any of you. Right?" He looks around the room. Colt, Joey and Tripp all nod. "This is just another story that's spiraled into an urban legend over the years, used to scare people, just like the rest of the stories about Camp Southwoods—stories that gullible people buy into."

"And what if it isn't," Darryl says. "What if Carver has returned, pickin' up where he left off?"

"Hold on. Douglas Lee Carver is still locked up in Haven Hurst, so he couldn't be behind this," Joey says, the voice of reason.

"You don't know if he's still there," Darryl grumbles. "He could have been released or escaped."

"I think we would've heard something on the news. Or read about it on the internet or in the papers. It was a major story back in the day, and it would have been reported if he broke out or been released from prison," Colt says.

"But do you know that for sure?" Darryl asks. Colt remains quiet, and his silence solidifies Darryl's point. "That's what I thought. And it's not like you can call Haven Hurst to confirm if Carver is still in their custody because the phones are down."

Colt looks at Joey. The panic in her face and eyes pulls at his heart. He knows what she's thinking because he's thinking it, too. This whole situation is reminiscent of last summer. They're again cut off from the outside world and stuck in the park. This time, instead of a hurricane being the cause of the destruction, someone meticulously set all of it into motion, waiting for a storm with calculating, inhuman self-restraint to strike. But Douglas Lee Carver?

"Little counselor running, Douggie Carver's gone a-hunting, Gonna catch that counselor, Gonna cleave that counselor, Little counselor done running," Darryl says in a hauntingly mocking tone that brings an unearthly chill to the room.

A thought strikes Colt. He should've realized earlier, but didn't, until now.

"You guys can't be buying all this nonsense. That's insane. There *is* someone out there." Flint points out the window. "But it's not fucking Douglas Lee Carver."

Colt is about to share his thoughts when Amos steps into the room.

"I heard voices. Thought I should attend the meeting."

"How are you feeling?" Joey asks.

"I'm hurting. But I'll manage." Amos circles his head slowly as if to prove he's okay. His eyes say otherwise.

"If it isn't Carver—"

"It isn't," Flint derides.

"—then who in the hell *is* doing this?" Joey asks.

"A copycat," Colt finally says. "Someone who's obsessed with the murders."

"What brings you to that conclusion?" Flint asks.

"The rhyme," Colt replies.

"What about it?" Joey asks.

"The rhyme wasn't part of Carver's MO in '97. It was created after the murders by local kids looking to scare each other."

Tripp snaps his fingers. "You might be onto something. How often have we run people away from Camp Southwoods, claiming they just wanted to see where *it* happened? Or ghost hunters, or true crime podcasters, all looking to make a name and money for themselves off the tragedy. This could boil down to someone's sick obsession with the legend."

"Or…it could be one of us," Joey says.

Colt feels the room's vibe instantly change. Everyone looks at one another with suspicious glances as their eyes shift from face to face. There's truth in what Joey said: it could be any one of them behind the stratagem. Or none of them. There was no way of knowing.

Flint is the first to break the uncomfortable silence.

"And why would any of us be involved?" Indignation rises in his voice, almost as if Joey had singled him out.

"We found the nightly patrol times in Rumor's bag, scribbled on paper. Someone working in the park, with access to RS1, gave them to him so he could avoid being caught while he vandalized the park."

"Bullshit!" Darryl yells from his cell. "Rumor's innocent."

"And someone unlocked the pit," Colt says.

"I can think of someone." Everyone looks to Flint. "Tripp Thatcher."

"You can't be serious," Tripp says testily.

"Let's lay this out, Tripp. You have access to RS1, to the schedules. And you have keys to unlock the pit. Let's not forget you were also the one who found Norm's body. That puts you in the area of the Panorama Building around the same time I saw someone snooping around up there, and before I found the radio smashed. And who's to say you didn't lay the speed spikes that got Lance killed? Now you show up, after no one has seen you for several hours, saying someone cut down trees, blocking both park exits. For all we know, you could be behind that, too. Or the exits could be fine, and you're just lying to us, trying to keep us here long enough for the roads to become impassable—so you can continue to pick us off one by one."

"Or maybe it was you, Flint," Tripp fires back. "You also know the schedules. And you just happened to be at the Panorama Building when Colt and I showed up, beside a radio that looked like it had gone a round or two with an axe. And where were you after we parted ways?"

"Wasn't me. I can assure you of that," Flint says smugly.

"That's what you say."

"It's not only what I say. I have proof of my whereabouts when everything was going down. Right, Joey?" Flint looks at her for confirmation. She shrinks into herself, being put on the spot to defend him in front of the group.

"Flint was with me when the accident happened on the bridge. That much I can confirm," she says.

"See." Flint smiles like a man after a not-guilty verdict.

But Colt has a few questions of his own for Flint Wheeler.

"Why didn't you return to RS2 like I told you?"

"You said to come here." Flint points to the floor.

"No. I didn't. I said to return to RS2 and tell Dusty what was going on. You disobeyed my direct order."

"Then I must've misheard you. I could have sworn you said head to RS1. We were outside when you told me, and with the wind." He taps his ears as if they're to blame for the miscommunication.

"Oh, that's convenient," Tripp murmurs.

"We can't trust either of them," Amos says.

"I told you I was with Joey!" Flint screams. "Right?" He looks at Joey, but she doesn't say anything this time. "But what about you, Amos? Maybe you're behind all this. You also have a key to the pit."

"Motherfucker, why would I lead myself into my own trap if I was behind it? And yeah, you say you were with Joey. But you had time to set up a speed trap—which I might add is stored in the back of your Interceptor—before meeting her at the antenna shed." Amos looks to Tripp, his eyes accusatory but he doesn't call Tripp outright. "Three people are dead and one is missing. We cannot trust either of them."

"Let's quit the finger-pointing," Joey says. "It's not getting us anywhere but at each other's throats. Let's focus on the facts."

"You believe them?" Amos asks skeptically.

"For the moment, I think we should take Tripp and Flint at their word," Joey says. "At least until evidence presents itself otherwise."

Colt agrees. Accusing each other will only divide them further —*precisely what the killer wants.* Instead, they need to stay focused on the facts, and the evidence, neither of which points directly to either Flint's or Tripp's involvement.

"Three people are dead?" Darryl asks. "Who else?"

Colt's eyes flick to Darryl between the cell bars. The desperation to know what happened to Rumor oozes from him like slime.

"We found Rumor," Colt finally relents.

"*What!*" Darryl's grip on the steel bars tightens, his knuckles whiten. "You found my boy?"

"Yes." Colt's voice is a low, somber tone. "I'm so sorry, Darryl."

"What...what happened?" Darryl asks. Tears wet his eyes as he tries to grapple with the fact that his son isn't coming home.

"Someone hunted him down and murdered him. Dumped his body into a concrete compost heap and covered it so we wouldn't find it." There's no other way to say it, Colt thinks. *Just the facts,* like Joe Friday.

"Oh, God." Darryl turns away, hands over his face. His back heaves as the tears come. He slinks into the corner of the cell, slowly rides the wall to the floor, and sobs next to the cot.

"Why hide Rumor's body in the pit but display Norm's for us to find? That doesn't make sense," Amos says.

Colt had thought the very same thing. But the only one who knew the motivation was the person behind it all. Maybe the same person who gave Rumor the schedules and the photographs of him and Joey in the motel room? *Tripp?* Tripp would have known the patrol schedules because he was always in and out of RS1 and he had a key to the pit. But so did Amos and Wyatt. Flint, and Dusty also knew the schedules. It could be any one of them. Or even two of them.

But why would they do it? And what would they get for murdering Rumor, Lance, Norm, and maybe Porter? What would they get for blackmailing him and Joey? What wasn't Colt seeing? It was right before his eyes, but the clues were frosted over like the windows in RS1.

"We need to get out of this park," Amos says. "Now."

"I second that," Flint adds.

"The only way we're getting out of this park is if we cut ourselves out," Tripp says. "And in this cold, we'd freeze to death before we had an opening big enough to get through."

"We can use the snowmobiles," Amos says. "Go around the deadfall and ride into Jackson on them."

"In this?" Tripp points out the window at the cake batter flakes. "You try cutting through the forest on a snowmobile, you risk hitting something buried under the snow and being either stranded or thrown from the sled."

"What about the Cat?" Amos says. "We can use it."

"The Sno-Cat's too big to go through the forest to get around the blockage," Tripp says with a shake of his head.

"Maybe we can use the Cat or the plow to move the trees," Flint says. "Strap a chain around them and drag them away."

"I already thought that myself. But you can't," Tripp says, again shaking his head back and forth. "Those trees are too big, too long, and too heavy to move with our equipment. You try pulling those logs outta there with a chain, it will snap and come through the windshield. If you're lucky, the glass will be the only thing that hits you."

"Then what do you suggest? Stand here with our thumbs up our asses waiting for this fucker to strike again?" Flint asks.

An unabated silence fills the room, except for Darryl's soft whimpers from the cell and the storm's wrath outside.

"I have one idea." Everyone turns their attention to Tripp. "It's a long shot, but it's an idea."

"What is it?" Colt asks.

"There's another way out of the park—Camp Southwoods Road. It's a direct connection to Route 9."

Again, the room falls into an uncomfortable silence.

"Is Camp Southwoods Road still passable past the Y?" Flint asks, looking to Colt as if the answer lies with him. *It doesn't*, Colt wants to tell him, but keeps his mouth shut.

Camp Southwoods Road splits into a Y about three and a half miles in. The left side led over to Route 9. The right side to the now abandoned camp. Most of Camp Southwoods Road was heavily overgrown, but it was passable enough to get to the camp in an SUV, kept that way in case the rangers needed to get back there. But to the left, past the Y, the road had been shuttered for nearly thirty years. Colt has no idea what Mother Nature reclaimed in that time, nor if the one-way stone bridge spanning Beaver Creek was still there. When Hurricane Phillis hit, the creek rose, and with it all kinds of debris that could have weakened the structure or washed it away entirely.

"There's only one way to find out," Tripp says.

It's a gamble that Colt isn't sure is worth the risk. If Tripp became stuck for whatever reason, he'd be a sitting duck, and there would be no way for him to contact them with the long-range radios down.

"Colt, it's the only way," Tripp says.

"Do it," Colt orders.

"You're going to let him go?" Flint says. "I can't allow that."

"Can you drive the plow, Flint?" Colt barks. Flint's mouth snaps shut like a kid told to shut up. Colt turns to Tripp. "What do you need?"

"Lots of coffee. Maybe a bite of food. Got my stogies, so I'm good there. Gun couldn't hurt. Just in case."

"No way," Flint says, waving his hands in front of himself. "We're not giving *him* a gun. We don't even know if we can trust this guy."

Colt agrees—*can anyone be trusted in this group at the moment?*

"Can't do that, Tripp."

Tripp nods, though there's hurt in his eyes that he's not trust-worthy. He might not like Colt's decision not to give him a weapon, but he will respect it if it proves his innocence to the rest of the group.

"What about Dusty and Wyatt? We can't leave them at the ranger stations alone, cut off from the rest of us," Joey says.

Colt had forgotten about them. With the long-range radios and phones down, there was no way to contact either of them, and with the weather worsening, neither Wyatt nor Dusty could drive from their ranger stations to RS1. The snow was deep enough that even a 4x4 won't be able to traverse the roads.

"She's right," Colt says. "We have to go and get them."

A quiet resolve slowly moves around the room from one person to the other. Everyone's on the same page. Everyone except Flint, who's shaking his head back and forth. Colt takes the majority decision.

Colt looks to Amos and asks, "You up to drive the Cat to pick them up?"

"Yes, sir," Amos says. "But wouldn't it be better if Tripp took the Cat since Camp Southwoods Road might be harder to get through? The Cat can easily get over any debris blocking the way."

"No. The Cat's too slow. If I get through, it will take me hours to get to Jackson in it."

Colt agrees.

"I should go with Tripp," Flint says.

"No. You stay here with Joey," Colt replies. "Ranger Station Two is just across the lake, less than a mile. See if you can reach Dusty on the short-range CB. If you do, tell him to barricade himself inside and only come out when he hears my voice. We'll swing by and pick him up after we get Wyatt at RS3." He believes he sees Flint sneer at him over this order, but it could've been the lighting. "When we get back, all of us will hole up here and wait until Tripp—hopefully—brings back help."

"What about him?" Joey asks. She turns to the holding cell where Darryl sobs in the corner.

"Set him free. But don't let him out of your sight."

CHAPTER 17

Dusk is upon the park when Colt, Amos, and Tripp step outside into the storm. They're geared up for the elements and are ready for the mission ahead; they've ironed out the details in the warmth of RS1. The temperature has fallen significantly since Colt was last outside. He estimates it's somewhere in the low teens from the bite on his skin. The wind is tumultuous, ripping the trees back and forth. They creak and crack under the stress. One snaps in the distance and falls. A thunderous impact upon the forest floor tremors the ground. The snowfall is fast and hard. The accumulation is mounting, and the conditions are deteriorating by the second.

"I'll go to the shed, get the Sno-Cat, and bring it over," Amos hollers.

"Okay!" Colt shouts back, adjusting the pump-action .12-gauge shotgun slung over his shoulder. "Be careful."

Amos gives him the "OK" sign, turns, and heads toward the shed. Across the parking lot, Colt sees the snowdrift is nearly as high as the shed's door handle. The dusk-to-dawn lamp at the top is a floating white orb that shakes in the breeze. RS1 is the same. The drifts are nearly up the windows, and large icicles hang from the rain spouts like stalactites in an ice cave.

"You sure about this?" Colt reiterates, stepping closer to Tripp so he can speak without screaming. "God only knows what Camp Southwoods Road is like after all these years."

"We don't have a choice," Tripp replies. He pulls a cigar from his case and fires it up. Colt feels the heat from the butane torch on his cold skin. "It might be our only way out."

"And you're sure we can't get past the deadfalls on Route 206?"

Tripp removes the cigar from his mouth and nods. "I'm sure. But you're welcome to go and check for yourself if you don't trust me."

Colt searches Tripp's eyes, as if they will reveal the truth in his heart—whether he's lying or not.

"I don't think I need to do that. Right?"

"Are you asking if you can trust me?" Colt remains silent. "I want to assure you that you can, but none of you will until I prove myself trustworthy."

Tripp's right. Colt hates himself for having to suspect his friend. He's heard it said: love is blind. But he also knows the same applies to friendships. Is he blind to who Marion "Tripp" Thatcher is because of their friendship that's spanned fifteen years now? He prays he is making the right decision in letting Tripp go alone to Camp Southwoods Road.

"I'll return and let you know what I find either way," Tripp says.

Colt looks at his watch. It's going on seven.

"If I don't see you by nine, I'm coming to look for you." He believes two hours is enough time for Tripp to investigate Camp Southwoods Road, find out if it is passable, and get back to RS1.

"Fair enough."

Across the parking lot, the shed's steel door begins to rise, and the Sno-Cat's diesel engine fires up with a throaty rumble. Tripp takes a step toward the plow but stops and turns back. From his troubled gaze, Colt knows something is bugging him.

"You know, I saw Maynard down there last summer."

"Down where?"

"Camp Southwoods. I nearly forgot about it, with all that's happened since. I was over by Ice Fisherman's Cove when I saw him come out of the mess hall. Don't know why he was down there or what he was doing, but I'll tell you this, he was as white as a sheet."

"You didn't ask him?"

"Never got the chance. The hurricane was moving in the next day, and it was all hands on deck to get the park locked down before it hit. Then, that distress call came in," Tripp says regretfully. "Anyway, maybe it means something. Maybe it doesn't. Thought I'd share."

With that said, Tripp starts toward the plow, climbs in, fires it up, and heads back out onto Route 206 toward Camp Southwoods Road. The plow's headlights cut through the darkness, catching the snowfall at a 45-degree angle. The blade grinds on the macadam and throws snow into the air like a giant white wave.

What were you up to, Maynard?

The lights on the front of the Sno-Cat come on, drawing Colt's attention back to it and from his thoughts. The Cat's engine revs and inches forward, the four independent tank-like tracks *clinking* and *clacking*. The Cat's lights wash over Flint's SUV parked in front of RS1 as it nears. Another thought enters Colt's mind.

What *was* Flint doing between when he left Dedication Hill and before showing up at the antenna shed? There was a void where Flint was unaccounted for. And, like Amos brought up earlier, Flint would've had a strip of spikes in the back of his SUV.

Amos stops the Cat in front of him. Colt pulls himself up and flings open the door. Inside he can feel the heat blasting from the vents; it's cool, but there's a touch of warmth to the air that his body instantly craves like water when dehydrated.

"Give me a minute. I want to check something out."

He slams the door, drops into the knee-deep snow, and lumbers to Flint's SUV. In the rear of all Interceptors is a small partition under the storage area for day-to-day equipment like road flares, closure tape, and other essentials that a ranger would need for daily operations. The speed spikes were also kept there. He pops the hatchback and lifts the panel in the floor. The everyday necessities are in the compartment.

Except for the set of spikes.

Tiny electric impulses shudder through his body.

Could Flint have…

He doesn't want his mind to form the rest of this thought, but it's already in his brain before he can prevent it.

…set the trap?

Flint would've had the time to set the spikes before moving on to RS1 at the antenna shed, giving him an alibi with both Darryl and Joey.

A movement inside RS1. Colt looks up to find Flint standing by the window, looking out into the night, searching through the snow and dark. He quickly cups his hand over the SUV's interior light, so Flint can't see what he's up to.

A moment later, Flint moves away from the window, and Colt breathes a sigh of relief. He replaces everything in the SUV. Though the speed spikes were missing, that doesn't mean Flint set the trap. *Someone else could've gotten to them, setting Flint up.*

Colt eases the hatch shut. He is not entirely sure of Flint's involvement. Or of his innocence. He returns to the Cat. The smell of diesel fuel is thick as he pulls himself up, unslings the shotgun, and climbs inside. Amos watches him as he drops into the seat. For a moment, he thinks Amos might question why he was looking through the SUV, but he doesn't, like he already knows.

"Ready?" Amos asks instead.

"Yes," Colt says, buckling himself into the passenger seat of the Sno-Cat.

Amos steers the Cat out onto Route 206. The Sno-Cat's massive tracks cause the cab to vibrate and hum like a rickety carnival ride. The four lights across the top of the cab's exterior and the two mounted on the sides easily cut through the darkness. To Colt, it feels like he's in a submersible, searching the ocean's depths as sediment, driven by the current, floats past the window. *Might as well be at the bottom of the ocean. Stranded without a way to reach the surface.*

The Cat is used to plow and till the northwestern side of the park, where snowmobilers go to slice up the powder in the hills around Snyder Point. Because of its manipulatable winged blade, which is currently in the up position, it's the perfect vehicle to get into tight spaces to clear snow or go over terrain unsuitable for a regular plow. The only problem is that it has a max speed of around twenty miles an hour. That's why Tripp didn't want to take it to get the sheriff in Jackson—it would've taken him hours to get there.

Hours we might not have.

"How's the neck?" Colt asks, looking at Amos as he operates the Cat with such efficiency that he makes it look easy. A joystick by Amos's right hand works both the tiller and the plow. Switches light up the dashboard in green. Two digital screens, one a GPS, the other with engine information, are mounted above Amos's head; Colt sees they are going about ten miles an hour.

"Hurts," Amos says. "But I'll manage."

Colt shifts in his seat. He feels the seat belt tug at his neck, rubs into the soft flesh. The thought of Amos in the burning pickup, the seat belt his death binding, works its way across his psyche. He hooks his thumb around the belt and holds it away from his neck.

"Can I ask you something, Amos?"

"I suppose," Amos hesitantly replies with a suspicious side glance.

"How long was Tripp with you at the Panorama Building?"

"Until the snow started to fall. Maybe till around ten thirty this morning."

"He left to go plow?"

"That's what Tripp told us."

What Tripp told him, too.

"And how long were you and Lance there after Tripp left?"

Amos ponders the question a moment before answering.

"I'd say we were there till around eleven or eleven fifteen. I wasn't really keeping track of time."

"Did you see anyone up there around that time—a straggling park guest, maybe?"

"Not that I remember. We were busy cutting that tree apart, trying to beat the snow."

"What about the Panorama Building. Did either you or Lance go in around that time?"

Amos glances at Colt warily.

"Why would we go in the Panorama Building? It's winter. There's nothing in there."

"Except for the radio."

They continue driving. The silence is interrupted by the clinking and clanking of the tracks along with the rumble of the heavy engine.

"What are you getting at, Colt?"

Colt turns to face him.

"Flint claims he saw someone sneaking around the Panorama Building around eleven thirty. When I got there, I was with Tripp, and we found Flint by the radio. It was smashed to pieces. Now, either Flint is telling the truth—and he saw someone—or he's full of shit."

Colt looks back into the night, lost in his dark thoughts. He drifts back to reality when he feels Amos's eyes on him.

"What?" Colt asks, shifting his gaze to Amos. Half his face is hidden in the shadows, except for one dark eye, directed at him with an intent gaze that causes a flutter of unease to pass through his body.

"I know what you're trying to do," Amos says. He blinks his eyes back to the snowy road. "You're trying to figure out who's doing this. Maybe even starting to suspect me. Because I was also up at the Panorama Building around that time." Colt stiffens, and his right hand slips to his side. The pistol's butt against his palm is a small comfort. "But you're looking at the wrong person. I promise you that. Remember, I was in that pickup when we crashed."

Colt adjusts himself in the seat. The belt again cuts into his neck. He rips it away this time, wants to shed the belt off altogether, but knows that's a bad idea in this weather. Anything could go wrong as they work through the snow that could cause the Cat to topple.

"Is that supposed to clear my conscience about you, Amos?"

Amos looks back at the road, half his face hidden in the shadows again, but he doesn't say anything. His silence is enough.

CHAPTER 18

From the window, Joey watches the light from the Sno-Cat fade away. Darkness returns to rule. She feels like she's been left behind on some remote frozen island while the others sail off to bring back help. She steps away from the window, feeling bleak that any hope of rescue isn't coming. Flint sits on the corner of a nearby desk, his arms across his chest.

"I can't help but think I'm sitting here because of my bad knee," Flint fumes. "First, I offer to go to Camp Southwoods Road to see if there's a way through. Then I offered to go get Wyatt and Dusty, but Colt ordered me to stay with you and try to reach Dusty. They don't want a gimp slowing them down, is what this amounts to."

Joey passes him to the cell, opens the door to let Darryl out, ignoring Flint's whining.

"Are you okay?" she asks, unable to imagine Darryl's turmoil after learning of Rumor's murder. It can't be easy losing a child, Joey imagines, something she never wants to experience first-hand. Darryl's bloodshot eyes are cast downward, laden with sadness, lost in some far-off place. He steps out of the cell and she escorts him to a chair by the heater, sits him down, and drapes a blanket over his shoulders, taken from the storage closet. "Can I get you anything?"

Darryl doesn't respond, doesn't even move. He's in shock. She feels for the old bastard—and yes, Darryl Shoff is a bastard, but her heart aches for him regardless.

She returns to her desk and falls into the chair. Exhaustion cramps every muscle and stiffens every joint. She thinks of getting some rest in the bunkroom. But rest is the last thing she'll be able to do. Her brain is abuzz with worry for Colt and how they will get out of the park.

"Do you *really* think it was a good idea for Colt to send Tripp to Camp Southwoods Road alone?" Flint asks.

She studies him closely, like a woman at a bar deciding whether to talk to the stranger who bought her a drink. She wonders if she can trust him. What was Flint doing between leaving the Panorama Building and when he showed up at the antenna shed? He quickly made it known that he believes Tripp is behind everything.

"Let me answer your question with my own," Joey replies. "Do you *really* think Tripp is responsible for what's happening?"

"I know what I saw, Joey."

"But what did you really see? Do you know for a fact that it was Tripp who broke into the Panorama Building and destroyed the radio?"

Flint shifts uncomfortably on the desk's corner, his eyes narrow and dark like a man caught in a lie.

"Look, Tripp was the only one up there around that time," Flint says irritated. His tone is of a man who wants to prove his point. That everyone has their blinders on about Tripp. "Why couldn't it have been him?"

"I'm not saying it couldn't. All I'm saying is that it could have been…anyone."

"Who? Douglas Lee Carver?" Flint snorts out a laugh. "Please."

"No. I don't think you saw Douglas Lee Carver up there. C'mon."

"But you think sending Tripp was the right choice?"

"Can you drive the plow?" He looks to the floor and moves a pebble of melting ice around with his foot that had blown in when the door was open. "I didn't think so. If there's a way out using Camp Southwoods Road, Tripp will have to plow it open, so the rest of us can use the SUVs to get through. No matter what you think of Tripp or what you believe he did, we need him."

"And what if Colt's wrong about him? Just like Maynard was wrong making the call to go up to the Rocks and rescue someone who wasn't even there."

Joey's jaw twitches at Maynard's name, at the memory of a day that had gone wrong.

"Maynard did what he thought was right with the information he knew then. Just like Colt's doing now."

"He should've waited, Joey. You know that. Colt knows that. I know that. Had Maynard held off until the road was open, and a real rescue team could get in here, had he not been distracted, he'd still be alive."

Distracted. That was precisely how she viewed Maynard that day, too. He was not focused on the severity of their situation, nor on the safety of himself or Colt when he made the call to try to rescue the climber. It was like he was on another planet, his focus elsewhere entirely. What was going on with him?

"We're back in the same situation, just a different storm. If we all hang tight, we can make it out alive. But splitting us up like this…" Flint shakes his head.

"What choice does Colt have? We can't just leave Wyatt and Dusty out there. They have limited food and water. And if the power goes out, which in these winds it may, they'd be stuck at the ranger stations without heat. They'd freeze to death, Flint!"

"If I was in charge, no one would've left my sight—not to go get Wyatt or Dusty."

"Well, you're not in charge. Colt is. We do what he says."

Joey's eyes drift past Flint to Darryl, who rises from the chair and saunters toward the window, the blanket still around his shoulders like a cape. What's he doing?

"You know I should've gotten Maynard's position after his death."

Her attention jerks back to Flint.

"But you didn't."

"But I should have. I was the next in line. The most senior officer, after Maynard."

"Do you guys hear that?" Darryl asks, now by the window.

"Alas, they gave it to Maynard's golden boy instead," Flint continues, his voice full of anger and irritation. His face and neck are bright red, and his hands are cannonballs of dissatisfaction. "I should be leading this team right now."

"I hear…music." Darryl again.

"You're out of line, Flint."

"Bullshit, I am. I've been overlooked by the park since my knee started acting up a few years ago. I do my job, Joey, to the best of my ability."

"No one says you don't."

"Then why wasn't I considered for the head ranger position?"

She doesn't have a solution for him. Such is life, where nothing is fair.

"No one has a good answer when I state the obvious. But I *do* know why. The state chose a newer model that isn't broken down. And one that *was* constantly in the boss's ear."

"It's coming from outside," Darryl says dreamily.

"Look, Flint, whatever your beef is, take it up with the head of the DCNR. It's not Colt's fault. And now isn't the time."

"No. You're right. It's not Colt's fault. It's Maynard's."

"What's that supposed to mean?" Joey's face pulls tight, her eyebrows nearly touch with resentment.

"Maynard was always taken with Colt. I'm sure he suggested to the higher-ups that Colt would be a good replacement to run the team when the time came."

"Maynard wouldn't do that. He was an honorable man and would've respected the seniority rule."

"Then why am I not in charge?"

"I don't know. That's above my pay grade. But I won't sit here and listen to you bad-mouth a dead—"

"*Guys!*" Darryl shouts. "I hear music." He faces their blank stares. "I think it's coming from the band shell."

Joey's eyes flip to Flint. His puzzlement mirrors her own. Together, they join Darryl next to the window.

"You hear it. And look. See it?" Darryl taps the glass with his index finger.

Through the snow haze, a dome of lights pulses in the distance, and heavy metal music thumps over the wind and seeps through the glass.

What the hell is going on now?

CHAPTER 19

Tripp jumps down from the plow and traverses through the snow to the yellow gate across Camp Southwoods Road. He plucks his keyring from the loop of his pants and fans them out. He finds the one that opens the padlock.

He takes the lock in his hand. The metal is so cold he feels it through his gloves. The lock might be frozen shut from nonuse and the extreme frigid temperatures. He knows the last time the gate was open was the day before Maynard's death. Tripp was at Ice Fisherman's Cove to clear poison ivy off the trail when he spotted Maynard across the inlet when he saw him step out of the mess hall at Camp Southwoods.

What was Maynard doing down there that day? Tripp hadn't heard anything about trespassers in the area, which usually went out over the radio when someone was seen traipsing around where they don't belong. There had to be another reason.

He tilts the lock so the plow's lights catch the keyhole, and his concern comes to fruition when he finds the keyhole frozen over, impenetrable past the ice buildup.

But Tripp came with a contingency plan just in case.

At the plow, he moves a toolbox and a crowbar out of the way from the small compartment behind the driver's seat and drags out a tow chain. After fastening one end of the chain to the plow, he takes the other end to the gate, where he wraps it twice around the gate's yellow steel bars, hooks it to itself, and tugs the chain. It will hold.

He climbs back into the cab, shifts the plow into reverse, and feathers the gas. The plow's diesel engine growls; black smoke shoots from the exhaust pipes. He backs up until the chain is taut. Tripp applies pressure to the throttle, and the plow inches slowly backward. The gate protests, the padlock keeping it shut, but he can see the yellow bars bowing. *Come on, you stone-cold son of a bitch!* Tapping the throttle, the plow jumps back, and the lock shatters as if made of plastic. Even over the blowing wind, Tripp believes he can hear the grind and squeal of the cold metal, revealing the mouth of Camp Southwoods Road as the gate is wrenched open.

He jumps out, gathers the chain, and returns to the warm cab.

The twisted road lies before him. *Goddamn, this place.* He knows locals believe the camp is haunted. Yet it's not the ghosts of the dead that haunt the area, but the atrocities that happened there—a curse that has seeped beyond the camp and contaminated the rest of the park. It's overgrown with brush. Tree branches hang low from the weight of the snow and will rake the plow's windshield and roof like fingernails across a chalkboard as the plow crawls along. The plow's lights are strong enough for Tripp to see the old welcome center atop the knoll through the bare trees. Shadows of branches and brush dance over the welcome center's fieldstone sides evocatively. But it will get worse the deeper Tripp goes past the Y.

His memory of Maynard at the mess hall is almost as unpleasant as Aleja's passing. *Something was wrong that day.* He remembers calling out to Maynard from across the inlet, and when Maynard turned to him, the look on his face was like he saw a ghost. The thought of that look now gives Tripp goose bumps.

Everything okay? Tripp had shouted across the inlet. Maynard's only response was a solemn nod, before returning to the Interceptor and driving off. What did he see inside the mess hall that spooked him so? Tripp wishes he would've had the opportunity to ask, but he didn't see Maynard for the rest of the day. He meant to ask the next morning, but Phillis was on their doorstep, and there was no time to dawdle as they raced against the clock to secure the park.

Whatever Maynard had seen or found down there, he took it to his grave.

With this troublesome thought, Tripp steps on the gas and crosses the threshold into the blood-spelled land...

While Amos brings the Sno-Cat to a stop in front of RS3, an alarm builds in Colt's chest like a steam cooker. The Cat's lights illuminate the front of the building. The light reflects off the glass windows and icicles hanging along the trim. But RS3 is dark. It was not just dark but void of any semblance of life, like what death's shadow didn't scare away from this land; it ate up, filling its gluttony on goodness and hope.

"Why are all the lights out?"

"I was about to ask you the same thing," Colt replies. He spots no movements in the shadows, just out of the light's reach. But someone could be out there. Waiting. Watching.

"Could the storm have taken the power lines down?"

"Doubtful. The entire park is on the same grid. Unless it went out after we left RS1."

"That's bullshit, and you know it," Amos says.

"Yeah. I know it." Colt clicks the safety off the shotgun.

"You can't go in there by yourself."

"I don't want anything to happen to the Sno-Cat. It's your job to protect it. If we need to get out of here, we'll need this rig to make that happen. That's why I'm leaving this with you." He hands Amos the shotgun.

Amos takes the weapon with admiration—the power it possesses in his hands. But Amos doesn't know that Colt left the shotgun empty to test whether he can trust him.

Colt opens the door. The wind rushes into the cab. Air blows up the back of his jacket and touches his neck. His muscles clench from the cold's icy contact.

"Keep your eyes open," Colt hollers. He glances at the shotgun again.

"I will," Amos says, tightening his grip on the weapon, driving home the point that Colt would have to pry it from his dead hands before he gave it back.

Colt slams the door, jumps off the tracks into the snow, and shambles to the porch steps, now a white snow ramp. He takes the stairs slowly, finding each one with his boot before taking the next until he's on the porch. He scans the area around RS3, rechecks the shadows. Dread works through him that someone is creeping around out there. But he sees no one is lurking about. He's alone.

Am I?

He swallows the knot in his throat, opens the door to RS3, and steps inside, absorbed by the darkness. An unsettling energy charges the building, a residue of emotion and anger, like walking into a room after two people have argued. He aims the flashlight toward the door, finds the light switch beside it, and flips it on.

Nothing happens.

He tries again.

Still, RS3 remains pitch black. It's not cold inside the ranger station, and Colt can hear a low hum from the running furnace. The power is still on, so what was wrong with the lights?

"Wyatt?"

The only response is silence, besides the screeching wind at his back pushing against the station. The wooden walls rasp around him. A flickering light toward the back of the room draws his attention. The office door is cracked, and light dances on the walls and spills out onto the floor.

He starts toward the office when something crunches under his feet. Colt trains the beam at the floor, the light catching something reflective, tiny specks of white everywhere. It takes him a moment to realize he's looking at broken shards of fluorescent light bulbs.

He aims the flashlight's beam at the ceiling. The bulbs are broken—the jaggy tubes still in their housings.

"Who's out there..." a voice calls from the office.

Colt's head snaps back to the office door; the light flickers on the walls and the floor.

"Who's out there..." the voice calls again.

Colt knows that voice. *Wyatt.* But it sounds different, like he's speaking through a microphone. It takes all his willpower to stop the chatter of his teeth, keep his feet steady, and steel himself against his panic and not run away. He removes the .357 and cocks the revolver. The heft of the gun was reassuring in his hand.

"Colt?" The distorted voice calls through the palpable silence.

He opens the door with the gun's barrel to find the office empty except for the desk facing the wall. A computer, a radio, and a landline phone are on top. None of them are in working order. But what is working, and causing the flickering of a , is the trail camera monitor Wyatt had set up to watch the pit, per Colt's orders.

But no Wyatt.

Where is he?

On the monitor, the screen is split into four camera angles. Wyatt had set up two cameras on the pit and another toward the service road to RS3. All three are in night vision mode, the video in black-and-white and clear enough to see the snow falling and the wind whipping the trees around. There's no one on the trail or near the pit.

"Colt, is that you?"

His attention shifts to the fourth screen at the bottom right side of the monitor, where a tiny, blinking word reads: Playback. Then, he understands the ghostly voice he initially heard was Wyatt, calling out on the monitor. His hopefulness to find Wyatt alive begins to ricochet inside like a bullet, shredding him.

On the screen, Wyatt steps onto the porch of RS3. He must have thought to place the last camera high in the corner of the porch, so he could watch the front door, a visual eye in case someone snuck up on him. Yet Colt knows something has gone awry; otherwise, Wyatt would be here, and the video he is now watching wouldn't be in playback mode.

No. Someone had drawn Wyatt out of RS3.

And someone wants you to see what happened to him…

On the monitor, Wyatt moves to the railing. He's holding his hand up in front of his eyes, blocking out a light shining in his face from the parking lot. *Someone was here!* Wyatt steps out of the light to the post beside the stairs, the same ones Colt had just taken moments ago.

"Colt? Is that you?" Wyatt calls out on the screen; confusion taints his voice.

Wyatt thought I had returned. And someone used that to lure him outside.

Disquiet begins to work its way over Colt. His cold flesh pulls so tight to his bones it hurts.

Back on the screen, a figure in dark pants and a hooded parka lurches into the frame behind Wyatt, who's oblivious to it stalking toward him. Colt wants to yell, *Look out! Behind you!* But that would be futile. There's nothing he can do to prevent what's about to happen. As the figure inches closer to Wyatt, they raise an object back over their shoulder, like a batter getting ready to hit the game-winning home run. It takes a moment for Colt to realize what it is.

An ice axe—the kind that mountain climbers use when they scale frozen cliffs. Colt's muscles tighten with anticipation as the figure nears Wyatt on the screen. He wants to close his eyes. Look away. *I can't watch this.* But he has to…

On the screen, Wyatt turns around as if he's felt the presence of his attacker nearing him. The figure swings out with the ice axe and connects to the side of Wyatt's skull. Wyatt's head snaps violently to the right, and a dull *thud* breaks the silence of the dark room as the ice axe embeds into the post by the stairs. Colt jumps at the sound. Feels a slight phantom pain on the side of his head, where Wyatt was struck. Wyatt falls back into the railing, grips it with his right hand while his left comes up to his temple as if trying to keep his brain from spilling out. Even in the black-and-white footage, Colt sees the fear and confusion on Wyatt's face. But there's nothing he can do. *I'm helpless. Fucking helpless.* Then, Wyatt's legs unbuckle like a marionette with its strings cut, and he crumbles to the porch floor.

Anger wells through Colt. He clenches the flashlight so tight he fears it might shatter in his hand. He cannot tell if Wyatt is dead or has just lost consciousness. He lies motionless in the snow. Either was a possibility after a strike like that. The face of Wyatt's attacker is still a mystery to him since their back is to the camera. Yet, Colt feels whoever is under that hood gets some kind of perverse pleasure from the harm they're causing.

Then, the figure slowly begins to turn to face the camera.

And Colt nearly jumps out of his skin at the grinning skeleton face staring back at him.

It was a skeleton. I'm telling you, it was there. Standing on the bridge. Thriving in the chaos it created. Amos's shivery words slice through Colt's mind, like the voice of some long-dead soul trying to get his attention.

Colt feels a scream work its way up from his diaphragm as those empty black sockets—*this can't be real*—stare into him. The scream wants to escape his lips but catches in the back of his throat and forms a large, hard lump. He understands how Amos felt when he first saw it on the bridge—*utterly terrified.*

The grinning skeleton begins to walk toward the camera, its hollow eyeless sockets trained on the lens as it nears. *It's looking at me. It knows I'm here. Knows I'm watching. Because it set all of this up for me to find.*

Yet as the figure grows closer to the screen, Colt realizes what he's seeing isn't some otherworldly creature that's escaped the grave…

But a person under a mask.

The masked person rears back with the ice axe and brings it forward into the camera.

The screen goes static.

The speed trap. He sees Amos struggling to get free from the seat belt. Lance bent over the steering wheel, blood gushing from his head, unconscious. The fire. The explosion. Was it a diversion to get to Wyatt?

Colt doesn't know. But it would make sense if it was. Whoever's doing this is as methodical as they are deadly.

He turns away from the monitors on the desk—ready to run back to the Sno-Cat and tell Amos to floor it and get them the hell out of here—but the flashlight's beam catches the wall behind him as he does, freezing him in place. His focus was on the monitor when he entered the room. He had not seen what was written on the wall behind him in what Colt assumes is Wyatt's blood.

> *Little Ranger Burke running,*
> *Douggie Carver's gone a-hunting,*
> *Gonna catch that ranger,*
> *Gonna cleave that ranger,*
> *Little Ranger Burke done running.*

Below the message, there's a bloody arrow pointing at the door.

The flashlight begins to tremble in Colt's hand as he turns toward the door. Blood runs down the side, pooling on the floor. He didn't see it when he entered the room a moment ago, too preoccupied with the monitor to see what had been left for him.

Colt slowly pushes the door closed.

Oh, Christ!

A man's limp body hangs from the door.

Like Norm, the face is gone, stolen by violent ice axe blows. There is nothing left but a bloody, bulbous pulp that looks like a lump of meat, wearing a messy, wet topee.

The beam catches the name tag on the victim's chest.

Ranger Burke, it reads.

CHAPTER 20

Tripp made it past the Y, though not without difficulty. Camp Southwoods Road, as they thought, was in rough condition with fallen trees and overgrowth. Luckily, most of what lay across the road was long dead, and Tripp could push most of it out of the way with the plow or drive over it. That was until the narrow, single-lane stone bridge materialized out of the darkness like a specter taking shape in the night. And as Tripp neared the bridge, trepidation crept up his spine like a spider.

Bringing the plow to a stop, Tripp hops out. He moves through the deep snow toward the bridge with his arms held out to his sides for stability, like a penguin walking across the icy tundra. The cold works its way into his body, and he feels it searching around inside like an organism looking for the off switch. *Put it out of your mind. Think of someplace warm.* Aleja flashes into his mind. Them sitting together, hand in hand, at her father's beach house in Miami. Tripp smoking one of Ernesto's pre-embargo Cuban cigars and sipping a Mojito, while Aleja lets the warm ocean breeze wash over her as if she's cleansing herself from the cold, wet winters of Pennsylvania. The pleasant warmness of the memory is short-lived when he arrives at the bridge and looks over the black expanse of Beaver Creek, hears the rush of the cold water below.

The bridge…is gone.

Tripp figures that it must have been swept away during the hurricane by the raging, chocolate-colored creek water, which carried full-size trees and other debris with it.

Whoever was lurking around the park knew this, too.

Panic swells through him like the creek had last summer, pulling with it a current of conflicting emotions. Should he stay and help the others find a way out of the park, or should he cross the cold water and try to make it to Route 9 on foot? *And you'd freeze to death in minutes if you did that.* A gust of wind seems to confirm his thought. His hope was that this was their way out. Their salvation. But it's another dead end. They're trapped inside the park.

So much land but nowhere to hide.

Disappointed, Tripp turns and heads back to the plow. He'll return to RS1 and inform everyone about his discovery. There's no passable route out of the park now, not with the plow, SUVs, or the Sno-Cat. That left the snowmobiles. But taking them through this kind of storm was dangerous; they would have to try to traverse through the dense woods. And God only knew what was under the snow resulting in a snag that could break the tracks, leave the rider stuck, or eject the driver, causing injury or death.

This thought doesn't sit well with Tripp, and the blood in his veins turns as cold as the creek water. But it's quickly overtaken with anger, anger that warms him slightly. He doesn't know who's doing this or why, but when he finds them…

"I'm going to put my cigar out in their fucking eye," he says as he pulls himself onto the plow and opens the door.

A glint of light catches his eyes just as something sharp swings at his face. Tripp pulls back, almost loses his grip on the door. The object comes around, misses him by mere inches, and *clinks* off the cab's metal frame.

Tripp, wide-eyed with terror, looks back to see a skeleton

slowly rising up from the passenger side footwell as if emerging from its grave. In its right hand is an ice axe, its blade catching the dashboard lights, turning it into a multitude of colors that remind him of Christmas lights.

As the figure rises, he realizes it's not a skeleton—not that he ever really thought it was—but someone under a mask. The mask is so lifelike it's downright disturbing. Horrifying.

How did it find him?

Before he can fully form this thought, the skeleton springs forward and tackles him around the waist. Together they fall from the cab and into a mound of snow pushed aside from the plow's blade. They plunge into the mound and sink into its cold, puffy gloom. Snow shoots up Tripp's nose and down his mouth; he breathes it in and feels ice daggers in his chest, setting his lungs ablaze with unbearable freezing pain.

He thrusts his hands down into the cold darkness below, feels the ground underneath, and pushes himself backward with all his might. He propels himself out of the snow mound and falls on the ground.

Rolling over onto his hands and knees, snow clings to his face, eyebrows, and long gray mustache in icy clumps. His skin burns so severely from the cold that his teeth chatter, and his muscles knot. He heaves, his back arching like a pissed-off cat, and a golf ball-size ice chunk erupts from his mouth. Tripp gulps frozen air and then coughs again, expelling more snow and water from his lungs. Saliva drips from his lips in long, syrupy strands.

Knowing time isn't on his side, knowing the skeleton is already working itself free of the snow mound, Tripp pushes himself to his feet. He runs his hand over his nose back and forth, rubbing the snow out of his nostrils. He darts toward the plow, he staggers from side to side like a drunk walking down a crooked sidewalk; his legs are so numb he can hardly move them, his toes cramping, useless.

Behind him, he hears the snow shift.

Looking over his shoulder, he sees the skeleton has worked

itself out from the mound and is quickly in pursuit, the ice axe ready. He cannot take on whoever is after him mano a mano. *He'll kill me for sure.* His best chance of survival is to jump in the plow, lock the door, and get out of there.

Pumping his frozen legs as hard as he can through the exhaustion, using the will to survive, he continues toward the plow.

Tripp takes hold of the plow's open door and begins to pull himself into the cab when a hand clamps down on the hood of his jacket. Fear sinks into him that the axe is about to penetrate his body. For a split second, he wonders what it will feel like to have his flesh torn open by that sharp blade. *You can't let that happen!* He has to defend himself before the axe finds a home in his flesh.

Tripp then sees the crowbar he used earlier in the day when helping Amos cut through the tree at the Panorama Building on the floor of the plow.

He grabs it.

Spinning on his heels, he brings the crowbar around simultaneously and swings it at the skeleton's outstretched arm, fist clasped on to his hood. The heavy steel crowbar connects to the inside of his attacker's forearm. A muffled grunt seeps from under the mask, and the skeleton instantly releases the hood and staggers back, cradling the arm.

But the blow is only a momentary inconvenience. The skeleton quickly recovers and charges at Tripp, swinging the ice axe in an X pattern.

Tripp backpedals as the skeleton nears, the axe swings back and forth, back and forth, intent on delivering the killing strike. He continues to backpedal. Unaware of his surroundings, Tripp bumps into the plow's blade. He can go no further. Complete and utter hopelessness skips through him. *This is it.*

The blade of the ice axe is already coming down.

Then, just before the axe embeds itself into his face, Tripp sees a window.

He lunges to his right. The ice axe strikes the side of the plow.

The axe bounces off and into one of the headlights. A shower of sparks explodes and the light goes dim.

Knowing he won't get another attempt to save himself, Tripp comes up with the crowbar and swings it as hard as possible. The round, blunt end of the crowbar sinks into the meat of the masked individual's inner right thigh. A painful scream erupts from under the mask. The skeleton grabs at its leg and drops to one knee in the snow. *Hope that hurt, you son of a bitch!*

Tripp shoots to his feet, adrenalin pushes away the fear and the cold, and raises the crowbar over his head, aiming to bring it down into the skeleton's skull. This time, he'll be the one to deliver the killing strike. But just as Tripp is about to bring the crowbar forward with everything he's got to bash this sick motherfucker's skull in, the skeleton springs up. It rears back with its free hand and swings, catching Tripp across the jaw with a backhanded strike. The blow knocks one of his molars loose from his jawbone, and his brain rattles around his skull like a ball in a cup.

And for a moment, the lights go out.

When he comes to, Tripp finds himself lying on his stomach; the plow's lights bathe him in a shower of yellow-tinted snowflakes. He shakes the cobwebs away, runs his tongue across his teeth in the back of his mouth, and feels the molar rolling around on his tongue. The taste of copper fills his mouth and mixes with his saliva. He spits a bloody wad into the snow and finds the molar in the center of the steaming red puddle.

You can't stay down. You have to…

The rev of the plow's engine and the smell of thick diesel smoke kicking from the stacks snaps Tripp out of his disorientation. A sickening feeling begins to churn through his body.

Pushing himself to stand, visible and helpless, he sees the skeleton sitting in the plow's driver's seat. The skeletal face is cast downward. That menacing sneer seems to grow more pronounced, and the black eyeless sockets are rife with hatred, eager to see him a blood stain in the snow.

Street pizza.

Rrrrrooooam! The engine growls, and the plow heaves forward like a giant metal beast about to pounce. The blade digs into the ground, folding up small piles of earth and snow.

The plow's blade will cut through him as easily as soft cheese.

Run, you dummy!

Tripp bolts in the only direction he can—toward the bridge. Behind him, he hears the engine whine and the stutter of the air brakes releasing.

The plow begins its chase.

But where does he go? The bridge is out. The only thing between him and the other side is ice-cold water. He knows he cannot jump the gorge over Beaver Creek. It's too far—a good twenty feet from side to side—and he'll go down into the frigid water if he tries, probably freeze to death if he doesn't die in the fall.

Tripp looks over his shoulder, though he knows he shouldn't because it'll just slow him down, maybe even cause him to trip like one of those dames in a horror movie. *They don't call me Tripp for nothing, do they?* But he can't help himself. He needs to know if he's about to meet his maker.

He finds the plow is only inches away, shooting a wave of snow high into the air. It's so close he can feel the heat from the engine on his back, like a bull's hot snorts while it runs down a matador. Tripp pumps his numb legs, trying to put as much distance between himself and the ever-gaining plow on his ass.

The gorge is only five feet away, maybe eight.

You can make it!

Again, he looks back at the plow, just in time to see the blade hit something hard in the earth, buried under the snow. A loud metallic grinding sound cuts through the air. The impact lifts the front right tire off the ground. The plow slams back down, bounces, kicks up snow. The impact throws the skeleton around in the seat, causing it to lose control of the plow. The vehicle swerves first to the right and then back to the left. He hears the skeleton leave off the gas, so it can regain control of the vehicle and return it to the target. He hopes the mistake will give him enough time to put some distance between himself and the plow.

But when Tripp looks back, he finds he can go no further. He skids to a stop just before going over the edge and into the creek, his arms pinwheeling to keep himself from dropping over the side. Snow and rocks sprinkle into the water below.

The engine's roar is so loud it hurts his ears, and the rumbling of the blade turning up the earth and snow as it inches closer vibrates in his chest. When he turns, he's blinded by the plow's powerful lights barreling down on him. Behind them, he can see the grinning teeth and those lifeless black sockets locked on him in a death stare.

This is it, Tripp thinks and closes his eyes.

CHAPTER 21

On the porch of RS3, Colt's entire body tingles like it had when he got to the top of the Rocks and found Maynard's flashlight on the ground, but Maynard was nowhere in sight. Something's...wrong. He turns his attention to the Sno-Cat, expecting to find Amos inside, but the cab is empty. *Where in the hell did...*

Footsteps crunch in the snow behind him. Someone is coming up on him like they had come up on Wyatt in the video. Every fiber of his being stands on end like an electrical current passing through his body, and he realizes the tingling he felt was the presence of another.

Colt spins to find himself face-to-face with the skeleton, the ice axe back over its right shoulder, ready to strike, just as it had Wyatt. Had it tried to foretell his death by showing him Wyatt's? He grips the .357 and brings the revolver up, thumbing the hammer back. The cylinder's click seems somehow louder than the wind as it rotates.

The rotation of the gun's cylinder causes the skeleton to shift its attention to the weapon. The figure swings the ice axe as Colt applies pressure to the trigger. The axe blade hits the gun barrel, forcing it to the porch floor. It goes off. A crack of gunfire echoes through the woods with a deafening report. The bullet blasts through the wooden porch floor, blows a plume of snow and wooden splinters into the skeleton's face. The disorientation from the blowback causes the skeleton to stagger and step back, its hands come to the mask's eyeholes to shield itself. This momentary instinctive reflex allows Colt to raise the revolver and level it on his attacker again.

Got you!

But the ice axe comes around, as swift and smooth as a tennis star rebounding a ball before Colt can pull the trigger. The blade catches him across the upper right arm. Hot pain sears as the flesh is sliced apart. He screams through his teeth. Warm, thick blood rolls down his arm. Lightheadedness overwhelms him.

That is until he hears the crunch of snow—the sound of footsteps.

Colt looks up to see the skeleton charge him, the axe ready to taste more of his blood. But there isn't enough time for him to aim the gun and take the skeleton out. The axe starts to come forward, the blade whistles through the air.

As a last line of defense, more of a reflex, Colt raises his hands over his face to protect himself, the gun still in his right hand. He closes his eyes as tight as he can. He doesn't want to see his end coming. He wonders if death will be instantaneous, or if he'll feel everything when the axe cuts through his hands and buries itself into his face.

Please let it be quick…

Then there is a loud *clack*. He's driven back into the wall of RS3 with enough force that the back of his head bounces off the wood. A single firework explodes behind his eyelids.

When he opens his eyes, he sees the pick side of the ice axe has lodged itself through the trigger guard of the gun, saving his life. *What are the fucking odds?* His focus shifts to the mask, or rather the black, rageful eyes hidden in the dark sockets. There *is* a human under that mask. A human intent on killing him—killing all of them—but a human nonetheless, who pushes with all their might to slip the axe's pick into Colt's body.

You have to hold him off.

He knows his strength to fend off his attacker won't last long, especially with the skeleton having the advantage of position and leverage. Colt slips his free hand into his pants pocket to retrieve his pocketknife.

But he doesn't feel the knife. *It should be there!*

The skeleton thrusts forward, the pick comes within inches of Colt's throat, threatening to give him a tracheotomy. But Colt holds it off, barely. His arms burn, shake with fatigue, and he can feel blood ooze from the gash, the tendrils rolling down his back. Still, Colt knows another powerful thrust like the last one will undoubtedly drive the pick through his throat and kill him.

He runs his hand around the inside of the pocket again, this time finding the pocketknife's handle. He rips the knife from the pocket and hits the button on the side. The blade springs free of the handle, and Colt trusts the blade upward, as hard as possible, catching his attacker's forearm.

He doesn't think the blade went in too deep, but it's enough to cause the skeleton to jerk back like it's just been hit with a cattle prod. He pulls the ice axe with him and yanks Colt forward, the gun ripping from his hand. The skeleton tries to shake the gun off the end of the pick, but it remains stuck there.

My turn.

Colt charges the skeleton with the pocketknife. He needs to disarm his attacker and subdue him before this madness can go further. He slashes at the right hand, catching the skeleton just above the right wrist, which causes its hand to spring open. The ice axe falls into the snow. The person under the skeleton mask screams out. A large cloud of breath kicks from the mask's sides like it's venting steam.

But Colt doesn't let up his assault. He can't. If he does, he knows he's as good as dead. *We all are.*

He swipes out again. But this time, his swing is short, and the tip of the blade skims the mask, cutting a thin slice into the latex just about the left eye socket. The strike doesn't do any physical harm, but it knocks his attacker back into the banister.

Colt spots the ice axe with the pick still through the trigger guard of his gun, lying on the porch floor. He then realizes the skeleton has the same idea—go for the gun and axe.

They both dive for the weapons at the same time, each hoping to get to them first.

Colt hits the porch floor hard and slides toward the weapons. He and the skeleton collide in the snow, but Colt reaches out and wraps the gun and the ice axe in his arms like a fumbled football, cradles it to his chest, and rolls away.

Coming to a stop on his side, Colt desperately tries to pry the ice axe from the trigger guard of the .357. Behind him, he hears the skeleton get to its feet and charge him. *Hurry! You need to…*

And then he feels a steel-toed boot connect with the fleshy part of his back, near his right kidney. A blossom of pain bursts through his torso, and a seepage of urine wets his underwear. He's knocked forward from the blow, the ice axe and the gun thrown from his hands. The weapons skid through the snow to the steps and teeter on the ledge, but they don't fall between the stairs.

The skeleton rears back and kicks again. This blow lands on Colt's right butt cheek, digs into the flesh, and strikes his pelvis, sending another burst of pain up his back.

"You kicked me in the ass!" Colt cries out involuntarily, furiously.

The skeleton steps over him and hurries to retrieve its weapon. It picks up the ice axe and tries to pull the gun free. When it doesn't come off, the skeleton takes the ice axe by the handle and slams the arm down on the side of the banister. The gun kicks free and falls into the snow below and disappears.

Then, the skeleton slowly turns to Colt. Its fingers flex around the ice axe's handle.

Oh, shit!

"Don't you fuckin' move!"

Colt's eyes shift to the parking lot. The skeleton spins. Amos is trudging through the snow toward the porch, the .12-gauge shotgun tucked into his shoulder.

Where the hell was he? Colt wonders.

"That's right! I want to look you in the eyes when I paint this white powder with your motherfuckin' brains," Amos screams, the shotgun trained on the skeleton.

But Colt knows something Amos doesn't.

The shotgun isn't loaded.

Colt pushes himself to his feet. His lower back and ass muscles feel like they're being torn apart as he rises.

"Stand down," Colt says. He flips the knife into his left hand, hoping to bluff a surrender from whoever is under the mask. Still, if it comes to it, he's ready to kill this fucker to end this right here, right now.

The skeleton rears back with the axe to throw it at Colt. He had not seen that coming. A soft *click* whispers into Colt's ears, and he knows Amos's pull on the shotgun's trigger left it unresponsive. Like a sidearm pitcher, the skeleton's body rotates forward and releases the axe.

He sees the axe coming toward him, sideways, end over end, as if in slow motion, and dives out of the way just as the axe passes by his left ear, nearly taking a chunk with it. He hits the floor with enough force that icicles break away from the roof, smash into the banister, and break into pieces. His forward momentum drives him across the slick porch and slams him into the front wall of RS3.

Colt turns to see the skeleton running for the side railing, attempting to hop over it and disappear into the dark woods from which it came.

Unless I can take him down first.

Through the pain of his injuries, Colt climbs to his feet. He hurries to run the skeleton down before it can jump the banister and vanish into the night. But just before he can lay a shoulder into his attacker, like a cornerback plowing down a wide receiver on his way to a touchdown, the skeleton dives over the railing into the darkness.

Gazing over the banister into the snow, there's a large indentation in the pristine powder where the skeleton came to rest. But it's gone. A footprint trail leads around the rear of RS3.

Amos comes up beside him.

"Let's get after him!"

Off in the near distance, there's a whine of a small engine—a snowmobile, Colt believes.

"No," Colt says, through laboring breaths. "We'll never catch him."

Amos turns to protest, but his eyes fall to the blood on Colt's jacket, and his face slackens with shock.

"Oh, man! That…that looks bad."

Colt's hand is held tight to the wound. Blood seeps through his fingers. The slash burns, stings, and throbs with each heartbeat. He doesn't think the wound is deep enough that he'll have any lasting damage, but he doesn't know for sure.

Colt pushes himself away from the banister and looks at the shotgun in Amos's hands.

"You didn't trust me," Amos says, following Colt's eyes to the shotgun.

"I didn't know if I could."

"If you had, this would be over."

"Where were you?" Colt asks instead.

"I thought I saw headlights approaching behind RS3. Thought I heard an engine, too. So, I decided to check it out. Found a snowmobile about fifty yards away. That's how this sucker's been getting around all night."

Colt searches Amos's dark eyes, trying to read them. If he's lying, he can't tell.

"Let's go."

CHAPTER 22

"What the hell is going on out there?" Darryl asks, his voice a raspy cry.

"Well, I can tell you it's not a concert," Flint retorts. He steps beside Joey to better look at the pulsating dome of light in the hazy distance.

Everything seems so surreal. So out of place. *So…fucked up,* Joey thinks. It's as if the world has collided with some infernal force that has turned it upside down. The whine of guitar strings, the *thump, thump, thump* of a bass drum, and an angry, guttural voice that sounds the way she imagines a demon would if it were on stage, screaming into a microphone to its loyal fan base works its way into RS1. The noise—and that's what this is to Joey—is upsetting and nerve-racking.

"It could be a trap," Darryl says.

"I agree with Darryl," Flint says.

And so does Joey. It *could* be a trap, the music luring them to their deaths like a mermaid serenading a sailor at sea before she pulls them into the ocean's dark abyss. Still, she's hesitant.

"But what if it's not," she says, glancing at Flint. "What if it's someone trying to get our attention?"

"Dusty." Flint's face lifts. "He might've made it back from Trail Loop Two."

Joey nods.

"Get on the radio. See if you can contact him."

Flint limps to the radio, snatches the microphone, and calls out to RS2. Joey's throat constricts with anticipation to hear Dusty's voice.

C'mon, Dusty. Pick up!

"RS2 this is RS1 can you read me? Over," Flint says into the microphone again.

No response. Static.

Flint tries a third time.

Pick up. Pick up. Pick up.

When a response doesn't come, other than the heavy static, Flint's eyes lift with the heaviness of a man who fears the worst has happened to Dusty. Joey knows this, too. There was a reason that the lights and sound system were turned on at the band shell —someone wanted to get their attention.

"We need to check it out," Joey finally says.

"You're not serious, are you?" Darryl tucks the blanket under his chin like a child afraid of an imaginary monster in their closet.

"If Dusty *is* over there, this might be the only way he can get our attention," Flint says. He tosses the microphone onto the desk. "The fucking radios are useless in this storm."

Darryl rolls his eyes and scoffs. The glow of the band shell lights continues to pulsate through the haze as if it's a creature, baiting them, entrancing them to come and explore.

"No, think about it for a moment. Dusty knows how to operate the band shell's sound system." Flint shifts his gaze out the window, on the glow. "Maybe this *is* his way to communicate to us. He has to know turning on the music and lights is bound to get our full attention. It's smart, actually."

"Unless it's a trap," Darryl says matter-of-factly. "Then the only smart person is the one who set it."

Darryl's right. But Joey knows it's life or death. Theirs or someone else's if they do nothing.

"If it is Dusty, we need to go get him," she says.

"If you go out there, Joey, you'll be sure to find something you don't want," Darryl protests. "I say we stay here. Wait until daybreak, and then get the hell out."

"Do you think whoever is doing this will allow us to make it to daybreak?" Joey snaps.

"As much as I hope Dusty's made it back to RS2, we have to think about the possibility that this is a setup just to get us over there. I think Darryl's right. We'd be better off staying put. Colt said they would swing by to pick him up on their way back from getting Wyatt."

"But what if Dusty's already hurt or in trouble? What then, Flint? We just leave him because…because we were too scared for our own lives to go and help?"

"Look, I know how this appears. But if it is a trap, we'd walk right into it. God only knows what's waiting for us over there. We need to stay here."

"Well, it's good that you're not in charge, right? Because then I'd be disobeying a direct order."

Flint's upper lip lifts in a sneer, and Joey can practically hear him growl at her for the backhanded remark.

"Fine. But I want you to know I vehemently disagreed with your idea."

Whatever. She cares little about what Flint Wheeler thinks.

"We'll need the snowmobile to get over to the band shell," Joey says.

"They're in the shed," Flint says. His face slackens with the thought of going outside and across the parking lot in snow deep enough to bury a body sufficiently. "And, we'll need protective gear."

"We have everything—facemask, goggles, gloves, snowsuits, and boots—in the locker room storage closet. C'mon."

Joey steps past Flint and starts down the hallway to the locker room. Flint follows close behind. She feels his eyes burning a hole in the back of her head. He disapproves of them going to the band shell. He doesn't want to risk his life on a gamble like Maynard did last year. But that was the difference between Flint Wheeler and Maynard Barrett. Maynard was a man of principles and doing the right thing, even when circumstances say not to. Flint Wheeler was the antithesis of that—he only cared about preserving himself and his interests. *No wonder the state never made him head of the Ranger Rescue Unit.*

Joey pulls her keyring off her belt in the locker room and unlocks the storage closet full of emergency gear and equipment.

"Grab the parkas," Flint says, coming up behind her. "It's near zero out there. And with the windchill, I'd put it several degrees below that even."

Joey grabs two jackets and reaches for two pairs of goggles. She loops a pair over her wrist and goes to hand Flint his.

"I've got my own," Flint says. He moves to his locker and begins to fumble with the combination lock.

Darryl enters the room, the blanket still around his bony body. He seems lost and desperate, stuck in a situation he cannot control. Joey understands. She feels the same way. Still, she wouldn't allow the situation to dictate her response. *That's what this fucker wants. For us to be afraid.* And she is afraid. There is no doubt about it in her mind. But she will not sit idly by with the possibility that Dusty could be out there and in desperate need of help.

As Flint spins the combination dial, he says, "Darryl, why don't you come with me?"

Darryl shakes his head and says, "I ain't going out there."

Flint turns and stares Darryl down. The look piques Joey's curiosity. She can't shake the feeling that it's saying more than Flint means it to.

"Darryl, I ain't asking," Flint replies. "There are two snowmobiles in the shed. I can't drive both. Plus, the engines may not want to turn over with this cold. From what I hear, you know your way around an engine. It would be best if you were there, just in case. Understand?"

Darryl slowly starts to come around to the idea as Flint's words seed in his mind, and quickly flower into agreement.

"Right. We'll get the snowmobiles ready and meet you back here."

"Get Darryl some gear," Flint says.

Joey returns to the storage closet and pulls out a parka, hat, and gloves. Gathering everything up, she turns to hand them to Darryl when something on the inside of Flint's locker door catches her eye. A picture. For a split-second, Joey dismisses what she sees, or at least what she believes she sees, as nothing more than her imagination playing tricks on her.

Impossible.

Flint slams the door. The bang of the locker echoes in the room. Joey jumps at the sound, snapping her from her thoughts. Flint turns around to face her, snow goggles in hand. He gives her a strange look.

"You okay?" he asks.

She maintains her composure so Flint doesn't pick up on her reaction—*you know what you saw!*—and quickly changes the subject.

"While you guys are getting the snowmobiles, I'm getting the shotguns from Colt's office."

"Good idea. If we're going to the band shell, we shouldn't go unarmed," Flint says.

Once Flint and Darryl are geared up and ready to go, Joey leads them to the front door.

"Good luck!" she says, pulling the door open.

Flint nods and steps out into the storm. Darryl follows him but stops when Joey grabs hold of his arm.

"Can I trust you, Darryl?"

Darryl thinks about the question, his beady eyes doing a shifty dance. The wait for a reply feels like an eternity to her, dragging on and on.

"Given the circumstances we find ourselves in, I don't think you have much choice but to trust me."

With that, Darryl steps out into the storm.

Joey closes the door and spins the lock. She places her back on it, the surface as cold as the walls of a meat locker. The picture inside Flint's locker forms in her mind. *It can't be. It can't.*

But you know what you saw, Joey.

She turns and looks out the window. Through the storm, she can barely make out Flint and Darryl trudging toward the shed. The floodlights across RS1 provide just enough illumination to see that the snow is past their knees. She estimates it will take them at least ten minutes, maybe fifteen, to make it to the shed in snow that deep. And God knew how long it would take to get the snowmobiles running—they never start easily when the engines are cold.

That gives me enough time to search Flint's locker.

She bolts from the window and hurries back to the locker room. She knows there's no going back if she breaks into Flint's locker. There will be a confrontation if she finds what she believes she saw in there. The question is: can she keep herself from ripping into him until Colt is back?

Her cheeks warm uncomfortably, like when she found the pictures of her and Colt in Rumor's bag. Her hands clench into fists. The rage in her throat is like acid and it burns the back of her tongue. *And if you're wrong about what you saw? What then?*

"Deal with that bridge when we cross it," she says to the voice in her head.

She doesn't know the numbers for the combination lock, but that won't stop her from getting inside Flint's locker. She has to know if what she saw was real or just her imagination under an insurmountable amount of stress projecting images that weren't there. But without the lock combination, there was only one way to get in.

She remembers the pair of bolt cutters in the storage room, kept there when someone forgets the combination to a new lock. It happens more than one might think, including to herself. She felt like a doofus when Maynard had to get the bolt cutters and cut her new lock off once, not long after she started at the park.

After grabbing the bolt cutters from the storage room, she places the open jaws on the lock's shackle and squeezes the handles. It's harder than the men made it look for Joey to cut through the metal, even with the cutters. Her arm muscles strain with exertion, and she pushes her legs and feet into the floor for leverage; perspiration begins to dot her forehead.

Snap!

The sharp jaws cut through the shackle.

Joey steps back, pulls the lock off, and flings the door open. It slams into the lockers behind it with a *bang*.

Two pictures are taped to the inside of the door. One is of Flint, in his late twenties or early thirties, Joey guesses, standing with an older woman wearing glasses, a flower dress, and a white blouse. She assumes the woman is a relative—his mother or an aunt. But the second picture causes the bolt cutters to slip from her hand and hit the floor with a dull thud.

In the picture, Flint Wheeler stands in front of a black muscle car, similar to what Joey remembers seeing peeling out from the motel parking lot two months ago. Could it be…yes, Joey believes it's the same car she saw that night.

"You bastard," Joey whispers to herself.

Then something else catches her attention. A folder lying on the small shelf at the top of the locker, pushed to the back. She pulls it toward her gently, as if it were a sleeping snake that she doesn't want to wake.

Paging through the folder's contents, blood begins to pound into her ears with horror.

Flint. He's behind…everything…

CHAPTER 23

The snowdrift against the door prevents Darryl and Flint from accessing the shed. Darryl knows they'll have to dig it out first if they want to get inside. The overhead dusk-to-dawn lamp shakes back and forth in the strong breeze, casting long shadows that look like evil spirits dancing for the devil across the snow. Together, Darryl and Flint dig the snow away with their hands. It takes them nearly ten minutes to clear enough to pull open the steel door. Once inside, and by the time the door is secure again, Darrel is wheezing like a longtime smoker walking up a flight of stairs.

Darryl bends and places his hands on his knees. He feels shaky like he felt earlier when he was out looking for Rumor on the cattle trail. His heart hammers in his chest with such force the skin between his eyes thumps. He's lightheaded. And though it's frigid outside, a cold, clammy film of sweat covers his body like some outer-space organism looking to assimilate him.

"You okay?" Flint asks, beside him. He places a hand on the center of Darryl's back that feels as heavy as a brick.

"Just need…tah…catch…my breath," Darryl rasps.

"Stay here. I'll go and check on the snowmobiles."

Darryl wants to object to Flint going off on his own, and being left there by himself, but he can't bring himself to say anything or even attempt to move. He needs time to catch his breath, to let his heart rate settle, and for the fogginess of his vision, his mind, to pass.

Flint leaves Darryl standing by the door. The wind pushes at it like a snow monster trying to break it down. *It wants in, wants us.* Only Darryl knows there isn't a snow monster trying to kill them…but a person. *The same person who took my Rumor.* A bead of sweat lets loose from his brow and runs into his eye. The salt burns. He blinks and rubs it away with his finger.

Darryl wonders what Flint's angle is. Why has he been supplying them with the nightly patrol schedules for over a year? Why is he trying to blackmail Colt and Joey with the photos, photos he gave to Rumor yesterday to place around the park? But Flint kept his secrets, even when pressed. The best they got out of him was, *I have my reasons.* But that's not all that bugs him about Flint. The man's too quiet, and he watches everyone a little too closely for Darryl's comfort, the way a pervert lurks in the bushes to watch children at a playground. Even today, he saw how Flint kept to himself, hanging back, blending in with the others. A chameleon, watching things unfold around him, quick to point the finger of accusation at everyone…deflecting blame away from himself.

Could Flint be…

A strange pressure, like a softball under his ribs, diverts his thoughts back to his chest. He touches the tender spot under his left nipple and can feel his heart beating against his sternum. *Does it feel out of rhythm?* He doesn't know.

Rumor had been after him to see a doctor for years, especially at his age. But Darryl, the tentative man he is wasn't keen to the idea. *Don't need them quacks poking around at me. Damn quacks. Quack! Quack!* His trust in doctors is about the same as his trust in the government—zero to none.

The lightheadedness makes him wobble, and the pain in his chest tightens. He braces himself on the wall for support. His vision has become blurry at the corners like he's looking through a kaleidoscope. The flop sweat slickens his face to a shiny finish. And now there's a numbness in his left arm.

I need to sit down.

Darryl spots a stool by a workbench with tools hanging on a pegboard above it. His feet feel heavy when he begins to move, as if his boots are full of sand. His heart hammers so hard that he hears it beating inside his skull like a drum. *Ba-bump! Ba-bump! Ba-bump!* It's a maddening, and yet, a very frightening sound that unnerves him.

What the hell is wrong with me? But he knows. God help him he knows but he doesn't want to admit it, not even to himself.

By the time Darryl reaches the stool, his legs almost give out. Had the stool been a few feet further, he might not have made it. He flops onto it, thankful. If he'd gone to the doctor, maybe they could have found whatever was wrong now. But Darryl was too stubborn. *Too stubborn for my own well-being.*

The thought makes him think of his land and all the time and energy he spent—both of which he wishes he could have back and put into positive things—fighting the DCNR. *Should have just taken the state's money.* He could have done a lot with that money: retire, vacation, fishing and hunting trips with Rumor. *But you pissed it away over your pride, your greed.*

And what did he get from it? No land or money. Just a dead son.

Flint walks back around the corner, finding Darryl on the stool. How long was he gone? *Ten minutes?* He has no idea. Time has no measure for him at the moment. But by the look on Flint's face, Darryl can tell he's taken aback by his ashen, sweaty appearance.

"What's wrong?" Flint asks, though there is no empathy in his voice.

"I don't know, honestly," Darryl replies. But he does know. He just can't admit it aloud, fearing God will strike him down for his sins if he does. He forces himself to smile for a reason that makes no sense to him—maybe to reaffirm to Flint that he won't drop dead just yet. *But you don't know that...*

"We need to talk, Flint," Darryl says. His chest is heavy and rigid. It's hard to speak. "You guaranteed us you had everythin' under control. That no one would find out that me or Rumor was behind the vandalisms. Now Rumor is dead." Darryl pauses and takes a deep breath. A sharp pain slashes across his chest. "Are... you...behind...what's going on?"

Flint says nothing. In his silence, Darryl can't tell if that's an admission to murder or the guilt he feels over Rumor's death. Though after what happened last summer, he isn't sure Flint Wheeler has compassion for anyone.

"Well?"

Flint steps closer to lift him to his feet.

"You don't look good. I'm taking you back to RS1 right now."

"No." Darryl pulls away. "Murder was never part of the plan, Flint. If you're responsible—"

"Why would I kill Rumor?" Flint cuts him off. "Or the others, for that matter?"

"Maybe so no one can tie you back to us...to what happened to Maynard." Darryl studies Flint for a tell that he was responsible. He has no qualms about his or Rumor's part in the vandalisms, but he knows neither of them had anything to do with that fake distress call that led to Maynard's death.

But what about Flint?

"Lock that shit up," Flint says, just above a whisper. His gray eyes search the shed. When he trains his eyes back on Darryl, his jaw is set, and the muscles jump spasmodically with irritation. "This place might have ears."

"Was it you? Was all this part of your grand plan?" Darryl hears a wheeze when he speaks now, and his concern deepens.

"I have nothing to do with what's going on," Flint says. There's something in his cadence that makes Darryl not believe him. "There's someone else in this park with us."

Another surge of pain cuts across Darryl's chest. The tentacles reach around his back, bite into the muscles under his left shoulder blade, and travel down his left arm and into his ring finger.

"Does anyone else know? About the three of us, I mean?"

"No."

Flint's face is blank, emotionless. If there are any feelings under his thick skin and beard, Darryl has yet to see them. Flint Wheeler doesn't care who he hurts to get what he wants, Darryl feels—*whatever that is*. He realizes that he needs to tread carefully. Because Flint is willing to do whatever he has to to keep himself from seeing inside a prison cell, which is where he'll go if anyone finds out that he's involved in vandalizing the park.

Did that include leading Maynard Barrett to his death? Darryl suspects it may. *But why?*

"We need to get those snowmobiles up and running," Darryl says, shifting the conversation back onto the issue.

"That's going to be a problem."

A troubling glint flashes across Flint's face.

"What?" Darryl asks.

"Someone destroyed them."

A bitter taste flowers in his mouth and seems to grow more robust and thicker, coating his tongue like a paste. He'd like to spit it away, but his mouth is too dry.

"Are...you sure?"

"Yes," Flint says with a look so firm it works into Darryl's chest, causing the pain to ratchet tighter.

"How...could..." Darryl labors to ask.

"I don't know."

"Who...was...last in here?"

Flint thinks about the question for a moment.

"As far as I know, Amos. To get the Sno-Cat." Flint looks around the large building. "But I suppose anyone could have gotten in while we weren't looking."

"Let me take a look at them. Maybe I can..." Darryl pushes himself to stand (wills himself, really) and finds his legs feel as strong as foam pool noodles, but they surprisingly support his weight, if barely. His heart jackhammers in his chest; the flop sweat feels tacky and thick, like his skin is coated with corn syrup, causing his clothes to cling to him.

"Maybe you should sit back down."

"I'm...fine." But even as the words pass through Darryl's lips, he knows they're as false as his teeth. He stands. Lumbers onward.

Snow and ice ticks against another large metal garage door in the back of the shed. The wind howls outside, causing it to bang against its metal roller track. In front of it are two snowmobiles, their hoods open. Parts from their engines are strewn across the floor.

"It looks like someone demolished them," Flint says.

As they near the two snowmobiles, Darryl notices something as his boot kicks a bolt, and it skids under the closest snowmobile. It appears the snowmobiles weren't destroyed as much as they were carefully taken apart, piece by piece. No cut cables or tubes. No leaking fluids. No smell of gasoline. The parts are not broken or bent, nor are there any stripped bolts that Darryl can see. Everything looks to be intact and ready to be put back together.

Whoever did this meticulously disassembled the engines. It all looks so chaotic. But that's just what someone wants them to believe. It was all for a show, to fool the untrained eye. Why?

But the answer comes to Darryl instantly, as strong as the pain in his chest. *Someone plans to use them to get out of the park. After we're all dead.*

How long was Flint out of his sight? Darryl's not sure. But it was enough time to disable the snowmobiles without tipping him off, especially while distracted by...well—*say it, dammit, admit that you're having*—his chest issues.

Slowly, as his heart rate ticks up with this thought, Darryl turns to find Flint eyeing him like a man caught in the crosshairs of a rifle...

CHAPTER 24

The cut across Colt's shoulder leaks blood with each heartbeat. His sleeve is red, like he's taken a stroll through a slaughterhouse. After Amos helps get him into the Cat, Colt undoes his belt and pulls it from around his waist. He makes a loop, slides his injured arm through, and tugs it taut, just above the laceration. The makeshift tourniquet will help stem the blood loss, but only momentarily. Joey will need to look at the wound. That meant, much to Colt's displeasure, that they wouldn't be able to pick up Dusty at RS2. Maybe Flint got through on the radio.

But in this weather.

Wishful thinking.

Amos punches the accelerator, and the Cat humps it toward the main road. They ride in silence while Colt tries to understand how the past and present intersect. But he doesn't see the connection. And if one has shown itself to him, it's buried deep in the slush of his mind.

"How you holdin' up?" Amos asks, keeping his eyes on the road. Even with the Cat's bright lights, visibility isn't more than ten feet by Colt's estimates.

"I'll manage." Colt looks into the darkness. "Where are we?"

Amos looks at the GPS screen above his head. A digital map with a blue moving dot representing the Cat shows him where they are.

"Just coming off the bridge," Amos says. "We should see RS1's floodlights any moment."

Colt didn't know they were over the lake; the whiteout was so thick the bridge and the water below were indistinguishable.

"When we get to RS1, stay here. I'll get Joey and bring her out to you."

"I can walk inside. I'm hurt. Not dying." *At least, I hope I'm not.*

The floodlights across the front of RS1 come into view. A bright, hazy range of white light that catches the snow as it passes by with relentless determination. Amos turns into the parking lot.

"You just stay—"

"There's someone out there!"

A figure logs toward them. Their arms wave back and forth in an X to get their attention. *What the hell?*

"Who is that?" Amos asks, bringing the Cat to a stop.

The figure slogs through the snow toward the Cat, trying to keep themselves from being blown over by the wind gusts. It's not until they're directly beside the passenger door that Colt sees who it is.

Flint!

Flint shouts through the glass, but Colt can't distinguish what he's saying over the engine and the hellish wind outside. The panic on Flint's face is as pure as honey.

"Something's happened."

"I'll check it out." Amos lifts the shotgun and looks at Colt for approval.

Can I trust him?

He's unsure but nods reluctantly.

Amos opens the door and climbs down. For a second, Colt thinks he hears heavy metal music coming from somewhere across the lake, but it might be wind manipulation. He watches Amos and Flint exchange words; sees the sheer fright on Flint's face deepen into something more agitated. The erratic movements of his arms and hands, and the way he keeps pointing behind him to something unseen, worries Colt that maybe there's been another attack.

What's going on?

Amos turns away and pulls open the Cat's passenger side door. Again, the wind rushes in with a howl, chilling Colt to a level he believes he's never felt before. *It's the blood loss*, he reminds himself. Still, he thinks he can hear…music. Far off. Somewhere out there. The beat of drums. The whine of guitar strings. An angry voice.

"We got another problem," Amos says.

"What?"

"I think Darryl is having a heart atta—" Flint stops short when he notices the blood covering Colt's right arm. "What the hell happened?"

"Someone jumped me at RS3." Exhaustion consumes him. He would do anything for a few minutes of sleep, to rest his eyes, injured body, and mind that's running like a locomotive on a desolate track at full speed without an end in sight.

"Did you get a look at 'em?" Colt shakes his head. Flint's eyes shift back to his arm. "What'd he get you with? A machete?"

"An ice axe."

"An ice axe? As in one of those things the mountain climbers use?"

Colt nods.

"Where's Darryl now?"

"He's over in the shed—"

"What the hell is he doing over there?" Colt asks, looking toward the shed. He sees a slight halo of light from the dusk-to-dawn lamp in the white mist, but nothing else. He can't help but wonder who might be out there, lurking in that white void between them and the shed.

"We were checking on the snowmobiles," Flint says. "Something's going on at the band shell." The sound of music comes to

Colt again. The confusion he feels on his face must give him away when Flint adds, "You hear it, don't you?"

Colt nods.

"How long has it been going on?"

"About thirty minutes or so." Flint turns and points in the direction of the band shell. "You can't see it as well now, since the snow has gotten worse, but the lights are on."

Colt looks toward the band shell. He sees a faint glow in the distance. The music plays on, even over the wind.

"Joey believes it might be Dusty trying to get our attention. Darryl and me were getting the snowmobiles from the shed so we could check it out." Flint pauses, and his face darkens to a shade Colt had never seen before. "Colt, someone destroyed the snowmobiles."

"Destroyed them? How?"

"They're out of commission. That's all I can say for sure. But Darryl thinks they can be repaired."

Who could've gotten to the snowmobiles? And when did they get to them? Colt realizes that he can't pinpoint everyone's whereabouts. That meant anyone he didn't have eyes on all day could have gone into the shed and taken out the snowmobiles. Who was the last person over there?

"Someone doesn't want us to leave this park," Amos says gravely.

Amos was the last person in there, Colt remembers. *Could he have sabotaged the snowmobiles so they couldn't use them to leave the park and bring back help?*

"We need to get Darryl back to RS1. But I can't carry him alone because of my knee."

Colt nods, trying to mask the connection he's just made about Amos being in the shed last. But he also realizes that there is the possibility that Amos isn't responsible for the snowmobiles. Because Amos *wasn't* the last person over there, was he? No. Flint and Darryl were. As much as he doesn't like the idea of not knowing whom he can trust, they need to get Darryl back to RS1. And to do that, he has no choice but to send Amos with Flint.

"Right. Amos, go help Flint get Darryl."

"What about you?" Amos asks.

"I can make it inside on my own."

Amos nods, but he's reluctant to let Colt go alone. He wonders if this is some penance after his disappearance while they were at RS3 or a way to disarm him from thinking he was responsible for the snowmobile's dismantlement.

Colt doesn't know. And that's a problem.

While Amos and Flint head off toward the shed, Colt climbs down from the Sno-Cat. He makes his way to RS1; the snow is significantly more profound, and the wind has brought a cold that feels like it's filleting the skin from his bones. Before going inside, he takes one last look across the parking lot. But he doesn't see Amos or Flint. The white monster has already eaten them up.

He prays that he's making the right call sending Amos with Flint. Even with their differences, Colt couldn't leave Darryl over there to suffer, to die, alone and cold. And he was in no shape to assist, not with his arm gushing blood. What choice did he have?

Entering RS1, Colt finds Joey standing at her desk, loading shotgun shells into a.12 gauge. There's a look of determination on her face that he's never seen before; a warrior ready for battle.

"Planning on taking down a bear?" Colt asks.

"Just a person." Joey looks up. Her eyes widen at the sight of his bloody appearance. "What in the hell happened to you?"

"Someone attacked us."

Colt undoes the belt tourniquet and drops it to the floor. With his good arm, he starts to unzip his coat.

"Here, let me help you out of that," Joey says. She assists him in shedding the heavy, blood-soaked jacket and button-down Ranger shirt. His white undershirt is stained red like a butcher's apron. Peeling the bloody shirt sleeve away from the gash delicately, the fabric sticks and pulls at the cut skin. He winces.

"My, God! Colt, this looks bad."

"How bad?"

"You'll need stitches to stop the bleeding." She stands and looks him in the eyes. "I don't know if you'll have any permanent damage, but you're going to have a nasty scar, that much I *can* tell you."

"Chicks dig scars," Colt says with a sly smile.

"Let me get the first aid kit."

Joey hurries from the room, and Colt finds the nearest chair. Exhaustion, unlike anything he's ever felt before, envelopes him. Probably from the blood loss, he concludes. Joey returns with the first aid kit. She places it on the desk, opens the box, and lays everything out like a nurse for a surgeon—antiseptic, bandages, needle, and thread. After snapping on a pair of latex surgical gloves, she takes the bottle of antiseptic and holds the mouth above the slice in Colt's right arm.

"This is going to sting," she says before pouring the clear contents over the wound.

Colt sucks air in through his teeth as the antiseptic fluid works its way into the gash and starts to fizz, clearing out anything that could set in and cause an infection. It takes all his willpower to not pull away, to not grab at the wound and hold it, nurse it like a dog licking an abrasion over and over.

"Sorry," Joey croons.

Colt tries to put the pain out of his mind and focuses on something else, like fishing the stream by his home, pulling out rainbow trout on a warm spring day. But that's easier said than done.

"What happened down there?"

"Someone wearing a skull mask jumped me."

Joey looks up at him with consternation. "Just like Amos saw on the bridge earlier?" Colt nods. "What about Wyatt? Did you find him?"

Colt's eyes drift to the floor, saddened by defeat.

"Is Wyatt dead?" Joey pushes.

"Yes," Colt finally says, his heart heavy that he failed Wyatt.

Just like he failed Lance, Norm, and…Maynard. *Christ! Can I protect anyone on my watch?*

He looks back at her, sees the deep worry lines running like a roadmap across her face. Joey's a strong woman but Colt knows she's slowly coming apart at the seams. Tears moisten her eyes at the loss of yet another fellow ranger, but she blinks them away and returns her attention to his arm.

The room grows still and very quiet. Even the wind seems to cease, if only for a few seconds—a moment of peace from the white hell outside.

"I take it you heard the music when you got back. We were going to check it out, thinking Dusty might be trying to signal us since the radios and phones are down."

She tears open a gauze package and pulls out a square. Colt grinds his teeth when she places it against the wound. The pressure of her hand is enough to make his stomach roil. He takes a few breaths, trying to calm himself so he doesn't pass out. Joey asks if he's okay.

"I'm fine. If you're right, and Dusty is out there, then we can't just sit here. We need to go and get him."

"It could be a trap," she replies, not looking up from the bleeding wound quickly soaking through the gauze.

"It might be."

"We'll be armed. If this fucker shows up, we'll take care of him," Joey says. She lifts the gauze to examine the wound. It's still bleeding but the blood is starting to coagulate.

That's a lot of bravado for someone who's never shot a person before, Colt thinks. There was a difference between saying you could take a life and actually doing it. But Joey? He wasn't so sure. And that concerns him. She might choke when the time comes to pull the trigger at a human target.

"Hold still," Joey says, picking up the needle and thread. "This is going to hurt like hell."

She pushes the needle into Colt's flesh. He instantly seizes taut. She made good on her promise. They're quiet while she works. The pain of the needle and thread pulling the flesh together, loop after loop, is like being repeatedly stung by a yellow jacket. Colt tries again to focus his mind on anything but the pain, but it's of little help. He must grin and bear the stitching. After sewing the wound shut, she ties it off and dresses his arm with a white bandage. It's tight but doesn't restrict his mobility.

"Thank you," Colt says in a low voice.

"You're welcome."

Colt has been around Joey long enough to know when something was bugging her. The skin between her eyes wrinkles into three sharp lines. There's something she isn't telling him.

"What's wrong?"

"I have good reason to believe it was Flint who took the photos of us and passed them on to Rumor."

Why would Flint follow them to a motel and take pictures of them? What will he gain from his betrayal? But there's something else Colt struggles to understand.

"How did Flint know we are seeing each other?"

"I don't know. We were so careful." Joey stands, flustered, and walks to the wastepaper can and dumps the bloody trash. She strips the surgical gloves with a snap and drops them in, too. "The night the pictures were taken, I recall seeing someone outside the motel, hurrying back to what I thought was a late seventies Camaro, carrying a camera."

Colt remembers her story from earlier. She'd seen someone in black running from behind the motel.

"But it wasn't a Camaro like I thought. It was a black Firebird Trans-Am, just like the one Flint had taped inside his locker. I saw it when he opened the door to get his goggles."

Though he wasn't a *car guy*, Colt understood her confusion. The 1970s Trans-Am and Camaro have similar body styles and could easily be confused for one another at a quick glance.

"To what end?" Colt doesn't see why Flint would have a reason to want to ruin their lives.

"If those photos found their way to higher-ups in the DCNR,

we'd be dragged over the coals—professionally and publicly—and fired. And who's next in line to be head of the Ranger Rescue Unit?"

"Flint."

Joey nods.

"But why would Flint help the Shoffs? That makes no sense. If he was trying to blackmail us, he could've taken the pictures himself and spread them around without anyone noticing."

"Maybe to keep his hands clean. If Rumor and Darryl were caught, and they squealed, Flint could easily deny his involvement. It would be their word against his. And no one would believe two vandals, especially ones with a tumultuous history with the park." Joey pauses, thinking. "He was using them, not the other way around, to get what *he* wanted."

"My position."

"I believe so. It's just a theory, mind you. I have no concrete proof, even with the picture in his locker. But he was bitching a lot about you being Maynard's favorite earlier and that it was why you were given the promotion over him."

Colt thinks about it and sees the possibility of Flint Wheeler not being the man he pretends to be. What else is Flint hiding?

"So is Flint involved…with the murders?"

Joey thinks, then says, "I found something else in his locker. A file."

"A file?"

"There were old newspaper clippings about the murders at Camp Southwoods inside, the subsequent investigation, and the trial. But that's not the scary part, Colt."

"Oh?"

"There were several web articles about the urban legend that sprung up in the wake of the murders."

"Where's the folder now? I want to see it."

"I removed it and put it in your desk's top right-hand drawer for safekeeping." A troubled look works its way across her face.

"What's that look about?"

"It's just that Flint was with me most of the day, including when you were attacked at RS3. So was Darryl. That leaves Rumor, but he's dead. That can only mean one of two things: Flint is being set up or..."

Fury rises inside Colt with a sudden and unexpected realization that connects everything. He stands, his muscles scream with fatigue now that the adrenaline has worn off. There's been something nibbling away at his brain since he found Norm on Maynard's bench. It was right in front of his eyes the entire time, but he didn't see the connection until now.

"Norm's body. It was placed specifically on the bench dedicated to Maynard for us to find. Because he's telling us something."

"What?"

Colt sees Maynard's flashlight lying at the top of the Rocks in his mind, swaying back and forth from the wind, the beam sweeping across the wet trees, casting shadows through the woods. He had not actually seen Maynard fall; but he heard his terrified scream and his body tumble through the darkness, down the side of the cliff, his limbs shatter, the air driven from his lungs with each impact to the sharp rocks. It was a horrible sound like the screeching of tires just before a car accident that made every nerve stand on end in anticipation of the crash. When he finally got to the top, and found the flashlight, he had believed that Maynard had lost his footing on the wet rocks and fell to his death. An accident. A terrible accident that Colt has spent the better part of a year berating himself over for not being there when his friend needed him the most. But it wasn't an accident.

"Maynard didn't slip that night."

Joey's eyes dance with trepidation.

"He was...murdered. Pushed." Colt says, confident he's on the right path. "We were lured up there that night."

"Flint made the distress call." Joey shakes her head as if trying to shake away the bad memory of the night Maynard died; tears spill down her cheeks like jelly as she comes to the same conclusion as Colt has already. "He knew Maynard wouldn't leave someone stranded up there and would mount a rescue mission, even in the hurricane. And he did it so he could get Maynard's position. But when that didn't happen, and you got the position, he came after…us."

Colt runs the scenario over in his mind. Flint was nowhere around when the distress call came in, and the voice was so broken up, because of the hurricane, there was no way to tell who the caller was. The next time Colt heard from Flint that afternoon, was when he radioed that both exits were blocked on Route 206 with downed trees.

"But Flint was in RS1 with me the entire time you and Maynard were hiking up to the Rocks. How could he—"

"He had help."

"Rumor? Darryl?"

"Or someone else."

Colt's words hang in the chilly air with reverence. Outside, the wind pushes against the building. The windows rattle and the wooden walls groan like a tired old man getting into bed for a long winters nap.

"But if Flint's behind everything, why connect Norm, Wyatt, and Porter to the Carver legend but not Rumor, who was hidden in the pit so as not to be found? That doesn't make sense."

She's right. There were still factors at play that he didn't understand.

"I don't know. We're missing something. But we're going to find—"

A sharp gunshot echoes across the woods outside.

Colt knows of only one person with a gun that could have made that much noise.

"That's Amos! C'mon!"

CHAPTER 25

Colt charges through the threshold of RS1 with a shotgun in hand—the bitter cold bites into the flesh of his bare arms. Joey follows close behind, her Glock drawn and at the ready. As they step into the blustery night, Colt sees a silhouette staggering through the snow toward them, just beyond the reach of the floodlights.

"Identify yourself!" Colt screams. He raises the shotgun, presses the butt tight into his shoulder.

"It's...meeeee!" a voice calls back, barely audible over the wind.

Colt can't ascertain whose voice it belongs to. Not willing to risk their lives, he narrows in on the nearing figure with the shotgun's iron sights. His finger tightens on the trigger. The cold metal burns his flesh with anticipation.

"Hold it!" Joey says, placing her hand on the barrel just before Colt pulls the trigger. "It's Amos."

"Are you sure?"

"Yes!"

Amos steps into the floodlight's reach. He looks like a frozen corpse. His bottom lip is split and blood stains the front of his jacket in small oblong splotches. His eyebrows and the slight outline of a mustache are white with frost. He collapses at their feet from his strenuous trek. They prop him up against the building.

"What happened?" Colt asks.

"Flint...he's...gone crazy!"

Colt glances at Joey, who has an I-told-you-so look on her face. He feels Flint's treachery slip further into his heart.

"Let's get him inside," Colt says.

Together, he and Joey lift Amos off the ground, which is no easy feat for either of them, and assist him inside RS1.

"Get the door," Colt says. He takes Amos's weight while Joey closes the door and locks it, the deadbolt slamming into the notch. Colt eases Amos down into a chair. "Are you alright?"

Amos nods. The split on his bottom lip is swollen and purple. *That must hurt like hell.* Amos peels the black tassel cap off his head like an extra layer of skin and drops his hands to his lap. Exhaustion settles in his eyes, over his body, like a fighter ready to throw in the towel.

"Flint attacked me," he finally says. "He believes that I tampered with the snowmobiles."

Joey comes around the side of the chair. She opens the first aid kit and pulls out antiseptic and gauze pads.

"Let me look at your lip." She applies some antiseptic to the gauze and lightly dabs at the wound. Amos pulls away. "Hold still!"

How long had Amos been gone when he went to the shed to get the Sno-Cat? Colt doesn't remember. He was too busy talking to Tripp. But he supposes that Amos did have enough time to dismantle the snowmobiles.

"I didn't touch those snowmobiles. I swear I didn't," Amos pleads as if reading Colt's thoughts.

"That's how the altercation started?" Colt asks.

"No." Amos shakes his head and looks at him with a gaze that could scare the most hardened man. "I stumbled over someone in the snow."

"Who?" Joey asks cautiously, almost as if she doesn't want to know.

"Darryl."

Colt and Joey glance at each other suspiciously. Darryl had gone with Flint to the shed. Now he was dead, too. *Flint really is behind everything. Or is this another setup? And Amos is the other person helping Flint?*

"How'd Darryl die?" Colt asks.

Amos shrugs. "As far as I can tell, he might've frozen to death. He was buried in the snow. I dug him out. When I found Darryl, I ordered Flint back here. But Flint lunged for the shotgun. We got into a tussle with it, and it went off, kicking out of my hands. I lost it in the snow. He then hit me on the mouth and disappeared into the woods." Amos touches his lip gently. "Flint's behind all of this. He's the one who destroyed the snowmobiles after he killed Darryl, so we can't get out of here. I think he was leading me over there to kill me, just like he killed Darryl."

Or is this just the story the two of you cooked up?

"Amos might be right. If Flint has been supplying Rumor and Darryl with park information and the pictures, who's to say he didn't murder Darryl, so his involvement doesn't get out," Joey says. "Just like Rumor."

"What pictures?" Amos asks.

Colt looks to Joey for her approval. It's time to clear the air, he feels—time for all the secrets floating around this park to reveal themselves.

"Go on. Tell him," she says.

"Joey has good reason to believe that Flint took photos of Joey and me and gave them to Rumor to spread around the park."

"Wait. Are you telling me that you two..." He swings a large finger back and forth between them.

"Yes," Joey says with a nod.

Amos tries to understand Joey and Colt's predicament. Outside, the wind howls, bringing the whine of guitar strings and that horrible voice that sounds straight from Hell. Finally, the pieces fall into place in his mind.

"They were going to blackmail the two of you."

"We believe so," Colt says.

"Why?"

"So Flint could get my job," Colt replies.

Amos considers this, head bobbing like it all made perfect sense.

"What are we going to do about the band shell?" Joey asks. "If Dusty's over there, we can't just leave him."

"We can take the Sno-Cat over," Amos says. "We no longer need the snowmobiles."

"But if we need to get out of the park, the snowmobiles are the only way to bypass the trees blocking the road," Joey says.

Colt remembers something.

"Flint said that Darryl thought the snowmobiles could be repaired. If that's true, Tripp might be able to get them up and running."

"But Tripp's not here," Joey says.

Colt looks at his watch. It's ten past eight. He wonders if Tripp found a way through Camp Southwoods Road to Route 9. They agreed that Colt would come after him if he didn't hear from him by nine o'clock.

That left Tripp fifty minutes.

In the meantime, Colt knows they must deal with the band shell situation.

He turns away and looks out the window at the pulsating light in the distance. They could stay inside RS1, safe and warm, or risk their lives for what is sure to be a trap. If Joey's right and Dusty *is* out there—cold and alone, possibly injured—Colt can't risk leaving him there. Not with a killer on the loose. *I can't let another man die on my watch.*

"Let's suit up," Colt says.

CHAPTER 26

The band shell's exterior lights cut through the trees in long, white streaks, like it were lit for a winter horror film. The music coming from the built-in sound system is hard, fast, and heavy and coincides with the strobing lights twirling and flashing on stage as if a demonic rock band was performing Satan's Greatest Hits. But there was no band on the stage, only a single chair, a person bound to it. This is a bad idea, Colt frets as Amos pulls the Cat parallel with the structure.

The person bound to the chair sits center stage, a black hood over their head. Coat and gloveless, the dark green cargo pants and the long-sleeve button-down shirt are the only protection from the elements. It's a ranger, Colt's sure of that. But if it's Dusty, he can't tell.

"This *is* a trap." Amos's lips pull into a grim straight line. "We should bail."

"If we do that, we're letting someone die out here," Joey says.

Colt doesn't see any signs of a trap, but that doesn't mean one isn't there. He knew—they all did—what they faced coming over here. There was no turning back now.

"Amos, stay with the Cat," Colt says. "Joey and I will check it out."

Colt grabs hold of the key and turns it. The Cat shudders to a stop.

"What the hell are you doing?" Amos asks angrily.

"I'm making sure you can't leave us out here," Colt says. He yanks the key from the ignition and slides it into his front pocket.

"You've got to be kidding me! I'm on your side."

"Sorry, Amos. I can't risk it."

Amos studies Colt intently, his dark eyes full of indignation. The trust Amos believes he's built has been rewarded with doubt yet again.

But there are too many red flags for Colt to blindly trust Amos—his disappearance at RS3, the disabled snowmobiles, and his altercation with Flint. Though Colt feels confident that Flint's behind everything, he's sure Flint has an accomplice or accomplices working with him. Is Amos one of them? He doesn't know. His first instinct is to keep Joey and himself safe. If that means some feelings until he is positive about whose side Amos is really on, then so be it. Until then, Colt isn't taking any chances—with anyone other than Joey.

He jumps into the snow and sinks past his knees. *There must be twenty inches on the ground.* He rounds the front of the Cat and meets Joey by the driver's side door, using the mirror to keep himself from being blown over by the severe winds thrashing over the hill.

"Hang on to me," Colt yells.

"Okay!"

With Joey's arms tightly wrapped around the crook of his elbow, Colt starts toward the stage. The wind whips across the open field. It's stronger than anything he's experienced in a blizzard before. It takes every ounce of his strength to keep himself and Joey upright; his injured back screaming as he tries to stabilize them against the gusts. He worries it could take both of them right off their feet and send them tumbling across the icy field as easy as a can blowing down the sidewalk. The screeching is loud enough that Colt's ears ache, like someone is driving a Q-tip into the drum. He feels Joey tighten her grip around his arm, and he pulls her closer, reaffirming his grip on her.

"You good?"

She nods, but Colt can see the doubt in her eyes, the fatigue to keep hold of him slumping her shoulders. If she slips, the wind might blow her away. He thinks about taking her back, but that's not an option. They need to free whoever is under the hood and return to RS1, where it's warm.

A large pine tree is about ten feet away. They can take some refuge there to catch their breath. He presses on, dragging Joey with him. His legs are on fire by the time they reach the tree, and his lower back, where the skeleton's boot struck him, is knotted tight and begging him to stop. Pushing through the discomfort slowly draining his body of energy, Colt moves them behind the tree. It's not an ideal spot—in fact, it might be the worst spot—for them to pause, but the thick, full pine will provide them some shelter from the deluge of wind and snow.

"We need to hurry," Joey says. She looks at the bound victim on the stage. "He's not wearing a coat or gloves. And in this extreme cold, we're also in danger."

She's right to worry about them getting frostbite, even though they wear protective gear. It was near zero, but with the wind chill, Colt estimates it's several degrees below that. Their protective clothing would keep the cold off them, but only for so long. But for the person on the stage, it must feel like he's being flash-frozen. Still, Colt has no idea how long the rangers been bound to the chair in the cold, the wind, and the snow. Minutes? A half hour? An hour? Longer? It only took thirty minutes of exposure for the skin to become frostbitten. Time was of the essence.

Stepping away from the pine, a strong gust of wind slams into them with such force that Colt nearly goes down. Joey loses her grip on his arm and is driven into the snow. He grabs her by the front of the jacket and hauls her upright.

"Hook your arm around my waist!" he screams into her face. She does and he pulls her into him. "Ready?"

She nods, pushes a strand of black hair out of her eyes that has come free from under her cap.

They start off again. Soon Colt feels the earth begin to slope, and the snow deepens up to his thighs and nearly to Joey's waist. He feels the compression of the snow holding his feet, threatening to snatch his boots with each step. *Can't catch a fucking break.* Traversing through the snow while pulling Joey with him is like dragging a sled full of bricks through mud.

Just a few more feet.

Finally, the ground ascends, and the snow lessens as Colt nears the band shell. Under the roof, the stone sidewalls block the crosswind and snow, which is a much-needed reprieve. He feels like his entire body is about to shut down and go into a deep coma. He's so tired from the exertion and the bitter cold that he only wants to sleep.

Keep moving.

The person bound to the chair mumbles something unintelligible and pulls at the ropes binding his arms. It causes the chair to rock from side to side like a little kid wanting out of his high chair. The legs make a *clup, clup, clup, clup* sound on the concrete like a galloping steed.

The music blasts from the speakers, hard and heavy. The guttural, angry voice is so loud it physically makes Colt feel ill. He wonders if eardrums can explode from the noise alone.

"We need to cut him free and get back in the Cat ASAP!" Joey screams.

Colt nods and looks around. Along the back wall are three large openings that allow a full view of Lake Clarke on a clear day. Now it's a stark blackness, with tiny specks of white catching the light like scratches on film as the snowflakes pass by the openings. To the right of the third window is a small room where the sound system is located. Colt's first thought is to go there and kill the music, but when he looks back, he sees Joey moving toward the person bound to the chair.

Something catches his eye.

"Don't!" Colt shouts as her hand comes up to remove the hood, revealing the person underneath.

Joey stops. She turns her outstretched hand into a fist, so upset at Colt that he believes she's about to slug him for the interruption.

"What?" she snaps.

"There," he says, pointing at the ground. "You see it?"

Joey scans the area directly below. But Colt realizes she doesn't see the trap because of the angle at which she's standing. *Clever.* Another step, and she would have set it off.

A muffled cry erupts from whoever is under the hood. He pulls frantically at the restraints; the chair's front legs raise and slam back down onto the concrete.

Just hang on, partner.

Colt moves alongside Joey. Squatting down, he slides his fingertips just under the surface of the snow and gently lifts. A thin green fishing line is present against his black gloves.

Joey's eyes widen with shock.

Colt follows the direction of the line across the floor and up the wall into the corner.

"There," he says, pointing. "See it."

Joey turns and follows his outstretched finger.

"Yes."

A basketball-size sphere of spikes is hidden in the shadows of the band shell's roof. It looks homemade. Tripping the wire releases the ball, causing it to swing down and impale whoever is in its way.

"Can you disarm it?" Joey asks, looking back at him.

"Not without setting it off. Best to step over it."

"How did you see it?" She takes a wide berth over the line.

"The line moved when the wind blew; I saw the disruption in the snow."

Now safely over the tripwire, Joey reaches for the hood—*moment of truth*, Colt thinks—and pulls it off.

Sitting there, shaking, bloody, and scared, is…

"Porter!" Joey cries.

And if Porter is here, then where is Dusty?

Porter's eyes bug out of his skull. A large laceration on the back of his head is deep and gnarly-looking, the dark blood frozen to his skin. It appears he was clubbed from behind. A piece of black duct tape is across his mouth.

Joey pulls off her glove, about to remove the duct tape, when Colt says, "Do it fast. Like a Band-Aid, or you'll risk tearing the skin from his lips."

Porter nods emphatically that she should do what Colt says. He even makes a *mmm-hmmm* sound. Joey picks a small corner of the tape away with her fingernail until she has enough to get a grip on it.

"You ready?" she asks, eyes locked on Porter.

Mmm-hmmm.

She pulls the tape in one quick swipe. There is a sound like Velcro, and Porter painfully moans as the adhesive rips a layer of skin from his lips, leaving them bloody. Porter opens his mouth wide and uses his tongue to work a dirty rag from the back of his throat. It falls on his lap and then to the ground by his feet, moist with saliva and steaming. He leans back in the chair and sucks in a large drink of air that whistles through his teeth.

"How'd you get here?" Joey demands.

"C-cut me loose," Porter says. He shivers with terror and the cold.

"Who did this?"

"P-please, Joey. C-cut me loose. I-I c-can barely feel my f-fingers."

Joey takes her pocketknife from her hip pocket, flicks the blade out, and slips it between the rope binding Porter's wrists to the chair. After Porter's hands are free, he nearly falls out of the chair from exposure and exhaustion. Colt grabs him before he hits the ground.

"Let's get him back to the Cat," Colt says "Get under his arm and help me get him to his feet."

Joey quickly jumps into action.

"On three. Okay?"

Joey nods.

"One," Colt begins. "Two…"

Everything around them falls into darkness. The music cuts off, and a thick silence fills the void except for the wind and the ticking of the ice and snow hitting the band shell's roof.

"Colt?" Joey calls in the darkness.

The lights snap back on, without the music this time, blinding Colt. It takes a moment for his eyes to adjust. But when they do, he sees Joey's gaze shift past him, her face in the throngs of horror.

"Colt, look out!" she screams.

He snaps his head around, fear slices through his body like a scythe. The skeleton is only a foot away, rearing back to reveal the ice axe, poised to bring it down and bur it into his chest.

CHAPTER 27

Colt shoves Joey and Porter aside. She hits the band shell's cement floor on her elbow, which drives her shoulder into her jaw like a right hook. White light blasts behind her eyes. Stunned, Joey flips on her back in time to see the skeleton bring the ice axe down. Colt has left himself open to the oncoming strike by saving her and Porter's lives.

Look out! Joey wants to scream, but her throat constricts so tightly that even a whisper can't escape. But even if she could warn him, it's too late.

She watches helpless as the ice axe embeds itself in Colt's chest. The bloodcurdling wail of his agony cuts through Joey's soul like an avalanche coming down the mountain, loud, piercing, grinding away the peace in order of chaos.

Nooooo!

Hot tears bubble behind her eyes. *No. No. No.* She's shaking, not believing what her eyes witness. With the axe still in his chest, Colt looks at her with the eyes of a man who knows death has him in its grasp. She remembers the first time they met. Her heart began to beat, her palms grew sweaty, and when she went to say hello, it came out a broken, *hel-lo* like she was a dopey teenager with a crush. Now she's watching the man she loves die right before her eyes.

"Ru-un," Colt breathes.

The skeleton turns its attention to Joey. He rips the ice axe out of Colt's chest, knocks him aside, and bolts at her. But Joey's transfixed on Colt's motionless body facedown on the concrete.

"Joey! Move!"

She blinks out of her trance at Porter's shouting voice, just in time to see the ice axe fall. Rolling aside, the blade strikes the concrete, missing her by only a few millimeters. She crab-crawls backward, away from the murderer in the skeleton mask, as it rises and starts after her once more. Her feet slip in the snow. The skeleton quickly closes the gap between them; those eyeless sockets latched on her with determination, as if it foresaw her demise in bloody radiance. She reaches for the Glock on her hip, but there's no time to draw it from the holster and take the bastard down.

She closes her eyes…

"Joey! Duck!" Porter's voice breaks the night.

Her eyes snap open, and she looks past the skeleton to see Porter lunge for the tripwire. He wrenches the green fishing line. The spiked ball in the corner releases, hitting the skeleton in the upper right side of its chest. The blow lifts the figure off its feet and throws it into the back wall, where it bounces to the floor like a pinball. A painful gargle came from under the mask. Blood seeps through its fingers, clasped over the hole in its chest.

Joey shoots to her feet, dodges the ball of spikes as it comes back toward her like a deadly tetherball game. Blood drips from its spikes and dots the floor like paint falling from a brush. She runs to Colt and drops to her knees beside his still body, the out-of-control ball of spikes passing over her head.

"Joey!" Porter cries.

But her attention is on Colt. Is there anything she can do to save his life? *Oh, please, God!* She rolls him onto his back, expecting to find blood covering his body. To her surprise, there isn't any.

"Joey!" Porter again. "It's getting back up."

She looks over her shoulder to see the skeleton rising. In its left hand is the ice axe. The skeleton staggers across the stage toward Joey, the menacing stride of an injured killer to see its mission through to the bloody end. It's not out of the fight yet. *Not by a long shot.*

The skeleton is only inches from Joey now. The ice axe is raised over its shoulder. Behind the mask she can make out its hateful eyes. She realizes that she's never seen someone with such an ominous gaze, and it makes her body quake with unabated fear.

This is what a victim of a serial killer witnesses, just before they're murdered.

The skeleton shifts its weight, about to bring the axe around and into her skull when…

A figure tackles the skeleton before it can end her life.

Amos!

Amos and the skeleton hit the floor. They roll over top of each other before coming to a stop against the rear wall with Amos on top. He tries to pry the ice axe from the skeleton's hand, but the skeleton isn't relinquishing the weapon without a fight. Amos brings his elbow down into the skeleton's chest like a professional wrestler's elbow drop. A cough expels from under the mask from the blow to the chest, and the skeleton's hand goes lax from the ice axe's handle.

Amos stands, his chest heaving with each breath. He grabs the ice axe from the floor. He turns away to distance himself from their attacker, but is caught and pulled back. Joey sees what Amos hasn't in the fight. The axe's nylon leash is wrapped around the skeleton's wrist, preventing the weapon from being taken away.

The skeleton jerks on the leash, pulling Amos forward into a boot to the face. Joey jumps at the sight of the violent strike. Amos cries out, and his body crashes down onto his side, his busted lip bleeding.

The skeleton climbs to its feet, raises the ice axe, and swings it at Amos, defenseless on the floor directly below.

A crack of gunfire splits the night.

The index and middle fingers of the skeleton's left hand snap from around the handle at an odd angle and the ice axe is blown from its grip. Still, the leash keeps the axe connected to the skeleton's body. It falls back, cradling its bleeding hand—two fingers hang by strands of flesh, muscle, and tendons—and screams in panting horror as the pain, the shock, settles across its body.

Joey turns to find Colt on his side. In his hand is the Glock he took from the gun cabinet before they left, the barrel smoking.

"Shoot it again!" Porter screams.

The skeleton draws itself up and bolts for the window. Colt opens fire in rapid succession, but the rounds miss the skeleton. As it lunges for the window, Colt fires the last round, which hits directly below the skeleton as it hops over the stone wall and disappears.

Relief floods Joey. She bolts to her lover, drops to her knees, and cups her hands on his jaw. His whiskers on her fingertips are like the soft bristles of a fine brush.

"Are you alright?"

Colt strains to sit up, like a great weight is on his chest.

"I don't understand. How?" Joey asks, confusion tightening her face.

He reaches down and unzips the parka and pulls the jacket open. Joey's eyes go wide in amazement. *What are the odds?* His ranger badge gleams in the light. There is a dent in the center. It had stopped the ice axe from penetrating his chest.

Joey throws her arms around him. Tears of joy stream down her face and freeze on her skin.

"I thought I lost you," she says into his ear. She pulls away and looks deep into his dark blue eyes, thankful he had not been taken from her.

"I thought you did, too, for a moment." He goes to kiss her, but Porter interferes.

"Can we get the fuck out of here, please?"

CHAPTER 28

Colt thought he was dead when the ice axe hit him. Though he felt no pain and had no life-flashing-before-his-eyes moments, he thought how lucky he was not to feel anything when struck. What a blessing. But before he collapsed onto the floor, about to go to the great beyond, he remembered telling Joey to *run*.

It was shock. His eyes believed they saw the pick enter his body, and his mind reacted accordingly and shut itself off. Had the killer known he was still alive they might have delivered another strike that would have ended Colt's life.

But it had allowed Colt to get the upper hand for the first time that evening. Whoever was under the mask was severely injured now, with two fingers nearly blown off and a puncture wound to the chest. No concealment could hide those wounds.

Thankful to still be among the living, he watches Joey examine Porter's injuries back at RS1. The laceration to the back of Porter's head, where he told them he was struck, is a concern. The cut is deep, and Joey must sew it shut to stop the bleeding.

Now only in his skivvies, after Joey made him strip his clothing, Porter shakes uncontrollably. His skin is pale, and his lips are a blueish-purple color. His teeth click together like one of those wind-up chatter-teeth toys.

Joey reaches for the thermal blanket and drapes it over his bare shoulders, with a look of distress.

Amos comes into the room with a cup of steaming coffee, the mug small in his enormous paw. He passes the coffee to Porter. His hands tremble, and some brown liquid spills over the sides. The rope burns around his wrists stand out on his skin like two bright red rashes, the right one torn open in a long, wide gash and seeping blood. Another wound Joey will have to patch up.

"Sip it. And not too much too fast." Joey looks back at Amos. "Did you load that coffee with sugar?"

"Yes, ma'am,"

Colt knows Joey's worried about hypothermia. It decreases insulin secretion, which will put Porter into a hyperglycemic state. If his insulin levels fall too low, his body will begin to shut down, and death will follow. Sugaring the coffee will help stabilize his insulin levels so he doesn't crash. But they're not out of the woods.

"I'm concerned, Colt," Joey says. "We need to make sure he stays warm. But we don't want him to warm up too fast and risk cold blood shooting into his heart and giving him a heart attack."

"When can I question him?"

"In a little while."

"How long is *a little while?*"

"Maybe an hour."

Colt looks at his watch. It's going on nine, and he still hasn't heard from Tripp. Did he find a way through to Route 9? Or will Tripp come barreling through the door any moment with news that there's no passable way through Camp Southwoods Road?

Still, there's an option, one that Colt dislikes, but the reality of their situation dictates he must face it.

"What's wrong?" Joey asks, noticing Colt's troubled gaze.

"Tripp isn't back."

"Maybe he got stuck down there and can't get out," Joey says.

"That's what concerns me." Colt looks at Amos, who wears a contemptuous gaze like a glove. "What?"

"Do you really trust Tripp? He could be the one working with Flint."

"It wasn't Tripp who attacked us at the band shell," Colt says.

"You don't know that. It could've been anyone under that mask," Amos says.

"I agree. But not Tripp."

"And how would you know?"

"Because I looked the son of a bitch in the eyes tonight, twice, and neither time were they Tripp's eyes."

That seems to settle the debate, at least for the moment. But he can tell from Amos's dubious look that he isn't convinced.

"Can you get us back to Camp Southwoods Road in the Cat?"

"It'll be tight with all the overgrowth. And we'll have to go slower than slow. But I think we can make it, sure." Amos shrugs.

"You're not seriously thinking about going back out there," Joey says. "We nearly lost our lives fifteen minutes ago."

"I can't leave Tripp," Colt says.

"But you don't even know if he's stuck or not. He could be on his way back as we speak."

"Maybe so. But it's a risk I'm not willing to take. If it was one of us, Tripp would do the same."

Joey's eyes drift away. She knows Colt's right, even though she doesn't want to admit it out loud.

"It'll be okay."

"You don't know that."

She's right this time. Colt doesn't know if everything will be *okay*. But that's not going to stop him. If Tripp found a way through Camp Southwoods Road and over to Route 9 and was returning to tell them the good news, great. But if not, and he's stuck down there, or worse...

Colt shakes the thought away. He prays that nothing has gone wrong.

Joey studies him, her golden eyes a dull yellow, worried for Colt's safety, as if this may be the last time she sees him.

"Don't you do anything foolish out there, understand."

Twenty minutes later, Amos turns the Cat onto Camp Southwoods Road. The yellow gate is open, the steel bars bent. By the look of the gate, Colt figures that the lock must have been frozen shut, and Tripp had to pry it open to gain access to the road. The only sign that Tripp was there. Any tracks the plow made are long gone, buried under the fresh powder.

"Take it slow," Colt says. "There's no telling what condition the road's in."

Amos feathers the gas, and the Cat pounces onto the road. Low-hanging snowy branches scrape the windshield and scratch along the roof like a metal rake across macadam. The gooseflesh rises across Colt's arms.

Colt plucks the CB off the hook.

"Think that'll work?" Amos asks.

"We're well within the distance for the short-range to reach Tripp's plow."

"That didn't answer my question."

"Only one way to find out." He presses the button on the side of the microphone. "Tripp, this is Colt. Can you hear me? Over."

Static.

Colt tries again but gets the same response.

"Son of a bitch."

Amos steers the Cat around a sharp bend in the road, and the lights catch the welcome center ahead, now a mere shadow of its former self. As they near the dilapidated building, Colt sees the glass windows are long gone. A tree has come down across the peaked roof, caving it in and creating a long fissure spanning from the top of the building to its foundation.

"Why didn't they tear this down after the Carver murders?" Amos asks.

"Why worry about bringing a demolition crew in when Mother Nature can do it for free?"

"It's always about money."

Amos's words spark a memory. About a month ago, Colt got a call from his boss, Mike Thomas, wanting Colt's thoughts on the idea of the DCNR reopening Camp Southwoods to help offset costs, after the COVID Pandemic put a strain on the park's funds. When Colt told Mike he believed it was a bad idea—*fucking stupid idea*, were his actual words—the call abruptly ended. That wasn't what Mike wanted to hear. It didn't matter that Camp Southwoods was hallowed ground. In the end, it came down to money. To hell with the memory of those kids and what happened to them.

They pass the welcome center, and the road bends sharply to the left. The overgrowth falls away temporarily. The Cat's lights illuminate the pool area and the run-down ore house on the right, no more than ten feet from the road. Colt can vaguely make out the black rectangular shape of the inground pool cut into the earth, filled with snow. The three-tier diving platform, built for a state championship tournament in 1989, still stands. However, the diving boards are gone, probably at the bottom of the pool—*rotting away like everything else.*

The growth closes in around the road again, swallowing the Cat. It goes on this way for a mile before they come to the Y. Amos brings the Cat to a stop. Before them, the overgrowth of intertwining trees and brush was so thick that even sunlight couldn't penetrate the canopy, leaving the road in a perpetual shadow year-round.

"Which way?"

"Left. If you go right, it takes you to the camp."

Colt hears the clicking of Amos's throat and realizes this is the closest he's ever been to the camp. The ghost stories of the camp precede themselves.

Amos hits the gas again and maneuvers the Cat to the left. The cab rocks back and forth as the tracks easily climb over fallen trees and rocks.

As they drive, Colt's mind drifts back to how they found Porter and how lucky he was not to get frostbite. Though Porter was outside, the walls of the band shell must've given him enough blockage from the wind and snow that he hadn't succumbed to the elements. He was damn lucky.

But why didn't he kill Porter like the others?

It was a question that Colt wants to ask Porter when he can communicate. Something about the situation feels off. Everyone else was dead—*murdered.* Norm's and Wyatt's bodies were left for them to find. Lance in the accident on the bridge. But not Porter. And where the fuck is Dusty? On their way back from the band shell, they stopped at RS2, only to find it empty, Dusty nowhere to be found. Was Dusty working with Flint? Or was his body going to turn up somewhere, too, along with the rhyme. *Little Ranger Albert Running. Douggie Carver's gone a-hunting...*

Why did he keep Porter alive? The thought pesters Colt again. *Just to use him as bait?*

It made no sense.

This brings Colt to another concerning matter: why hide Rumor's body in the pit and not display it with a connection to the Carver murders like the others? And then there was Darryl, found dead in the snow. Had he fled the safety of the shed because someone was chasing him? Or did someone—maybe Flint—force him outside, where he met his end? Colt suspects he missed something vital that links the murders together.

"Shit!" Amos says, bringing Colt out of his thoughts.

"What?"

"There." Amos points.

Two red spheres float in the snowy darkness on the road ahead. At first, Colt doesn't understand what he sees. It looks like road flares are hung from the trees. *Another trap?* Yet, as they grow closer, petrifying disquiet hardens across Colt's body.

Tripp's plow has gone over the side of the Beaver Creek gorge.

The rear wheels and hopper hang in the air, the taillights—the red orbs—make the trees above look blood-covered.

"Did he not see the bridge was out?" Amos asks. He brings the Cat to a stop about ten feet from the plow.

"I don't know." Colt scans the area around the plow but sees nothing that tells him how it got that way. Concern for Tripp's well-being claws at him.

Colt opens the door, but Amos speaks before he can climb down.

"You want me to come with you?"

"No. Stay here. I don't want someone sneaking up on us or taking the Cat. If you see anyone, blow the horn."

"You trust me this time?"

"You saved our asses back at the band shell. Had you not been there…"

Amos gives an appreciative nod that their distrust can finally be put to bed.

Climbing down from the Cat, Colt pulls out his flashlight and turns it on. He aims the beam at the plow. Is Tripp okay? Is this nothing more than a mishap? An accident?

Alongside the plow, Colt pauses to catch his breath and to inspect the wreckage. By the looks of it, the plow hit the left field-stone brick wall of the bridge, pulverizing it to rubble before going over the side. He wonders, like Amos, if Tripp had been blinded in the whiteout, lost where he was on the road, and didn't see the bridge was out until the last minute. By then, it was too late.

He continues on to the lip of the creek. Though he cannot see the dark water below, he hears it rushing by, swift and strong. Aiming the flashlight at the creek bed, Colt scans the area nearly fifteen feet below. The plow sits at a 45-degree angle, and the blade has dug deep into the silt. Water pulls freshly disturbed sediment around the blade, muddying the creek water.

But there are no signs of Tripp down there, dead or alive.

Colt aims the flashlight at the cab about five feet below where he stands. If this was an accident, Tripp might still be inside, unconscious. Or dead. He knows he'll need to check the cab. But the cab's door is out of reach.

He'll have to climb onto the hopper and shimmy down to the driver's side door to access the cab. It won't be easy, especially in the snow and with the metal as slippery as ice.

But it's the only way.

Colt walks to the rear of the plow. Directly above his head is a three-rung ladder that leads to the top of the hopper, a safety measure in case the operator needs to check inside for any reason. He grabs the bottom rung and pulls himself onto the plow's side. There's no movement from the truck; it's dug too far into the silt to be unstable. *At least I have that going for me.* Along the bottom of the hopper is a small lip, just big enough for the tips of Colt's boots to fit into. By holding on to the top of the hopper and inching his way toward the cab, like a rock climber scaling a narrow, icy ledge, Colt believes he can reach the driver's door without any problems.

Yeah. Right.

He edges his way down the side of the plow. Snow falls from the lip above and rains onto his bare neck, sending a shiver down his body. It's slow and strenuous work. He has to rely almost entirely on his arm strength to keep him on the plow while simultaneously maneuvering himself toward the cab without falling. The muscles in his arms are on fire, and he can feel them jumping spasmodically from overuse.

He comes to the empty space between the hopper and the cab and steps off the ledge and onto the lockbox, where the operator keeps vital equipment like gloves, flares, and other tools of the trade. Colt takes a long breath and shakes the lactic acid buildup in his muscles. His heart hammers, and he's sucks wind like an asthmatic trying to run up multiple flights of stairs. He takes a deep breath; a hint of diesel fuel wafts up his nose. It's enough to worry him that one of the plow's fuel tanks is leaking, contaminating the earth and Beaver Creek below.

Another mess to clean up.

Colt takes hold of the pull-up bar along the driver's side door. Stepping off the lockbox, he places his foot on the plow's step…

And his foot slips on the icy metal.

Gravity pulls at him with everything it has. He goes down, down toward that rushing ice-cold black water below. His hand instinctively clenches around the pull-up bar, and before he can plunge into the water below, he slams face-first into the side of the plow. His forehead takes the brunt of the impact. It's like he's just been hit by a metal fist. Heat breaks out across the thin skin of his skull, and he feels a small goose egg forming.

Dangling from the side of the plow, his right arm feels like it's about to pull out of the socket, and the stitches, closing the gash, are so strained they feel like they're about to pop one by one like cut piano wire. He throws his left foot back up onto the tank. Using every ounce of energy, he digs his boot heel into the step and uses his leg as a lever to help pull himself up.

Once on the side of the plow, with his back against the door, his heart beating so hard he believes it will explode, he hears a voice call out from a far-off place.

It takes him a moment to realize it's Amos by the creek ledge.

"You okay?"

"Y-yes."

"Jesus, buddy. I thought you went down."

I almost did.

"I'm okay. Just lost my footing." Colt circles his right shoulder; nothing feels out of whack, but there's some tenderness in the joint and around the freshly sewn laceration. He just hopes he didn't tear anything internally or externally in the fall. "Get back to the Cat."

Amos nods.

Colt takes hold of the handle and pulls the cab door open…

There's no one inside.

Despair floods his mind like a dam bursting.

Without Tripp, how are we going to get the snowmobiles back together? The worry sets deeper into his mind like a disease. *None of us are going to make it out of here alive.*

The battery has kept the plow's electrical system working, but the engine is dead. Colt looks to the CB radio and realizes Tripp wouldn't have gotten his calls even if he had been in the cab. The radio is dead from a single strike from something sharp—*an ice axe?*—through its brain.

Colt goes to turn around and climb back down when a cold, wet hand wraps around his wrist. He revolts, trying to jerk away, but the slimy hand remains clamped around his wrist, preventing him from moving. He thinks the skeleton had lain in wait for this moment to strike.

"Colt…" a voice speaks. "Colt, is that you?"

He leans forward. There, tucked into the small, dark space of the passenger side footwell, lips blue, soaked to the bone, and shivering, is Tripp Thatcher.

CHAPTER 29

"How do you feel, Porter?" Joey asks.

"Warm. Finally."

Porter lightly touches the back of his head with his fingertips, where three stitches connect the gash in a lightning-bolt slash. Joey eases his hand away. He'll infect the wound if he messes with it. He winces at her touch. His bandaged right wrist required five stitches to close the wound left from the rope's binding.

"Leave it alone. You don't need an infection on top of every-thing else right now." She grabs a liquid thermometer lying on the table beside the bunk. "Open."

She places it under his tongue. When they got Porter back to RS1, her preliminary check of his vitals revealed his body temper-ature was dangerously low at 94.9—on the cusp of becoming hypothermic. She hopes Porter's temperature has risen with the blanket, a warm, sugary drink, and a few thermal heat packs.

She gathers the medical trash, takes it to the wastepaper can, and disposes of it. When she returns, she pulls the thermometer from Porter's mouth and checks the mercury readout.

"Ninety-six-point-two. Your body temperature is steadily rising back to normal." She looks Porter over. His color is returning; the blueish purple of his lips is gone; the tips of his fingers appear normal. "You're fortunate you didn't get frostbite out there."

"Don't I know it." Porter wiggles his fingers.

"Do you remember what happened at the antenna shed?"

"Someone jumped me."

"When you got there or before?"

"When I got there. I had just unlocked the door and was about to enter when something struck me…" Porter points to the wound on the back of his head. "That was the last that I remember until I woke up."

"At the band shell?"

Porter shakes his head. "In a room somewhere."

"Did you recognize anything?"

"No. My face was covered with that hood the entire time."

"What about voices? Did you hear anyone speaking? Someone you knew, perhaps?"

He looks at her uncomfortably, his facial muscles jump as he tries to understand her question.

"Someone I knew?"

"Maybe Flint's voice?"

"Why would I have heard Flint's voice?"

"Colt and I suspect he's involved. Maybe behind everything that's been going on today," Joey confesses.

"Flint? Why would…"

"We believe he was working with Darryl and Rumor to help advance his position in the park."

Porter's steel-blue eyes dart back and forth to understand Flint's participation. Then he makes the connection, and his eyes turn dark, almost black.

"So he could get the head ranger position," Porter says.

"We believe so." A strange look that she's never seen before works across Porter's face. *Anger? Rage?* Joey believes it's both.

"Did Flint have something to do with the distress call last summer, too?"

Joey doesn't respond. She wants to keep Porter talking about his attack and abduction, not get sidetracked about his father's death or who might be responsible. *Murdered,* Colt had said. *Pushed. God, if that is true.* Still, she aimed to dissect as much information as possible from him. The more they knew, the better their chance of surviving the night. However, she does want to come back to his father. There's something she needs to know that might be important: why Maynard was acting so strangely the day of the hurricane.

"How long were you out there on the band shell stage?"

His shoulders lift. "I have no idea. Half hour...maybe."

Joey looks back at his fingers. *Damn lucky to not have frostbite.*

"How'd you get there?"

"I was put on the back of a snowmobile."

"How long was the ride?"

"I don't know." He brings his right hand up to his face and pinches the bridge of his nose. "I was in and out of consciousness."

"You really are lucky to not have gotten frostbite."

Porter drops his hand and looks up at her, smiles thinly. There's something about his smile that rubs her the wrong way.

"You said that already."

"I know. It's just a miracle. It's negative zero out there with the wind chill. Are you sure you were on the stage that long?"

"I suppose it might've been less. Like I said, I was disoriented, confused, and my head was thumping, so..." He gives her a pitiful look, like a puppy with a thorn in its paw.

Reasonable. She dismisses her earlier thoughts about his smile as nothing more than her tired mind's perception of things. When you don't know who to trust, you trust no one. But what did she expect? For Porter to describe details when he couldn't see what was happening, and suffering from a concussion no doubt?

"Porter, there's something else I need to ask you. It's about your father." He shifts awkwardly in the chair. "The day of the hurricane, your father was acting strange, like he was distracted about something. Did he ever mention anything to you about what might have been on his mind?"

Porter slowly shakes his head. "No. Nothing."

"Are you sure?"

"Yes. And besides, even if something was bothering my dad, it's not like he would've told me."

This is news to Joey.

"I thought you and your dad were close?"

"We got along. But I wouldn't say we were close."

She didn't know that. And, if true, she feels terrible for Porter. Maynard had treated her like a daughter. She saw him as an intelligent, loving, and kind human being, someone you could always turn to when you needed advice or a laugh when you were down. And not just with her, but with anyone—ranger, park guest, or stranger. It was a shame that Porter missed out on that side of Maynard. But she can't help but wonder what had soured their relationship.

"Why was that?"

"We just didn't see things the same way, that's all. Dad was Dad at home."

Joey leaves it there. She understands that the dynamic between father and son can be tumultuous, especially when they are also coworkers. She wants to ask more, but feels she would be prying into personal issues she has no right to.

"Why don't you lie back and get some rest."

She returns to the main part of RS1, and sits at her desk. The thought of closing her eyes, even for just a few minutes, is enticing, but she fears that if she drifts off—

The power goes out.

The shadows spring around Joey like a trap.

She nearly screams but cups a hand over her mouth, stifling it.

"Joey!" Porter calls from the bunkroom.

"It's okay! The power just went out. The generator should kick on any minute."

But the generator doesn't come on. The shadows remain, free

to linger, to smother. The wind outside is stronger than Joey's heard all evening, rushing past RS1 so fast and hard she thinks she can practically feel it sucking RS1 off its foundation. Now bathed in silence, the soft scratches of a tree branch on the outside wall—*screech, screech, screech* – work their way into her like nails across a chalkboard. She has no doubt that the storm must've blown a tree down across a power line or taken the lines down itself—either was possible in the turbulent wind.

The generator should've come on by now. Did someone sabotage it, like the snowmobiles in the shed and the radios? *Flint, you son of a bitch.*

Joey fumbles to find the desk's drawer handle in the dark. She opens the drawer and her fingers roam inside until she feels the long, cylindrical object she is searching for. A flashlight. She turns it on. The shadows snap back, scared of the light.

"Joey?" Porter calls again.

"Be right there. I have a flashlight."

But what we don't have is heat. Without the generator to run the furnace, it won't take long for RS1 to become an ice box. And with Porter recovering from exposure, that's the last thing he needs. Until Joey can resolve the issue with the generator, she'll have to do everything she can to keep Porter warm so his body doesn't recess into hypothermia.

She crosses the room and starts back down the hallway. Porter is propped up on his elbows in the bunk where she left him.

"Why isn't the generator running?" he asks.

"I don't know. But I need you to get dressed."

He nods, throws the covers aside, and quickly starts to pull on clothing that Joey had gotten from his locker and put on the stand beside his bunk.

A loud *bang* causes the entire building to shudder.

"What the hell was that?" Porter asks looking up, eyes probing the darkness behind Joey.

"Stay here."

She starts toward the bunkroom door.

"Joey…wait," Porter calls after her, trying to get into his pants.

Ignoring him, she walks down the hall to the reception area. She sucks in a breath of cold air that freezes every nerve.

The front door hangs open, the wind rocking it back and forth. A sheen of fresh powder that looks like the purest sugar she's ever seen has blown across the wooden floor and sparkles under the flashlight's beam.

That door was locked. It couldn't have blown open.

"Joey? What's going on? Talk to me."

"The door blew open!"

Is that really what happened?

She has to be sure. *Can't leave anything to assumptions—the mother of all fuckups.*

Moving to the threshold, she finds the door frame broken. Splinters of wood and the strike plate lay on the floor at her feet, dusted with snow.

The wind didn't do that. Only a person could have—

The floorboards under her feet shift with the weight of another person close behind. Joey spins, reaches for the Glock to face or kill whoever is behind her. But as she comes around, two large hands spring from the darkness and grab hold.

CHAPTER 30

Once Tripp is inside the Sno-Cat, Colt jumps in the rear seat beside him. He tells Amos to crank the heat and get them back to RS1 as quickly as possible. While Amos drives, Colt helps Tripp strip his wet clothes and boots. He notices that the first three toes on Tripp's right foot are waxy. Frostbite. He pulls a thermal blanket from a small compartment over the rear seat and throws it over Tripp's shoulders. His entire body is white, his lips blue, but he isn't shaking - a sign he's hypothermic. Colt pops a few instant heat packs from the first aid kit and places one in Tripp's hands, one on his stomach, and two more under each of his arms, hoping to raise his core temperature.

"Put your feet on my lap." Colt helps lift Tripp's frozen legs onto him. He pops the final heating pack and lightly holds it against the waxy, white toes.

"He was waiting for me inside the cab," Tripp says. "Like he knew I was going to be down there. How in the hell could he have known that? After I got away from him, he tried to run me down with the plow and almost had me. Had I not jumped out of the way, and into the creek, at the last second, I'd be dead right now."

"Was it someone wearing a skeleton mask?" Tripp meets Colt's intense stare with a how-did-you-know-look. "He came after us, too."

"Who is this guy?"

"Someone working with Flint." Colt wiggles the big toe on Tripp's right foot. Tripp doesn't seem to notice.

"My, God." Tripp shakes his head as if trying to shake away a bad dream. "I never thought Flint capable of something like this."

"Where are we?" Colt asks Amos.

"Coming up on the welcome center now." The lights on the Cat catch the dilapidated building in front of them.

"We're trapped in this park," Tripp says. "This was our last opportunity to get out."

"We can use the snowmobiles to get around the deadfall. Then get to the sheriff's station in Jackson and bring back help." Colt wiggles Tripp's second toe. Again, Tripp doesn't seem to notice.

"You're crazy if you think that's a good idea. In this storm— it's suicide."

"We have a bigger problem to deal with before we get to that point," Colt says.

"Bigger than losing my cigar case in the creek?"

"Afraid so." Colt knows what the case means to Tripp. He wishes there was something he could do to retrieve it. But it was gone. Most likely lost in the creek when Tripp went into the water. The thought makes Colt feel worse. "The snowmobiles are wrecked. Someone disabled'em so we can't use them. But Darryl —before he died—thought they could be repaired." Colt realizes by the shock on Tripp's face that he doesn't know about Amos finding Darryl buried in the snow. He quickly fills him in and then continues on about the snowmobiles. "I hope you can take a look at them as soon as you get warm. Maybe repair them. And then we can get someone on the way to the sheriff's station in Jackson to bring back help." Colt pinches Tripp's third toe. "You feel that?"

"Feel what?" Tripp's eyes drift to his toes. Colt didn't think Tripp could get any whiter, but it happens. "Oh! That's bad."

"Yeah," Colt says. "How bad, I don't know. Joey will have to look at them."

"Think I'll lose 'em?"

"Hard to tell."

The Cat shifts and bobs as Amos turns it onto Route 206. It won't be long before they're back to RS1.

"Why don't you lie back and rest," Colt says. "You're our only hope of getting us help."

Twenty minutes later, Amos pulls the Cat directly beside the door of RS1 and cuts the engine. It shimmies to a hard stop. The entire ranger station is as dark as a mausoleum and just as unnervingly still and dead quiet as one sitting in the middle of a forgotten graveyard. The storm must've finally taken out the power. *Surprised it took this long in these winds.* And still, there's another fret looming, deepening the worry for Joey and Porter inside. It makes Colt consider another possibility; one the winds weren't responsible for.

"Why hasn't the generator come on?" Colt asks.

"It's automatic. It should have fired up a second or two after the power went out. I don't—"

"Stay here," Colt says. Something has gone wrong. "I'll go check it out."

When Colt reaches RS1's front door, it blows open. A disease of blackness has infected the interior. He turns on the flashlight and sweeps the beam around, finding no one.

As he steps through the doorway, his right boot kicks something, sending it skidding to parts unknown. Colt arcs the beam across the floor. He spots the strike plate beside the front desk, where he kicked it. He turns back and aims the beam at the doorframe. Colt swallows what feels like large chunks of ice that scrape the lining of his throat raw. Someone had gotten in by force.

He turns and hurries down the hallway. Are Joey and Porter

safely holed up somewhere back there? *You should have never left them.* His hurting lower-back muscles draw so tight with this thought that they feel like they're about to snap. Though there's a chill in the air, Colt realizes this part of the building is still relatively warm. The power wasn't out long. As he moves down the hall, he checks the kitchen and the bathrooms. Both are empty.

His concern deepens into despair, especially for the woman he loves. Hurrying to the end of the hall, Colt charges into the bunkroom.

But it's empty, like the rest of RS1.

That awful feeling of being too late—again—to save those he's responsible for crashes over him like a breaking wave pummeling him into the sand, driving the air from his lungs, and filling his mouth with salty water. He realizes then that what he's tasting isn't salt water but his tears. Someone broke in and attacked Joey and Porter. *I should've been here to protect them!*

But he wasn't there for Joey. Or Porter. Or any of the others. He let everyone down, just like he had let Maynard down by not being by his side. He was responsible for their safety, and his actions and orders had cost them their lives.

You don't know if Joey and Porter are dead.

With this thought comes a sense of vigor. Maybe they got out? Perhaps they're hiding somewhere nearby? He wonders if his wishful thinking is a way for his brain to cope with the fact that he was a failure as their leader.

No. You can't give up.

He returns to the Cat and climbs in beside Tripp.

"What's going on?" Tripp asks, sitting up with the thermal blanket around his body.

"Looks like someone forced their way into the station. Joey and Porter are gone."

They're silent for a long moment, the ramifications weighing heavily on them. Tripp is the first to speak.

"So, what now?"

"We need to get that genny running. Amos, think you can look at it?"

"Sure. But I'll need some tools from the storage closet in the bunkroom."

Colt nods and turns back to Tripp.

"We need to get you inside. I'll have to slip your boots back on so you can walk through the snow, okay?"

Tripp nods, but the look on his face tells Colt he'd rather do anything else than try to get wet boots back on his frozen feet. Colt picks up his left boot and helps Tripp into it without a problem. His right foot, with the frostbitten toes, is another matter.

"Go easy. My toes are burning and tingling so bad it's like someone is roasting them over a flame."

Tripp winces as Colt slides the boot over his frostbitten toes, careful not to touch the skin, which will rind the dead flesh off as easily as a banana peel.

"One? Two? Or three?"

Tripp nods.

"One…"

Colt shoves the boot on, and Tripp's heel clicks into place. He cries out through his teeth.

"Thought you said three?"

"I asked you: one, two, or three. You just nodded. I took that as one."

"Cute."

Colt laces up the boots. He looks back at Amos.

"Help me get him inside."

After getting Tripp down from the Cat and inside RS1, Colt secures the front door, placing a chair under the handle. It won't do anything to keep someone out, but it will keep the wind and snow from blowing in until Amos can get the generator running and the light back so they can see to repair it.

"Let me grab some tools from the storage closet and go look at the genny," Amos says.

"Bring the first aid kit and some warm clothes for Tripp," Colt says.

Amos nods and disappears down the hall with a flashlight. Colt turns back to Tripp and kneels to get the wet boots off his feet. The left one comes off with a hard tug, but the right won't budge.

"You'll have to cut it off," Tripp says. "My foot's starting to swell."

Colt hurries to his office for a pair of scissors from his desk. What he finds stuns him. The front left desk drawer is open, empty. Though Colt hadn't seen it, he knows what was in there. *The folder!* The one Joey took from Flint's locker and put in his desk for safe keeping. Flint must have taken it so no one could link him to the crimes.

There's nothing he can do about it now. He grabs a pair of heavy-duty scissors to cut Tripp's boot off and steps out of the office when he spots a red glow under the front desk. There is no power to RS1, and he knew there was nothing electronic under the desk. Something was there that shouldn't have been. He bends down and sweeps the flashlight's beam around under the desk.

"Holy shit!"

"What?" Tripp's voice floats through the darkness.

A handheld CB radio has been duct taped to the inside corner of the front desk, out of everyone's view. Had the lights not been out, Colt would never have seen the red glow from the light on the top, indicating that it was functioning. But the CB isn't just any CB, Colt realizes. It's Norm's CB radio, the one he had on him when he died, the one that was missing when they found him. He pulls it free. The speaker button has another piece of duct tape across to keep the line open.

Everything they said, everything they spoke of inside RS1 had been heard.

"This is how Flint's accomplice knew where we were going to be," Colt says, shining the light onto the CB so Tripp can see it.

"The son of a bitch has been listening to us all night. He knew our every move."

"That means he was close to us the entire time," Colt says. "At least within a half mile or so to make sure he could pick up the signal through the storm without interference."

"Smart fucker."

Colt slams the CB down on the desk, shattering its communication to the outsider's ears.

He returns to Tripp and begins cutting the boot away, splaying it down the side and along the front until he can slide the swollen foot out sideways. Tripp cries as the fabric brushes over his toes.

"Sorry."

From the bunkroom, there comes a loud crash, and Amos's baritone voice, edged with shock, cuts through the darkness.

"Holy fuck!"

Colt shoots to his feet, pulls the Glock, and bolts to the bunkroom. As he darts into the room, he finds Amos standing there, wide-eyed with surprise, the flashlight's beam trained into the closet. Someone clambers out from that dark closet, their hands held up, blocking the light from their squinting eyes.

"T-take it e-easy," a shaky voice trembles. "It's m-me. P-Porter."

CHAPTER 31

"What the hell happened?" Colt helps Porter to his feet. The man is fully dressed—snow pants, boots, parka, and gloves. "Where's Joey?"

"Someone took her."

"Was it Flint?" Amos asks.

"I didn't see who it was," Porter replies. "I was back here."

"You didn't try to help?" Amos steps closer, agitation at Porter's lack of action to help Joey fumes off him in hot waves.

"Of course! But the lights went out, and we were in the dark. By the time I was dressed and found my way out there, Joey was gone. I came back and hid in the closet."

Any semblance of finding Joey drowns in a sea of discontent. A sudden urge to slap him comes over Colt. How could he let someone—Flint? His accomplice?—get to Joey—*why didn't you protect her!* But he suppresses the impulse that threatens to detonate his anger at Porter. It wasn't his fault. Besides, Porter was helpless and disoriented when the lights went out, not to mention that he was in no physical shape to protect anyone. *That was your job, Colt.* But that was the play from the beginning, Colt believes. They waited for them to leave before coming after Joey. But why only take her? Why leave Porter behind, and alive?

Amos steps past them into the closet and grabs a bucket of tools.

"I'll go see what's wrong with the genny," he says, and hurries out of the room.

"There was nothing I could do, Colt," Porter pleads, his voice cracking like a child begging for forgiveness.

Colt turns away without another word and follows Amos back to the front door. He removes the chair holding the door in place, while Amos zips up his coat and adjusts the goggles over his eyes.

"When you get back, knock three times so we know it's you," Colt says, feeling the wind pushing against the door, trying to get in, trying to get to them, to kill, just like whoever's out there hunting them.

Amos gives him the thumbs-up sign.

Colt pulls open the door, and Amos charges through the threshold into the storm and vanishes around the corner. He slams the door and replaces the chair under the handle.

"What now?" Porter asks.

"Amos is going to try to get the genny up and running. And we're going to try to fix the snowmobiles," Colt says. "And get someone to the sheriff's station in Jackson."

"I still think it's a bad idea to try to get out of the park on one of them."

"We have to try, Tripp."

"But it's not ideal. One of those skis gets stuck or hits a—"

"I know. But what choice do we have?" Colt asks. He sees a thought work behind Tripp's keen eyes. It's a look he's seen before while Tripp was figuring out how to repair something, his mind working through the mechanics. "What?"

"There's still a ham radio in the old fire tower above Snyder Point."

"So?"

"So, I'm betting it still works. If we can make it up there on the snowmobiles, maybe we can use it to call the state police—they still work on the same UHF 800 megahertz open-standard network. If we're going to reach someone, that radio's our best shot."

"I don't know."

"It's a better idea than taking the snowmobiles through the woods. At least there are trails leading to the tower that we know are suitable to drive the snowmobiles on."

Colt calculates the risks. The fire tower above Snyder Point was six and a half miles away from RS1. They could make it in under an hour on the sleds, even in this weather, and if the radio up there still works, they'd be in contact with the state police in no time. But there's a problem.

"How will you power the radio even to make the call?" Colt asks.

"The tower has its own genny."

"Yeah, but does it still run?"

"Should. Shot of carbon cleaner into the engine should fire her right up."

"That generator hasn't been started since the tower was decommissioned in 2019. There's no telling what shape it'll be in, Tripp."

"I can get it running. Trust me."

"I do," Colt says honestly. After he found Tripp, nearly frozen to death inside the plow, he had no reason not to trust him.

"Besides," Tripp says, reaching down and rubbing the top of his right foot, just above the waxy toes. "I know Cleve Kingston left some Cuban cigars up there."

Colt hadn't heard the name Cleve Kingston since his retirement in early 2020, just before the pandemic hit and ground the world to a stop. Cleve was an old-timer who used to man the fire tower before the park system fully switched over to using satellite imagery for wildfire detection in 2019. He spent many nights on duty, alone, at the fire tower. *It's my home away from home,* Colt remembers Cleve saying.

"Cigars?"

Tripp's eyes burn with delight.

"I brought them back for Cleve when Aleja and I would visit her family in Florida. Her father still had some pre-embargo tobacco from the 1950s that he'd roll for us. Good smoke, man. Cleve used to smoke them when he was up there by himself, so his old lady wouldn't find out. When he retired, he told me he left a few in a sealed container in the desk. Said I should go get them. I never bothered."

Torment fills Tripp's face. And Colt understands why he never went to get the cigars. They remind him of his late wife, and the good times he had with her family, of the life they had together before her passing.

"But now you want to. So, all of this is for a…cigar?"

"Well, it's a very refined cigar. But no. All of this is so we can get the hell out of here. The cigars are just a bonus incentive for me to risk my life to do it," Tripp says with a smirk.

Colt's unsure if the risk is worth the reward. He looks down at Tripp's feet. God only knew the damage the cold did to his toes, which will cause him problems walking, let alone climbing a six-story tower in the middle of a whiteout. And even if Tripp does make it to the cab, Colt worries if he'll even be able to get the generator started after all this time. And if he does, will the ham radio reach anyone, or will their calls for help fall on deaf ears? It was a long shot.

"Don't worry. I'll be able to make it," Tripp says as if reading Colt's mind. But the empty, hollow look on Tripp's face tells Colt he really should rest.

There are three hard raps on the front door. Porter hurries to it, removes the chair, and pulls it open. Amos rushes in.

"Generator's dead," he says, lifting his goggles. "Someone cut the fuel lines and smashed the carburetor. There's nothing I can do."

"Fuck!" Colt screams. "In an hour, this place will be near zero."

"I'm right, Colt," Tripp says. "The tower's our only option."

"Right about what?" Amos asks, looking from Tripp to Colt. "What are we talking about?"

"Tripp thinks that instead of trying to get around the blocked exits, we should try for the fire tower above Snyder Point. Use a ham radio up there to call the state police *if* the generator works."

"You can't do that alone. Not in your condition," Amos says, looking at Tripp.

"Oh, you trust me now, too, huh?"

"I can't think you did that to yourself." Amos's eyes drift down to Tripp's toes. "I can help with the snowmobiles, too. And if there are any problems with the generator, I can help with that, as well."

Tripp looks back at Colt, raising his eyebrows in a whatcha-think look.

"I don't know," Colt says. He worries that it'll be a fruitless attempt, that they won't be able to get the generator going just with a shot of carburetor fluid.

"Tripp's right about not trying to take the snowmobiles through the woods, Colt. You know he is," Porter says. "Our best bet of reaching help is the radio in that tower."

"Okay," Colt finally relents after some thought. *What did he know about fixing a generator anyway to argue with Tripp?* "Do it."

CHAPTER 32

When Joey emerges from the abyss that holds her captive, she's on a hard, cold floor. She tries to sit up, but a stabbing pain behind her left eye forces her back down. Air rushes into a cut above her eyebrow. It stings. The blood on her face is like frozen syrup stuck to her skin, stiff and tacky. She can't remember anything after the hands shot from the darkness.

Until now.

Her wrists are bound with rope behind her back. She tries to wiggle them free, but it's too tight to slip the knot. Rolling onto her side, she uses her abdominal muscles to pull herself up. Her head pounds as she sits upright in a haphazard position, making her look like a bent screw. She swings her legs in front of herself and uses the heels of her boots to push herself back into the wall.

With her heart pounding and sweat beads running down her face, she sucks in a breath of stale air. She's in a dark room. Cold air whistles through the slats of the bare wooden walls. There are no windows, and it smells musty and dank from nonuse.

Was this where Porter was held?

Another smell comes to her. It's faint, but pleasant. A warming scent that causes Joey's cold body to yearn for heat.

Burning wood.

Her eyes flick to a door. Oily light spills under the bottom of the door and onto the floor like orange soda. There's a fire going outside her windowless prison.

Where the hell am I?

The sharp pain behind her left eye returns, like a fire poker being driven into her brain. She closes her eyes, tries to focus on breathing until the discomfort eases.

A creak on the other side of the door draws her attention back to it. Slowly, the door opens; the old rusty hinges groan like those in a haunted house. The warmth from the other room spills over her body, her greedy, frozen pores suckle up the heat. Light cuts across her face, blinding her, and the pain in her head worsens. She pulls away like a vampire from the rising sun.

Someone is with her now, watching her. Their presence fills the doorway and the room, a malevolent entity full of hate and anger.

Colt hears the rev of two snowmobiles. *Son of a bitch, they did it.* He looks at Porter. The surprise on his face is indescribable. Like Colt, he didn't expect Tripp to come through. But Colt never doubted Tripp, not once. The man was a magician with mechanics. He pulls the chair away from the door. Amos enters, with Tripp limping in behind him, discomfort from his bandaged toes pulls his face into a scowl.

"We're good to go," Tripp says. "Darryl was right. Someone meticulously took them apart. There wasn't a bolt, cable, or hose broken."

"That's odd," Porter says.

"Maybe not," Tripp replies thoughtfully. "I think someone was going to put them back together and use them to get out of the park after all this was over."

"Why would they need to do that, if they already had a snowmobile?" Porter asks. "Makes no damn sense."

Good question. But Colt doesn't have an answer.

"Well, let's not give them that opportunity." Colt looks at Tripp for a long moment, knowing this could be the last time they see one another, if things go awry. He sticks out his hand. Tripp takes it. "Good luck."

"We're going to need it."

Tripp and Amos turn and head back into the storm, to the waiting snowmobiles idling in front of RS1. Colt and Porter stand in the doorway, watching them mount the machines. Both snowmobiles are equipped with a gas can to fill the generator at the fire tower. It's their only hope at this point and Colt prays to God that Tripp is right about the radio. The throttles whine, and the snowmobiles take off toward Snyder Point. *Godspeed, men,* he thinks before closing the door and replacing the chair.

"What now?" Porter asks.

"We're going to find Joey."

"That's easier said than done. She could be anywhere in the park, if she's still alive."

Porter bound to the chair on the band shell stage flashes back into Colt's mind. His gaze shifts to Porter's hands. *No sign of frostbite.* And if he has no frostbite, it must have meant that Porter was kept somewhere warm until the trap was ready to be sprung. *Keep the bait alive long enough to lure the prey.*

"What do you remember between the time when you were attacked at the antenna shed and when you woke up?"

"Not much." The muscles jump on Porter's face as he recalls his traumatic abduction. "Snippets of a room."

"A room?" Porter nods, his face grim. "It had to be somewhere with a heat source. Otherwise, you'd have frostbite. Think. What do you remember about that room? Anything you saw. Heard. Smelled."

Porter straightens.

"Smoke. I remember smelling wood smoke."

"Perfect. What else?"

"I don't know." Porter shakes his head; the anguish on his face makes it look like someone is ripping his fingernails out with pliers as he tries to put the pieces of his missing hours back together. "It smelled…old. Musty. Unused for a long time."

"What kind of room was it? Big? Small? Was it dirty? Clean?" Colt presses.

"It was dirty. And drafty. I felt wind coming through the walls."

"But there was a heat source—you said you remember smelling wood smoke—like from a fireplace, perhaps."

"Yeah. Maybe." Porter thinks about it. "But there are no buildings around the park that have fireplaces."

"No places in use," Colt says.

Porter's eyes meet his with alarm, as he puts together what Colt already has.

"Camp Southwoods," Porter breathes.

"If you were taken there, held there, then maybe that's where Joey is, too."

CHAPTER 33

Amos and Tripp make it to the fire tower above Snyder Point in about fifty-five minutes. They're nearly frozen to the bone when they cut the engines. Amos realizes Tripp was right about not trying to drive the sleds to Jackson. *Even if we didn't hit anything, we would've frozen to death before we reached the sheriff's station.* Dismounting the machine, Amos lumbers to the base of the tower. The structure looms 175 feet above his head, a wooden behemoth creaking in the wind. He cranes his head to the cab above, and a strike of pain shoots down the center of his back and digs in under his right shoulder blade like a fishhook. He tries to put the discomfort out of his mind. The snow fog encapsulates the top of the structure, hiding the cab from his view.

"You think it's safe to go up?" Amos asks, looking at the wooden steps winding up inside the tower's four support legs.

"Only one way to find out." Tripp limps to the wooden stairs, places his foot on the first step, and pushes his weight on it. "Seems okay."

"I don't think testing one step proves it's structurally sound." Amos nervously rubs his neck as the thought of going up those slippery, old stairs snakes through his mind. Anything could go wrong.

"Oh, sorry. I'll go and see if the elevator's still in operation."

"Don't be daft."

Tripp smiles, cranes his head, and squints his eyes against the falling snow.

"Well, I'll tell you this, Amos, we won't know until we know. It's either we stay down here and take our chances with that madman, or we risk our lives trying to get up there and get that radio up and running so we can call for help."

"If it even works."

"Trust me. It still works."

The wind whistles through the beams overhead; they groan and moan under the storm's onslaught. Amos's neck tightens further; he worries whether the entire structure will support their weight after all these years of abandonment. He pushes his fingers deeper into the meat, kneading the knot of muscle at the base of his skull that feels as hard as a stone.

"Grab a can," Tripp says, heaving the gas off the back of the snowmobile.

They take the steps slow and steady because of Tripp's toes and the fear of them breaking under their weight. They work their way up the circular wooden stairs to the third of the six platforms before pausing to catch their breath. Lugging their gear and the cans through a vertical maze in the cold has drained their energy fast. So far, the fifty-year-old, weather-beaten and worn tower seems sturdy enough. Of course, Amos knows this can change with the next step or the step after that, causing either of them to plummet to their deaths if one breaks under their weight.

"Let's keep moving!" Tripp hollers over the shrieking wind.

Amos nods. The wind is as loud as a warning siren so high up on the tower. The ice pellets sting his face like he's being hit with flecks of sharpened metal.

They continue on. The wind and snow worsen the higher they climb. The structure sways back and forth with just enough movement that the tower reminds Amos of being on a wooden boat adrift at sea. His stomach lurches, and if he'd eaten any food in the last two hours, he's sure it would've come back up.

Coming to the fifth platform, they pause again to catch their breath. Beyond the structure, Amos sees that they are now above the pine trees that surround the tower. Visibility is only about ten to fifteen feet at best. When he looks down, the legs of the tower fade into a white cloud. The ground is there, but he can no longer see it.

Tripp taps him on the shoulder.

"Let's go!"

They start again and work their way up the last flight of stairs. Tripp is the first to make it to the cab's platform.

"Firm as a bodybuilder's ass up here!"

Yeah. Sure. Amos wants to believe him, but he's positive rot and structural decay put them in danger. Lucky for him, he can't see how high they are, but it does nothing to squelch the vertigo feeling. *Just keep calm.* He never liked heights—ledges, high buildings, cliffs all freak him the fuck out. So why did he come, knowing he'd be climbing the tower? The answer, at least in Amos's mind is easy: If he didn't help, if he stood by in paralyzed fear, he wouldn't be able to look his daughter, Aisha, in the eyes. His fear of Aisha thinking of her daddy as a coward, was greater than his fear of heights. Though he is seriously reconsidering that opinion at the moment.

"You okay?" Tripp yells, sensing Amos's anxiety.

Amos shakes his head. "I hate heights!"

"Go inside. It'll be better in there for you." Trip hands Amos his ring of keys, the one to unlock the cab's door pinched between his thumb and index finger.

Amos doesn't argue. He knows he'll feel better inside, where there's no wind and snow and no ledge where he can be blown off if a severe gust comes along. He leaves Tripp with the two gas cans by the generator and heads for the door. Unlocking it, he steps inside and closes it behind himself. The howling wind is shuttered. But it pushes against the cab with a low rumble. The windows, which give a 360-degree view of the park on a clear day, shake. There are few amenities in the tower. A wood stove, a small kitchenette, two wooden rockers, and two cots with a small end table between them. An AM/FM radio sits on top of the end table. A desk and chair are in the middle of the cab. On the desk is the ham radio.

First things first.

Amos goes to the woodstove. Next to it, there's a pile of wood and a bucket for water to put the fire out. They will need to keep warm while trying to reach someone.

He opens the woodstove door and inspects the firebox. The stove's interior is clean of ash but overflowing with spider webs. *Eww!* Spiders weren't his favorite creatures. He gathers the webbing on his glove like cotton candy on a stick at a carnival, and then shakes it off to the floor. He then begins to place the logs in the stove. The wood is dried through and should light with just a match.

Amos shines the beam around the stove and finds a pack of long wooden matches on the mantle above. He lifts the box and shakes it. It's not full, but more than enough matches are inside to get the stove going.

Striking a match, the cab brightens in a warm glow, and the shadows recede to the far corners, eagerly waiting for the match to snuff out so they can spring forth again. It stays lit. He eases his hand into the stove, holds the flame to the logs, and lightly blows, fueling the flame so the wood catches. Soon, the smell of burning wood begins to tickle his nose, reminding him of his grandfather's cabin, where he spent summers as a kid and his long-lasting love of the outdoors.

Amos closes the door and opens the damper to let the smoke out. The air from the open pipe fuels the fire, and the logs go up into a bright orange ball, the dry wood crackling.

Outside, he hears Tripp pull on the generator's starter cord. It coughs—*blub, blub, blub, blub, blub*—but the generator doesn't turn over. Tripp tries again.

Same result.

Amos moves to the window to see Tripp spray ignition fluid into the generator's carburetor. Tripp pulls the starter cord again.

This time the genny almost catches. The overhead lights flicker. The AM/FM radio also sparks to life, and a quick blurb from some religious pastor shouts out. Amos jumps at the preachy voice—*And the devil will smite the wicked*—before everything falls back into the oily orange glow coming from the stove.

A deep shiver runs down Amos's spine into his feet. His toes cramp. He doesn't like that voice or its message. He doesn't think of himself as a God-fearing man, but he isn't dumb enough not to see a sign when it was given to him. *Get it out of your head.*

Tripp pulls the cord again.

This time the generator spits and sputters. The lights come on. Fade out. Come on again.

And...stay on. Along with the radio and that awful preacher's voice. Amos hurries over and shuts the radio off just as Tripp walks through the door, stomping to knock the snow from his boots.

"You got it working!"

"Just needed a little T-L-C," Tripp says with a smile. "Get that ham radio up and running."

"Right."

Amos sits down at the desk and flips the ON switch. The radio starts with a hum, the lit gauges jumping with an electric impulse.

"Hot damn," Tripp says, slapping his hands together. Snow flies from his gloves into the air. "We're in business."

"This is Marburg State Park, in need of emergency assistance. Over."

Amos looks up when Tripp starts to go through the drawers beside his knees.

"What are you doing?"

"Looking for...a-ha." Tripp stands. There's a smile on his face as wide and as rubbery as a happy clown. In his hand is a small metal container that reminds Amos of an ammo box. Tripp's eyes are bright, alive with excitement. He flips the metal latch on the side of the box, throws the lid open, and looks inside. A euphoric gaze swells his face, like a man who has just found gold. "Well, isn't this the box that keeps giving?" Tripp reaches in and pulls out two cigars in a sealed plastic baggie and a half bottle of rum.

"Pour you a snort and light you a stick?" Tripp asks, holding them up.

Amos smiles.

"I'll take the snort and skip the stick."

"I was hoping you were going to say that."

CHAPTER 34

olt drives the Cat into the center of what used to be the stone courtyard of Camp Southwoods and stops in front of the mess hall. The windows and front door are covered with plywood, preventing anyone from getting in. *Or the ghosts from getting out.*

"You sure about this?" Porter leans forward to scan the derelict buildings.

"Yes." Colt opens the door.

Outside, the *tink* of the cable against the flagpole in the uninhabited area makes the land seem even lonelier, like the moon's dark side. Even with the fierce winds, the air around the camp is heavy with the feeling of death and sadness; the events of that tragic day have saturated the land, contaminating it. But the air also brings an odor.

"You smell that?" Porter comes around the Cat. "Smells like burning wood."

To the left of the mess hall, about twenty feet from Colt and Porter, is Building A, a shotgun-style wooden structure where female campers slept. To the right of the mess hall is Building B, the same shotgun-style design, where the male campers spent their nights. The buildings are dark and desolate; boards cover the windows and doors. The days of children's laughter and games are long gone. The innocence of the camp stolen the night of the murders. All three buildings have large fireplaces. Colt doesn't see smoke coming from the chimneys, but the smoke is close by…

He turns and sees five hazy objects hidden in a thicket of woods.

"There."

Next to Building B is a clearing, once a trail when the camp was still in operation, that led to five cabins by the lake. Cabin One is the largest, reserved for the camp's director. The four other cabins were for the rest of the staff—the counselors. All of them, Colt knew, had fireplaces.

"Let's go!" Colt hollers.

Coming off the trail to the cabins sitting next to one another, Colt notices only one has light emanating from the windows. Smoke rolls from the chimney. The rest are dark, dead.

He pulls the Glock and starts toward Cabin One. Porter is close behind, his own Glock drawn in a two-handed grip as they ascend the steps onto the porch. Colt pauses outside the door, listening. There's no movement inside. No sound. Taking hold of the handle, he turns it. The latch *snaps* free, and the door falls open into the room. He brings the Glock up, ready to take down anything that moves.

But the cabin is empty.

However, a fire burns in the hearth, keeping the cabin warm. Water bottles and snack food—chips, beef jerky, crackers, Oreos— and other essentials that someone would need to survive in a snowstorm litter the floor. A medical kit is open next to the fire- place, and bloody bandages are strewn around it.

"Joey!"

"Colt?"

His heart jumps into his throat with relief. *She's alive. Thank God.* A door along the back wall leads to a bedroom. Joey's voice had come from there. He runs to it, grabs the latch, and turns. But the door doesn't budge. He throws his shoulder into the door, but the old oak isn't going to break easily. *Need a damn battering ram to get through it.*

"Joey!"

"Get me out of here!"

"Are you okay?"

"Yes. I'm tied up on the floor."

"How close are you to the door?"

"I'm across the room. Aim low and to the right if you're going to shoot the lock."

Colt steps back and aims the Glock at the door's lock. Low and to the right. He fires a shot, blowing the latch and lock away.

He busts through the door and runs to Joey. He turns her on her side and slices through the rope binding her wrists together with his pocket knife. When she turns back to him, Colt gathers her in his arms. Her body trembles from the cold and the fear. He's held her before, but all those other times pale in comparison. No other embrace ever felt as good as this one does now.

"I thought I lost you," he says into her neck. "Where is he, Joey? Where's Flint?"

She pushes herself away from him. And Colt sees something in her eyes that he doesn't like.

"Where is he, Joey?"

Amos continues to call out on the state police frequency. He has yet to get through to anyone.

"The storm could be interfering with the signal."

"It could," Tripp agrees, plucking the matchbox off the mantle by the stove. It has warmed significantly inside the cab; both have shed their coats, gloves, and hats. "Keep trying."

"This is Amos Kent calling from Marburg State Park. All of our communications are down, Route 206 is blocked, and several people are dead. We need assistance. Over."

Static.

Tripp sits beside Amos, opens the plastic baggie, and pulls out one of the Cubans. He runs the stick under his nose, inhaling deeply.

"You sure they're still okay to smoke?"

"Feels a little dry. It might even be a little stale, but it should be okay. Was in a sealed baggie and in this box." Tripp taps the top of the metal box with his hand as if that solves everything.

Taking the wooden match, Tripp punctures the cap of the cigar. He sets it aside, picks up the rum bottle, and takes a healthy swig. Amos believes this is some ritual for Tripp. His way of getting ready to light a smoke but delaying the satisfaction, the urge to make it more memorable. Tripp passes the bottle to him, and Amos takes a snort. The liquor burns the whole way down, and he feels it coat the inside of his stomach like molten metal poured into a mold.

"Holy shit! What is that? Fire?"

"Pirate Rum," Tripp says with a smile. "A concoction from Ernesto—my late wife's father. I brought a bottle back for Cleve for those long and lonely cold nights up here by himself."

Amos coughs.

"I don't know how they drank that stuff."

"It'll put hair on your balls, that's for sure." Tripp takes the bottle back and throws another slug down his gullet. "My wife and her family drank it like water." His smile slowly turns to a frown at the mention of Aleja. "You know, next month would have been our twenty-eighth wedding anniversary." His eyes mist over.

Amos wants to comfort Tripp, but the words elude him. He is never good at saying sentimental things to people in mourning. He turns back to the radio and tries again.

Still, there's no reply.

"This is useless," he says, sitting back in the chair, frustrated.

"It'll work. Trust me." Tripp says with the cigar in his mouth. He strikes the match and brings it to the end of the stogie. It fires right up, and the small cab fills with a growing odor of stale tobacco. Amos watches Tripp pull on the cigar. The cherry brightens, and blue smoke gathers at the ceiling like pollution over a city skyline. Tripp then takes the stogie out of his mouth and looks at it strangely, as if he's taken some offense to it.

"Well? How is it?"

"Tastes like cow shit," Tripp replies, but puts it back in his mouth and pulls again.

Just then, a voice comes through on the radio.

"This is the PA State Police. We've received your transmission."

"He left. About thirty minutes ago," Joey says.

"Who left? Did you get a look at him?" Colt asks. "Was it Flint?"

Joey shakes her head, eyes woeful. She doesn't know.

"We need to get out of here," Porter says.

"Right," Colt agrees. He looks back at Joey and sees she isn't wearing protective gear. "The Cat's up the path. But you're not—"

"Don't worry about me. I'll make it back to the Cat."

Outside, the air cuts off the lake, bringing flecks of ice and snow that are nearly unbearable. Colt feels it slice through him, even wearing a parka, gloves, and a hat. He can't imagine how Joey will bear the trek back to the Cat in just her ranger uniform. The hike isn't far on a typical day, but now she might as well be trying to cross the Arctic.

Colt unzips his jacket.

"Put this on."

"Keep it! You need to operate the Cat, and you can't do that if you're frozen."

Joey was a medic, and she knew the risk of venturing into subzero temperatures without the proper attire. It would only be a ten-to-fifteen-minute walk, but that's enough time for hypothermia and frostbite. He doesn't like the idea of her going without a coat, but she's right—he's the only one who knows how to drive the Cat, and if something happens to him, they'll be stuck.

As they start back, Colt gathers Joey close to shield her from the wind and snow and provide her with some of his body heat to keep her warm. The snow is past their thighs in some spots, and with the wind cutting through their clothing, every fiber of their being is freezing. Joey's teeth begin to chatter, and her body starts to shake.

Just hang on, baby.

As they work their way up the trail, Colt hears the *tink* of the cable against the flagpole. They're close now, though he cannot see anything past the white monster surrounding them. *Just a little further.* The trail opens into the courtyard, and the wall of white fades, ever so slightly, enough that he can see the dark shapes of the cabins and the Cat.

But something's wrong. *Oh, fuck me, no. No!*

"Wh-what is it?" Joey asks. She must've felt his muscles tense when he saw the Cat.

"The Cat isn't running."

All the lights are on, and everything appears to be working correctly, except the engine isn't running. A jolt of fear zigzags through him. *We're trapped down here.*

"Colt?" Joey says. "What are we going to do?"

He looks back at Porter, lumbering up behind them. He appears as worn out as Colt feels, maybe more so since his attack and abduction. Dark circles stand out under his sunken eyes even in the dim light, and his face is long and gaunt, like he hasn't eaten a meal in weeks. In fact, Colt thinks he doesn't even look like himself.

"You okay?" Colt asks.

Porter nods.

"If being out here constitutes as *okay* then I'm fine. What's going on with the Cat?"

"I don't know. Let's go find out."

Colt leaves Joey in Porter's arms while he inspects the Cat and why the engine isn't running. It doesn't take him long to discover the problem when he spots the green slush.

"Son of a bitch!"

"What is it?" Joey screams.

"The fuel lines have been cut. We're not going anywhere," Colt says.

"Flint's fucking with us," Porter hollers. He turns and scans the snowy forest around them. "He wanted us to find Joey in that cabin so he could strand us down here."

"We need to take shelter," Joey says.

"Let's go back to the cabin," Porter says. "There's a fire. Some food—I saw Oreos."

"No," Colt says. "Joey's not going to last until we get back there." He turns and looks at the mess hall. "There. C'mon."

They make their way toward the mess hall. At the door, he and Porter start working on removing the plywood. It's not easy work, and they both pull, grunt, and swear until the rusty nails finally give way, and the old plywood begins to peel off. Once removed, Colt tells them to stand back. He kicks out at the old door's handle, and it violently snaps open.

Turning on the flashlight, Colt shines it into the mess hall. Inside there's nothing but a seemingly endless void of darkness and foreboding silence that the wooden walls have absorbed. Everything is exactly as it was in 1997, including the rows of wooden dining tables and chairs where kids once took their meals beside the counselors.

They enter the mess hall. Colt tells Porter to grab one of the chairs and wedge it against the door to keep it shut, just like they did in RS1. Porter pushes past Joey, takes one of the dining chairs, and drags it back, its feet skid and jump across the floor. He slips the back of the chair under the door handle, securing it.

Colt removes his jacket and puts it around Joey's shivering body.

"We need to get a fire going," Porter says.

"Th-there," Joey says, pointing. Colt follows her outstretched finger with the beam to a fireplace along the back wall, the light catching the spider webs inside the hearth. Above the fireplace is the camp's seal—a red crosshair design with a deer, a bear, a burning fire, and a tent in each of the four sections against a yellow backdrop. CAMP is written above in bold red letters. Below, in the same bold red letters, is SOUTHWOODS.

"No," Colt says. "No fires. We'll give ourselves away."

"We'll freeze in here without heat," Porter says.

Colt trains the beam onto the double doors along the back wall leading to the kitchen. About two dozen pictures in wooden frames are to the right of the double doors. The glass, filthy with built-up dust, catches the light.

"We can go into the kitchen and use one of the stoves to start a small fire. It won't be much, but it'll give us some heat and keep us from being detected."

"What are we going to use as fuel?" Porter asks.

Colt swigs the light back to the chairs.

"The legs of those chairs will do just fine."

"Put that light back on the photographs," Joey says.

"What?" Colt turns back to her, shining the beam in her face. Joey holds up her hand, squinting. "Sorry."

"Shine the flashlight onto those photographs again."

Colt does. She crosses the room to the photos, her shadow blotting out the pictures as she nears. *What's she sniffing?* Colt wonders as he follows her, intrigue nipping at the back of his neck. He watches her study the pictures intently, her eyes going over them like a photographer picking their best snapshot.

The photos are all similar: a group of young people stand before the camp's flagpole. The mess hall is blurry in the background. Colt then realizes the photographs are seasonal, taken with a different troop of kids each year. The first seven photographs are black-and-white and have dates on the bottom ranging from 1973 to 1979. The following eighteen photos—from 1980 to 1997—are in color, the earlier years fading into obscurity. His eyes move to the photograph stamped: Camp Southwoods— Summer 1997. Ten girls are seated in the front row, and none appear happy to be there. The word *miserable* pops into Colt's mind. Behind them are twelve boys, with similar melancholy looks. And behind them are five adults. All counselors, each wearing a yellow Camp Southwoods T-shirt. Four of the counselors are Alice King, Kurt MacReady, Virginia Steel, and Ted Charno. They smile for the camera, oblivious to the horror that awaits them later that summer. But who's the fifth counselor? And why was he spared in Carver's killing spree? A smudge of dirt on the glass blocks the face from Colt's view.

Below the Summer 1997 stamp is a list of the names of those in the photo. The unknown counselor's name would be there. But the print is so tiny that Colt can barely read it. He inches closer and begins to read through the names, stopping when he comes to Douglas Carver.

His eyes drift back up and he finds Carver in the photo. Colt had never seen the revenant of Camp Southwoods before. By the grisliness of the murders, the ghost stories, hell, even the rhyme, Colt had built Carver up in his mind as a monster. But he was just a normal-looking kid. *It's the ones you least expect*, Colt remembers Aunt Sunny saying.

At that exact moment, Joey sucks in a breath, as if spooked.

"What is it?" Colt asks, snapping his attention to her.

"They both were here that summer."

"What are you talking about? Who was here?"

Joey points at a young man in his early teens, standing just three people away from Douglas Lee Carver in the group photo. The boy isn't smiling and looks as unhappy to be there as everyone else. And though the face is young, Colt recognizes it instantly. He tries to understand what his eyes see, but it's too much for his mind to comprehend, like overloading and frying a circuit.

This can't be…

Joey's finger moves up to the counselor standing behind the boy—the only counselor to survive the attack that hot summer night back in 1997—and rubs away the dirt. Colt doesn't recognize him. But Joey's face is white as a sheet.

"He *was* a counselor here that summer, too, Colt," Joey says.

"Who was?"

Joey moves her finger to one name under the photograph and taps it. Colt leans in to read it and feels his entire world drop out from under him.

Oh, my God…

CHAPTER 35

The state police tell Amos they'll be there in forty-five minutes, along with EMTs and a road crew, to start the removal of the fallen trees so they can enter the park. Amos and Tripp both take a swig of the rum with delight.

"What now?" Amos asks.

"We should get back. Let the others know."

It was comfortable and warm in the cab, and now that Amos was up there, the idea of going back out in the snow, ice, and wind wasn't pleasant. He was even less keen about walking down the winding stairs, feeling the tower swaying, hearing the creaking, wondering if it would blow over. *At least it's dark, and I can't see the ground. But soon, you'll be home. With your baby girl. Safe and sound.* That's what matters most.

Tripp pulls on his jacket. The cigar is down to a nub and tucked in the corner of his mouth.

"Put the stove out." Tripp picks up the remaining cigar and stuffs it into the jacket's pocket.

"I thought you said it tasted like cow shit," Amos says.

"It does. But do you see a cigar shop where I can buy another smoke?"

Amos shakes his head. *Every man has his vices.* He pulls on his coat, gloves, and hat, then walks over to the pail of water (snow they let melt while trying to reach the police) next to the stove and gently pours the water over the fire. The flames sizzle out; steam billows up the pipe.

"Ready?" Tripp asks.

"Yep."

An object bursts through the window, shoots past Amos's face—he feels something warm on his skin—and implants itself into the wood. Spinning, he finds an arrow—the tip on fire—with the blue and white fletching still quivering from the impact into the wall. The flame has already caught the cab's dry wooden interior on fire and crawls up the wall toward the ceiling.

"Put that out!" Tripp screams. Another flaming arrow bursts through the opposite window and plants itself into the wall beside Tripp, setting it ablaze.

Amos reaches for the pale of water and stumbles over it. What remains spills across the floor. He looks back at Tripp, hopeless.

"We need to—" A third flaming arrow cracks through the glass, shoots past Tripp's left shoulder, and into the wall. It goes up in a *whoosh!* "Get out of here. Go!"

Rushing outside onto the platform, an arrow hits the railing directly in front of Tripp. This one isn't on fire. It was intended to take him down or wound him to prevent him from escaping the inferno that would bring down the entire tower.

Behind Amos, the glass windows break under the heat. He turns to find the entire cab is on fire; the old, dry wood went up as easily as parchment paper. Flames shoot from the top of the roof. More glass shatters under the extreme heat, tinkling through the struts and support beams below them on their way to the ground.

"We need to move!" Tripp hollers.

They run to the stairs and start to descend them. Another arrow emerges from the darkness, taking the cigar stub out of Tripp's mouth. Sparks and ash fly. They hit his eyes. Tripp staggers into the railing, rubbing at his face.

"Keep going!" Amos knows it's just a matter of time before

one of them is picked off. The odds are against them. *We're like rats trapped in a vertical maze.*

Just as this thought strikes his brain, Tripp screams out. He grabs his right inner thigh and drops, his back coming down hard on the old wooden steps. A plank breaks away and tumbles down into the darkness, hitting a strut below before disappearing into the white void surrounding the bottom of the tower. Amos leaps over the missing step, thankful that he can't see the ground, to Tripp's side.

"The son of a bitch got me!" Tripp cries, gripping his thigh just above where the bolt rests deep in the meat.

Another arrow hits the wooden railing inches above Amos's head. He ducks down.

"We need to move, Tripp."

Just as the words leave Amos's mouth, something above their heads groans loudly. Both men look up. Flaming boards begin to fall from the structure and rain down around them. The firestorm above is weakening the cab's structural integrity.

"That's not good."

"That whole cab is going to let go," Tripp says. He looks at Amos gravely. "You have to go. Now!"

"I can't leave you here."

"You must! You have a daughter, Amos. Think about her. Go!"

"No way!" Amos pulls Tripp to his feet. He wasn't about to leave Tripp there. How, for the love of God, could he look at himself, at his daughter ever again, knowing he left someone there to die?

Another arrow whizzes by, missing the structure altogether, and glides off into the night.

With Tripp's arm over his shoulders, Amos starts down the steps. Tripp moans with each movement as pain flares from the arrow working around inside his leg.

They're about a quarter of the way down the structure, almost below the tree line. Amos believes it might shield them from the shooter's view if they can make it there.

Almost there. Just a little…

Amos sees a figure on the platform below them as they round the stairs. His chest tightens at the sight of that face—that fucking skeletal face with those hollow black sockets and that maniacal grin, just like it had when he saw it on the bridge. The skeleton has a crossbow aimed on them in a deadeye shot. *It can't miss… one of us.*

But how did it know where we were?

Thwack! The crossbow releases.

A flash of intense pain punches the right side of Amos's chest. The air is driven from his body. His knees buckle under him like someone has clicked off a switch. His weight shifts, even though he doesn't want it to, and he involuntarily starts to fall forward, pulling Tripp along with him.

Tripp saw the skeleton as soon as they came around the corner. He realizes it must have snuck up the tower and began shooting flaming arrows through the cab to draw them out. He then tried to pick them off as they attempted to flee the fire.

And just as Tripp has this thought, he hears the *thwack* of the crossbow releasing and feels Amos's body stiffen when the arrow strikes him. An expulsion of air blown from Amos's mouth sounds like a wet cough. His weight shifts and pulls Tripp, who's trying everything he can to stay upright on one leg, down with him. Together they tumble down the steps, over top of one another, bumping and hitting the safety railing as they go. The arrow in Tripp's leg catches on the railing and pulls hard, nearly ripping it out. The pain is unbearable, and he almost blacks out until he is jolted back to his hellish reality when his head and back hit something hard that stops him dead. Tripp looks up to find himself on the fourth platform. The wooden safety barrier around the landing was the only thing between him and meeting the almighty.

A moan brings Tripp's eyes back around. He finds Amos lying

at his feet with an arrow buried to the fletchings in the right side of his chest.

"Tr-ipp?" Amos says weakly. His breathing is heavy, and a wet wheeze rattles in his chest. Tripp spent many years as a hunter before Aleja died—after her death, he could no longer bring himself to take a life—and has heard that sound before, when an animal was hit in the lung. That same sound is coming from Amos now. His lungs are filling with blood.

Another arrow breaks overhead, missing the structure altogether.

Tripp looks back at Amos; hot ash falls around him like fiery raindrops. Bright red blood is leaking from Amos's mouth; his eyes are wide, afraid. *Aleja had that same look just before she left me.* Tripp reaches out to him as if he can do something to help. But he knows it's too late. Too late to save Amos. And too late—he looks up at the inferno above—to save himself from the hellfire about to obliterate him.

"Tr-ipp," Amos murmurs again. His fingers wiggle for Tripp to take his hand.

He grabs Amos's hand and pulls him closer. His large body easily slides through the snow. Tripp leans Amos against his chest and rests his back on the corner of the platform's walls, like a mother coddling her infant. Only for Tripp, it reminds him of the day he held Aleja, the day her heart stopped beating. Her love and soul leaving him behind, forever lost, hurting, waiting for the moment they will reunite.

Above, there is a thunderous crack. The structure shudders to its foundation. Large planks of flaming wood continue to fall. Some hit the steps in front of them. Others pass by outside the platform to the snowy ground below. Tripp covers Amos's body from the falling debris. One fiery plank lands directly next to Tripp's hand, sizzling in the snow.

A wet, gargling sound, like trying to blow water through a crack in a straw, seeps from Amos's lips. His chest rises and falls with a laborious heave that Tripp knows isn't a good sign.

He's dying. Drowning in his own blood.

Another loud buckling comes from the cab above. More fiery wreckage rains down. The support beams, holding the cab in place, are giving way. It's just a matter of time before the cab lets go.

"Tripp?" Amos breathes as a wad of blood bubbles from his lips and runs down the side of his face.

"I'm right here, Amos," Tripp says. Pain flares in his leg. He looks down the steps. There are four flights to go. He knows he can't take them with the arrow in his leg. And he definitely knows he can't carry Amos.

"I'm…so…cold, Tripp," Amos says. His eyes are glassy and on some far-off place that Tripp cannot see.

Won't have to worry about that soon, Tripp thinks, looking up. *Neither of us will.*

"I…just want…to see…my baby. I…just…want to…go…hoooome."

Tripp pulls the second cigar from his pocket, bites off the end, and spits it away. He picks up the flaming piece of wood that had fallen beside his hand and lights the stick with it.

"Still tastes like cow shit," Tripp says aloud.

Above, the cab breaks free. It swings as if on a lever and crashes into the wooden support legs, trembling the entire structure. The cab then breaks free from whatever held it in place and begins to tumble down through the center, blowing away the stairs like balsa wood. Fiery planks explode from the sides, shooting shards of wood splinters into the night. The cacophony of noise is deafening. The shaking and rumbling of the hellfire rolling toward Tripp, about to eliminate him from existence, raddles him to the core.

He closes his eyes, pulls Amos's still body closer, and realizes then that he's already gone. *I'm so sorry, Amos.*

His last two thoughts before the ball of fire eviscerates him are that he hopes to see Aleja again and that there are cigars wherever he goes next.

CHAPTER 36

The face staring back from the photograph causes Colt's bones to cry out. *It couldn't be. How did I not know?* He doesn't want to believe what his eyes are telling him. But he can't deny it.

Maynard Barrett was here in the summer of 1997. Working as a counselor. But it wasn't only Maynard…

There's the cold *clicking* of a cocking gun behind them.

Colt and Joey slowly turn and face Porter. The Glock is in his hand, trained in their direction. He sneers at them with eyes so reptilian that it causes Colt's skin to slither with disgust. But Colt's seen those eyes before, behind the skull mask when he was attacked at RS3. The shapeshifter has finally revealed his true self.

"It was you," Colt says, realizing now the slice on the top of Porter's right hand wasn't from the rope bindings, but from being slashed by his blade in the fight. "You're behind this."

A malignant smile spreads across Porter's face that matches the blackness of his eyes. Strangely the smile resembles the mask's grin that Porter hid under to terrorize and murder everyone tonight.

"I don't understand," Joey says.

"That's the point."

"The point of what, Porter?"

"Why *we* did it."

We—meaning the other person Porter is working with. Flint?

Joey inches closer to Colt.

How could we not have known?

He looks back at Porter. "So why did you do it?"

"Put your gun on the ground, Colt. Then kick it over to me."

Colt doesn't move.

Porter trains the barrel directly on Joey. Her body tenses against Colt's as his own muscles seize. Porter's dark eyes shot back to Colt. *Do as I say, or I shoot her,* that chilling look tells him.

"Okay," Colt says, raising his hands to ease the tension. "Just take it easy, Porter."

He reaches down and removes the Glock from the holster on his hip.

"No sudden moves or a bullet steals Joey's beautiful face, got it?"

Colt nods. He holds the gun up with his thumb and index finger for Porter to see. He then lays the Glock by his feet and kicks it across the floor. It bumps and hops across the uneven, warping floorboards but stops about a foot from where Porter stands.

"Why, Porter?"

"Why?" Porter smiles thoughtfully as the memories warp his once handsome features into something sinister, like the rot of his soul has finally manifested across his skin like gangrene. "Because *we* were the only ones who could stop the abuse."

Colt notices he said *we* again, meaning he didn't do any of this alone. Not tonight. And not back in 1997.

"You were here at the Camp in '97. You murdered those counselors and blamed it on Carver."

Outside, the whine of a snowmobile approaching breaks the palpable friction in the room.

Porter moves to the door, throws the chair aside, and opens it. A strong gust of wind blows into the building. Colt blocks Joey from it with his body while eyeing the Glock on the floor. He thinks about going for it. But he holds fast. It's too far out of his reach. If he moves, Porter *will* hear him and shoot both of them before he can reach the gun.

"Over here!" Porter yells into the storm. He looks back at Colt and studies him skeptically before his eyes shift to the Glock on the floor. "I know what you're thinking. Don't."

Porter steps away from the door just as footsteps near the threshold. Another figure emerges from the darkness into the flashlight's soft glow around the room.

Flint Wheeler steps through the threshold and into the mess hall. He looks exhausted, eyes sunk into his head, face pale and sickly. Blood leaks from a nasty head wound.

You son of a...

Just then, someone behind Flint kicks his bad knee out from under him. He screams and falls to the floor with a *thud*. Then, Colt notices Flint's hands are bound at the wrists.

Out of the darkness, another person wearing a skeleton mask, parka, and snowsuit emerges, the shadows falling off him like cascading water. His chest is bloody from being struck by the swinging ball of pikes at the band shell, and his right hand is wrapped in a makeshift tourniquet that has bled through. A crossbow is in his left hand, and two ice axes dangle off his belt by their leashes.

"You get the message I left back at RS1?" Porter asks. The skeleton nods in response. "You take care of it before Tripp and Amos could contact anyone?"

"Taken care of," a voice speaks from under the mask.

Tripp. Amos. Did they even make it to the fire tower? Colt can only wonder.

"Can I take this damn thing off now?" The masked person asks, looking for the go-ahead to shed the shroud.

Porter nods. "Sure. It's time we wrap this up anyway."

There was only one person unaccounted for. One person that Colt wasn't able to ever check on. Dusty. He had to be Porter's accomplice. Everyone else was dead.

The skeleton begins to remove the mask, finally revealing…

CHAPTER 37

Wyatt Burke fixes his dark green eyes on them with triumph and hostility. It's a menacing, fearsome gaze, transforming Wyatt from the soulful and caring person Colt knew into the unrecognizable demonic being standing before him. He thought Wyatt was dead, had seen him attacked on the video—a video that was left in playback mode for him to find, for him to witness. A shiver runs down his spine at the thought, the cruel deception. But if Wyatt was alive, then who did Colt find hanging on the door of RS3 hours ago?

The answer forms in his mind straight away. There was only one person unaccounted for. The one person he had not been able to check in on the entire day, like fate had intervened every time. The one person Colt suspected a moment before Wyatt revealed himself. Dusty. It made sense now. The insidiousness of their plan. They switched the name tag pinned to the body Colt found. And with the face a bloody pulp, there was no way for Colt to know who it really was, throwing him off from suspecting Wyatt's involvement the entire time.

But why did they do it?

"You asked me why *we* did it," Porter says, as if sensing Colt's confusion. He closes the door and replaces the chair, tapping the front feet with his boot, making sure it's snug under the handle. He steps beside Wyatt, takes one of the ice axes off his belt, slips the leash around his wrist, and lets the axe dangle before training his scary eyes back on Colt. "The answer is simple. We couldn't allow Camp Southwoods to reopen."

Porter glances at Wyatt. A moment of remembrance passes between them. A knowing pain they both share. Whatever it was, Colt knows it had decayed any semblance of the good in them long ago, leaving their souls tattered. But Colt saw something under the surface of that look, something left unspoken.

"Why?" Joey asks.

"Why, she asks." Porter's eyes fall to the floor, heavy and saddened with unspeakable memories. His jaws twitch as the past simmers to the surface of his skin, causing a purple vein to swell in the middle of his forehead. He almost looks like the kid in the photograph; a hurt little boy who desperately needs a hug from his father. Then his eyes snap up, the reptilian-like irises revealed as thin black slits like a snake ready to strike. "Camp Southwoods was a camp for problematic children—drug addicts, thieves, arsonists, liars, those with disrespectful behavior, aggression, and even impulse control. The camp promised to help them achieve behavioral, emotional, and spiritual wholeness." He shakes his head as if something were absurd. "That was all bullshit."

"What Darryl told us earlier...about the camp being abusive..." Joey says.

"It's all true."

"But your father was here with you that summer, why would he allow you, or anyone, to be abused?" Joey's voice rises with disbelief. Like Colt, she's having a hard time accepting that Maynard, someone they both called friend and mentor, could look the other way while a child was being harmed. That wasn't the man they knew, wasn't the man they worked for. That wasn't their leader.

"My father had two sides to him. The man you all knew wasn't the same man who came home to my mother and me every night. He hid himself well behind a mask, a façade."

The apple didn't fall far from the tree.

"But why?" Joey's voice cracks as she tries to make sense of everything.

"He believed what troubled kids needed was daily routines, exercises and outdoor activities, and physical discipline when they stepped out of line. And boy, did he love to dish out the physical discipline."

Colt and Joey exchange uneasy glances. How had Colt missed the signs of who Maynard really was inside? How did he not know that his friend and mentor was a man with such a callous heart?

"I can see this is hard for the two of you to understand. How my father could do this to me, to the others," Porter says, glancing at his partner in crime. "But everyone has skeletons in their closet, and my father had his share. Like running this camp for nearly three decades."

Colt thinks of the skeleton masks Porter and Wyatt wore to commit their crimes tonight; they weren't just to drive fear into everyone. They were making a statement by wearing them. Everyone has two sides. The side they present to the world and the side they keep hidden, to themselves, and to those closest to them.

"He made me come here with him that summer," Porter continues. "I was ten and had fallen in with a crowd of mischievous kids from school. I started shoplifting to impress them. Spray painted some walls. Broke into a few abandoned houses to drink and smoke pot. Stupid stuff that stupid kids with too much time and energy do. But when my father found out, after I was caught by the police throwing rocks at passing cars, he hit the roof and beat my ass until I was black-and-blue and couldn't walk or sit right for a week without moaning. But that wasn't enough punishment. It was never enough for him. So, he brought me with him to this fucking camp. *You're going to learn the meaning of respect, boy,* he told me. *I'll be damned if my son is going to turn into a delinquent.* The only bright side to that summer was meeting Wyatt."

Colt turns to the photograph on the wall behind him, looking for a young Wyatt Burke.

"Don't bother, Colt. I'm not in that photo. Came to the camp after it was taken that summer. Mom's boyfriend at the time thought it was a good idea to send me here."

Colt turns back to them as it all clicks into place. They weren't just accomplices in the recent murders around the park. They were also responsible for the massacre in 1997. Both were at the camp that summer. Both endured the same brutal treatment. And both share a deep seeded pain. Colt feels a shudder work through his body, knowing such atrocities were taking place at the very spot he was standing, and no one did a goddamn thing to stop it from happening.

How could Maynard do that to his own son? Or to other people's children?

"Why pin the murders on Carver?" Joey asks.

"Because," Wyatt says, as if the answer is simple, "we had to."

"You had to?" Colt says. "You took advantage of Carver's disability so that you could hide the murder of four innocent people behind it."

"Innocent? Those counselors were anything but innocent. What they did to us"—Porter waves his finger between himself and Wyatt—"to Douggie, and to the others that summer—the physical and mental torture they put all of us through—was beyond reprehensible. And for what? So we could learn respect. Or as Maynard used to put it: *you'll learn respect or we'll beat it into you kids.*"

"None of us deserved that kind of abuse. We were just dumb kids, some of us with shitty home lives, lost in a world that either didn't want us, didn't accept us, or like in Douggie Carver's situation, didn't understand. What those counselors did, and what our parents willingly allowed them to do to us was heinous."

"They took away our youth. Our innocence." Wyatt shakes his head as if an image from the past came into focus. "Neither of you could possibly understand what it was like to be abused—both at home and then to come here and get the same treatment at this fucking camp."

"Then why start back up after all these years? The investigation was closed. Carver's in Haven Hurst for life. No one suspects the two of you are behind any of it."

Colt shifts his gaze to Flint on the floor. He's quiet, afraid; his eyes are wide, bulging, staring at the Glock directly before him. He's thinking about going for it. *Don't be stupid, Flint.*

"My father," Porter says quietly as if he's afraid Maynard will overhear him speaking from his grave, "told me he got a call from Mike Thomas at the DCNR. They were seriously considering reopening the camp to bring in extra money to the park, especially after the pandemic."

Colt's aware. He's had those same talks with the head of the DCNR.

"He was excited at the prospect, telling me how great it would be for kids to learn teamwork, build self-confidence, and reconnect with nature, something he felt modern-day kids were severely lacking, with technology making them *mindless dopes and disrespectful assholes*—his words. This was his baby, a place he started with the backing of the DCNR in the seventies to help troubled youths. He reveled in the idea of getting it up and running again. He even came down here the day before the hurricane hit to inspect the cabins and see what could be salvaged."

Porter frowns.

"I was waiting for him inside the mess hall. I told him that if he allowed the camp to reopen, I would expose everything that went on that summer, everything he had been involved with, what he had allowed, and what he had done to children. We got into an argument. He stormed out. I was going to go after him, but I saw Tripp across the inlet, so I stayed back until they both were gone. But I knew right then that something had to be done. You see, I couldn't allow this place to reopen. *We* couldn't allow it to reopen. I wouldn't let another child be sucked into that same system of abuse that Wyatt and I were in." Porter pauses to catch his breath; he's talking so fast that his voice is manic. "We stopped the cycle once before and were willing to do it again. So, I set up the fake distress call the day of the hurricane."

Joey gasps.

"You murdered your father." Colt's hands instantly clench into fists. Porter not only caused Maynard's death but also put Colt's life in jeopardy, too.

"I knew my father would never turn his back on this place. Not for me. Not for anyone. He loved the camp, the years he spent building its spoken-in-whispers reputation, and what he felt it represented in his mind. That if a child couldn't learn to behave, then you beat good behavior into them. But I also knew he would never leave someone stranded on the Rocks, even in the middle of a hurricane. He couldn't ruin the image he had built up—the caring, loving husband and father, a hardworking park ranger with an adoration for nature, who went above and beyond for his team of rangers and was willing to lend an ear or a hand to a stranger in need. You all tried to talk him out of it, especially you, Colt. You said it was a bad idea. Dangerous. You were right. But murder my own father?" Porter shakes his head, thoughtfully. For a moment, Colt sees his humanity return, pain pulling his face tight at the prospect of murdering his father. "As much as I hated him, as much as I wanted to see him dead for what he did to me, to us, I could not bring myself to kill him. That might sound strange to you, you might not even understand, but I just couldn't do it."

For a brief second, Colt is at a loss. *If Porter didn't kill Maynard...* Then, a memory strikes him. There was one person who wasn't in the park that day. He was on vacation in California, hiking in Big Basin Redwoods State Park. But that was another lie.

He was here, in the park. He was the one who sent the distress call. The one who pushed Maynard off the Rocks.

"Wyatt?" Colt looks at him with an astonishing gaze.

Wyatt beams with pride, a devilish smile from ear to ear.

"I waited for Maynard up there that night. We needed his death to appear like an accident. A rescue operation that had gone terribly wrong, because of poor judgment on Maynard's part, but nothing more than that."

Colt swallows. His throat grinds as truth and fiction collide in his mind, exploding his perceived reality.

"I had fallen behind on the trail because my pack got caught on a downed tree. Maynard was ahead of me, working his way to the top of the Rocks. If I had gotten unsnagged and been a moment sooner, I would have—"

"If you had been there, Colt, you wouldn't be here now," Wyatt says in such a matter-of-fact tone that it gives Colt goose bumps.

"And everyone bought it," Porter adds. "Our hope was that the DCNR would rethink their plans to reopen the park since my father's death. Bad PR and all that. But I was wrong. All it did was delay the inevitable. Isn't that right, Colt?"

Colt says nothing.

"As soon as I saw Mike was calling you, not six months after my father's death, I knew what he wanted. So, after I forwarded the call to you, I stayed on the line listening. I'm glad you thought the idea was stupid and said as much. But I knew the DCNR wasn't going to stop. They were going to reopen the camp no matter what. So, we needed to do something so grand that it would taint this park beyond repair, forever closing it and Camp fucking Southwoods forever."

"You fucks." Joey lunges at them. Wyatt raises the crossbow at her. Colt pulls her back into him, but she struggles to get free despite staring down an arrow that could end her life. "The authorities are going to know that Carver isn't the murderer this time."

"That's the beauty of it," Porter replies triumphantly. His eyes shift to Flint on the floor.

"You're going to pin the murders on Flint?" Colt says. "Like you pinned the murders on Carver in '97."

Porter nods, smiles devilishly, eyes dull and dead.

"Flint's not that innocent. He was, after all, working with Darryl and Rumor to get my father's position and then yours, Colt—by blackmailing you two." Porter looks down at Flint. "You really shouldn't have shot your mouth off about being overlooked to me, Flint. That put me onto what you were up to."

"Rumor wasn't part of the plan, was he? That's why he was buried in the pit, unlike everyone else."

"He was an unforeseen hiccup that needed to be dealt with," Wyatt says.

"Rumor was in the wrong place at the wrong time. That was his mistake. Once Flint is connected to the murders—thanks to the evidence we put back in his locker and at his house—it's just a matter of time before the police figure out he was also helping Darryl and Rumor vandalize the park and blackmailing you and Joey, giving him a motive." Porter shrugs it off as a no biggie. "Flint murdered everyone to cover up his tracks."

"So your plan is to make it look like Flint snapped because the DCNR overlooked him for the head ranger position. And with all the evidence about the Carver murders and the legend surrounding the camp that you planted, it will appear to the investigators that Flint had an unhealthy obsession with the case, and tried to make the murder look like it was the work of a copycat killer. And then you two were going to use the snowmobiles—which you disabled earlier—to get out of the park and go for help. The sole survivors of the massacre, able to spin the tale in your favor."

"I'll never admit to being a murderer!" Flint growls.

"We don't need you to admit to anything," Porter says. "We just need it to look like I shot you in self-defense."

He raises the Glock, the barrel only inches from Flint's face.

"Porter. Don't..." Colt screams.

He pulls the trigger.

The bang is deafening. The room fills with smoke and the smell of gunpowder. Flint's body slumps lifelessly onto its side with a thump and twitches like a dying rabbit. A pool of blood slowly forms around his skull, a red halo, soaking into the old, porous wood.

But Flint's death provides Colt with an opening. And he knows if he doesn't capitalize on it, Porter will kill him and Joey in cold blood, just like he had Flint.

Colt dives for the Glock and wraps his hand around the gun. Rolling onto his side, he squeezes off a round without aiming. The bullet hits Porter in the upper right thigh, taking his leg out from under him and driving him down onto his side next to Flint's corpse. The Glock is knocked from Porter's hand upon impact with the floor and bounces across the room as if it's made of rubber, stopping just inches from where Joey stands.

"Joey! Get the other gun!" Colt screams, climbing to his feet.

She springs forward at his command, reaching for the second gun.

He sees Wyatt bring the crossbow up and follow her movement with its sights. It will be as easy as shooting fish in a barrel at his distance, Colt knows. His throat constricts with the thought of Wyatt taking her from him. He aims and squeezes off another round. This one hits the end of the crossbow, blowing it out of Wyatt's grip. But it only slows him down momentarily and he reaches for the ice axe dangling from his belt.

Colt's heart jumps into his throat. Wyatt will kill Joey if he doesn't stop him now. He narrows his eyes down the Glock's iron sights on Wyatt's chest and pulls the trigger.

Nothing happens.

A jam.

Why I use revolvers.

While Colt clears the breach, Wyatt closes the space between himself and Joey in two steps. He rears back with the axe as he nears her, eyes full of malice. Colt racks the slide back, the bullet ejects, and it snaps into place, now ready to fire. He brings the gun up and is about to pull the trigger when Porter is suddenly next to him. He grabs Colt's wrist and jerks the gun toward the ceiling. The Glock goes off with a thundering report. The bullet rips through the roof of the mess hall—dust, wood, and snow sprinkles down on them.

A deep, guttural scream bellows from Wyatt's throat. Colt's looks back at Joey just as Wyatt is bringing the ice axe down.

"Joe…" Colt tries to scream, but Porter wraps his forearm around his neck and begins to squeeze like a python, cutting off his oxygen.

Colt's choked warning gives Joey enough time to flee from the falling ice axe. She hits the wooden floor hard, her left elbow taking the brunt of the fall; a feeling that sends pins and needles down her arm and into her fingers. The forward momentum of the axe swing pulls Wyatt along with it. He stumbles forward into the wall. Her eyes search the floor for the second gun. But it's now more than three feet from where she's lying. She'll never get to it before Wyatt can turn around and kill her.

A gurgling sound pulls her attention back to Colt. Porter's arm is latched around his neck in a chokehold.

"*R-un!*" Colt gags.

She bolts for the door and rips the chair away, throwing it over her shoulder. The door blows open. The extreme cold sinks into her, every muscle cramps, and her breath freezes in her lungs.

"Get after her!" she hears Porter scream. "I got this one."

Rushing out into the snow, Joey sinks nearly to her knees. *Where the hell are you going to go?* But she has to figure out a way to save herself and Colt. *Hang on, baby. Just hang on.* Behind her, she hears Wyatt stomp onto the porch.

"There's nowhere for you to go, Joey!" Wyatt taunts over the fierce wind.

She pays the threat little mind and pushes through the snow. Her eyes fall onto the Cat. If she can make it to the Cat, she knows there's a flare gun under the driver's seat. It's not much, but she can use it to defend herself.

"I'm coming, Joey!" Wyatt calls.

Looking over her shoulder, he's already within arm's length. He's taller, so the snow doesn't slow him down as easily; he hops in and out like a runner over a hurdle.

"Little Ranger Walsh Running. Douggie Carver's gone a-hunting. Gonna catch that ranger. Gonna cleave that ranger. Little Ranger Walsh done running."

She's just about to the Cat when she feels the ice axe slice through her back, opening her up. Her scream echoes across the camp, the hills, and the lake. The strike knocks her forward, and she face-plants next to the Cat's front tracks. Hot blood runs down her back and soaks into her bra. The frosty air stings the laceration as if she were being burned with acid. She grits her teeth to suppress the pain. The smell of diesel fuel from the Cat's cut fuel lines wafts up her nose. It's strong. Repugnant. And she can see the snow under the Cat has turned to green slush from the leaking fuel lines.

She rolls onto her back, hoping to distance herself from Wyatt. But he's already there, his hands reaching for her neck. She tries to push them away, but he's too strong, too fast, and before she knows it, his hands are around her throat, squeezing.

Joey instantly feels her windpipe close off. She tries to draw a breath, but it's impossible. She thrashes this way and that to loosen Wyatt's grip on her throat. But the exertion, the fight for her life, is depleting any oxygen left in her body. She feels herself slipping into a dark tunnel gathering at the corners of her vision.

"You know, when I pushed Maynard off that cliff, he screamed the entire way down," Wyatt says with a smirk. "But I don't want you to scream, Joey." He leans closer to her face, applying more pressure to her neck. When he speaks, hot spittle dots her skin. "I want to watch you go silently."

Joey tries to scratch his face. But what little fight she has left in her is drifting away, and her limbs feel useless and thick like tubes full of sawdust. The dark tunnel of her vision is narrowing. Soon it will overtake her, and forever blackness will follow.

Then, she sees the ice axe dangling by the leash around Wyatt's right wrist. With her last ounce of strength, she takes hold of the handle and drives the pick end of the ice axe upward and buries it in Wyatt's armpit with everything she's got. He howls in pain. His hands instantly go lax around her neck, and he falls into the green slush beside the Cat, grabbing his underarm.

Rolling over onto her side, Joey sucks in a large gulp of air. Coughs. Her throat is raw, and the muscles and tendons in her neck feel like they're on fire from the strangulation.

Fighter's fatigue washes over her like a tidal wave, threatening to pull her into a deep coma. A coma that she will never wake up from if she allows it to take hold.

You need to get up!

She wills herself to stand. Using the Cat's tracks she pulls herself to her feet. She slumbers, heavy footed, to the door, throws it open, and looks under the front seat. There, in a small red box, is the flare gun. She grabs the gun and a single flare. Popping the chamber, the barrel falls forward, and she slides the round in and snaps it closed with a flick of her wrist.

And then turns back to Wyatt.

He's moaning in pain, kicking, and squirming around like a slug in a vat of salt.

She cocks the gun.

Wyatt stops thrashing at the sound, and his hateful, but pain-filled eyes settle on her with a knowing look that Joey has gotten the upper hand on him.

Without hesitation, she pulls the trigger.

The flare pops from the barrel and hits Wyatt in the face, embedding itself in his right cheek. The force of the round knocks him back into the green slush, setting him and the area around him ablaze. He screams and kicks and slaps at the snow as the flames engulf his body.

"Who's screaming now!"

Then Joey notices the fire crawling up the Cat's undercarriage, working its way back to the fuel tank.

Oh, shit!

She turns and runs…

The explosion of the Cat is so powerful it blows the boards through the front windows of the mess hall, showering glass and wood over Colt and Porter. Both men are driven to the floor. Porter loses his grip around Colt's neck, and he draws a much-needed breath.

He hears Porter push himself up and limp to the doorway, dragging his wounded leg behind him.

"Wyatt!" he cries into the night.

Colt climbs to his feet and rocks from side to side, trying to regain his balance. His head is swimming from nearly being choked out, but he's quickly resurfacing, coming back into himself. Outside he can see the burning Cat, feel the heat on his skin. But he doesn't see Joey. *Where is she?* He feels his feet moving toward Porter, like his body was on autopilot, pure instinct to survive, to save the woman he loves, taking control.

Porter stands in the doorway in front of him. Colt sees his face is a twisted roadmap of pain and loss. Only this time, Colt knows, it's not an act like it was when Colt told him his father was dead. This time, that pain is real. Pain for Wyatt. His friend.

This ends now!

He gathers steam and charges Porter.

At the sound of Colt's boots on the hardwood floor, Porter turns. Colt tackles him around the waist. Together they fall through the open door and come down onto the porch, covered in broken icicles blown off the roof during the explosion, and roll into the snow.

For a moment Colt is lost in the sea of white, unsure where he is. When he finds his way to the surface, Porter is already standing before him, already coming around at Colt with the axe. He tries to duck before the axe finds a home in his body. But he's too slow and the axe catches him on the right side, burying the pick deep between his ribs. Hot pain quickly spreads throughout his body like lava.

Porter rips the axe free. The pick's teeth catch on Colt's ribs, lighting up every nerve ending. He screams. The pain is so intense he's on the verge of blacking out. His knees buckle, as if his mind and body suddenly disconnect, and he crumbles to the ground.

Now on his knees at Porter's feet, Colt looks up. Porter raises the axe over his head in a two-handed grip, like he's about to split a chunk of wood. Only he's not aiming to bring it down into a piece of timber, but into Colt's skull. His eyes are wild, mad with the idea of Colt's death. Victory is only moments from his grasp.

Then, Colt feels something under the snow: something brutal and pointy.

He knows he only has one shot at stopping Porter. One shot to maybe save himself. One shot to save Joey, if she's still alive after the explosion.

The snow crunches under Porter's feet as he shifts his weight to bring the axe forward.

Digging deep, focusing every last bit of energy he can muster into willing his legs to work, Colt springs up with an icicle in his hand, blown from the mess hall roof in the explosion. He stabs out hard and buries it deep into Porter's jugular.

Porter's eyes widen with shock and dismay. *Didn't see that coming.* He gurgles blood as it quickly fills the back of his throat and mouth. His hands shoot to the ice pick, and he rips it from his body without thinking of the repercussions of extracting it. A spray of blood shoots from the fleshy hole and paints the snow a shower of red. He cups his hand over the wound, but it does little to stem the blood squirting between his fingers with each heartbeat.

Porter teeters, reaches for Colt as if he wants his help; his eyes capitulate with the fear of his own death. Colt takes a step back, out of Porter's reach, and he falls face-first into the snow. The blood pumping from his neck turns the snow a deep, dark red that hurts Colt's eyes. His body twitches once. Twice. And then goes still.

"Colt!"

He looks up to see Joey standing there, fire at her back. Her uniform is torn and dirty. Her dark hair blows across her bloody, bruised, and tired face. To Colt, she looks like a Shawnee warrior emerging from a great battle.

Rushing to her, Colt collapses into her arms as his legs give out again.

"Oh, God," Joey cries. She applies pressure to his wound, holds him tightly. "Colt, this looks—"

Colt shushes her. He doesn't want to hear how bad the wound is. He already knows. The pain is telling him, and more so what he feels inside—like his guts are filling with liquid. Something internal is punctured. And that's not good.

"We can use the snowmobile to get back," Joey says, pointing to the sled Wyatt had ridden there on.

But Colt's not so sure he's going to make it back. He can feel the color running from his face as fast as the blood leaking from the wound. He's cold all over. Death is creeping up on him. *Here I come*, it whispers in the back of his mind.

Off in the distance, the sounds of emergency sirens cut through the howling wind.

"Tripp and Amos must have gotten through to the state police," Joey says, her voice hopeful.

Colt lifts his hand and caresses the side of her smooth face. He pulls her to him and kisses her tenderly on the lips for the first time that day. *God, it feels so good to do that at last.* When he pulls away, he stares into her golden eyes, captivated by them like he was the first time they met so long ago. He studies her; trying to absorb every inch of her to take with him to the great beyond.

He was unable to save a lot of people today, including himself
—of the latter, Colt feels certain. It's something he'll never be able
to forgive himself for. Still, he had been able to save one life.

One counted. One is better than none.

Joey was alive, safe.

End of watch.

ACKNOWLEDGMENTS

Thank you to Kristen Weber, my editor, whose critiques helped narrow the book's focus. Without your guidance, patience, and insight, this book wouldn't be what it is today. To Elaini Caruso, who line edited the novel – this dyslexic, who sometimes has trouble spelling and with punctuation, can't thank you enough. To my wife, Laurie Smith, for always being by my side to traverse this wild ride into book publishing. And finally, a huge thank you to all the park rangers across the United States who keep us safe in our state and national parks.

ABOUT THE AUTHOR

Westley Smith is the author of the crime thrillers *Some Kind of Truth* and *In the Pale Light*, which landed on IngramSpark's #1 pre-order charts in the mystery, thriller, and hard-boiled detective category. He is also the author of the psychological thriller, *They Came at Night* and two horror novels, *Along Came the Tricksters* and *All Hallows Eve*.

Writing since he was ten, his first short story, "Off to War," was published nationally at sixteen. His short stories have recently appeared in On the Premise and Unveiling Nightmares. He was the runner-up contestant in Alfred Hitchcock Mystery Magazine's Mysterious Photograph Contest, and his short story "Winter Reflections" was chosen as a finalist for Crystal Lake Publishing's Shallow Waters short story contest. He also had a short story, "The Security Guard," in the horror anthology *Hospital of Haunts*,

(Watertower Hill Publishing) which hit #1 on Amazon, and his true encounter with the urban legend of York, PA's, Toad Road and The Seven Gates of Hell, was featured in *George Watertower and Other Childhood Terrors* (Watertower Hill Publishing).

He lives in southern Pennsylvania with his wife and two dogs.

ALSO BY WESTLEY SMITH

Along Came the Tricksters

All Hallows Eve

Some Kind of Truth

In the Pale Light

They Came at Night

Hospital of Haunts (Anthology)

George Watertower and Other Childhood Terrors (Anthology)